A Thief
Reborn

ARIANNA WEBB

A Thief Reborn

For Patrick,
Thank you for supporting me unconditionally on this wild ride.
I love you.

For my kids,
May you follow your heart and take a chance.
I love you.

Contents

Prologue

"Now, Aesland! Make haste, before our chance escapes us!" Ilona urged me towards the bubbling cauldron, wisps of smoke curling like tendrils over its heavy iron lip.

"Are we certain? Is this for the best?" My dark brown eyes darted between the others' grim gazes, my uneasiness visible by the grimace on my lips. My heart ached for what was to become of my friend.

Friend. And this is how I show it? Backstabbing him? Robbing him of his power?

Silence responded, the others succumbing to one final hesitation, hoping one of us would come up with another option.

In the distance, shouts of warfare travelled through the damp stronghold hallways. The rings from the clashing of swords were followed by screams cut short in agony, echoing ever closer. It was not that we were afraid of battle—we all had a plethora of experience with it. You got used to the bloodshed after a while;

the faces began to blur, the sounds dulled, the stink ceased to pervade your senses any more than the faint aroma of sweat.

It was what might come after. What we all feared more than anything. What we knew, if we could not prevent it from happening, we would be helpless against. What had spurred our decision to concoct this plan initially.

The ancient texts had forewarned us, told us what to look out for. And the signs were coming in strong and fast... too strong, too fast. Inexplicable phenomena of which no other person could make sense: whispers no others heard, conversations with no one else around, and an insatiable thirst for more power, more magic.

We had watched him become withdrawn, secretive even. His skin had paled, his body wasting away as he began to prefer the dark, damp corners of his basement, like the monsters from our children's stories. I could see the madness spreading in his once loving and calm mind, his bright eyes now clouded and shifty.

If only the ancient texts had been preserved in their entirety. Maybe then we would have more guidance in how to help him learn to control his power.

But they were not, those old, frayed pages centuries older than ourselves. And so we were close to losing the chance to save our people and our civilization. And now we had to invoke a spell we all had sworn against ever summoning.

For it meant that our pentad had become unbalanced, our carefully constructed power dynamic no longer held in check by our mutually assured destruction. We had to bind his powers—they were outreaching the rest of us, with no other fail-safe in place.

"We must make this decision now or forever lose our chance!" William's thinly veiled fear reignited my own worries. Whatever indecisiveness that was delaying us evaporated, our collective decision to bind Dashiell now resolute.

The clangs of metal crescendoed as Dashiell's forces pounded on our doorstep. Our soldiers stood no chance. They must be fearing for their lives, seeing death bound near. Without our magical support, they had no tools to stop them.

William's muscular body began to metallize as he prepared himself for war, becoming impenetrable in this form as he flexed his corded arms. To his left, Ilona's velvet dress brightened from the light emitting from two molten orbs burning above her outstretched palms. Only Tauri and I had yet to invoke our powers, still clinging to some last hope of altering this course.

My eyes flicked to the last of us, finding deep pools of aqua staring back at me, tears rapidly blinked away as Tauri came to terms with everything. I knew then that everyone was ready to do the unthinkable, what we swore we'd never do to each other.

Our powers were intertwined within every fibre of our being—to bind it would be like severing a limb.

We were cursing our brother to a life never again fulfilled.

With a small nod to myself, I took the final step towards our cauldron, where a mosaic of colour weaved like silky branches, our magic swimming like hungry eels waiting to be fed. Sparks crackled softly, as if building in anticipation of the final step in our spell.

My hand, the same hand that had clapped his back in camaraderie hundreds of times—that traitorous hand reached into my hidden breast pocket, feeling the coldness of the Relic, and pulled out the smooth onyx cube. The silver etchings glowed enchantingly from the soft luminescence of our potion, like wolf eyes reflecting the moon.

I took one last survey of the faces in front of me—good, honest faces that mirrored my own discomfort in betraying one of our own.

The heavy wooden door groaned as the battle finally reached us, soldiers battering against our last remnant of defence.

After a second bang, I dropped the Relic in.

The smoke immediately dissipated, the crackling hissed to a stop, and the colours began to blacken, as if we looked into darkness incarnate.

"It is done," I said to everyone and no one.

The cube shot out of the cauldron, arcing towards the back wall, its integrity splitting into three jagged pieces as it smashed against the hard surface.

Ilona ran over to pick up the pieces, our plan to hide it in its entirety shattered like the Relic. But before any of us could brainstorm new ideas, the door clattered open, splinters of wood littering the barren floor before it.

We turned towards our invaders, our bodies readying for combat as our lips muttered magical incantations. The familiar comfort of my magic deluged through my veins, and I could not help but mourn for our friend who would never again feel this surge of warmth and power.

My fingers coaxed deadly spears of broken wood and stone to hover, suspended in air before me, awaiting their impalement into whomever, *what*ever crossed through the threshold.

Our battle had just begun.

The Hand that Thieves

If I failed, we were dead. But if I never tried, we were still bound to die, just from a longer, more drawn-out death.

My eyes blinked rapidly as I tried to get used to the darkness. Only small slivers of pale moonlight broke through the gaps of the heavy blackout curtains that covered the expansive windows along the hallway I was in, nearly severing my sense of sight. My heart felt like it might burst through my chest.

"It's too dark," I breathed, fearful I was in over my head. "I can't see shit, Arch."

"Give yourself a second, Holls, you've got this," a male voice reassured me through the comms nestled in my right ear. "Remember the vault?"

A small smile tugged at the corners of my mouth as I briefly remembered two years ago when I'd had to steal from a bank using only Archer's blueprints and my outstretched hands.

He's right—that was way darker than this.

I rolled my shoulders to physically ease the tension building in my gut and waited patiently as I adjusted to the dimness of my surroundings.

Crown moulding lined the high ceilings, the gaudy extravagance typical of Domers. I had no doubt each and every inch of this mansion housed more wealth than the entirety of my downtrodden, cramped apartment. Pristine wooden floors glistened, the expertly applied protective wax reflecting in the streaks of milky light coming in.

It would take me years of saving and stealing to afford floors like these, if ever.

Wood—real wood—was a rarity Townies could only dream of, despite being enslaved to harvest, mill, and build with it. But the tertiary goods were not for us, never for us. We were the labour force, coerced to endure gruelling sixteen-hour days, seven days a week, or else undertake the grave risk of starvation, disease, or freezing to death. We harvested, but they reaped the rewards.

Fuck these bastards.

My hand instinctively checked my leather utility belt, tightly strapped to my hips, as I mentally assessed my inventory, not wishing to forget anything. My callused hands ran along the wrinkles and tears of the fake leather as I zipped and unzipped each pocket. The belt was hanging a little looser than I remembered from the last time. I would wear this gear out until it could no longer be repaired, having no extra cash flow to justify upgrading my equipment.

My leather jacket groaned as I bent into a low crouch, my arms cautiously out in front of me, ready for whatever may come. I was thankful for my lithe body, for the ease with which I moved, quickly and with grace. It did not come from a background of sports, or dance, or any other normal means, the likes of which I had heard about from the children's stories our teacher used to read to my class. That was before we were forced to leave school to join the workforce by the age of ten.

It had come from a need to thieve. And a bigger need to not get caught.

I assessed my surroundings, noting the utter silence of the manor: no whistles, clangs, or groans like those emitted from the over-laboured appliances and heating systems in Low-Town. No shouting or banging from the hundreds of other dwellers that filled every available inch of living space. No squeaks or scratches from the rodent or bug infestations that had become our normal.

Everything inside was so utterly perfect here compared to the slums of my upbringing.

The working staff had left for their own homes hours ago. Another luxury I could not fathom. We had chosen this night because we knew the owners would not be home—whispers of vacation I had overheard during reconnaissance assured me as much. I had never travelled for fun, had never left Edinguard before. Townies couldn't survive the dangerous forest that surrounded our city. We were trapped.

Despite over ten years of stealing from Domers, I still did not comprehend their lifestyles. I had no idea what people with nothing but time and money occupied themselves with. Had no idea what people did with so much hoarding of wealth, while they watched us like lab rats rotting before their eyes.

I couldn't remember the last time I had not been harassed by nightmares about being caught, the shutdown of the black market, of failing my grandma, or any combination of fears over our future. That was why I'd had to take this job, why I always had to take whatever job eventually climbed into my scrawny, indigent lap.

The jobs had never been consistent, after all, with the Domers increasingly cracking down on the black market, drastically reducing my only source of income. But they had really slowed down in the last year, just as my grandma's sickness had worsened. Seizures were ravaging her frail body, and her incoherent babbling spouts had become more insane, more constant than ever before. She needed a higher dose of her medicine—had for a while now—but these past months had forced me to choose between our survival or easing my grandmother's pain. It was haunting me, not being able to fix my grandma's illness, and frustrating me into near madness over our incurable poverty, despite trying everything, including illegal activity.

I had landed on thievery in my teenage years, adept at remaining invisible and at refraining from asking too many questions. I had my father's abuse to thank for that; he could not hit who he did not see or hear, I had learned that quickly. I would have left him years ago, had I not still had my grandmother to consider, refusing to leave her wellbeing in my father's cruel, alcoholic hands.

And times were the hardest they'd ever been—no new rooms available for rent, no new buildings erected, no new jobs created. And despite Archer's insistence on us moving in together, my pride would not allow me to burden him with our problems.

Truth was, I wasn't sure Archer really understood what he was offering. And I wasn't sure I knew what would become of us if we moved in together. I didn't let myself hope for happiness. And so I forced us to stay in whatever this was, refusing to acknowledge the feelings hovering between us.

That was why I had agreed to this job, despite protests from Archer, protests I deep down had agreed with. The job was inside a Domer's home. I had never taken such a risk before, usually tasked with stealing from their businesses or storehouses. But desperation caused even the most pragmatic of us to make choices unlike ourselves.

When Archer and I had first teamed up, we had always agreed on pragmatism over profit, both of us understanding our sentence of execution if we were captured, our loved ones' deaths imminent as well. But it had been months, *months*, with no jobs from any of our regular dealers, all of them wishing to wait out the latest string of crackdowns. The O'Malley patrols had skyrocketed in frequency as our own police and militia had been seduced into giving up their own kind to the O'Malleys' never-ending witch hunt.

We never knew who they were after until they dragged their victims from their homes in the dead of night and executed them in the middle of our streets, the victims shrieking as they burned alive—a not-so-subtle reminder of where the power lay. It was just as much a public flex of their muscle to scare the rest of us in line as it was an execution of a culprit.

I was creeping into the mouth of a lion, praying not to wake the beast from its slumber. We knew, despite the family being away, there would be enough security to make this a risky job, police and mercenaries but an alarm away. Paid *very* well to be at their immediate disposal. Besides their state-of-the-art security, Domers were magical, and I had little experience with magic. Money, power, and magic all went hand in hand, but only the Domers had any of it. And they had spent centuries protecting it, hoarding it from the rest of us.

And here I was, entering one of their homes. Stealing something precious from a house made for and by magic.

Archer hadn't been able to find blueprints that would show us what magical safeguards stood between us and our goal. But we could guarantee there would be some. This mission would be my biggest challenge yet.

My fingers found a knot in my neck as I cracked the ache out of my shoulders, years of sleeping on a decrepit, sunken-in mattress on the floor wreaking havoc on my young body. My mind wandered, worrying whether my body could continue this lifestyle, what my options would be as age overcame my youth, what I would do if I was permanently injured.

"Holls?" Archer's voice interrupted my mind spiralling.

"Here. Sorry." I cleared my throat softly, careful not to set off any noise-activated alarms.

Rolling my shoulders to shrug off my mind for now, I began to prowl forward, embodying the litheness of a lioness, eyes flitting a full 180 degrees. Always watching. Always ready.

"It's showing a servant's staircase coming up in about fifty feet on your left. Take that to the second floor, but remember to be on the lookout for any tripwires." The comms in my ear crackled. It, too, felt the years of work it had undergone. Archer's melodious voice refocused me and I gained some confidence, the comfort from years of working together calming my nerves. He hadn't gotten it wrong before. Surely today wouldn't be the day.

I stuck to the shadows against the left wall, crouching beneath the extravagant oil portraits lining it, a visual journey through time, from the oldest known relatives headed towards their newest brood.

Funny how they love to look at themselves while the rest of us try to avoid it.

Just before the wooden door, my eyes caught the faint flicker of red as the dust my movement roused fell delicately over the first of many secret tripwires. My hands quickly grabbed my

JTag to shut off the trap. I carefully hovered nearby to press the silencing button, refraining from moving so I did not trigger anything. Lately, anti-theft measures had increased in craftiness, many now triggered by the very decoders used to disarm them.

I held my breath, an eye half closed unconsciously as my body tensed.

I pressed down on the button. *Click.*

My breath let loose in relief when nothing seemed to have been set off. Not willing to risk more, I slipped my body through the doorframe, careful not to open the door any wider. My thin frame fit, and I kept the door ajar to ensure my backup escape route remained open.

The narrow staircase rose to a small oval window—small enough to hide the servants from any curious onlookers, the owners unwilling to make their work conditions privy to the rest of the city. I dared not give up my crouch yet, knowing cameras lined the soffit just outside, their faint red eyes whizzing in every direction, like a scavenger searching for its next meal.

Once I reached the first landing, I reminded myself which stairs to skip, Archer's voice repeating incessantly in my mind. *Avoid every fourth step like a heaping pile of shit.*

Thankfully my long legs made quick work of the second half of the staircase, easily sailing past the rigged steps. Archer had mentioned they were connected to the latest weighted anti-thievery counters, designed to set off at changes in pressure over fifty pounds. I could stand to gain a few pounds, but there was no way my body weight would not provoke a full-scale manor lockdown, effectively trapping me within.

My boots softly scuffed the top step as I stared down the worst part of this assignment. What appeared to be another rectangular hallway, windows smothered by more velvet drapes, was in fact a labyrinth of invisible lasers.

I fingered the small pouch tied tightly to my left hip.

Though he hadn't been able to find specs on what magical safeguards lay in wait for me, Archer had been able to drag up recent renovation blueprints. This was a state-of-the-art implementation, the first of its kind in any private residence. It would have been any other thief's demise.

But not mine.

My right hand unfastened the loop as my other cradled the pouch in it. My fingers pinched a minute amount of Dustclox and I softly blew it in front of me. As the dust flitted to the ground, I began to assess where each beam was located, systematically scanning the first wall of gridlock tripwires. The red beams crisscrossed like a potato masher, and brief memories of my grandma and I cooking together flicked through my mind. For her. It had always been for her.

I scouted my best route through the first wall, espying the biggest gaps. Inches... I had inches to spare. There was no room for error.

I approached the first hole sideways, my body flattening like a right angle as I sent my first outstretched leg through the hole. I held the pouch firmly to my chest, both hands clamped down to ensure the precious contents would not be dropped. I thanked the stars that I still had some Dustclox left to use—even that was becoming harder to purchase.

My head twisted towards my shoulder as I eased my body slowly through, shallow breathing the most movement I dared to make, the nervous quivering of my body fighting to undo me. I took some deep breaths, visualising each inhale scooping up the tiny tremors and each exhale blowing them out of my body. The lines hummed quietly as my face passed right by them. I scooped my butt under as my boot pivoted so that I was facing backward and could ease my other leg through the hole.

I took but a moment to close my eyes and silently thank whoever was watching over me before I turned towards the next section, my hands ready to repeat the process. The quicker I pulled this off, the better. I could not leave room for the unexpected.

Blow, step, bend, scoop, pull, blow, step, bend, scoop, pull.

Surprisingly, the method flowed smoothly, no hiccups impeding my progress. I found my groove as my body loosened through the holes like it was following the steps of a dance.

I thought fondly of Archer dancing with me last summer up on the hill by our houses, our faces inches apart, the beat of my heart rapping in fever as our lips met. The plushness of his full lips, the whiskers of his five o'clock shadow scratching my face, his tongue tentatively finding mine. It had been after completing a particularly exciting mission.

That was the last time I had felt somewhat safe, before our jobs had become this scarce, our futures so uncertain.

I repeated the process, almost flowing through the lasers, until I came face to face with the final door, its simple design lacking edging or panelling, almost as if to convince you that nothing of worth would dare be held behind its ugliness.

"Remind me one last time of the code," I demanded of my partner. I knew it, I had memorised it days ago, drilling it into my mind late at night when sleep had evaded me yet again.

"It's 3785560—but remember you need to press Home, then press Code, THEN enter the passcode, then press Home AGAIN, or else it trips. Don't fuck this up, Torch," Archer joked in an attempt to lighten the mood, despite the undercurrent of tension in his voice. He had never been able to hide his emotions well.

"Right. Stay tuned," I whispered, going silent again to focus. I tapped the front of the plain door to bring up a screen, where I began inputting the code. The illuminated keys turned mustard yellow as each key was pressed. Once I was finished, they all began to blink green in acceptance, assuring me I was successful.

A clunk, followed by the door slowly opening, showing its triple-steel reinforcement as it hovered ajar, inviting me in to see what treasure lay beyond.

We didn't actually know what treasure we were taking, as we had gained a reputation for being close-lipped. If our client did not wish to divulge, we did not ask. Ignorance of some things kept us safer. And it helped us to live with the choices we had been forced to make to survive.

"Looks like a box. On a pedestal. How... typical." I rolled my eyes. The Domers sure loved their symbolism.

"Blueprints are showing absolutely nothing else in there. But stay vigilant. It's been a little too easy for my liking." Archer's thoughts mirrored my own. *No magic?*

Our contact had looked fearful in even bringing us this job. Why? I wondered.

Another pocket inside my jacket held a place weight, chosen to mimic the same weight as our target—the only description we were given about the item. I had kept it close, not wanting my balance to be compromised. I edged towards the pedestal and my quick hands swapped the items in a flash, the dais not even fluctuating from the movement. A life of having to steal to survive had worked well for me in transitioning into a professional.

I surveyed my surroundings as my head slowly swivelled to take in the rest of the room. Quite an ugly room, barren except for this. No windows, no other doors. In total contrast to the grandiosity of the rest of the mansion.

How odd, to house this here by itself. Where are all the rest of their assets?

Something didn't feel right.

A smoky mist began to leak from each corner of the ceiling, the sour stench assaulting my nostrils. My nose wrinkled, my brows furrowing as I raced towards the door.

"What the fuck is this?!" I coughed, the fumes making me light-headed. My comms crackled in reply, the transmission bugging out. The beginnings of panic settled into my stomach as my skin perspired with cold sweat.

I swayed on my feet, the vapors muddling my vision as my exit swam around in triplicate. I focused, my eyes squinting in strain as I sprinted to the exit, not wanting to find out what other magical traps awaited me if I got locked inside here.

Just as I stumbled to the door, the fumes ignited into flames, one blaze scorching my hand before I slipped out of the room.

The fortified door slammed shut, metal mechanics grinding as multiple deadbolts locked.

I shook my hand wildly as my mouth gaped open from the white-hot pain that erupted, tears welling in the corners of my eyes. Not daring to delay a moment longer, I raced towards the first window on my left.

We'd refused to risk hacking more than one camera, not wanting to increase our digital footprint more than necessary. One shot was all we'd agreed to, and my preference always leaned towards securing my exit rather than my entrance. We had chosen the closest window as my escape route, should things have soured quickly.

I shoved the window open with my good hand and took a quick peek outside. Reinforcements had not shown up, no security awaiting me below, to my luck.

Crashing reverberated from within the locked room as the arms of smoke seeped out in pursuit of me.

I could not delay further.

"Here I come," I rasped to Archer, the small box secured inside my breast pocket.

The map had shown shrubbery beneath, where my body would land after jumping out the window, both cushioning and hiding it. With an inhale, I squeezed through and leapt.

Grim and Bear It

C *link!*

Archer convinced me to have one celebratory drink with him, although the tab would be his to pay, as he knew I had nothing to spare. As always, he'd assured me my company was payment enough for him, but he made sure not to press me, knowing I was too proud to accept more than one free drink.

We had decided to take our drinks back to my house, not wanting to be seen out celebrating on the night of a job, although the townspeople were so downtrodden, I doubted they would even take notice of us.

We lived in a caste system, from what my rudimentary schooling had taught me, one that had been proven to work for centuries—at least for the rich. You were either born with magic, or you worked for those with it.

Sure, we *could* go to school, but what good was education to families that could not afford to feed themselves? Kids were a critical part of our workforce, providing necessary income for most families to make enough Kroja to survive.

Magic helped them extract all the vital resources, ensuring that power stayed within the hands of the Domers, not us Townies, who were born without magic. Born without any real power.

What was a knife compared to a soldier who could burn you alive with a flick of their hands? Break your mind with a snap? Become physically impenetrable?

Many times throughout history, one of our own had come forth, believing themself to be our saviour. And each time, they had been *violently* massacred, a lesson to be heeded for future generations.

We had learned the hard way to play the hand you were dealt, finding whatever ways we could to alleviate the bleakness of our lives. Some found salvation through substance, like my father, some through contraband and prostitution. And some, like me, by filling a niche in the marketplace.

Had my father not succumbed to his own vices, had my grandmother not been incurably ill, maybe I would have been able to finish school and find honest-paying skilled work.

But this was my life, and I had made choices to the best of my ability.

In some ways, I was lucky.

I wasn't a whore. Or an addict.

As I choked down the piss taste of the Townie beer in front of me, I wondered how much better Domer beer—real beer—tasted. I looked around our humble house, resigned that I would probably never know; I couldn't even really afford one of these watered-down versions.

My father seemed to enjoy them though—they allowed him to stay drunk for the majority of his day and night. I had to scramble to make ends meet, pay for our rent, and get food on the table, while my father squandered every last Kroja he stole, from me, from Grandma, from anyone his meaty hands could get ahold of.

Damp wooden walls sagged in on us, lending the air a distinctly musky smell, the paint mostly flaked away. The floor, or rather dirt ground, lost its flatness years ago. It now mimicked the bumps and ridges of a turtle's shell, the result of the residual tremors that plagued us.

Our one-bedroom apartment had a small kitchenette, our brown stove often propped open to help heat the place during the unforgiving winter nights. A leaky shower was crammed next to a stained toilet, years of dirt and scum no longer erased by a heavy scrub. My father had scrounged a rocking chair from the dump one night—he had dragged it in, knocking into both our mattresses, startling Grandma and me awake in the dead of night.

Neither of us were allowed to sit in it.

From his throne, he often drank, watching us, berating us, playing cards, shouting at himself until he tired of our ugly house and left to harass others for the night.

We had but one blanket each, not much more than a few threads barely holding together. Most months lately I couldn't afford the heating bills, so my grandma and I had taken to sharing one of our beds for body heat—when she wasn't having an episode.

When she didn't recognize me, I did not share her bed. Once I had made that mistake, and I still could not shake the memories of the horrified look plastered on her face.

It had gutted me. I'd wept silently later that night at the encroaching fear that I was losing her. But I could not give up on her. Would not. I had plans to get out, once I'd saved enough to get us far away from here.

Where I was planning to go... I hadn't thought that far. But I knew it had to be far enough away to never cross paths with my father again. It wasn't as if he would mourn losing us. He'd be enraged over losing access to my income.

But before I could even plan where to escape to, *how* to escape there, I had to secure enough Kroja to start anew.

If the jobs kept slowing down, I had no idea what I would do. *We'll cross that bridge when we get there.*

Archer's strong, warm hand gently took my burned one, moving it as his eyes scanned the damage.

We had always stuck together, him and I. His was the only shoulder I could cry on, when I snuck out to meet him after especially aggressive nights with my father. He'd lost his parents eight years ago, when we'd just turned sixteen, and from that night on, we had taken on the role of provider.

He'd always had a knack for tech stuff, but with his limited opportunities for exposure, we had started with old-fashioned printed blueprints when planning. Once we had proven ourselves *extremely* useful to our clients, our dealer gave us a proper machine, and Archer's inherent gift had flourished. Now we had access to some of the best resources on the networks.

He was crucial to our success, just as I was. We were a team, a united front that could tackle anything life threw at us. With proper planning, of course.

My heartbeat crept up into my throat as I pulled my hand away from his grasp, the warmth of his touch making my cheeks flush. I could feel his gaze on me, and I kept my eyes averted, praying the dim lighting hid my blushing.

Friends. *Best* friends.

I swallowed down my feelings, worried that our situation was becoming something I couldn't handle. Something I wasn't ready to put words to. I knew he loved me, and I loved him... on some level.

But I didn't know if I could give him what he deserved to find. True love. Not just companionship.

The physical attraction between us was palpable, but I was afraid of taking that next step, wrecking what we had already. Preferring to have him in my life rather than risk more and lose him. We'd already toed the line last summer and it had terrified me—I'd shut it down completely.

I blamed it on my stress, on being too busy, but I knew he felt me pulling away, building that wall up brick by brick. He'd let me carve that space between us. What did that mean about how he felt about me? Maybe our sexual attraction existed only because of proximity. So I choked down my lust, creating space to keep us from crossing that point of no return.

Refocusing on my hand to ignore the storm of emotions whirling inside of me, I unwrapped the gauze and wiped away remnants of the topical balm I'd created and applied to my wound. It had worked wonders; I was already seeing the shiny markings of scars forming. I clenched and unclenched my fist, the shiny ripples catching the dull light emitted by the lamp nearby. Grandma always said I had a knack for healing. Perhaps in another life, I would have pursued a role in medicine.

"What the hell happened in there, Hollyn?"

"Some kind of smoke and fire room. It tried to catch me in there." I trailed off, the reality of my near-death experience smothering me. I tugged at my jacket, my anxiety building within.

From behind me, my father's drunken snores rattled the walls. My grandmother somehow found slumber despite the racket, her bony body rising and falling with each shallow breath.

"I think we can agree we don't take a job like this again," Archer urged, his voice chock-full of emotion.

"Some of us don't have that choice, Arch," I reprimanded him, hating the bitterness seeping into my voice. It was not his fault he had no family to look out for. I hated that I was trying to hold that against him. That I was holding him back. He had offered to help pay, but I refused to be the victim or to rely on anyone. I'd endured my entire childhood listening to my father berate me for being a leech on society.

That was something you never truly forgot.

Sighing, Archer continued. "You know I would—"

I waved my hand, shaking my head. "Not tonight. Not again."

His eyes lingered on me for a moment before looking away, but I had seen the hurt in them. A sour feeling settled in my stomach.

A pause, the thickness of what was unsaid hanging over us like a storm cloud.

Finally Archer broke. "Same spot as last time?" My eyebrows slightly raised at his not-so-subtle change in topic.

The prized box lay on the table, my piqued curiosity slowly eroding my usually steadfast resolve to not peek at what was stored inside. But the dealer had acted so strangely.

"What do you think it is?" To me it seemed worthless, but that only heightened my curiosity. "He seemed almost terrified in giving us this mission, didn't he? I don't get it."

Archer lifted the box and gave it the same scrutinizing gaze he'd given my wounded hand earlier. His dark eyebrows scowled as he squinted, his neck hunching over the item. "Should we... open it?"

Before I could respond, my grandmother began to whimper softly from her mattress. "Hollyn, baby. Hollyn, where are you!"

I shot to my feet, my chair falling back in haste as I rushed to her side. Finding her gnarled hands, I gently guided them to my face. "Here, Grandma, here I am."

"Baby, what's happened to your face? It's so thin." Her wrinkles deepened in worry. Her hazel eyes weren't as milky as usual, a clear sign I had her back mentally, even if for only a moment.

"I'm okay, Grandma. Just been working more, and food's been a little harder to get, is all."

Another whimper, this time in frustration as her hands dropped in defeat. "God, how useless I am in this broken old body. What good am I to you like this?"

My hands stroked her white hair out of her pale face. "You were the only one who looked after me for years. You've done your part." But a small part of me was exhausted from the increasing care she needed. I would need help soon, was already stretching myself too thin.

Tears filled her eyes. "You are my everything, baby. I should have gotten you away from this hell years ago." Her hands softly caressed mine, and warm memories of those same hands rubbing me to sleep filled me with a deep, nostalgic love.

I had no memories of my father doing the same.

"I love you too, Grandma. We are surviving, aren't we?" A weak smile that never quite reached my eyes. "Are you in any pain? Let me get you your medicine." I rose and walked to the kitchen shelves—jagged, rusted chunks of metal I had scavenged by the dump years ago. Locating her prescription and a medicine cup, I carefully poured the appropriate dose, noting its near emptiness.

I'd have to buy more in a few days. I had to ensure I was paid enough tonight.

Maybe I could ask for more?

I rubbed my face in exhaustion, the mental load of keeping track and budgeting every facet of my life draining me more than I'd ever let on. I forced a smile on my face before returning to my grandmother's side. I could never let her know how dire things had gotten.

"Grandma, Archer and I have to go out for a little bit right now." I cupped her jaw as I poured the liquid into her mouth, my thumb lovingly rubbing the tiny trail that seeped out the corner of her mouth. "But we'll be back before Father wakes up."

She suddenly grabbed my wrist, my body jolting in surprise.

"Grandma? You okay?"

"Promise me. *Promise* me you will get out of here." Her eyes widened in urgency. I hadn't seen her this alert in a long time.

"I'm working on it, but I need to save up a little bit more for us."

"No! Leave me, love. *You* must get out."

I shook my head. "I'm not leaving you here." I felt rather than saw Archer at my side. The urgency in her voice must have concerned him too.

"Archer, please, you have to convince her. I'm not getting any better—you two can't be worried about me. You two deserve better than... than *this.*" Her arms outspread around her, as if we did not know the squalor we lived in.

Reaching for the cup of water that was by her bed, I brought it towards her lips and nodded, insisting she take a drink. As she gulped down the lukewarm liquid, I reminded her, "I don't think there's much else out there, Grandma. We're together, we're safe, and we're unbothered by others. That's good enough for me."

"We'll get by like we always do." Archer kissed her cheek softly, the gesture bringing tears to my eyes. She was all the family he had left too. "You should rest some more and stop worrying about us so much."

After one last embrace, I rose from her side, grabbed the stolen box from the table, and shut off the lamp on our way out the door, its rusted hinges squeaking in protest.

We couldn't risk being late.

Our feet fell into step as I took in the early morning scene. The looming condo buildings were mostly dark with the slumber of those inside, the odd room lit by flickering bulbs. This was the quietest time of day, the pregnant pause between the night owls finding slumber and before the early birds rose to begin their laborious day of work. The smog lifted somewhat this early in the morning, allowing just enough starlight to sneak through, letting us discreetly head towards our meeting place without the need of a flashlight.

Our feet evaded the plethora of potholes that covered the roads, like pockmarks left from years of rampant acne. Most of us in Low-Town could not drive, having lost the need years ago with no money to own cars, so our roads remained in this state. Problems like leaky tin roofs, broken windows, and the rising issue of food security far superseded our pathetic road conditions.

Peeking out above the maze of condos, the vibrant light emitted by the Dome spanned vastly into the sky. The rippling shimmer of the glass panes sealed in any sounds from their world, simultaneously preventing our existence from seeping in and tarnishing theirs. It was the biggest architectural "fuck you" you could create.

We took the back alley, heading towards the old pulp factory, our usual meeting place. It was on the outskirts of town, hidden away like the unpaid bills stuffing my drawers full. A fire had destroyed most of it except for the old control room, which now stood blackened but intact. The only residents of the pulp were rodents and the odd lost, doped-out addict. To us, it was obscure and private–the perfect place for illicit meetings.

Archer entered first, always chivalrous, before waving me inside. We sat in our usual seats–rotting wooden stools that groaned under the weight of us– and waited.

And waited.

And waited.

Life or Debts

"This isn't like him at all." Archer paced back and forth. "He's usually waiting for us. Creepy little guy. With his creepy, beady little eyes." His mouth grimaced in distaste.

"Let's give him five more, then we leave," I said, smirking at his disgust. Our dealer really was one of the ugliest people I had ever met, with his shifty eyes, his lips that were always wet from his irritating habit of licking them in anxiousness, and his greased-back, thinning hair. But he had proven himself reliable—as reliable as possible for a criminal liaison—so we tolerated his slimy presence.

A big part of that reliability meant we met for our trade-offs at *exact* predetermined times. We never made him wait for the item, and he always came stocked with cash. We both valued our time, a different form of currency, so it really was unlike him to be late. A small seed of worry—for him, for us, for everything on the line here—was sowed in my mind even as I tried not to let it take root.

"You sure it was 3:45?" He anxiously bit a hangnail, a scowl furrowing his dark brows.

"Arch, when have I ever gotten it wrong?"

"I know, I know, I'm sorry." Archer put his hands up in apology.

But this did feel wrong. Something was off.

My hands checked for the fifth time for that cool, smooth box in my belt, my awareness heightened for any sound or sight, as if an ambush was imminent.

Archer was pacing like a caged feral cat, and my eyes flicked to him, watching his broad shoulders, his long lean legs, that shock of wavy jet-black hair that flopped into his eyes. Every time it would get too long, he would cut it himself out of frustration, not bothering to waste money on something as vain as a haircut.

And even with a lopsided haircut, he was still absolutely stunning.

I released my own hair from its bun to let loose the auburn waves that cascaded down just past my breasts. Mine was long, not because it was stylish—in fact, from the few glimpses I had taken of the Dome-heads, short, blunt haircuts seemed to be in fashion—but because my mother had had my hair, from what I'd gathered from the few pictures my family kept of her.

She'd succumbed to shingles, transmitted from me as a newborn suffering from chickenpox. It was something my father never forgave me for; he hated me from that moment onward.

The beginning of the end of any paternal bond we could have had. I had let that guilt haunt me for most of my adolescence.

So my thick russet waves now remained in defiance to my father, to remind him daily of his sorrow, my only real chance at inflicting some pain back onto him.

It was a low blow, I knew. But I had given up on earning his love years ago.

As I opened my mouth to call off our meeting, a shadow passed by the front window and I paused, shrinking back into the shadows. The door handle turned sharply, and a massive figure stepped through the threshold, shadows disguising his face from us.

"What the fuck, man, we're trying to have some alone time! Find another spot!" Archer stood protectively by my side, one hand possessively wrapping around my shoulders as the other grazed my jawline. We defaulted to this backstory a lot—merely a horny asshole and his piece of meat.

This was not new territory for us; we had found comfort sleeping with each other during an exceptionally rough summer last year. I placed my palm affectionately against his hand, my face leaning into his gentle caress, eyes closing in bliss. Our eyes met, the heat building in them real attraction.

It had been hard to give up that intimacy, and my body still responded eagerly to his nearness.

But instead of backing away in embarrassment or apology, the stranger strode closer until our eyes began to decipher the narrow, straight nose, the clenched jaw, and the steel-grey eyes staring me up and down. Whether he was sizing me up or stripping me down I could not tell.

"Sorry to keep you waiting." He spoke to me, barely registering Archer.

"I'm sorry?" I asked vacantly, acting like a vapid fool.

"Your meeting," he responded. *How did he know we were meeting someone here?*

"I think you must be mistaken. I don't know you."

"No, but you will. Your grandmother's life depends on it," he stated flatly.

My body jerked unconsciously as a pit in my stomach formed, terrified that this monster had hurt her. "Has something happened to her?!"

My mind reeled as I obsessively tried to remember if I had locked the door behind us, playing back our walk over, scouring my brain for any indication that someone had followed us.

"I suggest you sit and listen very carefully to what I am going to say," the stranger suggested, his deep voice leaving no room for negotiation.

"If anything's happened to her, I will fucking kill you," I promised through gritted teeth, rage pulsing through my body.

"Sit," he said calmly. I stared him down, standing in defiance. "*Sit*," he repeated with exaggerated enunciation. I didn't dare risk pushing further, my grandma's safety resting in the palm of his gigantic hands.

I obeyed his command, hatred spilling from me as I maintained my staredown. "Who the fuck are you? And how do you know about me?"

I worried that maybe my mouth had buried me deeper when he paused. But after a moment, still as calmly as ever, he replied, "Ryker."

He spun on his heel and exited, only to return seconds later with our toady dealer, his mousy-brown hair slick from sweat, his eyes swollen, and his guilty gaze refusing to look at anything higher than our knees.

Ryker shoved our dealer forward and he stumbled into the light, where I noticed the oil of his hair was actually blood. His eyes were bruised from what I suspected were repeated punches, and from his nostrils flowed two streams of snotty blood.

I stared at Ryker, for the first time truly terrified of who stood before me. I could feel myself being backed into a corner, as I realised that whatever this creature was going to ask of me, I would risk my life and my grandmother's if I tried to deny him.

"We need you to bring us something precious that belongs to us," he stated matter-of-factly, feeling no need to explain the condition of our dealer. His eyes lacked any remorse over what he'd done, which I figured came from a long career of having to be this person. For whom, I did not know.

"Then why don't you still have it?" I rebutted before I could stop myself. *Easy, Hollyn.*

"That doesn't concern you, does it?" He raised his eyebrows. "I thought you didn't ask questions. Part of your package deal."

"No fucking way is she going with you," protested Archer, the shock of everything finally shaking from him.

Ryker's eyes finally found Archer's, and then mutely he turned back to me. Expected me to answer, dismissing Archer entirely.

"You come here, threaten my grandmother's life, and then beat the shit out of our dealer. And you want me to work a job for you?" I asked incredulously.

"Yes," he replied, boredom edging into his body as he waited for my agreement, arrogant confidence dripping from him.

"No way in hell." I shook my head. "I don't know you, I can't trust you."

He stared at me again, his eyes boring into me, then finally raised his cell phone to his ear, speed-dialing someone on the other end. He purposely spoke loudly enough we could hear their conversation. Could hear him ask for his backup to move in on unit 29. My unit. Where I had left Grandma asleep, her only defence the measly lock of our front door and a deadbeat drunk.

"Wait."

"Holl—"

"Well, what choice do I have?!" I yelled at Archer.

"They're bluffing. They wouldn't hurt her." Archer's eyes didn't sell me, even as his mouth attempted to convince me otherwise. He too sensed the severity of this man. How far he would be willing to go to get me to agree. "What if he just kills Grandma anyway? What if this job gets you killed?"

Always my voice of reason.

"It's a risk I'll have to take. If something happened to her because of me... I can't take that risk... I won't. She's all I have left," I croaked out in worry.

Hurt flickered quickly over Archer's face and I regretted my words. I had not meant them to sound so isolating. I had him as well.

"You're not going without me."

I nodded, thankful for his friendship—our relationship—or whatever this was.

"We depart immediately. For the Dome. I'll let him fill you in once we get back." Ryker exited, not waiting for us, knowing we would follow. "Oh, and by the way, this one was going to screw you over. He had a mercenary with him when I found him."

A mercenary. To kill us.

Had.

"Things, uh, are getting more dangerous out here," our dealer gulped. "It—it was for my protection, you see, I h-have always had your back." His hands came up to beg, his scrawny, moley neck bobbing as he nervously swallowed, his face confirming his guilt. He had never been a good liar; he could barely contain his nervous twitches.

"Why?" I asked him.

He hesitated, not wanting to answer.

Ryker walked up behind him and cuffed his head, and his body reeled from the impact. He stank with fear.

"I-I've been dealing with some... pressure... from my clients." He stumbled over his words. "To tie up loose ends. With the newest crackdown, it would be... unwise... for them to have any connection to the black market."

I processed this information, nausea sinking in my stomach. This meant that I had *no* job. No way to make money.

I turned to look at Ryker, boredom plastered on his face. He already knew this information, it seemed, and was watching as his calculated plan fell into place. I was officially backed right up to that corner, now with no means to make money or to help my grandma.

As we walked past our dealer, I spat in his face, "You better hope they get to you first."

His beady little eyes blinked rapidly, his face paling in realisation.

As I stormed off I heard a thud, followed by another thud, and I turned to watch his body slam to the floor. Archer jogged to catch up to me, shaking his hand in pain.

The small box felt heavier in my belt than it had before, like an omen of what was to come. On a rash impulse, I pulled out the box and ripped it open. Maybe I could sell whatever was in there.

A small figurine, crafted into the likeness of the Priestess Navi.

Symbolically priceless. Financially worthless.

I threw the cement figure onto the road with frustration. I'd never believed in the Priestess, anyway.

"A woman of faith, I see," Ryker joked dryly at me.

I scowled back at him, "Most people would be upset by that."

Ryker stopped in his tracks, his boots scraping the path as he twisted to face me, "It seems like we both aren't what we seem."

Squinting my eyes at him, I tried to make sense of his cryptic message. But before I could ask anything more, he strode ahead to make a call, his words too quiet for me to overhear.

Who was I following into the Dome?

And who the hell was I about to meet?

Honey, I'm Dome

I never dreamed I would be entering the Dome legally.

We approached the heavily guarded entrance in their pristine vehicle, the air inside warm and smelling of some sort of woodsy aroma. I discreetly took a sniff of my armpits, and my nose scrunched from the dull stink of sweat and grime. Ryker had stuffed us in the leather seats in the back, his mute presence, save for the odd grunt in irritation, leaving us to our own thoughts. I watched blankly as he drove us towards the frosted globe.

I noticed the armed grunts that patrolled the perimeter, as well as the barely visible guards situated on elevated perches all over, ready to defend from any and all angles. Some shimmered, their skin having morphed into titanium or some other hard metal. Some had assumed predatory bodies: wolves, lions, even a gigantic grizzly bear. Others forwent military weapons for orbs of flames or lightning crackling from their fingertips. And others still seemed defenceless, meandering as if there was not a care in the world. Those ones I knew were anything but incapable, relying on their minds to control.

We came to a stop, Ryker rolling down his tinted window to talk with an approaching officer. As soon as he saw Ryker, he gave a curt nod and flicked his hand to signal we could head through.

There was no checking of any identification, no questions, no searching our car, like we had seen during our reconnaissance.

Who is this guy?

The entrance blinked green and our car peeled through, continuing towards the expansive roadway system as the reinforced Dome doors slowly closed behind us.

The roads—so smooth and so clean—led us winding through gorgeous mansions, some modern in design with copious concrete and glass that was kept immaculately clean, everything sharp edges and lines. Others were architecturally similar to Second Empire homes with wraparound porches, mansard roofs with dormers set into them, and elaborate pediments over the many windows.

Each house had the lushest, greenest lawns I had ever seen, with intricate play structures and numerous toys scattered, the fear of someone stealing them nonexistent in this world.

My eyes widened as I drank in the views: shiny, expensive-looking cars lined every driveway. Shrubs and bushes were manicured to perfection, and mature trees canopied the roads like a woven blanket sheltering us from the bright early morning sun above. The sun seemed stronger here without the taint of smog our factories produced.

It was so quiet, the odd tweet of a bird or rumble of a car the only sounds that broke the silence. In such contrast to the constant hum of Low-Town, where the generators wheezed from the strain of keeping up with the overwhelming energy demands.

The people, I noticed, smiled at each other as they passed, so unlike the zombies that marched back home. Flashes burst in my vision as Domers flew past, their speed barely perceptible to my human eyes. I watched as one little girl walked to the end of her sidewalk before soaring away as a beautiful eagle.

Life seemed to flow harmoniously here, magic infusing everything, from the streets being swept by unmanned, floating brooms to the gentle pitter-patter of water sprinkled onto lawns. People of all colours and heights intertwined with animals of all shapes and sizes. Kids laughed, the vibrancy of their faces reflecting the lack of stressors placed upon them.

Do they not know how bad it is in Low-Town?

I watched as one homeowner manipulated the earth beneath him as he tested out new landscaping designs, his hands flowing like a conductor in front of his orchestra. Two teenagers played frisbee in a luscious park, their hands settled in their laps, their eyes squinting in concentration as they telepathically shot the plastic disc back and forth. Laughter erupted out of seeming silence, their conversation stored secretly inside their minds. Another of their friends barbecued mouthwatering slabs of meat and whole cobs of corn while he formed ice cubes that plunked into their cups. I had never seen such thick cuts of meat before, nor had I enjoyed fresh corn.

It was... beautiful. Like a dream state. Their buildings stood proud, painted in gloriously unabashed colour, demanding attention and respect. Just like their owners.

Archer grabbed my hand, but his face remained turned to the window. He too was enchanted by the beauty of this foreign world. But I also knew he was cataloguing every bit of information that presented itself to him. How his enemies filled their days, what powers they harnessed, how their lives intertwined with magic.

We devoured the breathtaking scenery, our eyes starved of the colours, the cleanliness, the architecture, until our car pulled into a horseshoe-shaped driveway, the mansion in front of us groomed to perfection. Two stories of concrete, shaped in asymmetrical overhanging squares, like a delicately balanced tower of blocks, greeted us as we exited the car. Ryker was already walking towards the double-door entrance, leaving us to open our own doors. Whether he couldn't be bothered to play nice, or he really did not know how to, I didn't know.

Our boots, discoloured at our toes, wrinkles flaking the fake leather, crunched on the gravel as we walked to the front steps. The glass doors had been left open, inviting us in with open arms, but despite the lack of apparent security, I did not drop my guard. Whoever owned this building, I imagined, took lengths to protect it. Wealth was distributed generationally, little exchanging hands throughout our history. The Domers protected their money and their magic by whatever means necessary, including faith.

It was one of the reasons I never believed in Her: there's no way any higher power worth following would allow my people to rot away like they have been for centuries. But critical thinking did not bode well for my kind, and so most found solace in faith, choosing instead to turn a blind eye to whatever suspicions might arise.

They didn't understand that they sought comfort from the Priestess to help them from hardships their devotion played into. They prayed for help and divine intervention from an enemy that puppeteered their very religion.

They didn't understand that the comfort they sought from the Priestess only added to the domination of the very people from which they sought refuge.

Most Townies had nothing else to get them up everyday. I could understand why they practiced. I just couldn't participate in it.

It would be interesting to see if Domers were as devout of followers as they pressured Townies to be.

Archer and I stepped inside, heading towards the low murmur of male voices. Unlike the manor I had broken into earlier, there were no family portraits, no gaudy trim nor Gothic drapery. No lavish rugs warmed up the cold stone flooring. Everything was sleek and cold, like this house had never quite developed into a home. Varying monochromatic shades filled the rooms we passed by—a spacious living room with white couches that looked as if they had never been sat on, an all-white bathroom, whiter than ours had ever been. A winding staircase wrapped around an all-glass elevator with not a smudged fingerprint in sight.

My breath caught as I took in the destination room; sunlight poured in from an entire wall of floor-to-ceiling windows, the manor's backyard filled with a lawn cut in a weave-like pattern, the acreage lined by towering aspens. It was both entirely private and overwhelmingly open. It was like nothing I had ever seen in daylight.

I quickly caught my expression, pulling on a mask of blankness in defence. I had no idea what else they knew about us, but I refused to give them anything else to hold against me. So when they turned towards us, I was an unreadable statue.

Sitting at the mahogany desk by a wall of books was one of the most handsome men I had ever seen. If Ryker's features were dark like the night, this man was his polar opposite, with golden blond hair that curled behind his ears and eyes bluer than the sapphire ring I had stolen last month. His mouth upturned on one side in a lazy smirk while talking with Ryker before they both turned in unison towards me, Ryker's massive frame leaning back against the front of the desk as his arms folded across his body.

We took a couple more uncertain steps.

The man at the desk gestured for us to sit in the chairs nearby, but neither one of us moved, far more content to be standing and alert for our meeting.

He propped his elbows on the desk, his fingers meeting at a point before his face, his smirk now replaced with an expression far more serious.

"I apologise if my partner here made you feel uneasy—subtlety is not his greatest asset." His voice was deep and melodic. His eyes, I noticed, crinkled in mirth, obviously very comfortable in making Ryker the butt of his jokes.

Ryker grunted in response. I didn't care for small talk. Low-Town folk didn't waste the time or the energy. Most of us were straightforward, bordering on harsh.

"I'm not doing shit until you leave my grandma alone," I declared.

The two men shared a quick glance.

"Right. I can assure you your grandmother is safe and will remain so. I am a man of my word."

I scowled at Ryker, who shrugged lazily in response. "You jumped to that conclusion. I never said I would hurt her."

"You sure as hell didn't correct me!" My blood boiled.

"Why the hell should we believe you?" Archer questioned. "All you Domers are snakes. You've cheated and used others your whole life. Your word means dick all."

Ryker sat taller. "You can assume all you want, but we—"

"It's alright, Ry, they're allowed to express how they feel. They've certainly earned the right to do so." The blond leaned back. "Maybe I should have started off with my name: it's Slade. My partner and I are in desperate need of your services. Services we have been keeping tabs on for a while. Services that require the utmost discretion."

"If you say my grandma is safe, then we will see ourselves out. Find someone else." I turned and began to march back towards the hallway.

"I can pay you more than you could imagine. All those medical bills. The prescription. I could get you the finest care for your grandma. I could set you free."

I froze in place, the promise of a future dangled in front of my nose. My own future. One where I did not have to choose between my own life or my grandmother's. I could go to school, get an apprenticeship, make an honest living. Things I could never have if I continued down this path.

This could be my final job, if I played this right.

"Come on Hollyn, we're done here." Archer gently tried to guide me out of the room. But my feet failed me, as if they had grown roots into the ground.

Free.

When I was a kid, I dreamed about freedom. These last few years my soul had damn near given up, weathered by the pressure, the responsibility, the weight of my family's survival burying me just a bit more day by day.

"I know how hard it has been for you in Low-Town—"

"The fuck you do," I spat and turned on my heels to march out of the room, irate that a Domer was pretending to understand my experience.

"I could bring your grandmother three years' supply of her medicine."

Three years. My knees buckled at how much that would cost. How many jobs I would have to take to acquire that much wealth. And he offered it to me without hesitation.

What's the catch? Nothing comes this easy.

And yet his offer was impossible to ignore. I was struggling to convince myself to walk away, despite whatever risks came with it. That kind of fiscal freedom could give me the chance to elicit a career change. It would give me the space I needed to breathe, to look after myself for once. To escape my father.

"You're a Domer. How could I ever believe you?" I asked them.

"Slade's a good man. *Honest* man—" Ryker began, his chest puffing in defence of his friend.

With a wave of Slade's hand, Ryker closed his mouth.

"I will station a live-in nurse with her while you are working, as a gesture of good faith. I will even preemptively give you the first year's supply upfront. That way you still are up more than you started with."

"You know, for when us Domers fuck you over," Ryker teased dryly.

I dragged my hand up my throat and flicked it at him—one of the more vulgar habits I had picked up from working with so many degenerates.

Ryker merely barked in laughter.

Not the reaction I wanted.

I felt Archer's incredulous gaze on me and my cheeks flushed. I knew he couldn't believe I was considering this deal—I had long been a devout hater of Domers and everything they fought to protect.

But I met Slade's gaze, searching his unreadable face for any notion of sincerity. I scrunched my own in thought, searching for what hidden angle he could have that would fuck me over.

"Hollyn, let's talk about it." Archer tried to pull me aside, scrambling at the look of resolve now plastered over my face. He'd read me like a book—I'd already made up my mind. He didn't understand. He never really did; he could afford to be selfish at times, with nobody else depending on him. He hadn't given up on a better future yet.

I shrugged off his grip, the decision already made. I gave him a look that told him we would have this discussion in private, without Domer eyes and ears as audience.

I turned back towards my new clients, curiosity and a hint of excitement bubbling within.

"What is the target?"

Slade came around the table, his arms pumping his wheelchair in front of the mahogany desk.

"I need you to get the Inukviak Relic."

Spill the Dreams

"The what?"

"The Inukviak Relic," Slade repeated patiently. It faintly rang a bell in my memories, but I shook my head for more information. I looked at Archer, his expression pinched. He must have known more than I did.

"Hollyn, how much do you know about the history of our magics?" Slade started.

"I know that you people are the only ones who have it, that it's been passed down from generation to generation, and that people like us fear it enough to put up with the shit we do," I said bitterly.

My teachers briefly skimmed the history of magic in our classes. They were tasked with trying to maintain peace and order, by toeing the line between informing and inciting a rebellion. It was rudimentary education never delving too deep, never encouraging too much honest discussion. Questions always brought forth generational spite and envy, emotions that could cripple productive workers and upset the world order.

So the Domers had created preapproved educational materials and insisted our teachers strictly adhere to them, never digressing.

We also learned, repeatedly and from a young age, that uprisings never won. We had no chance of overcoming their magical prowess. And the details concerning their magic were not revealed so as not to equip us with the very information that could undermine them.

The Domers' survival, their very dominance, had always been the priority in Edinguard.

"So you blame us for things done generations ago. And you hold something we are born with against us?" Ryker challenged, his dark eyebrows raised.

"Generations ago? Do you not own all of this?" I waved my hand around me, gesturing towards the opulence they were accustomed to. "You may not have created this caste system, but you sure reap the rewards from what your families built."

Ryker rolled his eyes, my guilt trip having no effect on his conscience. "What? Do you expect us to renounce our power? The money? To *choose* to live in poverty like you?"

I seethed, my fists clenching in barely veiled hatred. *Maybe I can't do this*, I thought.

"I really could not give a shit what you do," I said through gritted teeth. "But I will never empathise with your kind. Not when you sit in your ivory tower and watch my people break themselves—*die*—for you."

"You do not have to like us to work with us," Slade interjected.

I snorted at the callousness of his logic. I needed to remember I was merely filling an order and nothing more.

"It will be nice to bleed you of a fraction of the blood money you own," Archer growled, mirroring my spiteful sentiments.

"Then so be it," Slade finished, concluding our argument as he wheeled towards a wall of books, chromatically organised, and pulled out a black leather book, its pages yellowed with age. He held out the book for us to grab.

When I hesitated, he wiggled it in impatience.

"You can hate us all you want. But we need to get to work, so if you're in, come take this and let's move forward."

I stretched out my hand and accepted the book, Slade's gaze lingering on my burn, already pink with new healing skin. I jerked the book out of his hands, snapping his concentration back. My hands grazed over the worn leather and the gold-threaded stitching of its title.

"*The People's History of Abraxas* by Basilides," I read aloud. "Abraxas... isn't that the old name for Edinguard?" Our country's first settlement, long before the Great War. Over five hundred years ago.

This book is that old?

"Correct," replied Slade. "It holds answers to some of the questions you will have. I will lend it to you, while you stay here, until you are adequately prepared for your journey. I suggest reading some of it tonight, after dinner and training."

Archer protested, "I'm sorry, you want us to stay here? No way. We do our planning at home."

"You're lucky to even have that book in your hands. Don't think we're just going to let you fucking go," Ryker growled.

"So we're prisoners," Archer observed, his hands shooting up in emphasis at the insanity of the situation.

"Is that not what we are back home too?" I remarked dryly. "At least we're getting paid."

Slade cleared his throat. "Let's get back to the Relic."

He didn't say we weren't.

"Ry is of the Lagodas bloodline, so his... feral ways, I believe, really come from his ability to take the form of any animal." Slade began as Ryker's mouth opened wide, his canines enlarging rapidly into foot-long spears.

He was a shapeshifter. I had never met one before. I shuddered, thinking about the havoc those fangs could wreak.

Archer's body surreptitiously inched towards mine, as if he stood a chance against what this man could become. I had so many questions, but before I could ask more about Ryker, Slade continued.

"Then we have the Makotovic bloodline, who have physical powers."

Drawing my eyes away from Ryker, I said, "Yeah, I remember hearing about one family that was faster than a car—and could easily lift one."

"Dumber than bricks, too. Nothing but metal inside those thick skulls of theirs," alleged Ryker, his finger tapping against his head.

I walked over to the deep navy armchairs and sank into a plush cushion, my weary body finally giving in to the tiredness that had seeped into the core of my bones. I couldn't remember the last time I had felt fully rested. Mentally and physically drained. Leaning my head against the back of the chair, I heaved a deep sigh.

Pumping his arms, Slade cut across the room to join me. "The O'Malleys, I'm sure, you've seen before."

I had. They were the "faces" of magic. The one family we had all seen before in our textbooks, and out on the streets. They had been the ones to deliver the killing blow during the War; the eldest daughter Ilona had harnessed the turbulent sea's great power to drown the enemy's foot army, mere moments before the city had been ransacked.

They were masters of the elements, and from blazing fires to quaking tremors, they had become the backbone of the efforts to quell talks of Low-Town uprisings. Their grip on power had grown exponentially these past years with their increased fervour. They were the only family to patrol Low-Town, and whenever they came we scrambled back into our burrows, out of sight like cockroaches, hiding in hopes of living another day.

They were also the ones that systematically hunted and executed any perceived threats to the world order. In the name of the Priestess.

"So then you must be a Cabral," I concluded.

With a sad smile on his lips, Slade responded, "No, actually. I am none of them. I am just a man whose legs stopped working, hoping for a second chance."

My eyes slid down his body, pausing on his muscular legs clothed in expensive-looking jeans, ironed to perfection, the bottoms cuffed above polished brown boots.

"It happened not too long ago, if you're wondering why my muscles haven't atrophied."

I tore my gaze up and we locked eyes as I sussed out who really sat before me. Whether I believed he was a nobody. Whether he would uphold his end.

"Then how come you live here?" I gestured to the grand building we were in. "Don't you have to be a Domer?"

"If you mean magical, technically, yes. My parents were Cabrals. They had telekinetic powers, could read people's minds, that sort of thing. They were quite important people here. But they were unable to conceive, and the Panel allowed them to adopt outside of their family," Slade explained.

"So you're a Townie?" Archer's troubled expression illustrated his brain trying to reconcile both his hatred towards Domers and his loyalty to Townies simultaneously.

"I was orphaned quite young, my mother passed away early on. She had been one of the few nonmagical allowed to work inside the Dome and died in the hospital here. They told me my parents stumbled upon me and fell in love. But enough about me."

"I know you have no reason to trust us, given our historical animosity. But I'm in desperate need of your services and am willing to pay you everything you could ask for. And I am offering you a once-in-a-lifetime opportunity to get out of your hellhole."

He brushed his tawny curls behind his ear before adding one last point. "We may not be revolting the social paradigm we thrive off of, but we can at least offer you the opportunity to alter *your* lives."

I stared out the window, basking in the glow of the strong morning sun as I contemplated everything I had heard.

"You'll have to forgive me if I find this all a little too... convenient," I replied. "Surely there are other capable thieves for hire. Magical ones, too. Why me?"

"I cant trust any Domers... It needs to be you." Slade replied. "I will explain more later."

What new shitstorm are the Domers brewing?

My brows narrowed in thought, my mind thirsty for more information.

"So where is this Relic, and why do you need it?" Archer interrupted my racing mind. He was perched on my armrest, never too far from me.

I looked at him warmly, his sensual lips pursed in thought, those amber eyes surrounded by sooty lashes. *It's always the men that get them,* I thought to myself with a small chuckle, a sense of brief levity amidst the grave decision before me. The sound brought his attention as we exchanged an intense look, curiosity of the job mixed with trepidation of the danger. But behind that, we saw in each other kindred spirits; we loved the rush we experienced during these jobs. The cheap thrills we both sought to help to break up the monotony of our grim lives.

"The Relic, when invoked properly, can offer the power to heal," Slade stated. "I've tried everything medical that money can buy, to no avail. I want my legs back. This is my last option. My only option."

My head whipped toward him. "Heal?!"

A look of uneasiness flitted across Slade's face but for a moment. If I hadn't been paying close attention, I would have missed it.

"Yes." He hesitated. "But we don't know the full extent of its powers yet. What its limitations are... or the risks."

"But it could maybe heal my grandma's condition?" A stroke, we were told by the doctor, which had begun to attack the brain, her body becoming a hostile environment. The promise of Domer medication and access to state-of-the-art doctors and procedures was great. But if she could be healed... I would do anything for that.

"I'm not getting this thing unless you agree to cure my grandma too." Boldly, I sat back and crossed my arms. Archer's hand rubbed my knee, a noncommittal understanding of what opportunity this Relic could be for us. What it meant for Grandma, for me.

Another shared look between the Domer men before Ryker began, "It could be dangerous for you. We don't know what might—"

"If there's *any* chance to save her, I'll take the risk."

Slade plucked a piece of lint from the shoulder of his shirt, as if to give himself an extra moment to weigh out his options. It hadn't taken me long to understand Slade was calculating. Ryker uncrossed his heels before standing tall in front of the desk, his bulging arms crossed in front of his chest. His eyes never left Slade, as if leaving the ultimate decision to him. *So Slade holds the power.*

A practiced smile broke out across Slade's face, but I knew better than to believe he was happy over me forcing his hand like this. "Of course. Of course we will try."

I rose and stalked towards him, my hand shooting out to secure this deal with a forearm clasp—a Townie gesture of oath. His sapphire eyes focused on the shimmering scar on my hand again as my heart pounded in my ears, victory in this game of chess tantalisingly close.

Those same eyes swept up my body, ever so confidently and slowly, burning a trail everywhere they roamed, as if to remind me who still held the majority of the power here.

"A deal is unbreakable to Ryker and me," Slade warned in a deeper tone than we'd heard, his eyes unblinking. There was no warmth there, only cold ice.

I gulped, forcing the trembling in my hand to subside.

He reached out his hand to clasp my forearm in a firm grip.

What did I agree to?

We were shown to our rooms shortly after. Ryker and Slade must have seen the exhaustion on our faces and agreed to delve deeper into the details of the task after a quick rest. Archer had protested separate rooms, still wholly distrustful of our clients, referring to them instead as our captors. So we both entered one room, safe in our partnership. But I had seen the need in Slade's tanned face and somehow believed we would be okay. They had to obtain this Relic, and thus required our skills, which offered me some comfort at least.

"I don't trust this, Torch." Archer's nickname for me started years ago, after my father had shoved me into a wall one night in a drunken stupor. It was like a switch had flicked inside me—I'd finally had enough of his abuse. I front-kicked my father right between his legs. I had never seen his face get so red before. I'd felt empowered, flushed with that high, and I'd turned my back on the inner docile little girl ever since.

Archer referred to it as the day my inner fire relit like a torch.

We headed into the open, airy room, minimally decorated, save for a plush rug beneath the king-sized bed and an oval mirror above the large white desk on the far wall. One of the walls was solely made of towering glass panes, the vibrant sunlight lighting the room in welcoming warmth. The bed was gigantic, the stark white of the sheets and duvet thick like the fluffy clouds that rarely poked through the grey blanket of smog back home.

"They're just promising you whatever you want most; they're fucking with your hopes, manipulating your worst fears. Typical Domer mindfuckery." Archer's curls shook as he took in his surroundings, vigilantly assessing it for our safety. Self-preservation habits from which we would never be free.

I walked towards the windows to look out at the manicured lawn and watched a small brown bird flit from just above my view. "Why would they make this up?"

"Because they know your grandma is sick. They know how much she means to you. You're playing right into it." Archer shook his head in disapproval.

I scoffed, my gaze still following the bird haphazardly flapping across the windowpane. "Slade's in a wheelchair—do you really think they'd go that far? Couldn't they have just stuck to threatening me?" Domers were tricky, sure, but they preferred the quickest means to their end. So why offer a carrot if a stick would get the job done faster?

"So what, now Domers are reasonable? *Honourable?*"

I didn't appreciate the snarkiness from him. "We're on the same team, you know. I'm trying to figure this out too. I don't need you acting like I'm an idiot."

"Sorry, Holls, you're right." Another sigh escaped him, his full lips flapping from the movement. His nervous energy told me he wasn't done talking about it, and so I waited for him to unload.

"It's just too good to be true," Archer continued, the words pouring out of him. "How do we know they won't bail once we've given them the Relic? What if it doesn't help Grandma? What if it hurts her? What if the real reason they're asking us is because they know it's suicide and no Domer would be dumb enough to accept it?"

He slumped down on the end of the bed, his elbows resting on his knees as he cradled his head in his hands, all his worries cathartically expressed. I wondered how exhausted he must be too—I had a habit of being consumed by my own misery, forgetting Archer stood beside me through it all.

When was the last time I helped him?

I sat down beside him, my knobby knees knocking his midthigh. His height loomed a foot taller than mine—another reason why I was better suited for the stealth role in our duo.

"I know," I replied, unsure of what else to say. "I know."

One hand dropped down, his cheek squished by his other as he rotated his head towards me, peeping at me with one eye.

"But still you're interested."

"Honestly Arch, I'm feeling a lot right now. If they could heal Grandma? How could I not at least try? But of course a big part of me is beyond suspicious. Another part, terrified. Even another part is disgusted that I'm considering working this closely with a Domer." I grabbed his hand in mine, our fingers interlocking. "But we've been doing jobs for Domers and whoever else for a while now, whether we want to admit it to ourselves or not. We've just had someone be our middleman. Was that really any different?"

Archer's eyes bored into mine as he sat there mulling everything over.

I knew I would not do this without him. He knew it too.

I would never beg him. And he would never let me.

"We can at least hear the rest of the details," I hedged, pushing into his leg with my adjacent knee. "Right?"

With a sigh, he nodded towards the bathroom. "Fine. But I'm not leaving here empty-handed. Let's at least steal some of those fancy bottles by the tub."

Snickering, I rose and approached the freestanding tub, housed in an enormous en suite of shiny marble and tile, and I almost sobbed at the tub's size. Various concoctions of wonderfully smelling soaps, shampoos, and oils were laid out on its bath tray. I picked up a bottle of turquoise liquid that smelled like how I imagined a vacation by the ocean must smell. Not like I had ever seen the ocean before.

I pocketed the bottle, along with a few others, and heard a soft chuckle in response.

Pivoting on my heel, I twisted my hands together, my gaze downcast as I fumbled for a way to persuade Archer. "I know I'm asking for a lot, Arch. And—and maybe I am being a fool for considering this. But I'm just... I'm drowning. And it's only getting worse. We might not have jobs to come back to. Maybe we can figure something else out, but can my grandma wait?"

I paced towards the bathroom vanity mirror and stared back at my own emerald eyes and my strong brows, slanted ever so slightly upwards. I noticed the bags underneath them, the dryness of my tight skin, the cracks in my chapped lower lip. Bending over, I ran the faucet and splashed cold water over my face, revelling in the pure smell of the water. No copper tang, no funky odor. I stood up to my full height again before patting my face dry with the plush face towel hanging perfectly on the gold towel rack to my left.

As I walked back towards Archer I nearly begged him, "Please just listen to the details, and I promise we will make this decision together."

Reaching his hand out, he grabbed mine, his thumb gently caressing the back of it, and again I blushed from the nearness of him. Skirting my eyes away, I pulled my hand from his, uncomfortable in the intimacy. Physical touch was difficult for me to endure. *Probably because I've been hit more than hugged by my own father.*

"Okay, Torch." A small smile and an earnest nod. "You win."

The corners of my lips tugged up. "I'll wait and see before I start celebrating."

Archer opened his mouth as if to respond, but then abruptly shut it before muttering that we should get some rest.

I hesitated, hoping he would say something else, give me an excuse to continue the conversation. But when he rose to start undressing for bed, I nodded and began doing the same.

I plopped down on the edge of the bed to unlace my boots, then stretched my feet in freedom. I unzipped my leather jacket, struggling to pull the sweaty fabric off my tired arms, before I flung it at the chaise lounge by the foot of the bed. Gingerly I placed my belt on top, careful of the contents it held, before I shuffled my jeans down my hips until they fell onto the floor in a messy heap. As Archer stripped down, my eyes caught a quick glance of his long, lean body. *No, Hollyn.*

I climbed under the plush covers and buried myself by my edge of the bed, careful not to focus on how close in proximity our near-naked bodies would be. I felt the dip of the mattress as he slid in beside me, my body clenched with anxiety and anticipation, my breath catching in my throat. Waiting.

But Archer never crossed over onto my side of the bed, and shortly after I heard the first soft snores emitting from him, I quickly succumbed to my own exhaustion and drifted off.

An unapologetic knock startled me awake and I found myself interwoven with Archer's limbs, his eyes also shooting open at the interruptive rap. The right side of his face was imprinted with red markings, illustrating the depth at which he had slept—probably as restfully as I had. Our vigilance had failed, our weariness squashing our hopes to remain alert for any danger. Instead we had been as defenceless as newborn babies asleep at the tit.

We threw off the covers, rushing and stumbling to find our clothes, hopping on one foot as we pulled our legs through our pants, our jacket zippers rending through the air in careless speed. My hands whipped through my hair as my fingers worked to detangle the multitude of knots they found as a second knock, louder now, sounded at the door.

"Alright, alright already, we're coming," grumbled Archer as he went to open the door, his hands fastening the button on his pants.

A plump, squat lady, her brown hair coiffed into a low braid, held a tray of all sorts of delectables, from French-pressed coffee to still-warm cinnamon buns. The aroma was intoxicating. Spices like cinnamon and nutmeg I hadn't smelled in years, having had to prioritise staple foods over seasonings. My mouth watered as she entered the room and laid the assortment of goodies on the desk. Her eyes squinted as two cups floated up, then a teapot, which poured out coffee into each one before the cups softly sailed towards us.

My hands caught the teacup and the pastry that followed behind it and brought them towards my lips. Explosions of flavour burst in my mouth as I devoured the sweet and sipped the drink, my eyes closing briefly in delight.

"I'm the housekeeper here—the name's Minerva. But you can call me Minnie. If you two need anything, anything at all while you're here, you just let me know. Slade told me to make you two as comfortable as possible. So eat up, drink up, wash yourselves, and let me know what you need." Her grey-blue eyes were warm, gentle even, and her well-worn hands belied the life of magical luxury I assumed of all Domers.

Noticing where my gaze lingered, she smirked. "Not everything is done with magic, you know. My hands still do lots of hard work on their own."

She glanced towards the closet, and the doors folded open with a wave from one of her callused hands. She pointed to the array of clothing inside.

"There should be a bunch of different-sized clothing in here—hopefully something to fit that tiny frame of yours. Pick whatever you'd like. But I'd recommend something breathable, as I overheard mention of training. You know, the best house-keepers know what's going on in their house at all times, they do. I pride myself in knowing all the comings and goings. So get yourselves ready and head downstairs—they'll be waiting for you two."

As Minerva strutted to the door, she said, "You really oughta eat all that there. Not a pound to lose on you. Not a pound." She shook her head, clucking like a mother hen as she left, not waiting for my response.

I stretched my arms stiff above my head, shuddering at the feeling, then strode into the bathroom, one mission on my mind. I was going to savour each second of my bath, prepared to scrub to death years of grime. On the way, I grabbed a raspberry turnover, shoving it into my mouth. *Fuck that's delicious.*

Turning on the faucets, my butt perched carefully on the lip of the freestanding tub, I carefully poured a stream of amber-coloured oil in, swirling my hand in the warm water as I played with the scented bubbles multiplying rapidly.

With a quick glance over my shoulder, I checked for privacy from Archer, who was busy rifling through the closet, before I began stripping down. As my pants fell to the floor, I couldn't help myself from cataloguing the faint scars scattered across my legs. I knew each and every one, as the memory of them had been burned into my nightmares, plaguing my childhood for decades. I used to replay each and every fight with my father, trying to decode what had set him off, how I had upset him, what I could have done differently.

Now they served as a reminder that those closest to me could hurt me the most. That family did not equal unconditional love. That trust would forever be a problem for me and mine.

That maybe, just maybe, I *was* unlovable.

I felt myself numbing, my brain instinctively compartmentalising the deep, unresolved anguish within. I made quick work undressing the rest of me and plunged myself into the toasty waters, fighting from falling into that dark headspace. I submerged underwater as if to wash it all away, and when I reemerged, my eyes flitted towards the bedroom, where I found Archer watching me.

He tentatively strode towards the bathroom, pausing in the archway, his hands braced against the walls. "I should have stopped him after the first one."

My stomach twisted at those words. "You were a kid, just like me." My hands trailed over my head and down my neck, pushing stray strands out of my face as I exhaled. "My father is not your fault. And I would never have let you interfere."

"Maybe I shouldn't have waited for your permission." His words felt multilayered, as if he were referring to more than just my father. "I feel like I'm always careful, always planning. And what good did that do? It allowed years of abuse to happen to you."

Lifting one of the bars of scented soap, I began lathering my outstretched arm. "I don't need a white knight. I'm not helpless."

"I know, Holls, I didn't mean that. It's just... again I'm sitting back, letting you consider this new mission, when I feel like in my gut something's wrong with it." Archer sighed, his head hanging down as if imprisoned in a stock. "I'm scared I'm letting something bad happen to you again."

Pausing in my cleaning, I turned to face him. "You're my best friend, Archer. We're a team. What we have works, and works *well*. I appreciate you listening to me. That we can make a decision together, instead of you acting on my behalf. You know that would piss me off."

He lifted his head, his amber eyes boring into me, emotion storming within them. "Just promise me we talk this through.

And that you don't do this without me, if that's what you choose. I-I can't lose you. You're my best friend, Torch."

My cheeks flushing in response to the intensity of his attention, I forced myself to swallow the deep wound his words cut. He couldn't have been more clear about how he viewed us—friends, nothing more, reassuring my doubts and insecurities that the feelings I felt weren't mutual. I quelled the heat building deep in my belly, choking down my attraction to him.

But I willed myself to keep his gaze, refusing to show any indication of the battle within. "You won't." I wanted to say more, to tell him how much he meant to me too. But I couldn't.

So I kept my mouth shut and returned to my soaping, my mind racing as I heard Archer sigh and pivot to head back towards the bedroom.

As I cleaned every inch of my body fastidiously, I wondered what dangers we would face, what angle Slade and Ryker had, and what strife this would create between Archer and me.

Would I be successful and save my grandmother? Or would I be unsuccessful and lose Archer in the process too?

Hope for the Best, Plan for the Work

M innie had been right. My legs wobbled from exertion, my body bound to be bruised already.

I was dressed in sweat-wicking spandex, narrowly dodging punches from Archer as Ryker shouted tips and orders from outside the boxing ring. They had their own gymnasium in the basement, filled with endless rows of machines, free weights, and other paraphernalia I had no idea how to use. Sweat poured down our faces, our bodies not used to this style of work—neither of us having much experience in sparring. We tried our best to avoid fighting whenever possible, but times were hard in Low-Town, and so we did have *some* basic self-defence skills.

But nothing like this.

Ryker had laughed in our faces when we'd initially refused to spar—and then proceeded to shove us into the ring. One of many days of training, he'd told us.

The need to defend ourselves was necessary in our "worst-case scenario." And if anyone knew how to fight, it was Ryker. So Archer and I threw ourselves into the training, absorbing all the tips and tricks Ryker shot our way to maximise our crash course in combat. Even if we refused the job, we'd at least have learned a trick or two in the process.

Ryker was topless—why, I had no idea. He had not once exerted any energy, instead frequently stepping in to reposition our bodies, his giant hands firm and confident. Down both arms, corded in muscle, Ryker had tattoos of numerous animal heads, the colours of their different furs, scales, and feathers a spectrum of vibrant colours.

"Now pivot while pulling his arm, your other hand slamming down on his elbow."

I did as I was told and Archer buckled.

"You'll see you're behind him, which is always a great place to be when sparring. Keeping his arm overstretched like that, wrap your other arm around his neck as you lower him to the ground. You have the option then to replace your arm with your thighs, all while maintaining his one arm, and he'll be asleep in a matter of seconds."

I followed directions, going for the chokehold with my thighs, Archer's arm bent awkwardly over my thigh, and just as Ryker said, he slammed his hand against the mat in surrender.

"You don't have size working for you, but you're a natural, and you're quick and flexible. Those are great advantages to have in a fight. Don't forget that," Ryker counselled.

I caught my breath after releasing a sweat-soaked Archer and asked, "Do all the Lagodas have those tattoos?" Tattooed Townies were few and far between—and those that had them had endured stick-and-poke tattoos crafted from DIY materials and inks. Nothing that could create the intricate detailing of what covered Ryker.

"No. I just like the pain." He grinned at me.

I rolled my eyes in return, but a small smile tugged at my lips. Remembering that I was letting my guard down in front of Domers, I shook my head to refocus my attention on my training.

We reentered the ring for another round of combat.

Jab, punch, duck. Hook, uppercut, duck.

Archer danced away from my strikes as I exhaled with each punch. His eyes twinkled in challenge at me, so I swapped the order without warning and grazed his jaw with my hook, to his surprise.

With a welp, Archer rubbed his jaw, feigning irreparable damage. But in his eyes I had seen genuine shock and pride at how quickly I was taking to this style of martial arts.

"Truce? Or are you thirsty for more," I joked, my eyebrows flicking up and down, perhaps adding more flirtation than I meant to.

"I'll never turn down more," Archer drawled. My cheeks warmed again at the innuendo laced in his words.

Ryker must have picked up on the signals, as he cleared his throat rather hoarsely. "Let's take a break, grab a drink. You seem... thirsty."

Plopping down on the gym mat, I sat crisscrossed as I guzzled a bottle of ice-cold water. The brand was Nordic Ice—I had never seen it sold in our stores.

As the chilled liquid streamed down my throat, I understood why—it was way too pure for Low-Town. I shivered as the frosty water settled in my stomach, goosebumps breaking out down my gangly arms.

"So when are we going to discuss logistics on this?" questioned Archer. "We need blueprints, security camera data, and access to some of our equipment if we're gonna do this right." He counted on his fingers as he listed his demands, his fingers hovering as he pondered what else he would need.

"You won't need any of that." Ryker smirked, waving a dismissive hand.

"What? What do you mean? Of course we will. Everywhere in Edinguard has at least a decent security system set up. Unless we're stealing from a Townie?"

"You're not going to steal something in Edinguard. You're going to Abraxas."

My body shivered again, whether from the water or from the target of our mission I wasn't sure.

Nobody ever went to Abraxas—it'd been sealed up for centuries. It had been the last stronghold during the War, the pivotal setting where the tides had been turned and our ancestors saved.

It was ancient, stuck in a magical limbo almost half a millennium ago.

It had been, from what I remembered from stories, where Dashiell Dufort's power had been bound, effectively halting his advancing rampage on our people. Where the fifth magical bloodline had ended.

It was the home our ancestors had been dispelled from, forced to relocate and settle in a new city: Edinguard.

My knowledge ended there, as my teachers had only briefly mentioned this moment, and more to highlight the power of the other four bloodlines. We did not speak of Dufort's magic, since it was long dead. We were simply told that the others had effectively stopped it—a warning for us not to mess with their magical descendants.

Some said the magic drove him crazy. Others said he was always mad, the magic only giving him the power to act on his insanity. Some even believed he was death incarnate, his followers raised from the dead.

Either way, the magic was gone, the truth lost in time.

Until, perhaps, now.

Cold dread filled the pit of my stomach as I tentatively asked, "Why is the Relic there?" I rose, my body no longer wishing to rest as adrenaline pumped vivaciously through me. "What exactly is this Relic?"

My mind raced as I mulled over what magical traps might lie in a place like that. One that hadn't been penetrated in five hundred years. I prayed that the Inukviak Relic was not connected to the Duforts and their sealed powers.

"How could *we* even get in? Nobody has cracked the barrier." Abraxas was sealed behind a magical wall, the collateral result of the magic that'd been invoked on that fateful day.

"A great question, Hollyn," commended Slade as he wheeled into the room, startling both Archer and me.

For thieves who prided ourselves on our top-tier skills, we sure had gotten careless here.

"We have been researching this for a while and can fill you in on all we know over dinner. Let's head to the kitchen—Minnie has cooked up a delicious roast for us."

We were seated at an elegant dining table of off-white oak, our china plates and cutlery edged with strings of gold. Tender slices of beef, garlicky mashed potatoes, and roasted vegetables flecked with various seasonings filled my plate, Minnie's obvious intention to fatten me up. This amount of food would have been enough for my family, but for once in my life I greedily devoured everything.

Slade was at the head of the table, ever the picture of calmness, dressed in a linen button-down rolled to above his elbows. His forearms rippled as he confidently sawed through his slabs of meat before carefully sopping up as much gravy as possible with each bite.

Ryker, on the other hand, might as well have shoved his face directly into his plate, his fork more a weapon for puncturing his food to death than a vehicle to get it into his mouth. His spoon ladled up vegetables to dump in like an avalanche of snow crashing into a valley. The black T-shirt he wore bulged around his muscles, the threads of it holding on for dear life. Each time he shovelled a spoonful of food, I waited for his sleeve to rip. But clearly, Domer fashion was built more resilient than the thin textiles Townies were stuck wearing.

Archer sat to my left, somehow looking unappetised by the glorious meal in front of him. His eyes darted around the room, taking in the enormous abstract painting hung on the wall before him. I watched him snarl his lip, seeing his brain process the shapes and colours, his bewilderment over its lure unabashedly plastered on his face. He had never been impressed with anything the Domers treasured, none of the grandiose art, the fancy cars, or the fashion.

"So let me get this straight." Archer paused. "This Relic isn't connected to what happened back then? It just *happens* to be in Abraxas?"

"That's what he said, isn't it?" Ryker snapped, irritated by the repetitive nature of our conversation.

The men shot each other glares as tensions rose. Agitation rolled off their bodies, like waves cresting against the shore. This mission was becoming riskier by the minute, and I could feel Archer begin to shut down over it.

"Seems like a lie... but even *if* that's true, how are we supposed to break this magical barrier and enter a city that has been stuck paralyzed in time? Where no comms will work, no blueprints are available, there's no information to gather—since, you know, nobody has ever gone inside?" Archer's voice rose in hysteria.

"Hollyn can do this without you, without all... that. We don't need you," Ryker dryly reminded Archer. "Please feel free to leave. Anytime." Ryker's smile was more akin to a dog baring its teeth than pleasantries.

Archer looked to me, confident that I would now refuse this insane mission.

But instead, I prompted further discussion. "How would we break in then?"

"Jesus Christ, Hollyn, you can't be—"

"I'm not saying yes, I'm just getting information," I reminded him pointedly, my hands raised in placation. "Like we agreed."

"I have one piece of that Relic nobody else has. See, it was broken a long time ago into three shards, and I believe that the barrier surrounding Abraxas will react to one of the missing pieces. Nobody has ever found a missing piece before, and from what we've researched, the hypothesis is pretty sound," Slade clarified.

Archer arched his eyebrows in sceptic disbelief. "How the hell did that piece fall into your lap?"

"Does it matter?" Ryker retorted.

"Yes, it matters. If something shady happened to get it..." I began, my hackles rising. "We may be thieves, but we have morals. And if you want us to even consider this, then we need to know the truth before we get entangled in something bigger than what you're telling us."

Archer scoffed. "Why are we even trying, Holls? Of course they're going to lie to get what they want. They're Domers."

"You have no idea what's going on—"

Slade raised his hand to silence his friend.

I tried to garner more details from another angle, my gut agreeing they were omitting some key information. "So why us? Why not send him in?" I pointed towards Ryker.

"It appears as though any member of the other magical bloodlines cannot enter. We have tried, believe us, but it seems like only someone like yourself can get in."

Like us. Nonmagical. Good old-fashioned thieves.

I wondered how many before us had tried. I wondered how many had perished. Would I do this job alone if Archer refused to join?

Was the payoff worth the rapidly mounting risk?

I remembered the last seizure that had ravaged my grand-mother's body. Her curved spine, arched from decades spent working in the factories hunched over machines, the rank air, horribly uncirculated and thick with perspiration and steam. Archer and I had been in my house, reviewing the latest gig we had planned when we'd heard the commotion. We had raced over when factory workers had begun to shout my name from down the street, hoping I had more medicine to quell the attack.

It had been a particularly vicious one. Her eyes had rolled back into her head, her tongue flopped out, drool spilling from her mouth. Her arms tightly clenched in awkward angles as she lay on her back, her spine bending forwards and backwards like a fish out of water. Her forehead sported a large gash gushing blood down her cheek—from her body plummeting to the ground, they had told me. I watched her mouth fill with foam as her tiny, helpless body convulsed for too long. It had been her longest seizure yet.

The doctor had warned me if these attacks lasted for too long, irreversible damage would occur. That she could become a vegetable, an invalid incapable of even going to the bathroom by herself. It would destroy her—and consequently, destroy any vestiges of hope I had of turning our lives around. I would have to wait out her life, and the thought of that nearly killed me.

I had tried long before to sober up my father, pleading for his help in all of this. But he'd simply taken the last bit of cash I had stowed, reminded me of my lack of worth, slapped me hard across the face, and followed it up with a backhand. He proceeded to inform me that he'd never wanted me, that I was really my grandmother's responsibility, and that the "the two of us selfish cunts deserved each other." And that if I didn't take care of my grandmother, her pain—her death—was on my conscience, not his.

I had given up on hoping for his help after that.

"But you surely have nonmagical workers under you? Why not hire them?" I asked before I stuffed my face with a gravy-drowned scoop of potato, my appetite insatiable. *Fuck, that was delicious too.*

Slade swallowed his mouthful of food. "We have tried, but they do not carry Dufort blood in them. That seems to be the key."

I glanced at Archer in confusion, my mouth paused mid-bite before heavily swallowing a too-big bite.

"Dufort?" I glanced between them. "But they're all long dead."

"That's what we've been told since forever," Slade confirmed. "But Ryker and I believe that's not actually the truth."

My mind reeled, this new information shattering my understanding of our society and its bloody history. *Am I to bring a vial of this blood with me?*

"What do you mean it's not the truth? Nobody has seen a Dufort in over a century," Archer probed.

"The O'Malleys have been executing anyone even suspected of being connected to a Dufort for decades." I shook my head in disbelief. "How could they have possibly survived?"

"Yes, the O'Malleys' perverse paranoia has escalated to genealogical genocide. But we have uncovered some records that indicate they were not all killed." Slade shared a brief glance with Ryker before he continued.

"Part of what I've been researching has been tracing the genealogy of the Dufort bloodline, in hopes of figuring out a way to gain access into Abraxas. But what we stumbled upon led us to you."

"What do I have to do with the Duforts?" Another tower of food entered my mouth as my jaw went to work, mincing the deliciousness as I pondered this information, trying to piece together the puzzle.

I knew my father and grandmother were magicless, and my brain strained to remember any moments of memory that might have indicated otherwise.

Slade lifted his water to his lips, his throat bobbing as he gulped. With a clink, he set his glass down. "You see, Hollyn, I have reason to suspect that *you* are from the Dufort bloodline."

I sucked in my breath in stunned shock, effectively choking myself on a half-chewed piece of meat. I pounded on my chest, my face heating as I laboured to breathe, my throat frantically attempting to swallow through the clump of food blocking my airways.

My hand shot out to grab the glass of ice water before me in an attempt to flush the blockage and quell the burning in my throat, but it only added to my choking. The food finally shot out and back onto my plate with one final ejective cough.

"Wh-what... the... fuck," I gasped.

Ryker barked with laughter, his broad shoulders heaving up and down as his head ripped back in mirth, evidently enjoyed my near asphyxiation.

"That's ridiculous," I panted as I regained some normalcy in my breathing, only to find fury replacing the space.

"How could she be a Dufort? She's a Flynn." Archer shook his head in disbelief.

"I've never done anything... magical. Nobody in my family has." My eyes squinted, my forehead scowled. "The Duforts died out long ago."

"Actually, some of the records—"

"Why are you saying this? Is this some sick joke?" I began to think that Archer may have been right, that this was some perverse mockery, some cruel joke Domers played on desperate Townies. Lure us in, make some grandiose story, and then watch us fail as they laughed at our misery.

"What? Why would—" Slade's face scrunched in surprised confusion at my anger.

"Because you think all us Townies want is to be like you. That magic is the only thing we desire. How conceited is that?" Archer explained, pushing his chair back to rise. "What a waste of our fucking time."

I rose from my spot at the table, tears welling in the corners of my eyes at the embarrassment of believing what they'd offered was real. That I had let my guard down just slightly, only to be reminded of the malevolence of Domers.

"We aren't joking—" Slade attempted.

"Yeah and I'm the fucking Priestess," Archer interjected.

Ryker's fists slammed down on the table, its quake shaking everything set on top.

"*Listen* to us, dammit," Ryker growled. "Whether you believe it or not, Hollyn, you have Dufort blood in you. If you will just shut the hell up and let us speak, we can explain it all. So stop wasting our time debating something Slade and I know to be true, and let us get the fuck on with it."

"That's impossible. I am a Flynn. I'm magicless." My loose curls wobbled as I shook my head in denial, but Ryker's reaction felt sincere, felt honest... for a Domer. "This is ridiculous. It can't be true." My brain whirled as this new information began cracking apart my understanding of my life, my world, my identity.

Slade cleared his throat, his calm demeanour once again intact. "We found records that had been tampered with by someone at the hospital. Modifications had been made to names, families, birth records, death certificates, and all sorts of extensive alterations. It prompted us to delve further, to really check whether our software was malfunctioning or if it was catching some extensive behind-the-scenes puppeteering."

Slade pressed the stark white napkin to his full lips before placing it on the empty plate before him. He leaned back, comfortable in explaining his theory.

"One of them was your birth record—both your name and family had been modified."

Silence.

I felt numb in every fibre of my being. I could muster nothing to say. I couldn't believe it. *Wouldn't* believe it.

"That could mean anything... I..." I fumbled for a logical reason. "I mean my father, my grandmother, they're not..."

"We don't know how far back the alterations were made, yet—whether your father and grandmother too are living under another identity like you."

"So maybe they changed their minds, wanted to change my name—"

"People don't go to this level of secrecy just to change a name or record of familial lineage. Unless, of course, they don't want anyone to piece together their true identity. Their family's true identity. An identity that would put a target on their backs for the rest of their lives."

My head whipped towards Archer, but words escaped me. His pinched expression was all I needed to confirm he too felt it was straying from fantasy and venturing closer to reality.

I sank back into my chair, beginning to feel queasy and light-headed.

A part of me had never felt like my father was family. That there was another reason for his innate hatred of me.

If I truly was a Dufort, then that could explain it.

It meant he had spent his entire life hiding my identity. Risking his life by harbouring the enemy of Edinguard.

Confusion crashed through my mind, snippets of memories whipping through my head as I reassessed my father in this new light.

"Shouldn't I have... *felt* some magic by now?"

"No. The Dufort magic—holy magic—lies dormant inside, bound by the chains of the other bloodlines. Unless that magic were to be unbound, you would not have any indication otherwise." Slade's response was far too calm in comparison to the tornado twisting inside me.

"*Holy* magic? But—but it made Dashiell mad. It's... evil." I blanched, thinking about what could become of me. What would happen if it corrupted me too.

Slade shrugged. "Is that the truth, or is that what we've been told to believe?"

"So the magic is good?" Archer asked tentatively.

"We don't really know, to be honest. Is magic ever truly evil? Or is it simply the wielder that is to blame?"

Shooting to my feet, I caught the lip of the table to steady myself, my brain running rampant as it tried to process this paradigm-shattering information.

"I-I need to think about all of this. Alone."

Without waiting for permission, I left them all and darted back to my room, each step getting progressively more dizzying. My hand shook as I twisted the doorknob, desperate for privacy when I inevitably crumbled. Once inside, I sank to the floor, my back slamming against the door as I closed my eyes, focusing on calming my rising panic attack.

I hadn't had one in a while.

I had come to despise everything about the Domers—their exploitative nature, their greed, their complete disregard for the downtrodden and their prejudice against the nonmagical—only to discover that perhaps that same blood flowed through my own veins.

I was the Goliath in this story, not David.

If this was true.

But Slade's words struck a chord deep within me. Perhaps a truth that I'd long since suppressed. Something that had always contributed to the difficulty I had fitting in with Townies.

Spiralling, I inhaled heavily through my nostrils and focused on exhaling every last breath of stale air out of my lungs, as if trying to eject the new reality bestowed upon me.

Who was I, if not a Townie? Surely not a Domer.

I felt neither like a Flynn nor a Dufort. I felt like nobody: an identity fallen through the cracks and loopholes.

I felt my body shaking before I realised I was weeping. Each tear a cathartic experience, each drop purging the overwhelming cascade of mixed emotions tornadoing through me until a soft knock jolted me out of my near fugue-like state.

"Holls?" Archer's tender voice, muffled by the thick door standing between us. "Let me in, Holls."

Wearily, I stood and cracked open the door, heading towards the bed to envelop myself in a cocoon of expensive blankets. I sank into their plushness, my line of sight diminishing as the thick duvet hooded around me.

Weight pressed down beside me, and I welcomed Archer's long, warm body as he spooned me over the covers.

"I can't figure out why they would lie about this," I pondered aloud in between sniffles. "My brain keeps trying to figure out why this couldn't be possible, but it comes up with nothing."

He rubbed my back, allowing me the space to speak my mind without interruption.

"Who am I, Archer?" Tears choked me. "*What* am I?"

"You are Hollyn. You are a survivor, a warrior, someone who had to grow up too early. Someone who's suffered for too long, bearing the responsibility of people twice her age."

I turned around to face him, my tear-streaked face inches from his. "And if I truly am a Dufort, then I'm the very thing I have spent my entire life hating." I searched his face, terrified to see any disgust he might now feel towards me for being a Domer. My lower lip trembled in emotion as I waited for his response.

Archer blew air through his lips, his eyebrows raised in question, "Can we really consider the Duforts to be Domers? For the last five hundred years we thought they were dead."

I hesitated, his answer not exactly as direct and reassuring as I'd hoped. "True, but I'm from a family that was driven crazy. Crazy enough to try to slaughter their own civilization. That's worse." *Tell me I'm wrong.*

"That does not change who *you* are, only who your family was." A soft kiss on the back of my blanketed head. "The past is the past. You had no part in that—you can't forget that, no matter what we learn."

Silence—a comfortable silence between partners.

"You don't hate me now?" I asked boldly, needing to hear his answer.

Without hesitating he replied, "No. Never. Not for this."

A whoosh of air released from my lips and I didn't realize I was holding my breath. I nodded, my eyes closing briefly in relief.

Rolling onto my back, Archer nestled against the side of me, I broached one final topic. "I need to confirm what they've told us," I declared. "I can't just take their word."

"Maybe there's some information in that book they gave us?" Archer rolled over to retrieve the book before placing the ancient text on my stomach. My hand instinctively reached out to touch it.

"And if it isn't in there?" I asked.

"Then we go ask your father."

"What if he doesn't know?"

"He will."

I nodded, the blanket hooded around me stretching with the movement.

"Do we take this mission on? Knowing everything we do now?"

Archer sighed heavily. "If you truly are a Dufort, and they've already discovered this, it's only a matter of time before others find out. And I can't keep you safe if you're preoccupied with looking after your grandmother."

"Yeah," I responded, my voice eerily hollow and empty. "And I can't leave her with him. My father."

"Yeah." Another sigh. "And besides, maybe you will find what you've been missing your whole life—a future worth fighting for. A real family. And an end to all of this thieving."

"Thank you... for doing this with me. Despite everything." Emotions welled up in my throat until my voice bubbled. I peaked at Archer, who smiled warmly back at me. My stomach fluttered as my body flushed with warmth.

"What, you mean breaking into a city that nobody has entered in five hundred years?" A deep chuckle. "Besides, I'm always up for a challenge."

My hand snuck out to rub his in thanks.

"Maybe we'll get out of Low-Town after this. Escape it all, bring your grandmother along. Get her better. Live a new life, just us three."

"Yeah... maybe." I smiled softly, envisioning that spectacular dream.

Will you still be with me if I'm a Dufort?

Book, Line, and Sinker

The spine creaked as I opened the tome, the musty smell from the ancient pages smacking me in the face. I had always liked the smell of our textbooks, the sour odour so different from the stench of factory waste and smoke that smothered Low-Town. My fingers traced over the inside, the smooth coldness of its glossy finish so refined compared to the recycled, rough texture I was used to.

I had so many questions about who my real family was, about the full history of Abraxas, about what power the Inukviak Relic held. It was only fair to Archer and myself to gather as much information as we could before planning our expedition inside. I hoped the book would affirm my trust in Slade's words, having nothing else to rely on save for my intuition.

Luckily, despite the book being over five hundred years old, it was still written in our native tongue, the odd word spelt in older styles and some of the phrasing archaic, but understandable. I started from the beginning, skimming and scanning for key words, stopping to read passages of importance as I went along.

After a while, I had gotten a fairly decent description of Abraxas's founding—it had initially been a trading port colony situated on one of the bigger rivers, the Helban River. The town had seen large success, with a sharp influx in settlers as monetary gains skyrocketed with the mercantilization of the unique onyx bone hunted from the tusks of Shadowstompers. These elephant cousins had long been hunted to extinction, their illustrious black bones proving to be stronger than both titanium and diamond.

The book did not list any medicines or treatments like I had hoped. But it did describe medical miracles for which Abraxas had become famous. That had been the other major pull to bring in new settlers—people travelled from all over seeking Abraxan healers, with some stories so wild as to claim cures of incurable illnesses.

Reading about these stories, whether they were myths or not, gave me more hope for my cause. It failed to mention, however, who or what was used in these situations. I hoped, like Slade, there were medical documents we could access, or perhaps instructions on how to invoke the Relic.

It seemed as though the five magical dynasties had played key roles in Abraxas's creation, although it did not state whether that was where magic was born. Perhaps the families had originated there, or perhaps something in Abraxas had lured them in.

Minnie rapped politely at my door, breaking my concentration, and entered bearing hot teas and pastries to fuel our efforts.

"Nothing like a little reading with a nice warm cup of tea, eh?"

I nodded, savouring the spicy smells coming out of the teapot's spout. Minnie poured us each a cup, and I delighted in the trail of warmth that spilled down my throat as I sipped the beverage. My callused hands cupped the heat greedily.

"Thank you, Minnie." I smiled warmly, my feelings towards my own grandmother overflowing onto her, Archer murmuring his thanks as well.

"You know, despite how Ryker may seem, they really are a nice couple of boys." She flicked her hands, sending a muffin each floating our way. I caught mine midair before sinking my teeth into the baking. Blueberries exploded in my mouth.

"Been here fifteen years, I have. Known 'em since they were little boys running around the place, getting into mischief." Her face reflected the love she felt for them.

"Have they always been together?" Archer asked.

"Yeah... ever since the murder." Minnie busied herself by lathering a giant glop of butter onto a scone, armed for our next bite.

I sensed there was more to the story. "What murder, Minnie?"

"Well, they said it was suicide, but I knew his parents like the back of my hand... and depressed they were not. The officers just wrote it off, barely did their due diligence, I said. Bad cops. Bad bad cops." She shook her head in disappointment.

"Who would want Slade's parents dead?" Archer inquired and I winced. He was always too direct, too straightforward.

Minnie opened her mouth to answer, but snapped it shut before shrugging in dismissal.

"So then Slade moved in with Ryker?" I continued, hoping to coax more information out of her. It seemed Minnie was in the mood to spill. Might as well gain some insight. We had to take every advantage we could.

"No. They moved in together. With me serving them here." Minnie fired the scones at us, just as we finished swallowing the blueberries. "The Lagodas... well, there's a reason they have shapeshifting powers, you see. Sometimes they come off a little... inhuman, at times."

We kept quiet, waiting for her to continue.

It took only a moment. "They felt Ryker was ready to be on his own and sent him on his way. Wasn't right, I said. He was too young! He was only fourteen. I mean, they gave him nothing, just shoved him out into the real world. Didn't check up on him, nothing. I'd know—I've been here the whole time!"

Archer and I shared a glance. It was around when we had been forced to become independent.

I could see him process this information. Could see how it contradicted what he believed the Domers' lives to be. We wore our hardships on our sleeves with pride. Used it as armour.

But if they too had suffered, then maybe our prejudices about them were wrong.

The rushing of water from Archer's shower diminished as I softly closed our bedroom door behind me. I had questions for Slade, having skimmed through most of the book into the late hours of the night. I wasn't sure if he was still up, but I headed towards the library, my curiosity spurring me on. I figured I would browse the rest of his collection too, in case there were other books that could fill my gaping pit of knowledge.

It's not as though I didn't want Archer to come. It was more that I believed I would get more answers, *better* answers, without him antagonising them. I had learned how to keep my mouth shut. Had learned that quickly—raging alcoholics didn't like a smart-assed daughter. But Archer had never learned that lesson, and right now, that didn't work in our favour. We didn't need a bulldozer. We needed a snake charmer.

Slade had given me no reason not to trust him. Neither had Ryker, really, though it was obvious he felt no loyalty to us, which kept me on edge around him.

That could be dangerous.

But where Ryker seemed to have no filter, everything that spewed out of Slade's mouth was calculated. To me, that was far worse. I had to assume our conversations were tactical, us the players of some metaphysical game.

The problem was, I never had time to play games. I was a neophyte up against a grandmaster.

My legs quietly strode down the hall, my rose-coloured silk pyjamas softly swishing as I approached the top of the exquisitely modern staircase. It had wrought-iron bannisters, wide concrete steps, and concave pocket shelves diagonally down the wall, filled with various marble carvings and soapstone pottery.

It all felt very... impersonal. Like they had hired someone to decorate simply because they knew they should, but had no input on anything. Had no desire for that input. It lacked any warmth. Somehow it felt just as lonely as my shack back home. Although our reasons for our design choices were far different.

As my slippered feet plodded down each step, my body luxuriated in the silken apparel and my feet sighed into plush heaven. My stomach grumbled at the smell of something baking in the kitchen, steering my attention towards it. I went to walk in but heard voices whispering and hid behind the wall to listen.

"We need her to trust us or she won't agree to this."

"Why the hell did you give her the book?"

"She has a right to know about her history... her family."

"And you think when she finds out what her family has done, what that magic can do, she's gonna say 'yup, sounds great'?"

"You know it doesn't go into that kind of detail. Come on Ry, you expect me to send her in there knowing *nothing?*"

"What if she figures out what—" Ryker halted midsentence as I heard him inhale sharply, as if he smelt my scent. I shrank back slightly, wondering if his senses were heightened like an animal's.

I rounded the wall and entered the kitchen, my face a blank canvas as I met each of their gazes head-on, almost daring them to ask if I had heard anything. We all knew I had been there.

But they too acted ignorant.

"Hungry?" Slade swept his arm towards the fresh blueberry pie sitting near the double industrial-sized ovens.

Imagine how many people you could feed with those.

I took in the kitchen, the immaculate stainless-steel appliances, the floor-to-ceiling cupboards that wrapped around three of the walls, the marble-topped island and countertops, lowered for Slade, and I was gobsmacked at its magnitude. It was easily double the size of my entire home.

I marvelled at the square footage of the entire house, a bitter taste developing in my mouth at the comparisons. We were sardines, every inch of space filled, and they were eagles free to roam expansive areas. I had been stupid since coming here; I had let myself revel in their luxuries, let my dreams run wild, and had completely forgotten these people were part of the reason why my life was so fucking awful.

And what the hell had they been talking about before I'd interrupted them? What ulterior motives did they have? What *wasn't* I supposed to find out? I needed to know the whole truth of this Inukviak Relic. And fast.

Truth was, I was terrified that I was in over my head. But I coveted what the Relic offered my grandmother and found it difficult to resist, even with the red flags that kept sprouting up.

I still couldn't determine whether I could trust them. Even if I was a Dufort—a Domer. I needed to continue to extract information from them to give myself a better idea of the whole picture, not just the snippet they'd fed me. And keep my guard up.

Forcing myself to swallow my rising uneasiness, I agreed to a slice and settled into a barstool while Ryker cut into the pie. Even his kitchen manners were feral; the pie looked like it had been gnawed by stray dogs after he was done with it.

"I hope I'm not interrupting you two," I said innocently. "I just had some more questions about our plans."

A grunt erupted from Ryker, which I took for acceptance.

"Why do you need a Dufort to open the barrier? I mean, what if I'm not who you believe me to be?"

Slade wheeled around the island to come face to face with me.

"We've been working on this for a long time, long before my tragedy. The truth is, we need to get inside before people far worse than us do. There has been talk around the Dome of some malicious intent. I don't know who to trust... I can only rely on Ryker here—us Domers will do anything to fuck each other over, right?" A wry smile, and a handsome dimple popped out. I hadn't noticed that before.

"Bryce, the commander of the O'Malleys, began to lead patrols to hunt out the Dufort lineage after talks of restoring the Dufort magic started to develop. They'd heard rumours of your bloodline still living, despite generations devoted to ending it." His tanned hands rubbed his eyes—he seemed so tired—and tucked his curls behind his ears before continuing. "Ilona O'Malley, as you may have learned, was the main catalyst for having Dashiell's magic bound, they say because Dashiell went mad. It has been a paranoia for the O'Malleys ever since, and they have devoted their lives to becoming no better than ravenous bloodhounds, obsessed with eradicating the Dufort bloodline. And in turn, any chance of its magic reemerging."

Could I go mad?

My eyes narrowed as I continued to listen.

"But the Dufort bloodline had been expansive. And they'd adapted quickly, knowing that their identity must never be revealed if their lineage were to survive. Unfortunately for some, that meant hiding right in the slums of Low-Town, destined for a life of destitution and secrecy like you. Some say others were able to escape. Past the forest."

My eyebrows shot up. Only those with magic had ever been able to get past the forest. If their magic was bound, I wondered if other Domers had helped them escape.

"However they've managed to survive, one thing is for certain: only a Dufort can undo the magic bound in Abraxas. The other bloodlines can't even get close to it, a safeguard we believe the others put in place so that no one could harness that power again."

I nodded.

My father had insisted on my isolation, and I'd always assumed he took twisted pleasure in seeing me miserable and alone. But perhaps he had been keeping me safe. Or at least keeping himself safe—for if the O'Malleys discovered he was safeguarding a Dufort, it would be his execution as well.

"Who is my real mother then? Or father?"

"That, we do not know. There's a reason you haven't been found yet... well, not until us. Whoever hid your identity, they did a great job with it." Slade picked a piece of fluff off his shoulder.

I rose from my barstool, my body unable to contain its energy. "Why didn't they just smuggle me out of Edinguard? All of us live in peace beyond the forest?"Ryker shook his head, "Only way through the forest is to fly above it or to portal past it. And that requires specific magic."

I scoffed, not convinced abandonment was my parents' best course of action.

I paced back and forth, my eyes flashing between the two of them as I wrung my hands, an anxious habit that popped up occasionally.

I stopped and threw my hands up in disbelief. "How do I know any of this is true? This is every hard-knock kid's dream: to find out they're important, that they're a part of something bigger than their pathetic little lives." My hands rubbed my temples. "You'll have to excuse me if I think all of this is still unbelievable."

Is it? Some of what was being said just made sense. I couldn't explain why.

"Why don't you ask your father for yourself?" Slade asked softly, surprising me with the gentleness.

I couldn't rely on my grandmother's senility. Perhaps if she was lucid enough.

I needed my father to verify all of this. He was a piece of shit, but he never shied away from a chance to crush my spirit—and being the person to inform me that my real parents had abandoned me would be too sweet a treat to resist.

I was going back to my father, and I wasn't leaving until I got the information I wanted.

If Truth Be Cold

We'd agreed to leave in the early morning hours, before the sun rose in its splendour, to help conceal our travel back to Unit 29. I had updated Archer with everything we discussed when I'd returned to our room.

Frustration spilled out of him over the constant danger now weaved into my life, at having to interact once again with my deadbeat father. But it was mixed with understanding and compassion, for Archer knew I had accepted this mission wholeheartedly, logic be damned, and I knew he would do everything in his power to help keep me safe.

My heart raced at the thought of what else might be uncovered. What other family members might be hidden out there.

Deep down, I was terrified of how my grandmother would feel towards me, if I was in fact a Dufort. She hated Domers just as much as I did—would she hate me too? If I truly belonged to the family that nearly destroyed us all, maybe she would grow to resent me, hold me responsible for things done centuries before.

I would be destroyed if she shunned me, if her love for me did not supersede her hatred of Domers. If I no longer was family to her, I would have nobody. And if she could give up on me, I had to anticipate Archer would too.

Could I survive on my own?

Ever since she'd become incapacitated, my loneliness had intensified. I had never been one to make friends easily, had been an extremely shy child. Looking back, I had been surviving abuse—it made sense now.

But back then, I'd worried I was too different, too awkward, too quiet. That exposing any real part of me would allow others to hurt me. So I never opened up, and before long, we were all working at the pulp mill. The hours were too long, and shift work was too loud for conversation, pushing me further into my own isolation. And a few years after that, I'd started thieving and had never had to work among strangers again.

Surprisingly, another part of me felt a thread of excitement. Hope for the answers that were to come. Finally there might be a chance to feel like I belonged to a people. A bloodline. A family.

Maybe I would find that familial love my grandmother could no longer give to me in others. In Duforts, if my father confirmed it all.

Absorbed as I was by my own worries, Ryker's voice startled me as I headed towards their vehicle. "We need to leave as soon as possible. We can't risk the Relic landing in anyone else's hands."

Turning to face him, I asked, "Do you think other people know? Who I am—who I might be?"

He met my gaze with intensity. "Do you want to wait to find out?" Opening the back door, I climbed into the immaculate SUV, certain I did not.

The car slowed to a stop by one of the back alleys in Low-Town, camouflaged in the shadows from the eyes of neighbouring busybodies. We eased out of our seats, pushing our doors shut as quietly as possible.

I refastened my trusty old utility belt to my updated wardrobe. I hadn't shied away from the expensive fabrics that had been offered, my legs now dressed in compression spandex, my old jacket replaced by a long-sleeved undershirt of the softest wool I had ever felt. I'd paired it with a gorgeous olive-green leather jacket over top to protect myself from the usual dangers of my job: scrapes and cuts. But this leather was soft like butter, like a mould fit just for me. My hair was pulled back in my usual low bun, topped with a black beanie to conceal the brightness of my hair. My hands were clad in fingerless leather gloves; I had refused full gloves as I relied on my sense of touch. My over-the-knee leather boots had been fit perfectly to my calves, like a second skin, to give my knees added protection from falls and trips. I was outfitted to survive whatever would come my way. I was a knight in armour.

The four of us briskly walked towards my house, heads down to conceal our faces, until we heard my father's eruptive snoring from around the corner. I decided to enter alone so my father would not wake up to Ryker and Slade—two strangers—breaking into his house. I told them all to hold back awhile. We could not afford my father's screams waking the neighbourhood—not the kind of attention we needed right now.

Cracking open the door, I slipped silently inside and flicked on the lamp atop the table, the dull amber light not strong enough to fill the corners. I eased myself towards his ruddy face, his swollen belly rising and falling with each rumble. My grandmother stirred, her eyes blinking awake, her pupils dilating to the light.

"Hollyn, honey?" she called out to me. "Are you okay? Where have you been?" It was a more lucid moment, one where she knew who I was and where we were. Her frail arms wobbled as they pushed her upright atop her mattress, with nothing but that frayed blanket to keep her warm.

I rushed towards her and embraced her roughly, all the emotions of the past twenty-four hours pouring out of me as I began to sob. It surged out of me like a waterfall as my grandmother softly rubbed my back.

"You know, don't you?" she said.

I pulled back to look at her through tear-filled eyes. My stomach tightened. I needed her to say it fully.

"Who you really are. A Dufort. I can see it on your face: the pain... the awareness..." she said, her small smile not quite reaching her eyes. Her cold, weathered hands held mine in comfort.

My mind reeled as if I'd been hit by the news again, the room around me blurring.

"You stupid bitch!"

Large hands gripped my grandmother's shoulders, shaking her violently in rage. Her face grimaced in pain as her head was thrown forwards and backwards, her body cowering in fright.

I hadn't heard my father's snoring stop. Hadn't noticed his cot groan as he rose, my mind consumed by Grandma confirming my hidden identity. And now his massive hands were seconds away from provoking another seizure.

What could be her last seizure.

My body leapt to defend her, my hands trying to pry his off, my teeth grinding in effort. I began shouting, pleading for him to stop, that she was innocent in this.

"You're killing her!" I screamed at him, all worries about discretion flying out the window. My hands pounded on his face, but my strength was incapable of overpowering his. I targeted his ear and his temple, hoping to hit a sweet spot. His head recoiled with each hit, and it fueled my frantic fervour. I reeked of fear.

In a flash, his right arm wound up and punched me across the face.

Blinding pain erupted in my head, my vision blurring from the hit. I stumbled back onto the floor, my cheekbone and nose burning as I felt warm blood trickle down my nose and pool into my mouth. I tasted the copper as my eyes clamped shut in agony, my hand holding my face.

Wet gurgling sounds followed by a thud rapidly wrenched my attention back to my grandmother—convulsing erratically on the ground, my father panting in fury on top of her. His eyes shifted towards his new target: me.

Before I could reach her, my father's hands found my lanky neck, his fingers wrapped into a deadly circle poised to asphyxiate me. I started to gasp for air as my panic-stricken hands clawed his, my long fingers failing to weasel between his to create space.

"S-st-op," I wheezed. My throat scorched and I couldn't choke anything else out.

"You—fucking cunt! Everything!! You've taken EVERYTHING FROM ME!" He spat in my face. "My life was ruined because of you, bitch! They'll be back! I'm not fucking dying because of you!" His brown eyes bulged at me, the whites of his eyes rimmed in red, the noxious stench of whisky burning my nostrils as his spittle landed all over my face.

He lifted me off the ground, my body helplessly hanging like a kite floating in the sky. Blackness began to close in around me, the thumping of my grandmother's body flailing around quieting as my eyelids grew heavier.

"They'll reward me handsomely if I deliver a dead Dufort! Maybe that will save me. For knowin..." He ranted to me. "It's either you or me, bitch, and you've never really been mine." My mind struggled to focus on his words, each sound more puzzling than the last. I'd have almost laughed hysterically—if I could have.

Archer, please come... hear us...

My hands slapped his, but the effort became too much, each strike weaker as consciousness slipped from me. My father's hands did not waver.

"P-Please..."

"I've tried long enough. Just like I promised. But if you know, they'll know soon enough. I won't die. Not for you!"

I gasped like a fish out of water, my eyes rolling back as my hands slipped down, the strength in me depleting.

"You ain't mine. And I've done all I—"

An enormous tentacle wrapped around my father's torso, spiralling up until it tightly wound around his neck. His eyes opened wide in shock and his hands gripped the snakelike limb to defend himself, dropping me. My lungs burned as I raggedly inhaled, coughing as I crouched over in recovery.

I looked up as the mouth of the biggest anaconda I'd ever seen gaped wide, hissing at my father, who'd pissed himself in fear. I found a little pleasure from that.

But as the enormous snake held strong and I regained some composure, I began to watch the life start to leave his eyes as the snake's body constricted tighter and tighter, and the pleasantness faded away.

I heard the bones in his body begin to shatter. I smelled the excrement seeping down his pants. I watched, frozen, as his body, bending now in impossible angles, turned blue as death prevailed.

I felt myself vomit.

His body slumped down, and the snake unravelled before slithering towards me, its grey eyes focused on mine. Shivering, I watched as Ryker's brawny naked body formed from the reptilian predator. Limbs burst out like tree branches to their trunk. His head sprouted forth, his raven hair replacing scales as his nose protruded from snake slits. His fangs were replaced by human teeth in a human mouth slightly panting from exertion. I noticed the old scars that marred his beautiful body, shining in the lamp's amber glow.

His naked form stood over me, his hand outstretched. I averted my gaze, embarrassed from the height I was at and what was dangling in front of me. I took his hand as I struggled to stand, and we stared at each other, the words to thank him escaping me. So I settled for a nod, to which he nodded back.

Still nude, he strode towards the barred door to unlock it, carefully sidestepping the shattered glass that littered the dirt in front of the sole window. He must have broken it to get inside, our screams and fighting drowning out the sound of the breaking glass.

Father barred it. He really was going to kill me.

The realisation gutted me. Nausea washed over me again as I understood how close my death had been. I glanced at my father's corpse. Not my father, really, as he had confirmed. But the father figure I had known.

I felt nothing for him, except for relief that he no longer could hurt me. Or my grandmother.

Instead, I was terrified that what Slade and Ryker had told me was true.

I was a Dufort.

Archer bounded inside, the front door rattling as it slammed against the wall. He rushed to my side, his corded arms enveloping me as my body shivered, now falling into shock. He murmured how sorry he was over and over, as if he should have known how evil my father was down to his core. Known that he really might try to kill me.

"I should have been with you. I should have stopped this from happening. I should have known..." Archer was shaking his head in hysteria, his eyes hollow and faraway, as his hands nearly ripped his curly hair out. I wasn't sure if his confessions were more for me or him.

Wheels rolled against the dirt floor as Slade was the last to enter. He surveyed the scene, assessing the damage I'd taken, his eyes at last landing on my grandmother's body, shallowly breathing on the ground.

Grandma, I remembered in fear and guilt, as I wiggled out of Archer's embrace and crawled over to her, my hands touching her body. Reassurance flooded me as I felt warmth. I cradled her into a seated position, her eyes closed in slumber, her body in an almost coma-like state. My hand brushed the wisps of white hair that matted her face as I rocked her gently, like she used to do for me.

"She'll be okay," I whispered to no one in particular. Slade stopped beside me and planted his hand on my shoulder in mute comfort. Compared to the warmth that came from it, I realised my body was ice.

"Let me take care of her. Bring her to my house. She'll be safe. She'll be looked after," Slade promised me.

I mutely nodded, too terrified to leave her on her own. My father had mentioned "they" would kill him if they knew who I was, for secretly housing a Dufort. I couldn't leave my grandmother defenceless against that same threat.

The only way to help her now was to obtain that Relic. To harness its healing power before it was too late.

And I couldn't ask Archer to look after her—I needed him with me. Being a loner often had its benefits, but in this circumstance, it fucking sucked. I had to put my grandmother's life into the hands of someone I'd met only twenty-four hours ago.

A *Domer*.

But it was that or her certain death. And a bloody one at that, if the O'Malleys found her. I didn't like gambling. Hated the uncertainties, the unknowns. But what choice did I have?

What choice do I have?

Shaking and Entering

Enormous warm arms gently lifted me off the ground and carried me past his corpse, past the shattered glass, past the glowing eyes secretly spying from neighbouring windows. My legs flopped listlessly as I leaned against whoever was carrying me. I didn't care, didn't even register that every part I touched was naked. Anxiety over my grandmother's condition stormed inside me; my surroundings briefly flashed past, my eyes failing to register images with any clarity or focus.

I could feel Archer hovering, unsure how to console me. And perhaps also because I was nestled in a Domer's arms.

Truth was, I didn't know what I needed. I was numb.

My entire life is a lie.

I was being hunted for magic that my family had once possessed. That I never knew I had dormant in me.

I had been abandoned.

With someone who was not even my father. Who had genuinely hated me.

Who had abused me. Scarred me physically and emotionally.

And yet, some part of me had still loved him, I realised, as waves of grief cascaded through my body. Grief for my dead father... whoever he was. For the man who held no loyalty to me. Who had been willing to sacrifice me for his own benefit.

The thud of his body plummeting to the ground echoed over and over in my mind. It would haunt me, even though death was not new. I'd seen it all around me, as neighbours and acquaintances had slowly perished, decades of impossible work and malnutrition finally claiming them.

But never had I watched life leave someone's eyes first-hand. Looked on as the colour of their skin diminished, their pupils enlarging into glossy, lifeless orbs.

And it had taken someone I'd believed to be my father. The child in me mourned him and the love he never gave me.

The Reaper had so narrowly missed my grandmother and me with his scythe too. And that, most of all, shook me to my core.

Perhaps it hadn't missed me. Perhaps it had killed my life as I knew it.

My body quaked as silent sobs escaped, my face burrowing into Ryker's chest as I let my tumultuous emotions overcome me. I felt his arms tighten slightly around me, surprising me with his tenderness.

I looked up at him from bleary eyes, the back of my hand wiping at my tears, and took in the masculine profile that kept his gaze forward, his eyes dilating and darting around, always focused on potential threats. Those eyes housed bags underneath, and I wondered whether his job as "the muscle" took an emotional toll on him more than I had first thought.

He finally glanced down towards me, the heat of my stare drawing his gaze, and we shared a soft, small smile as the bud of a friendship began to blossom. He'd saved me. My grandma too. And he had been forced to end another life to do it. I did not take that lightly, and I vowed to myself to try and pay him back, somehow.

Archer carried my only remaining family, Slade off to the left of us, both on edge as they scanned the wobbly streets we travelled, the morning sun starting to colour us in shades of orange and red. The sunrise was beginning, and our chances of escape without too much attention were depleting rapidly as golden fingers began to climb up from behind the horizon.

"It always reminds me of a flame bowerbird. Have you ever seen one of them?" Ryker asked me. I shook my head. I had no idea what they looked like.

"They have heads of bright red that fade to a bright yellow breast and tail. They're beautiful... my father had one as a pet when I was little. Used to carry it on his shoulder and feed it by hand. Not once did that bird ever try to escape. He must've known how lucky he was living inside the Dome," he recounted.

I stared, surprised at this thoughtful side of him. At his awareness of how easier a life could be in the Dome.

"As much as I have enjoyed carrying you, we are closing in on a big hill, and Slade will need my help." He gently plopped me onto my feet, the sunlight illuminating streaks of chestnut in his black hair.

"Thanks—"

The ground trembled underneath us as cobblestones behind us began to rip out and fly backwards, as if being pulled by an invisible magnet. The muscles in my legs rippled as I surfed the tremors, my head whipping around trying to understand what was happening.

"What's going—" I began, before I watched chunks of the road vanish in a trail leading right towards us.

We needed to move. Now.

I snapped out of my stupor as my survival instincts took over and I launched into a sprint towards the others. I felt blistering heat whiz past my ear as an orb of flames blasted a foot in front of me. I wheeled my arms to abruptly stop before I slid into its fiery splatter.

Is this an attack?

I searched behind us, trying to pinpoint where our enemies were stationed. An immaculately dressed man, his bald head glistening like a beacon of light, led the assault, his hands still aflame. He must have shot the orbs at us.

Our eyes locked from afar. He yelled orders as he pointed his finger directly at me. The pieces of road began dropping even faster, quickly gaining on where I stood rooted.

"Hollyn!" Archer bellowed at me. "Move!"

Spinning on my heels, I dashed towards the others, desperately outpacing the ever-growing sinkhole forming behind me. I spied a spear of ice puncture the ground a few feet to my right, and I propelled my feet to go even faster.

There was no doubt we were being hunted by the O'Malleys. They had already found us.

They must know about me. He pointed right at me.

I sidestepped the mess and blazed on in a zigzag pattern, hoping to evade the catapulted burning balls and lances of ice raining down on us.

Finally I caught up to Slade, whose face mirrored my own confusion and terror, his helpless legs flailing as his arms pumped his wheels in desperation. I ran towards the handles at his back to push him faster. But one of his wheels fell into a hole and his body was flung out of the chair, narrowly missing a puddle of molten lava.

I called for Archer but saw him straining, already carrying the burden of my grandmother, and couldn't find Ryker. I knew I was the only one that could help Slade.

My back blocked his prone body as we both struggled to figure out a way for me to drag him. There was no way I could carry him; even though he was lean, he still easily outweighed me. I tried to get him to sit up so I could hook my hands under his armpits, but the cool, collected Slade I'd been introduced to had vanished, and his panicked frenzy inhibited any progress we were making.

"Stop moving and let me get a grip on you!" I hollered at him.

But I saw the horror on his face and whirled around to see where he pointed.

Three blazing spheres headed straight for us. We had no time to do anything except brace for their impact. My eyes scrunched shut and my breath caught as I waited for the excruciating pain.

An ear-shattering shriek pierced the sky as two expansive wings blasted gusts of wind towards us, our hair blown back at the power. Enormously taloned harpy feet gripped the front of our shirts, lifting our dangling bodies. Each powerful flap propelled us upward, and I watched helplessly as Archer and my grandmother faded from sight.

"We have to go get them!" I cried to Slade once we had landed in a small grove miles past the dense forest that encircled Edinguard. I never understood how imprisoned it kept us until I saw how the trees fused into bands of evergreen so thick they became walls. They'd been the walls of my cage, and I had just flown the coop.

"No," Ryker firmly replied, beads of sweat on his temples. I wondered how much it took for him to transmorph into a harpy eagle and carry us the distance he had.

I looked to Slade for an ally in this, hopeful that he would feel guilty leaving my grandmother behind. He was slumped against a boulder, his button-down drenched in sweat.

The last pieces of my heart were left on those streets, and I wouldn't allow myself to think of what might have happened to them. There was no way Archer could get out alive, not with my grandma weighing him down. Not against the O'Malleys and their magic.

No. They had to get out. I had to get them. I couldn't lose them too.

The look on Slade's face sparked fear in me. I knew that expression—I'd worn it myself often, before having to make a decision that needed to happen, but one that would pile guilt on me. Someone else's misery was always the cost.

"Hollyn..." he began. I spun on my feet, rage distorting my features as I stormed away in the direction I believed would lead me back to Edinguard. I got only a few feet before Ryker stepped in front of me, his mass blocking my way.

"Move," I barked at him, my hands curled tightly into fists, my shoulders pulled up towards my ears. I tried to bypass him, but he invaded my space whichever direction I attempted.

"They are all I have left, don't you get that!" I shouted. "They need our help, you fucking cowards! How can you just leave them there to die! I-I won't do this job without them!" My throat ripped in pain, still recovering from my father.

Ryker's hands immobilised me, his grip rooting me to my spot. "You will die if you go back."

"I don't give a fuck! Get off me, you bird bitch!" I screamed back at him, my arms incapable of escaping from the death grip fusing them to my sides.

"We need you. We can't let you die," Slade softly said.

"Let. Me. Go," I threatened between clenched teeth. Fury exploded through me, almost buckling my body in its intensity. I trembled with adrenaline as I struggled to break free.

I didn't even move Ryker an inch, his grip unwavering steel.

"I will never get you your Relic!" I roared at them. "I can't leave them there!"

I continued to snarl vehement slurs at them as I thrashed around like an entrapped banshee. My arms made zero ground, so I surprised Ryker with a swift knee to his balls.

He grunted in pain as I connected and I wiggled free of him, sprinting towards the forest line. I had no idea if I was headed in the right direction, but I put every last vestige of energy into my mad dash. This was my only shot; I had to make it into the forest and get some coverage. I was small and I could climb—maybe that was my chance.

My heart thudded in my chest as my lungs burned, but I didn't slow down. I couldn't slow down, even if my legs were tripping up from fatigue. I pumped my arms harder to keep my momentum.

I was thirty feet from the tree line.

Twenty feet. The ground was beginning to be covered in fallen leaves and needles, my boots crunching noisily as I smelled the pine and other wet flora of the forest.

Ten feet. I had this. I would find the first good tree to climb and disappear. Ryker was huge, but he was slow. And his weight would be his disadvantage when climbing branches.

Stick to the flimsy ones. He'll break those.

Five feet. The first branches reached towards me. I spotted a towering maple, and my hands and feet connected with branches and nooks as I started my ascent.

I sensed Ryker right behind me but didn't dare risk a glance down. I couldn't slow down now. I would get as high as I could and figure out a plan from there. Surely he wouldn't be able to get up here.

I slowed once I had reached a comfortable height on a branch I thought would be too flimsy for Ryker and turned my back against the trunk. My eyes scanned the forest floor for him, but he was nowhere to be seen.

I took a moment to gather my breath and settle my nerves. I needed to be calm so I could hear my surroundings instead of my pounding heart.

Where is he? I was too exposed.

Carefully, I leaned forward, easing my body off the trunk as I avoided rustling the leaves of the branch I was perched upon. I began to crawl on my hands and knees across the length of it until I reached its end, the branch wobbling subtly under my weight. I was close enough to the next tree that a jump between was doable.

I was only, what, twenty feet up? If I landed wrong...

I couldn't think like that. I had to make this.

From a crouched position, like a flying squirrel preparing for takeoff, I sprang for the new branch, but the limb beneath me swayed, shifting my balance and undermining my thrust.

I wasn't going to make it.

The branch whizzed by my head, my body stretched out as far as possible in the hopes of catching a lifeline. But my fingers found nothing—and I began to fall.

The ground raced up at me, my hands frantically grasping for and brushing against other branches.

I was going to die. Right here.

My fingers grabbed at a twig, my hands ripping open from the bark, but I managed to hang tight, my legs kicking in search of a foothold. I finally made contact with a delicate piece, but it immediately snapped under my weight until my legs dangled helplessly again. I held on tight, but blood from all the scrapes began to oil up my hands, until the tree limb was slick.

I watched helplessly as my fingers slipped and I continued my fall.

Maybe I'll only be in a wheelchair falling from this height. How ironic.

Eyes closed, I refused to watch my own demise and braced for the impact.

A painful crash into my stomach opened my eyes in shock. My body was pulled from one branch to the next, a steel-eyed chimpanzee carrying me with his hairy feet as his lengthy arms swung us through the trees, back to the grove and away from my goal.

He tossed me into the air as he landed on the grassy floor, my body airborne until his once-again human arms caught my fall.

Ryker flopped me onto my stomach and proceeded to sit atop me, leaving me helplessly staring at Slade. Who had not moved an inch.

We stayed like that for a while, my mouth spitting venom at my captors, cursing them for their cowardice.

Whatever chance I had of getting back to Low-Town in time had just been eliminated. Going back now would be my own death in vain. Archer would have given me hell for even trying.

If going back for one another means we both die, we keep going on without them.

He had insisted on that rule for us. Had made me promise I would agree to it. *What good is it if we both die?* he'd asked me.

What was I going to do without him? He was the anchor in my life and the brain on our missions. Why did I get to keep living and everyone else had to die?

First my grandmother, now Archer. I had failed to keep both of them safe.

Only *two* people. And I couldn't protect either one.

I had no reason to do this mission anymore. I had no reason for anything. What purpose did I have?

"Fuck both of you for doing nothing. Fuck you for saving me and not them." Unparalleled pain radiated from me, survivor's guilt fueling my hatred for the men with me.

Perhaps I knew deep down there was nothing they really could have done, but for once my emotions overpowered logic. I would refuse to do this job for them. I would try to hurt them in any way I could for the pain they had just given me.

Archer had been right: we were disposable to them.

"There's no fucking way I'm still doing this for you two. You let the only things you held over me die back there. We are fucking done," I spat at them.

They shared another look. It was clear that I was not going to be able to leave of my own accord.

"They are *dead*. The only people I've ever loved. Dead," I choked out, desperately trying to swallow down my sorrow.

"We don't know that," Slade argued. "They're more likely being held hostage in hopes of cutting a deal with us—"

"What could we have done?" Ryker interjected.

"I-I don't know! Anything! You could have dropped us off closer and gone back..."

"We barely escaped the O'Malleys. Going back would have been all our deaths. I'd be dead. You'd be dead trying to drag Slade. We had to make this decision. It was some or all," Ryker said soberly.

"Don't let them die in vain," Slade added.

I shot him a look of death, daring him to try and rationalize their murder. His eyes fell downward in defeat.

Minutes passed as we all stayed in that thick, uncomfortable silence.

"I want to go home," I finally broke the quiet.

"They will hunt you down and kill you. You saw them point at you," Slade reminded me. "We have even less time than we anticipated."

"Then I will die. What's the point of living now anyway?"

"We... still need you. I'm sorry, but we can't let you go, not when we're this close," Slade confessed. "You don't understand—"

"Then help me fucking understand. How the hell were both of their lives worth healing your legs?"

"There are things much worse happening right now. I can't tell you—"

"So I'm allowed to risk my life, have my family's lives taken, and I can't even know why? Or say no? Archer was right. I am a prisoner. I was too stupid to see it."

Slade's expression darkened and his mouth opened as if to retort, but then he seemed to decide against it and turned his head in dismissal, his arms crossed to deter further questions.

I turned to Ryker, the next target of my verbal assault.

"What are you going to do, kidnap me now?" I challenged him.

"If we need to, yes," he told me. "The only way home is through that forest. You can't outrun me. You can't hide from me."

"You really are an asshole," I hissed. The look on his face told me he would do what he had to, despite the humanity he had shown me earlier.

How quickly I had forgotten where his true allegiance lay.

Slade faced me again, "The best thing for you and your family now is to obtain the Relic and hope you can strike a bargain with the O'Malleys before it's too late."

"And if I don't?"

"You will guarantee a death for them more excruciating than you could imagine. I have seen the extent of Bryce's bloodlust. He will carry their torture out for as long as humanly possible." Slade's gaze darkened, painful memories clouding his cobalt eyes. I shuddered in fear.

"Why are they after this Relic too?"

"They're not, really. They're after you. But they fear what that Relic symbolises. They fear the unknown connection between the Dufort lineage and the magic dormant inside it. They fear the *what if*. So now they will stop at nothing to obtain you and this Relic, for fear of losing their chokehold of power. And they will do everything possible to kill you."

I gulped, comprehension dawning on me. This was about more than healing Slade's legs.

A lot more.

What the fuck have I gotten myself into?

The Lone Stranger

"Why didn't he just fly us right to Abraxas?" I asked Slade as we huddled around the rudimentary fire Ryker had crafted. We'd continued on foot for most of the morning, travelling around a chain of mountains until we'd reached the turquoise lake we were now camped next to. It had been gruelling, with copious ascending sections, and I'd marvelled at the ease with which Ryker had carried Slade.

"Couldn't he, I dunno, become a horse and let us ride him?" I mocked Ryker, venom poisoning my words. Stupid beast couldn't give us a break.

"There is a magical barrier that extends out from Abraxas. Once we reached the grove, his magic was bound by it. There's a reason Ryker chose that spot—had we traveled any further, the barrier would have forced him to transform back to human midflight, and we would have fallen to our deaths," Slade informed me. "The forest around Edinguard is just outside the perimeter of the magic seal."

"Have people made it this far before?" I asked, hoping to fill some of my gaps in knowledge.

"Yes. But not many. The forests are so dense most people die trying to find their way out. Only those who can avoid the forest entirely like we did have made it."

"Either from flying or from… a portal?" I asked tentatively, my mouth experimenting with this new word. I'd never heard that term before, didn't know what it meant.

Slade pushed up on his hands to reposition his lower half into a more comfortable position. "Right. A portal is in essence a gate through which you can leap great distances instantaneously. But it requires a Cabral and a Makotovic to invoke."

My head shot up, surprised to hear of two families cooperating. "But I thought you guys don't work together."

Slade smirked and I swore he seemed slightly impressed by my quick understanding. "They don't. Usually."

"Have other bloodlines spelled together?" If a portal could be created fusing Cabral and Makotovic magic, I wondered what else could be possible.

I saw Slade watch me carefully, like I had asked something he didn't want to answer. He hesitated, as if calculating his response, and I wondered if his life had forced him to become this suspicious. "Maybe. Domers are pretty secretive."

And then his gaze drifted away as he turned his face from me, signalling an end to my questioning.

I poked the fire with my stick, my other hand outstretched towards the burning pile, savouring the heat emanating from it. I remembered flashes of burning orbs whizzing past my head and felt sick to my stomach again as I wallowed over Archer and my grandmother, hoping to God they hadn't been burned alive.

I had to keep talking, keep distracting myself from thinking about them, or else the grief would swallow me. I prodded Slade further. "So what can a Dufort do? Their magic, I mean."

Slade leaned back against the boulder he was propped up against, his head falling back, tawny curls falling off his face. He seemed so youthful like that, the soft glisten of his blond beard just sprouting from his tanned skin, his nose straight and proud.

Bringing his head forward again, he replied, "That is perhaps our biggest mystery right now. In old texts they used to call the Dufort magic "holy." But so much has been lost... eradicated by O'Malleys. As I'm sure you read, Abraxas became known for its healing miracles."

"So this Relic... holds Dufort magic? Can it be released?" What did that mean for me? Would it awaken in me?

"I don't know. I think the Relic has trapped it. You might never gain it back." Sadness touched his eyes. Perhaps he felt sympathetic that I might forever be caged like that.

What will happen to me if it does return? Do I want that? Would it drive me mad?

"But then why would 'holy magic' cause Dashiell to go mad?" Something so pure couldn't possibly turn someone evil. It didn't add up. "There must be more to it than that."

Slade murmured his agreement. "That is why we need to be exceptionally careful with the Relic."

I pondered all this new information as I looked towards the other of the duo. Ryker was waist-deep in the lake, using a man-made spear chiselled from a fallen branch to thrust periodically into the water, his weapon bringing back up impaled fish bodies that flailed in their final moments of life. Dinner would be the freshest I'd had in a long time, and my stomach grumbled in ravenous hunger, despite how unappetising food sounded right now.

"I truly am sorry—for your friend and your grandmother. I didn't want that to happen. If I wasn't so dependent on Ryker, maybe..." Slade's face was scrunched in pain and what looked like anger over his paralyzed body. Did he often feel useless?

I scrutinised him intensely, unsure whether his apology was genuine or not. I knew it didn't mean shit to me either way. He had chosen not to go back—that was all that mattered. My attention returned to the fire, my eyes blurring as I choked back the emotion threatening to bubble over.

Just you wait. I'll get you back worse.

Ryker returned to our palpable awkwardness, probably happy for my silence as he expertly laid the fish on one of the flat rocks and cooked our food. He did nothing to break our silence either, so we all huddled by the warmth as the savoury aroma of grilled white fish distracted us.

I guzzled down the food, impatient to arrive at our destination. Anger spurred me onward—the sooner I was done with these Domers, the better. My nervous energy filled my body, causing my legs to start jostling in an anxious tremble.

Would I take the Relic for myself? Refuse to heal Slade? Break the Relic before anyone could harness its power? I turned over all the options of revenge that jumped into my mind.

I had to do something to make them hurt for even a fraction of the pain that ached inside me.

"So what am I supposed to do once we reach the barrier? Should I say abracadabra?" I said wryly.

Ryker huffed at my joke. To him there was obviously no bad blood between us.

Slade turned back towards me, his eyes distant and troubled. It took him a second before he snapped back to reality, and he coughed before replying, "From everything I've read, it seems like all we need is the catalyst—a piece of the Relic—and the blood—you."

"Okay, so I just wave it around, and then it all evaporates?"

"At a basic level, I guess, yes," Slade replied.

"And then what do I expect?" I prodded.

"We're... not sure. Nobody has ever been able to get past that first step. You Duforts are hard to come by," Slade admitted before he reached into his pocket and held up a jagged black obelisk. "And this guy has never been located before."

It looked so simple. So dull. Like those crystals sold at the holistic health store that promised some sort of miracle cure.

And I lost my family over this... shard of shit.

"So I'm going in like a sacrificial lamb, blind without my partner, and we have *zero* idea of what I will come up against." I felt hopeless, and for the first time completely disinterested. I didn't care about winning this mission. The risks didn't scare me like they should have—I felt nothing about the danger. Felt nothing about any of this.

I just wanted them back.

But if they're not dead yet, I could heal them with this, couldn't I?

Maybe it wasn't too late to save them. Maybe they were being held hostage, like Slade had mentioned.

And if the only way for me to hold any sway in this future deal was to have the Relic, then I'd have to sack the fuck up and get it for them.

I needed that ace up my sleeve.

"This might shock you, but if we could, we would help you more. But nobody knows anything," Ryker remarked. I looked up again, trying to figure out if he was joking or not. It felt honest.

I watched as Slade elegantly scooped up fragments of fish flesh before placing them in his mouth, his full lips opening to accept the food, the back of his hand brushing his golden curls off his face. Every inch of fish landed perfectly, in complete contrast to Ryker—who might as well have just crouched completely over to hoover the fish into his gullet. Slivers of fish flew like shrapnel as he barraged the fillet bits into his mouth.

I watched in awe, wondering how these polar opposites had become so close, so loyal to each other. How one so refined as Slade accepted and welcomed someone as rugged as Ryker. Their relationship went deep, *very* deep, I suspected.

As I gently popped each finger into my mouth one at a time to lick off the remnants of my meal, I observed the tension rolling off Slade, shown in moments where he gazed off into the distance, his handsome face scowling in deep thought.

Something else was in the works, something they either weren't telling me or hadn't yet confirmed. It surprised me how quickly Slade's poker face had worsened, ever since the O'Malleys had pursued us. Something was definitely amiss between the Domers. I just hoped I wasn't walking into a trap from which I could not escape.

We each rose, the final leg of our trek glistening in the late afternoon sunlight. On the horizon lay an alabaster fortress, stained in sections from centuries of algae, marine flora and fauna cresting against its towering wall. Only the peaks of the city's spires and its steepest roofs poked over, the rest hidden, akin to its mysterious history. There were no gradual banks to dock a boat, nor were there any bridges to cross. It was surrounded by sapphire water in every direction. I hadn't a clue how we would even get inside, let alone whether the unseen magical barrier could be conquered.

"I... can't swim," I quietly admitted. I'd never had the time, nor the chance to learn. Low-Town had no fishing industry, as we were barricaded by those dense forests, nowhere near a body of water. Pools were a luxury only for Domers.

They both turned my way, the heat of their gazes warming my cheeks in embarrassment. Their mental wheels grinded as they searched for an alternative course. Even Ryker would be incapable of swimming with both of us helplessly clinging to his neck.

"Alright. If we can't swim our way there, we're gonna need a raft."

Ryker went to rip off large branches, and I explored the surrounding area for plant fibres and vines we could use for twine. Before I had begun my thieving career, I'd become accustomed to using whatever natural resources I could scrounge to create various basic traps in the forest for supplemental protein sources, especially in preparation for our frigid winters. My eyes found a fibrous creeping vine that scaled the trunks of the aspens dominating the area, and I began ripping off long tendrils. Slade assembled as we dropped materials at his feet, and just as the sun softened with the beginning of its descent, we had created a platform large enough for the three of us to hold on to.

We stripped our pants, jackets, and shoes off, not wanting to be weighed down by them in the water, but I refused to shed my belt. My body shivered entering the frigid water. Ryker boldly looked me up and down, and I met his gaze, refusing to let him make me feel uncomfortable. I then turned to meet Slade's eyes, which darted shyly back to my eyes. I realised my legs were covered in bruises of chartreuse, violet, onyx, and everything in between. Both old and new contusions, in various stages of healing, mixed with long scrapes and cuts. My skin exhibited the life I'd endured. I was so used to the patchwork of injuries that consistently covered me, I'd forgotten how alarming it would be for others to see.

Wait until they see my back.

My father had always loved a cheap hit from behind, too cowardly to risk retaliation face on. There were scars there, deep and permanent, from broken beer bottles, cigarette burns—when he was able to steal a pack—and from the metal claws of his worn leather belt. Once his gut had outgrown the belt, it had transitioned entirely to being used for discipline. I hacked it to bits one night. That'd led to at least two of the scars back there.

It had been worth it.

Ryker scooped up Slade in his arms and we waded into the cool water, pushing the raft in front of us. I shivered from both the temperature and the daunting task ahead of me.

Each of us grasped along the same side, and Ryker's muscular legs began to propel us slowly towards Abraxas. Terror seized my body as we drifted past the point of my toes touching. My life was mercilessly in the hands of Ryker.

I would be absolutely fucked if I lost my grip now.

My body was clenched so tightly I barely swayed from the movement. I tried to focus my mind on the looming structure ahead rather than the snake of death nipping at my ankles. I still couldn't see how we would get through the wall.

Abraxas barreled towards us, Ryker surprisingly rapid despite the two anchors he hauled along. The scale of this fortress was unfathomable as we got closer and closer. My neck strained, craning to look up the walls as my body vibrated, as if in response to what lay in front of me. I felt a deep, dull pounding in my head, the start of a migraine forming as our raft tapped gently against the wall. I shut my eyes, forcing my headache to quiet, hoping adrenaline would push me through.

"—shouldn't be more than twenty feet down, although I'm not sure how far we have to go before we can resurface," Ryker continued.

"Wait, what? No. I can't do that. I can't swim," I stammered, panic rising inside me. I gripped our life raft harder, my knuckles draining in colour.

"This is our only option. All you need to do is hold your breath and shut your eyes. Ready?" Ryker asked before he yanked me under, his arm hooked under my armpits, Slade draped over his back.

My eyes burned—I hadn't had time to close them before submerging, so I swiftly squeezed them shut. I pursed my lips to keep them sealed and focused on counting. I had no idea how long I could hold my breath.

Ten.

Cold permeated my core as we sank further, pressure building and irritating my migraine. Impulsively, I breathed out some trapped air through my nostrils and immediately felt some relief. I didn't know if I could risk losing any more air and prayed we neared the end.

Twenty.

I knew it hadn't been very long, but losing my sight was fucking with me. It disoriented me and inhibited me from obsessing over anything except how long I had been under and the fire beginning to burn in my lungs.

Thirty.

The pressure had built intensely and my lungs now burned angrily as I felt a change in our direction. We had reached the lowest depth of our swim—I hoped. I really had no idea.

Forty.

My nostrils stung, my ears needed to pop, and my eyes itched. This was my nightmare.

Fifty.

I began to internally gasp, my lungs involuntarily gulping for new oxygen that did not exist. A small whimper escaped, precious air bubbles gurgling over my lips. My throat constricted in spasms as my entire body incinerated from the inside out. I couldn't hold on much longer or I would drown.

Sixty.

I opened my eyes, water flooding them as I blearily slapped Ryker in panic. I accidentally took in water, choking as it filled my lungs like burning lava. Darkness encroached from the corners of my vision as I continued to choke and swallow. Calmness began to wash over me as death loomed its ugly head.

Seventy.

I thought of my grandmother and Archer, somewhat happy that I would at least get to see them again. I blacked out.

Warm, soft lips blew hot air into my mouth before I purged a waterfall of swallowed lake water down my chin and onto the ground beside me.

Ground.

I drowsily blinked my eyes awake to see Slade perched awkwardly by my face while Ryker's hands lay on my chest. Relief flooded their faces. I raggedly inhaled air, a fiery throbbing in my lungs where Ryker must have done chest compressions. I rolled over into a fetal position, away from their faces, as I recovered from the pain and the terror. Each breath ached, my head throbbing unbearably, as my lungs relearned how to inhale.

"W-water," I croaked, my throat desperate for some lubrication. Slade extended his body to hand over the water skin and I sipped it delicately until the smouldering lessened.

We were inside a dank cavern, atop a stone floor just feet from the water I'd almost drowned in. It was dark and clammy, stalagmites and stalactites extending towards each other along the cavern walls. An uneven staircase, moist with slimy residue, led up towards a heavy wooden door, slashes of light bursting through the cracks.

I pushed myself upright before rising. I needed to propel myself onward, lest my body shut down from the shock. I needed to use the adrenaline coursing through me and get the hell out of here.

"Are you okay?" Slade asked.

I shrugged.

He assessed me himself for a moment before nodding. He rooted in his pocket for his Inukviak Relic piece and extended it to me, but his hand hesitated before releasing it. I shoved the piece in my belt. My migraine had returned, so I tried to get used to the constant throb.

Guess I'm doing this thing without pants on.

"We will wait here for you. I don't know how Ryker's magic will react with anything in there," Slade informed me. "Hollyn... I... Be careful in there. I don't know what else waits for you. Stay vigilant."

I held his gaze before I stalked up the damp stone steps, the Relic heavy by my hips.

I turned back and looked Slade dead in the eyes. "I hope your legs are worth it."

Hurling the Midnight Oil

*C*reak.

My shoulder pushed the solid door open, its hinges moaning in protest as centuries of hardened rust flaked off.

Bright midday sunlight welcomed me, and I raised my arm to shade my eyes until they adjusted to the radiance. Confusion hit me as I recalled that the sun was setting mere minutes before I was sucked underwater. Surely I had not been unconscious an entire day?

I scanned my surroundings and was mesmerised by the glorious architecture that stood proudly in front of me. Gorgeous alabaster buildings lined the brick road that appeared to form one giant circle along the perimeter of the town. In the middle stood an impressive tower that loomed over the rest of the town. The salmon-coloured road was edged with meticulous shrubbery and shocks of crimson and apricot flowers. Cast-iron lampposts were stationed intermittently, real flames still smouldering in their glass cages.

I headed along the road, not a weed in sight threatening to burst through the cracks. Various vendor stands and shop fronts housed tables and shelves still stocked with goods, completely untouched. Like a museum without inhabitants.

Downspouts and irrigation channels trickled water into wells and fountains—what I assumed was Abraxas's water system, channelling the fresh water it sat upon.

Wood and rope staircases and bridges led upward, my eyes following them towards floating chunks of earth suspended in the sky, roots dangling down. The islands drifted softly in midair, no foundation or pillars to support them. It was as if someone had uprooted these chunks of land and glued them to the sky.

They hovered just above the buildings, hidden from the outside by the wall surrounding the city. Moss and wild grass cascaded over the edges of the floating islands, a soft, warm breeze rustling the blades and dispersing the sweet fragrance.

I stared up at them with my mouth agape. I could not understand how they functioned, how enough magic still resided here to maintain them, what their purpose had been. Houses seemed to be situated atop them, and I wondered if the rich lived above everyone else.

There wasn't a building around I wouldn't have heartily agreed to live in though. Everything was gorgeous, lush, well-made. It was like the beauty of this magical city had truly been sealed, frozen in time, untouchable for centuries. In its glory.

The buildings themselves were made of a marble-like material that glistened in the sunlight. I had never seen anything so beautiful—not even the Dome held a candle to Abraxas's magnificence. The Dome was a poor man's attempt at replicating the brilliance of this city.

Emerald-green, sapphire, and amethyst-coloured roofs were a shock of colour against the achromatism, and I genuinely believed true gems were used to create the mesmerising colours—they were that vibrant. Just like in the Dome, not a wisp of cloud nor a puff of smoke marred the panorama of sky.

I had to force myself to refocus on my purpose, intent on searching for places the Relic might be hidden. Places only my thieving eye might have thought to look.

I noticed a bronze door, unlike any other door I'd seen, at the base of the tower and advanced slowly towards it as I stayed vigilant for any hint of traps or threats.

As my hand grazed the door, I reeled; my mind flashed with snippets of war, destruction, and burning. I saw a floating island plummet until it crashed into the ground, breaking into massive chunks of earth. I felt the heat of the inferno devour the shrubbery and melt the wares of shops. I sensed the terror of the citizens fleeing in panic as waves of soldiers clad in heavy armour skewered them with broadswords and spears as they ransacked homes. I watched as a handful of men and women, dressed in distinct, exquisite finery, retreated past the bronze door, their furtive glances drawing my attention.

I stumbled back a few steps, my brain scrambling to process everything I had just seen.

The fuck just happened?

My head whipped around as I scanned my surroundings again, but everything was as perfect as it had been before.

Had I just had a premonition? Or a vision from before the magic was bound? Who were those people and why were they escaping through this door?

Without more information, I could not solve the puzzle. I had to press further, and clearly this bronze door was my next step. I twirled around, taking in the beauty one last time before I turned for the doorknob.

But there was no knob. No handle, no latch. Nothing.

I pushed the door, but it did not budge.

Slammed my small frame against it, but it did not move an inch.

I searched the doorframe and walls for a secret button. Something that would allow me access.

But there was nothing.

I leaned forward to press my ear against the door, to see if I could hear any mechanisms inside or any sounds beyond it. As my body made contact, I felt the piece of Relic still stowed in my belt begin to vibrate. A low hum sounded as an invisible film appeared, like a mirage over the door. It glistened in the sunlight, like the lake we had swum through earlier.

The vibrations emanating from the Relic crescendoed, my chest pulsing with the building intensity. Whispers swirled around me, the messages indecipherable—merely fleeting murmurs, seemingly nonsensical, despite my efforts to make sense of them.

My head raged with a budding migraine, until finally it caused me to stumble forward, my hand shooting out to brace myself from falling face first into the door.

As my hand made contact, the translucent film began to deteriorate outward, reminding me of the termites that had ravaged our place two summers earlier. The film continued to evaporate until it seemed like the door was no longer shielded.

The bronze door revealed underneath, however, was not the same; its lustre was dampened and its bronze rusted. Near the centre was a metal ring.

My hand gripped the ring to pull the door open, and a shock of air impacted me like a wave of force, knocking tendrils of hair loose from my bun.

A ripple of the invisible veil crept past the door and began eating its way over the buildings behind me. The magical barrier eroded as the ripple swept through the streets, revealing the truth that had been hidden behind this glamour.

I turned to watch the once-stunning landscape decay into demolished piles of rubble. The glorious roofs were now shards of dirt-covered gems that littered the pockmarked streets. The groomed plants had decomposed into dead branches, any life that may have been left in them choked out by the fallen debris.

The lampposts, now cold and extinguished, leaned hard against various shops, the sturdy poles bent and warped beyond salvation. Storefronts had crumbled in, their entrances filled with broken stone and creeping vines. The spouts that had channelled fresh water were strewn all over, separated and twisted.

Gasping at the destruction that had truly laid waste to Abraxas, I couldn't believe how real the mirage had seemed. It had truly felt frozen in time.

I thought of those terrified citizens fleeing the soldiers, how they must have suffered in their final moments. This glorious city that was utterly destroyed, the livelihoods incinerated, the families brutally murdered.

I couldn't help but picture Archer and Grandma facing a similar fate, and I emptied my stomach on the now-crumbling road.

Wiping my mouth with the back of my sleeve, I stood upright, taking a moment to regain some composure.

Re-exploring the city in its reality, I approached one of the wells nearby, which had previously housed fresh, drinkable water, and gagged from the stench flowing up from the tainted sludge within, no doubt the cemetery of many dead rodents.

I strode back a few paces as I took in the devastation before me. Even the immaculate roads were blown to bits, in even worse condition than the worst sections in Low-Town.

Did Dashiell do this? Could I be capable of this?

Wild creeping plants sprouted through the cracks and gaps of the destruction, centuries of human absence allowing their total domination. Nature could live anywhere, given the chance.

Not one island remained afloat, their masses broken and strewn all over.

So this *was Abraxas's reality.*

This was a good reminder to stay alert—I had been bewitched by a glamour, some alternate reality this city had projected for visitors to see. Magic was still deeply intertwined here, despite centuries of isolation.

And the Inukviak Relic piece had reacted to the mirage, like it pierced through the lies that enshrouded Abraxas.

Perhaps the Relic would aid me in finding its next piece, helping me figure out truth from fiction. It was definitely a tool I would need to harness in order to succeed here.

Steeling my nerves, I returned to the magical door, clasped the cold, hard ring, and yanked the portal open. A frigid gust of wind slapped my face in greeting and the hairs on my arms jolted upright. Darkness pervaded the entryway, preventing me from seeing any farther. My eyes strained open, trying to discern anything ahead, but to no avail. Only the draftiness stuck with me: no smells, no sights, no sounds.

I stepped through.

After several paces in utter blackness, my eyes spied a door, its border backlit. I tentatively approached it, eager to return to some light, to leave this void. I braced for another reaction between this new door and my Relic piece, but as I pushed my way out, nothing formed or disappeared.

Just a regular old door.

But there was no way I was letting my guard down. Now that I knew this place was protected by magic, I couldn't let myself believe anything was "normal."

I entered a massive, cylindrical room filled with doors of all shapes and sizes. Steep staircases sprouted out of every door and the spaces in between. Standing at the base of a staircase of stone, I strode up a few steps to get a better look around. I was inside a massive tower, the walls of the gigantic room made of tanned bricks and small glassless windows, just big enough to let enough light in to illuminate the space.

Peaking over the lip of the step, I swayed at the never-ending abyss of floating staircases and doors beneath me, all at different angles and elevations. I could not make any sense of it—no patterns or obvious routes. Looking upwards, the room continued far past what my eyes could see, although the higher up, the brighter the room seemed.

There were Gothic arched doors, beautiful double French doors, doors of every colour of wood at the end of every staircase. There were even doors made of bronze and gold overlay with artful scenes etched into them. The doors were beautiful and intricate—in stark contrast to the simplicity of the barren room itself. Almost as if the doors were too beautiful. *Is this another magic trick?*

"Think, Hollyn. Where's your exit?" I muttered to myself, a habit I developed from years of communicating with Archer through comms. "Do I go down?" I glanced down again, scrunching my face in deep thought, my fingers tapping against my pursed lips.

I shook my head, "If I go down, there might be water down there." I shook my head again in refusal–I couldn't risk getting stuck down there. I had to go up, where it seemed to get brighter. *Brighter means better, right?*

Returning my attention to the staircases above me, I noticed certain staircases seemed closer together than others, like I could jump the space between them. Maybe I could patchwork a route to the top, where I was hoping there was an exit out of here. I scouted my route, denoting which first few staircases and doors were close enough.

Puzzles like this were my specialty. I had ample experience carefully crafting paths, often having to avoid security systems and traps in my jobs. Not getting caught required agility and adaptability, the need to be ever vigilant.

This was just another job, I reminded myself. My target, I hoped, was the top of this room, and all I had to do was figure out the way. *I can do this.*

The latticed wooden door at the top of my staircase was closed, so I ascended the rest of the steps to open it before returning to the bottom. I took a big breath before I crouched in preparation. I locked on to my target staircase and dashed towards the top, launching my body with all the effort I could.

My hands slammed against the sides of the first step's edge, my fingers digging in, my breath knocked from me from my chest colliding with the front. I pulled my body higher, moving one hand up to grip the next step, and shimmied my way up until I could use my knees as leverage. Awkwardly, I raised myself onto the staircase, my feet still overhanging. I silently thanked the Priestess, just in case She did exist. Figured I needed as much help as I could muster.

I didn't dare look down, not willing to let my brain freak out over what demise I had just narrowly avoided. Rising, I glanced around for my next goal. Two other floating staircases hovered to the left and right at varying angles, each with a different-style door as well. The staircase I was on led to another door—this time one of the arched Gothic styles. I continued up the steps, hoping my path was correct, my glance heavenwards although I was incapable of seeing the way. Too many floating stairs blocked my vision.

Fuck, can I do this all the way up?

This door was made of ebony wood and edged by wainscoting into three rectangular sections. I snuck it open, my head sticking through to assess everything. Yet again, there was a floating staircase in the distance, but this time, it seemed that much farther away.

My gut sank, uncertainty creeping into my composure.

I'd barely made the last jump.

I glanced down, gulping at the never-ending abyss below.

Certain death if I failed.

I turned around to look behind me, contemplating giving up this mission, only to find that the staircase I'd jumped from had disappeared, as if it had plummeted into the chasm below me. I couldn't see any remnants of it, though.

I was fucked. I couldn't turn back.

I had to keep going. I had no other choice.

I needed to get to the next staircase.

You can do this. Relax. Trust yourself.

I rolled my shoulders, trying to calm the pounding anxiety inside, and began my sprint up the steps.

Just as I reached the doorway, I watched the staircase in front of me begin to rotate clockwise.

My hands gripped the doorframe at the last minute to catch myself from falling to my death, my feet skidding to a stop just as my toes overhung the ledge. I stepped back and watched as, layer by layer, the staircases began revolving clockwise and counterclockwise, like cogs in a machine turning in motion.

I would have to time this jump perfectly—and at full speed. If I didn't...

I shook my head to banish those depressing thoughts. *Plan it out. Step by step.*

I counted each second that passed as the staircase revolved. It took a full eight seconds to complete one rotation.

Eight seconds for me to sprint the staircase and vault myself to safety.

I walked halfway down the steps, not wanting to extend my sprint any longer. I practised a sprint to the edge, timing myself.

Five seconds, roughly.

That gave me three seconds to jump and land.

That seemed doable, but I really had no clue otherwise.

I proceeded back down the steps and turned to watch two preemptive rotations of the staircase, my body swaying as if it was feeling the rhythm of the moving obstacles.

I tensed, my breath held as I counted down the last three seconds of the rotation.

Three...

Two...

One.

I sprung into action, my arms pumping as my legs gained speed, my toes grazing each step to keep my momentum. My thighs burned as I scaled the height, until I was just a couple paces from the edge. My last step landed a hair's breadth away, and I sprang with all my might, stretched long like a lioness pouncing on its prey.

My body was weightless as I soared towards the staircase. I focused on catching the platform's edge as it completed its rotation.

Thud.

I landed awkwardly, the corner edge landing between my chest and armpits and my forearms clamped down like vise grips as my lower half swung with the motion of the stairs.

My arms started to slide, struggling with the momentum, and I thrashed wildly, trying to solidify my grip on the stones, but the pressure from the motion trapped me. It felt impossible to pull out of the undertow.

I slid down further, my hands falling back to grip the corners of the staircase base, my chin hooked over the edge in desperation.

Panic washed over me and I frantically searched for another option, certain I could not get myself up now.

The staircase on the left, I noticed, briefly rotated under me for only a moment. But if I could time it right...

Sweat built up in my hands, and my fingers squeaked as my grip loosened further.

I glanced down one last time and released my hold, plunging downward.

My ass slammed hard into the steps, and I bounced down a couple more before coming to a stop. My tailbone felt bruised, and I tasted blood from biting down on my tongue. But I was alive. I closed my eyes in reprieve from the motion sickness building up; the constant rotating was dizzying.

I took a moment to breathe as I shakily stood, rubbing my butt and wiping the blood from my lip.

There was no option left now except to head toward the Gothic arched door at the top of this new staircase. I took the steps slowly, body shivering, as if a cool breeze drafted in from the doorway.

I thrust it open, expecting another death-defying jump ahead of me, but what I stumbled upon was utter darkness, like what had appeared at the bronze doorway.

Confused, I leaned my body inside, hanging from the doorframe to see if there was any surface to walk or land on. My foot tentatively tapped and found some sort of invisible walkway.

I gingerly stepped inside, goosebumps covering my bare legs from the crisp air. Slowly, I made my way across the invisible bridge, making certain I stayed as straight as I could. A soft glow popped into view and grew rapidly as it sped closer, until another backlit door stood tall before me. It popped open, as if to welcome me inside. I shoved it wide and saw the steps of another staircase leading up.

No jump.

I sighed in relief and continued onward. As I passed through the doorway, a ripple of wind washed over me, softly tickling my skin, and I shuddered at the pleasure. Surprisingly, it seemed like I somehow came out the other side a huge distance higher; I looked down at a number of staircases and doors that crowded my view, still rotating, still untouched.

I must have jumped past dozens.

My head whipped up and I noticed in the distance what looked to be one unique door painted a beautiful cherry red. None of the doors I'd seen had been that colour, if I recalled correctly. I scanned for any other pop of red, and when I didn't find another, my heart leapt in excitement.

It must be my exit.

My strategy shifted, my eyes now searching for an arched doorway, hoping to find another shortcut like the one I'd just come through.

Two staircases to my far left, I spotted my target.

Just two more to the next door. I could do this.

But these staircases weren't revolving like the obstacles I'd jumped between earlier.

These staircases were dissolving into nothingness, until long moments later, they reappeared.

I would have to time every step right. There was no opportunity for me to go backward once I started.

Normally, I would have tools at my disposal, like my Dustclox powder to illuminate the hidden, or my EM radar that could pick up disparities in the electromagnetic fields. Archer would have had the blueprints and other back-end documents, and we would have already known what awaited me each step of the way.

Normally. But this was anything but normal.

The first staircase seemed to dissolve in an orderly wave, starting from the lowest step up to the highest. Like a string of chasing lights, each step blinked out until they all disappeared briefly, before relighting fully to restart the cycle.

I counted four seconds between each transition—my landing would have to be precise and would not afford me any room for slowdowns.

Both staircases, thankfully, seemed to follow the same rhythm.

Gathering my nerves, I kicked each leg multiple times to warm my body and flush out some of the stagnant air building inside them.

I crouched into a runner's starting stance as I waited for the final steps to disappear. When the last one blinked away, I dashed to the top of the stairs I was on and sprang over the gap to the first staircase to my left. I landed just as the first step materialised under my feet.

My knees slammed into the hard surface, pain shooting up my legs. I felt warm blood gush down my shin—my kneecap was deeply gashed.

I had no time to dwell, I had to get moving.

My knees hissed in anger as I rose, and I cried out in pain. My legs pumped my body up the steps anyway, the numbness creeping up my thighs a welcome reprieve.

I didn't have time to worry about whether my knees could handle the next jump. I bent into a squat, blood gushing even harder, before I leapt to the next staircase.

I landed awkwardly on my front like a frog, my face smashing into a ledge, my shins assaulted by the corner edges. My tongue tasted blood again, and I scrambled to stand up in time.

I began to run up the stairs, my speed exhausted now, sheer vapours fueling me on. I could not feel my legs causing me to stumble over a step, and my hands shot out to brace the impact. I clambered up the last steps using all my limbs and wrenched the Gothic door open, catapulting myself into the darkness, praying there was a floor to catch me.

Lumbering through the void, I found the illuminated door I was hoping to and barreled through.

There it is.

The illusive door, red like the rubies I used to steal, waited at the top of my final staircase. I hauled my body up each step, eyes darting every which way for one last trick.

My mangled knees buckled with each difficult step, my breath labouring with the strain. I worried my kneecap was fractured, and the blood gushing down my face had yet to quell. Each breath felt like flames igniting my lungs.

Fatigue almost won, but I grunted as I exerted myself in my ascension up the final few steps. My body fell against the exit, its hinges scraping as it opened.

Come to a Dread

The fuck is that smell?

The stench gagged me as I continued into the damp, cramped room. It wasn't any bigger than my home and was just as barren. I heard a squeak and the scurry of little feet as I headed towards the recessed circle situated in the centre of the room. In the middle of a brick border rose a smooth dais, made of some sort of terracotta, with intricate golden swirls etched onto it.

The pounding in my head that had plagued me in the streets roared back with a vengeance, a deep aching just behind my eyes. I clamped my head with my hand, my eyes squinting in reaction.

A small black box rested on the platform. It was unassuming, without any design, but it pulsed energy towards me, and I could not stop hyperfocusing on it as the rest of my surroundings drowned out. The same gust of cold I'd felt in the portal voids whipped me, and I knew that I had found the Inukviak Relic piece.

It was like it was calling out to me, whispers of beckoning filling my head. I felt my eyes glaze over, the room around me dulling as I glided towards it, my body moving almost of its own accord. Pragmatism be damned as I reached the box and bent down to pick up the compact container, my fingers grazing over its edges, the dark leather delicious under my fingertips. I had never felt anything so lovely. I was consumed by the urge to open it.

Any vestiges of restraint flew away.

My fingers found the flap barring me from what was inside, and I ripped it open in furtive haste.

Somewhere deep within the recesses of my brain, I heard my inner voice scream warnings at me, but my compulsion did not listen. I was a moth to the flame. *"Open it,"* I heard a voice whisper in my ear, and soon others joined in urging me to free what was inside. Voices swirled in my head until my fingers opened the box.

Inside a slender, jagged piece glistened irresistibly, nestled safely in a bed of ruby silk.

I reached out towards the prize, and as my fingers connected with the obelisk, my migraine eased. I gasped in ecstasy as waves of pleasure cascaded through me from my fingertips down to my frozen, bare toes, the toenails dirtied with grime and dried blood.

Laughing maniacally, I played with the Relic, swirling it in the palm of my hand and revelling at the warmth that filled my body. Emotions pent up from the shocking events of the last few days purged out of me in hysteria; grief for my grandmother and for Archer barked out of me in belly-wrenching laughs.

I wondered if this was all a dream. How such a small, modest piece could have led to the utter destruction of my life in a matter of days.

Finally, my giggles sputtered into huffs of air and my frenzied amusement ebbed away until a void in the core of me took residence.

The warmth that spread from the Relic was the only thing preventing me from a complete psychotic breakdown. Every other inch of my body felt cold, almost dead. Like everyone else in my life.

I reached into my belt to retrieve the Relic fragment Slade had given me and brought the two near each other, one in each opened palm. I rotated the pieces till they fit and marvelled at how perfectly they seamed together. Not a fraction of a piece was missing, each jagged ridge fusing flush. The third and final piece still needed to be found, as it was obvious there was a missing chunk where it would undoubtedly fit perfectly.

Pearly veins glimmered in response to their unification, and I watched the streaks flicker alight, casting an ethereal glow to the onyx pieces. Magic clearly flowed through these pieces freely, and I couldn't look away, losing myself watching the luminous strands pulse to life. Wisps of pale light slowly snaked up from the Relic, cocooning me in translucent spider webs. I tensed but for a moment, unsure whether the magic was friend or foe.

The warmth intensified and it felt like I'd received a shot of adrenaline. I revelled in the warm light for who knows how long; it felt like only seconds and many hours all at the same time.

Such immense power. What kind of magnitude would it have when its third and final piece was reunited?

This was the Dufort magic, caged inside such a tiny rock. It seemed almost impossible such a plain thing could contain a fraction of what had overtaken me—it felt like I had been possessed, lost my mind even. I began to understand how someone might indeed be driven to madness having to control this thing.

And where did those voices come from?

Once the light had ebbed, I instinctively crouched down to huddle over the Relic, in awe of its power, like a monkey guarding its treasure. I'd forgotten about the state of my knee and braced for a new rush of pain. But when my eyes investigated my wounds, it seemed that the gash was no longer where I had remembered, and my kneecap was no longer crooked.

Perhaps my mind had exaggerated how bad it was. Perhaps shock had played a trick on me. Hell, maybe another mirage guarded that hellish tower of staircases and had fucked with my perceptions.

Or maybe, even with just the two pieces, this Relic was so strong it was already healing my battle injuries.

Stone grating against stone shattered my thoughts, drawing my attention back to my present surroundings. One by one, the bricks encircling the dais began to rise towards the low ceiling until they came to a halt inches from the top.

I retreated a couple steps before the entire room began to quake, making me stumble and trip over the rumbling floor. Before I could turn around and sprint for the door, the brick posts erupted outward, blasting me with their hefty chunks. My body was thrown back against the wall, my hands just barely coming up in time to somewhat cover my face against the blast.

I felt my head crack as the impact reverberated through my body, my hands dropping open. The Relic clinked as the pieces separated and danced away out of sight.

Groaning, I assessed my skull but detected no blood, no open wound. I was lucky. I groggily shook the stars from my vision as I struggled to my hands and knees to recover from the recoil.

But my mind kept chanting for me to look, to find the Relic again, that nothing else mattered. My eyes searched feverishly for them as I scrambled to my feet, like an addict itching for their next hit. The need to get the Relic pieces back was overbearing.

Large slabs of the ceiling began to crumble and plummet from above, the room beginning to cave in on itself. But still I hunted everywhere desperately for them. My chance of escaping dwindled with each step I took deeper into the room, obsessing over the missing fragments.

There.

One of the pieces was wedged in between a gap in the stones, and I pounced on it. I raised it up in both hands in victory and quickly kissed it before stuffing it in my belt pouch, my body twisting around to scavenge for the second piece.

A massive lump fell and shattered a foot in front of me, dirt and mortar spraying everywhere. I scrambled over it and continued my pursuit, now almost at the far end of the room, past where the central dais once was.

Again, faint whispers pleaded—this time for me to get out—but other voices dominated, commanding me not to leave without the other piece. *I can't leave now!*

Something glinted to my right and I rushed towards it. I was so close, I could feel my body pulse in anticipation. Reaching out, my hand finally clasped around it.

Crash.

Another chunk of ceiling dropped, this time crashing into my hunched-over back, and I flattened like a pancake.

Darkness enveloped me.

I blinked awake and tried to rub the dust out of my eyes, but my arms were trapped underneath a tremendous weight. I also couldn't free my head from whatever was pinning it on its side.

Panic started to set in when I realised the gravity of my situation. The tremors had not subsided, and another quake contributed to what sounded like almost the entire room caving in. I didn't know for how long I had been unconscious. A cold sweat broke out as I realised I might die in this room.

What a way to go out.

No.

I refused to die here like this.

I focused all my strength into wiggling my right hand out from under the rubble. I clenched my teeth in exertion as I tugged over and over, until finally I freed it, the rocks scraping the back as I dragged it out. I wiggled my hand to check for injuries but was relieved when everything moved the way it should.

Light penetrated through cracks in the pile of rubble to the right of me, and I used my hand for traction as I inched slowly towards freedom. My cheek dragged across broken ground, leaving behind a streak of blood like a snail trail.

As I reached the beams of light, I picked away at the loose rocks with my one free hand, slowly widening the holes until I could suck in fresh air.

My lower half, however, was still pinned under a slab of stone, so I began to rotate my left foot in circles, creating space with each turn until I could liberate it with one final tug. I could not feel anything below my right knee, and my ankle felt like it hung at an awkward angle. But that proved to be a blessing, as I was able to yank it free without any pain. For now.

With both of my feet available, I bucked up against the piece weighing down my upper body and gained momentum when I began to feel the great slab shift with each thrust.

Finally, I acquired enough space to wiggle my head out and turned it to face the hole. My nails broke and my hands bled as I scraped and raked, pulled and pushed until a gap opened wide enough for me to drag myself through.

I emerged to dazzling sunlight—the entire roof of this room had crumbled. I crawled out of the mouth in the rubble mountain, then rolled down the heap and landed on my back with a puff of dust. I closed my eyes just for a moment, to collect myself and send silent prayers to whoever the hell was up there keeping me alive.

Bringing my hands to rest on my forehead in stunned relief, I noticed something.

Caught in my left shirtsleeve was the second Relic piece.

I almost wept; I wouldn't have had a hope in hell of finding it amongst the wreckage now. I stowed it safely with the other inside my belt.

Sitting upright, I scanned the room—now nothing more than heaps of debris surrounded by four partially standing walls. Battling to a standing position, I immediately felt sharp pains tear up from my right ankle, causing me to hop erratically to catch my balance as my eyes closed in agony.

After the pain dulled to a manageable ache and my balance recovered, I searched for a way to get out of here.

But everywhere I looked, there was nothing but a gigantic crater below. The rest of the fortress seemed to have been gouged away, along with the door I had entered through. All I could see in the distance down far below were the war-torn streets I'd walked before I'd gone through the bronze door.

How did I even get up here? Where were the staircases and the doors? Had I fallen victim to another mirage?

Most importantly—how the fuck was I going to get down?

I slumped down, my feet dangling over the edge, my right bent way too far, and I knew it was likely broken. Leaning over, I searched for any way to scale down. So much of the building I perched atop had been eroded, my heart sank. There was no good path to climb down, and I wasn't sure I *could* with my ankle.

There was no way I could safely jump down.

Well, fuck. Now what?

Sudden, vigorous gusts of wind blew my hair out of my face, the last strands that'd clung for life in my bun finally admitting defeat, and my locks unravelled down my back. Dirt, stone, and sand blew against me, tiny bits pelting my back as I squinted upward at the source.

Propeller blades whipped as a helicopter lowered, hovering a few feet above me. A soldier clad in green camo and a helmet with a tinted face shield painted like a German shepherd gestured to me.

Fear struck me—had the O'Malleys found me already? I scrambled back, my body tensing, anticipating I might need to flee. But I paused when I realised I did not recognize the helmets—I had never seen Domers wear any designs on theirs. *Is this someone else?*

Who could possibly know I was here? Did others see the blast too?

Had Ryker and Slade? I glanced down to see if they had found a way into Abraxas, perhaps in reaction to the explosion. But I saw no one.

The soldier shouted something, drawing my attention back to him. He mimed that he would throw something at me. I stood wearily on my good foot and got ready to catch whatever the stranger was sending down.

A thick rope was tossed at me and I grabbed the tapered tail. I wrapped it around my waist and tied a triple knot to secure it. Gulping, I peeked down below, then up above at the masked soldiers.

I had no idea who my rescuers were. I didn't know whether they were my enemies or my allies, but since I had no way back down, they were my only option.

I stepped off the edge, my hands clenching the rope with all my might as it dug into the skin around my waist. My body arched backwards as I was slowly tugged up.

I didn't dare look down.

When I finally was pulled inside, the soldier's hands worked nimbly to undo the noose around my waist, and another handed me spare pants and boots two sizes too big for me. I quickly dressed myself as the helicopter doors closed and our vehicle circled around, then started its trajectory back to wherever home was.

Glancing one last time down at the rubble of Abraxas, I wondered how mad Slade and Ryker would be. Wondered if they'd think I'd crafted this exit strategy myself. A small part of me still wondered whether I might have been able to trust them.

But then I remembered how they had left my family to die, had been so quick to make such a callous decision for their own good, and my lip curled.

I turned back towards the soldiers around me, trying to assess who they might be, where they might be from. But I couldn't hear the language they spoke over the sound of the helicopter, couldn't see the facial features hidden under their helmets. Altogether there were four soldiers, one shorter and slender—perhaps a female, while the others were taller.

The one that had pulled me up came towards me, their gloves going to each side of their helmet to lift it off. Short chestnut curls spilled out from beneath. Familiar amber eyes glowed at me.

"Where the hell'd your pants go, Torch?"

Knight at the End of the Tunnel

I barreled into Archer, my arms wrapping around his neck, almost knocking him off-balance. I sobbed as relief flooded me, emotions too powerful for my words to wade through.

He rubbed my back as I let everything out. The other soldiers averted their gaze to give us some privacy.

When finally I began to regain some composure, the last hiccups of my emotions sputtering to a halt, I drew back and looked up into his eyes, my teary view blurring his olive face.

"Y-you're here," I stuttered, as if it wasn't evident.

A lopsided grin emerged. "Yes."

"Grandma?!" A pit of fear wrenched my stomach as I held my breath, waiting for his answer.

"Yes." He rubbed my back again in reassurance. I let it loose.

"But... but how?" I shook my head in confusion. By all estimates they should have died back in Edinguard. Were they held hostage as Slade had thought?

"There's a lot I need to fill you in on, Torch. But it's a little too—"

"What?" I yelled, the sound of the helicopter drowning out his voice.

"TOO LOUD," Archer hollered. "BACK HOME."

I nodded, understanding he wanted to wait until we landed. I had no idea where he referred to. Edinguard was the only home I had ever known, but I imagined we weren't headed back there.

Briefly another soldier leaned towards Archer, a private discussion held between the two. I couldn't hear anything.

Who are these people? How do they know Archer?

A soft kiss atop my head, Archer's arm around my shoulders. I leaned into him, wanting to forget myself, even if just for a moment.

It didn't matter. We were together again. Grandma was safe too.

But a hint of guilt pervaded my happiness—I had left Slade and Ryker behind. Deserted them, with no communication. The hatred I'd felt when they'd forced me to abandon Archer and Grandma now seemed not so intense, now that they were safe.

Slade would be left unhealed, his only chance at regaining mobility nestled safely in my belt pocket.

My hands scratched at my hip as the weight of the Relic dug into my skin, and I gasped when I felt a burning sensation.

Was I way in over my head?

Would I need Slade's expertise?

What will happen if we find the third piece?

I shuddered, remembering the power of just two of the pieces, and vowed not to join the last piece together until absolutely necessary.

Scorching water pounded down on me as I lingered in the shower for as long as I could, savouring the heat and watching grime flow down the drain as I scrubbed layers of filth off my skin. My eyes were swollen from crying earlier, my mind still unsure whether this was all a dream or not.

They were safe. Both of them.

We'd landed somewhere in the far east. My geographical knowledge did not extend much past Edinguard—up until now it was all I had ever known. We were in a place called Dyrcsa, they told me.

From what I had noticed while flying in, it was rather large, covered in sand, and was equipped with fountains spouting exquisite turquoise water that people seemed to drink from.

There were funny-looking trees that seemed to have food growing right off them—in different shapes and colours than any fruit I'd ever eaten.

Our trees were strictly fuel for fire, although some of them dropped edible nuts and seeds. But none of them ever produced fruit. Our climate struggled with growing any fresh crops, centuries of factory pollution and smog poisonous to our outdoor propagation efforts. It had especially worsened in the last decade—many of us were forced to steal or forage in the forest to survive. We had taken to drinking pine needle soup and hunting small rodents to offset the gaps in our nutrition.

I'd never been able to understand why the Domers had let it get this bad. If Townies could no longer work, there would be no one to fill their factories, harvest and process their resources, or even clean their toilets and sewers. Domers had the luxury of deciding when and if they wanted to work, but that freedom relied on *our* grunt work.

But now I wondered if they'd always known there were other towns out there. Maybe their plans all along were to move on once us Low-Towners dried up, to conquer and enslave another population. We were cogs in the Domers' machine, and when we rusted, we would be replaced without a second thought.

Use us, then lose us.

It turned out new people were waiting all over. I'd seen them, in droves, winding through these sandy streets.

Peaceful-looking people. Families.

Bile rose in my throat. I'd always known our caste society was brutally unequal—but to imagine it seeping like poison into another unsuspecting town, a town full of innocent people who didn't deserve such a fate–that was hard to swallow.

My teachers had briefly mentioned that the creation of Edinguard had been bloody. That'd been our first revolt: the original Low-Towners had fought against the creation of the Dome and everything it stood for. But without magic, they'd succumbed to a brutal defeat. A defeat that had produced generations of terrified, obliging citizens, fearful of disobeying even the most cruel of societal demands.

And now my people quickly approached their end, the scarcity of resources visibly killing the weakest, the oldest, the poorest. It was only a matter of time before it reached even the strongest of us.

The Domers, I imagined, probably laughed at us rotting away, our stink halted from reaching their noses as they sat safely inside their glass castle.

I turned the shower knob off and stepped over the brick trim that squared off the shower area. There were no curtains or glass to give privacy like at home, the doors for each room nothing more than a hanging fringe of beads that parted like water as you passed through.

The toilet had a stool for one's feet built around the seat, and there was no paper with which to wipe. They used warm water instead, I'd learned, after my ass had been sprayed when I thought I'd pressed the flush button.

Towel wrapped around me, I began scrunching sections of my damp hair, having learned through trial and error how to tame my loose curls and avoid looking like I'd been electrocuted. I'd yearned for a mother to show me these kinds of things throughout much of my adolescence.

I exited the communal showers—people liked to be together all throughout their days here, it seemed. They shared showers, toilets, kitchens, even sleeping spaces. And not just with their own families, like poverty forced us to at home.

I had been here for only a couple hours, housed in a modest quadplex where Archer and whoever else were stationed. In that time, I'd watched the citizens striding through the streets, their smiling faces warmly greeting each other, their tight embraces and loving exchanges of food.

They wore magnificent cloaks of vibrant satin and silk, each family member adorned with the same shade, and I marvelled at how many new hues I was being exposed to. Some cloaks were lined with threads of gold, silver, and other sparkling colours, while others were embroidered and fastened with gems, sequins, and more.

Their cloaks seemed to be a form of social recognition, from what I could understand. Their coat of arms, so to speak. It seemed they were proud of their lineage, unafraid to show it off.

And here I've been born to a family forced to hide its identity for centuries.

Underneath their capes, they dressed rather plainly in flowing linen pants tapered at the ankles; the women wore fitted bodices in a matching set to the pants, while the men wore what looked like leather breastplates. Their footwear varied between soft black slip-ons or bulky black leather boots.

I headed back to my room, where Dyrcsan attire had been laid out for me to change into. Archer had informed me that it was warm and sunny here and that the Dyrcsan people appreciated visitors who respected their culture; dressing in their usual garb was a first step towards that goal.

So I slipped into the breezy, almost-silken mustard yellow pants before picking up the confining-looking top, wondering how the hell I would fasten it without help. As I struggled to tie up the top, my fingers slipped on the last few when I heard the soft clinking of my door's beads, my heart hammering as Archer entered.

"Seems I came just in time."

My whole body flushed in response to that melodic voice, mischief laced in everything he said and I kept my eyes focused on the final clasps in a weak attempt to hide my feelings for him that seemed impossible to ignore any longer. I hadn't seen him since he'd left me to settle in—he had some business to attend to, he'd told me. With whom, I hadn't the faintest idea.

I was so confused.

About how he was alive, how my grandmother was okay, how he was connected to this place or these people. About how much I had missed him.

Mustering the courage, I finally turned towards him and felt a rush of love almost dizzy me. But behind it was a new sense of weariness. Someone I'd known, loved, and trusted for so many years had been keeping all this from me.

I had never felt that with Archer before.

Who is Archer really?

I vowed to get answers. Taking a few steps back to give myself the space to resist, I awkwardly bumped into the nightstand by the huge four post bed that was clad in expensive-looking threads and multiple plush pillows. Archer choked down a laugh, his eyes twinkling with humour, "Where you goin', Torch?"

Turning towards the window to hide the blush creeping up my cheeks, I tucked my hair behind my ear, "This is all a lot to take in, Arch. I mean, I didn't even know this place existed." I shook my head as I watched turquoise water spew from a fountain, my mouth watering as I fantasized over its taste.

"Pretty crazy, huh?" I felt his breath send tingles down the nape of my neck and I shivered. I hadn't noticed him closing the gap between us. Squeezing around him, I searched for refuge in another part of the room, finally settling on a straight-backed chair settled in the opposite corner. I fingered the carving on the armrest, before trailing my fingers along the satin covered seat. It was a beautiful rose colour with a pattern of flowers and vines twisting and curling everywhere.

Nearly forgetting myself again, I abruptly spun around not trusting myself to leave my back exposed. I could barely contain how much I wanted him; nearly losing him had only amplified my desires, my needs.

Get a grip, girl.

He strode towards me, so handsomely clad, like he was born to wear Dyrcsan garb and my knees buckled as those amber eyes locked onto me, the intensity both thrilling and terrifying me. The seafoam green warmed his honey-coloured skin and brightened the golden streaks laced through those curls. All the agony I'd felt in losing him was replaced with mounting desire. I could feel it rising inside of me—perhaps my body was eager for intimacy, to rid myself of the loneliness that's haunted me the last few days.

I put my hand out to halt him. I still wanted answers.

But the look on his face took my breath away. Emotions whirled in his eyes, as if an inferno blazed behind them. His full lips were parted sensually, his chestnut curls so sweetly curled in chaotic abandon and the last threads of restraint shred as I watched his throat bob with a gulp, as if he too felt nervous being this close to me.

And it undid me.

"Hollyn, I..." His warm hands found my waist as he pulled me into an embrace, and I wrapped my arms around him in a hug that said so much without words. I could feel the relief in both of us at having found each other alive. We always joked that we loved each other. But after almost losing him, the carefully constructed barriers I had in place to keep him at a friendly distance dissolved as I melted into his arms. As we lingered in each other's embrace, I wished time would stand still, both of us savouring the comfort.

Archer pulled back slightly before pressing a kiss to the top of my head. I looked up into those amber eyes and saw the desire burning in them, a desire that matched my own. After all the pain we had been through, we deserved some pleasure.

I would get my answers. Later.

His fingers traced up my waist, slowly, excruciatingly slowly, until my body was flushed with goosebumps and his hands caressed the tops of my small breasts nearly bursting from under my shirt. My nipples hardened under his touch, and I sighed as I arched backward, inviting him to continue.

A moment of clarity whipped my head back up.

"Arch," I began, then gasped as he scorched a trail with his mouth, kissing down my neck. My brain fogged and I scrambled to think of anything to stop this. I didn't know how to ask, didn't know what words to say as our eyes met again, electricity crackling between us. Did he feel the same way I did?

We had both had partners before, sex one of the small comforts left that was free for Low-Towners. And after seeing my father deteriorate under substance abuse, I knew I would never turn to drink to ease my troubles.

So I had found some small pleasures elsewhere. But Archer and I had never crossed that boundary. With him, it was different.

I knew I loved him. Deeply. And that terrified me.

I couldn't give myself to him like that unless he loved me back.

My father had never loved me back. That truth had tortured me for years, and I couldn't survive feeling that way again.

"Arch." I trembled between his kisses. "I can't—"

He pulled back briefly, searching my face to see if I really meant it. "Why? Do you not... feel that way for me?" Pain scrunched his face, as if he was bracing, waiting for me to confirm his worst fear.

"Me? You? I-I—" A sudden laugh erupted from me. *He's worried about* me?

He pulled back further, as if taking my laughter as confirmation, his face pained. "I've been lying to myself for years, convincing myself that we had to stay friends. That you saw me more as a brother. That I couldn't cross that boundary and risk losing you if you didn't feel the same way." His head dropped down, his curls bouncing in dejection, his shoulders sagging in defeat.

My mouth agape, I stood rooted in stupor.

His head rising to meet my eyes again, Archer rapidly blinked back tears, gulping a hard swallow before continuing, "But I knew—I've always known—I loved you. And more than sibling love." Urgently he grabbed my shoulders, and I faltered a step backward, surprised at the panic lacing his voice. His sadness had been replaced by a wildness, a panic even, in his eyes.

"Arch—"

He shook his head voraciously, "Let me continue. Let me get it out. I can't keep living in denial." Breathing a ragged inhale, his hands tenderly cupped my face face, his warm fingers tracing my cheek. "I've wanted you for a while, but I've felt you pushing me away, so I haven't pursued it. But almost losing you back there... I don't give a fuck about the risk anymore." The heat smoldering in his eyes ensnared me and I felt numb, my body incapable of moving away. I could feel the warmth of a blush seeping up my skin, felt every goose pimple pop up as an ache blazed deep in my gut. An ache I knew would not be sated without crossing that line between friend and lover.

I opened my mouth to respond, to confirm the feelings were reciprocated, that I had loved him for too long, but nothing came out as I struggled to find the right words to convey how much he meant to me.

Archer continued, to my mercy, his earnest face hopeful as he gave me a choice, "So I'm at your mercy, my feelings out on the line. If you don't want to take this step with me, no problem. I will forever be your friend."

His fingers softly trailed down my arms as his eyes bored into mine. "But I can't live my life without asking, *hoping*, if you feel the same way. Because to me, you are perfect."

Tears welled in the corners of my eyes, years of self-doubt finally appeased. All this time, and his turmoil had mirrored my own.

I *was* worthy of love, despite my father's insistence I was not.

And fuck if I would let his evil spoil my life any further.

My arms encircled his neck and I brought him towards me, my mouth slanting hungrily against his, the levee on my emotions finally breaking. Archer responded to my passion with his own rising desire until our lips nearly bruised from the fervour.

I gasped for breath when he pulled back, my mind reeling from the headiness and my pale skin flushing from the blood pumping through my body. A whisper of wind caressed my stomach and I realized Archer had already unfastened my top, the yellow bustier falling by my feet. Trembling, I felt like butter melting under his touch, barely able to stand as his fingers caressed every inch of my upper body

"Arch, someone could come in–"

I moaned as his soft lips found my nipple, his tongue adeptly flicking and twirling my pale peaks until he softly suckled one then the other before pulling my head back towards him in a crushing kiss. Our arousal built with each passionate kiss, urgency pushing us towards that edge as our tongues danced with each other, our mouths slanting from side to side as our hands intertwined in each other's hair.

Archer yanked my head back and began to trail kisses down my neck, and I shuddered in delight when he found the sensitive spot by my collarbone. My eyes closed for a brief moment before I felt the urge to take some control, my hands finding the clasps behind him. I needed to feel his skin on mine, and I worked rapidly to remove him from his breastplate.

My lips found his throat and he groaned in pleasure as I unhooked the last clasp. I ripped the breastplate off him and chucked it far away, the need for clothes far gone now.

My hands roamed the curves of his lean muscles, fat nowhere to be found, just like me. Eyebrows shooting up in alarm, I trailed new scabs along one side of his stomach—scabs that must have resulted from his escape. He winced ever so slightly, so I bent and kissed each scar soothingly, lovingly. Sighing in pleasure, I refocused my attention on ridding him of the rest of his clothes, first the navy-blue cloak around his neck. It wisped to the floor like petals dying before the start of our unforgivingly harsh winters.

I pushed him to the edge of the bed before shoving him onto his back. Revelling in his attention, I took my time slipping out of my towel, standing there under his lustful gaze. I refused to cower, welcoming the heat that built as he devoured me with his eyes.

I stalked towards him before bending over to pull his pants off, wanting to feel our naked limbs coiled around each other in climax. I hungered for the heat of him, to fill that void of loneliness that ate me away.

In awe of his naked form, so bold and hard for me already, I couldn't wait any longer.

"I want to feel you inside me," I breathed, and his lazy chuckle gave me all the answers I needed.

Like a prowling cat on all fours, I climbed on top of him, and his hands grasped my hip bones as our lips found each other, my naked body pressed up against his hardness. I wiggled my hips against him and giggled when his breath caught and a low rumble escaped his throat in warning.

"If you want to really enjoy this, I'd suggest you stop that," joked Archer, as he sucked breath in through his clenched teeth.

My hands pinned his arms up above his head as I ground my hips even more until, in one smooth flip, Archer had bucked me, reversing our positions and my heart pumped wildly in response. I learned that we both enjoyed taking and conceding power; it was like a dance as we took turns leading and following.

His kisses trailed down my stomach, searing my skin on their way south before they jumped to my inner thighs, my legs bending as I fondled my breasts instinctively.

My breath skipped as his tongue began to softly lick me, swirling and lapping as I shuddered in ecstasy. He gently suckled and the pressure in my body began to build as his fingers entered me boldly. Rhythmically, his mouth and fingers worked in unison, coaxing me closer and closer, until my hands gripped the sheets by my head as I writhed beneath him.

"I thought I lost you," he murmured to me, his breath tickling me. "I love you."

I whimpered as I neared my climax. My legs widened and I ground into his face in response. "Oh my god," I gasped when his fingers worked faster inside of me, circling, beckoning me towards my finish, until I couldn't bear it anymore.

Clamped around his head, my legs tensed and my body shivered from the first wave of ecstasy that crested over me, his mouth not yet releasing me. I rode the surge, over and over, gasping for breath, my heart racing from pleasure, until finally Archer released his hold on me. My eyes closed, I panted as I recovered from the bliss.

I sat up on my forearms.

"My turn," I told him with a wicked grin.

I motioned for him to lie on his back before I straddled him. My warmth and wetness sheathed his hard cock, and I leaned back in pleasure as I took a moment to enjoy his fullness. My hands gripped his shins and I spread my legs open with my feet flat on the bed for leverage, opening myself up for his view.

Slowly I began to pump up and down as I felt the fullness of him come and go, the tip of him tapping the back of me with each stroke. Adding on, I began to circle my hips like a tornado rising and falling down his length and watched as his eyelids dropped in arousal, his teeth biting his lower lip in concentration.

I revelled in the power of my seduction, my own desires crescendoing again to match his.

His fingers found my clitoris and began to massage and twirl until I dropped my head back, my rhythm almost faltering from the pleasure.

Warmth burned up from where our bodies met, and I placed my hand on his chest to stop him, the need to tell him bursting from me, "I tried to go back for you but I couldn't get away." Our eyes met as I needed him to know I had tried. That I hadn't given up on him.

"I know," Archer murmured in response, his eyes filled with passion. "But you shouldn't have tried." His hands cupped my breasts, his mind already reoccupied with more pleasurable things.

"I know we agreed against it, but I-I couldn't lose you too."
Tears welled in my eyes, the pain of nearly losing him resurfacing.

Sensing my impending downward spiral, Archer pulled my
mouth to his in a crushing, passionate kiss, before murmuring
softly, "I'm here. I won't leave you again." I moaned, our bodies
once again meeting in explosive passion as our lips kissed hungrily, my fingers gripping his silken curls. I relished the feeling
of his hardness inside me.

Holding on to my hips, he began pumping as his need for
release became impatient. I relinquished control and let him
fuck me, each stroke building in intensity until my body tensed
again in rapture, the throes of another orgasm convulsing my
body moments before he plunged into his as well.

I felt him pulse inside of me as I gripped around his shaft,
pleasure once again cascading through me. We stayed together
until the ripples quieted, and I pulled off in sweaty exhaustion.

I flopped beside him, both of us taking a moment to lie in our
bliss. Not a care in the world pervaded our minds as we listened
to conversation chatter from the streets, the soft tweets of birds,
our background noise. A gentle, warm breeze swept softly over
our naked bodies, drying off beads of sweat.

I draped my leg over him as I scooched in for a cuddle, my
hand resting familiarly on his chest as I gazed up at him through
drooping eyelids. His eyes were peacefully closed, a soft smile
plastered on his mouth.

Slumber ensnared me as I too closed my eyes in euphoria.

We were together again.

Get the Lay of the Sand

Sirens blared, jolting us awake.

My body jerked upright as terror seized me. The O'Malleys had found us. I raced to the window to peek out, trying to gauge how much time we had to escape.

Life continued as normal, not a soul perturbed by the warning sound trumpeting all around them.

Archer's hand cupped my shoulder and I jolted in surprise. "Come on."

Quickly redressing, I followed him out the door and into the streets, puzzled at his lack of urgency.

Back home, sirens blew every time there was an emergency at one of the factories—usually when someone died. But it was more for the Domer police to clear the body before it delayed production too severely than a safety warning for the rest of us.

It was never to try to save the poor souls.

Brilliant sunlight beamed down on my face, and I turned to face it instinctually, relishing the warmth. Our summers were too muggy to truly enjoy, most of us facing heat exhaustion slaving away in the steam-filled factories. But here, it was perfect. Not too hot, clean air, and a soft breeze prevented my body from sweating, despite the cloak and pants.

Beige streets led pedestrians past similar buildings, all lacking any pop of colour. It appeared as though they were formed from the very sand in which they were situated. Beige everywhere you looked, except for the colourful fabric awnings that sheltered their porches and front steps from the constant summer sun.

"There, Holls, look." Archer pointed down the street as men and women strode towards the centre courtyard we faced. Everyone else skirted out of the way, turning to watch as the group gathered in orderly rows, men and women of all ages and sizes standing with one hand raised high while the other was held just in front of their bellybuttons. All wore thick leather collars around their necks and wrists.

The wind had picked up, whipping my curls into a frenzy and dusting us with airborne sand. The once-blue sky began to darken with an approaching storm as pressure built in the air, rain only moments away—yet no one headed for shelter. I loved the rain but could not understand why people were not retreating back into their homes.

Like street performers, the group waited for some unknown sign, their bodies tense with anticipation, atop their heads semicircle crowns made of slivers of pointed metal, luminescent even as the sunlight died.

With the forewarning rumble of thunder, the performing Dyrcsans jumped into movement, their wrists twirling as their hips swayed in circles. Each movement felt natural, almost instinctive as they began to weave between each other, their arms raising and lowering. Some began to clap at the peaks, and others began to stomp after their twirls, while the last ones let out a low hum until an enchantingly rhythmic melody was created.

A bluish haze began to emanate from their hands, the hue intensifying as the song and dance continued, until it was so vibrant it was almost blinding, like the blue flames of stick welders.

All at once, they knelt down before throwing their hands skyward, releasing the energy. A translucent blue film rippled over the town–something I had not noticed was there before.

Seeing the bewilderment on my face, Archer explained, "It's a magical shield that protects Dyrcsa from the sandstorms in the area. It doesn't really get rid of the storm, it just keeps the storm from penetrating through. That's why it's always perfect, warm weather."

As if on cue, the sky quieted, the ominous storm clouds that had covered us dissipating right before my eyes. The whistling wind died immediately, and the whirling sand collectively dropped back to the ground.

I watched as, within seconds, the raging storm that had been building ceased to exist. The expansive sky was cloudless as far as

I could see, and warm rays of sunlight once again beamed down on me. I knew now that it wasn't gone, only hidden and kept back.

The crowned people, without a word, rose and humbly walked back down the street, into houses and stores, and the world around me continued on as if nothing had happened.

"They do this daily to stop the sandstorms that destroy this area. There's magic here, Torch," Archer explained.

My head whipped towards him, meeting his eyes in disbelief. "Magic?!"

Archer nodded vigorously, his eyebrows raised to stress the point. "I know. There are others."

"Are they related to Domers?" I questioned.

He shook his head, his curls shaking across his forehead as he shrugged. "I would say about a quarter of the Dyrcsan people are magical, from what I've observed. It seems like they harness the same types of magic, but everyone here works together. Like that storm dance—all those Druids invoked that protection spell to keep Dyrcsa safe. It's how they've stayed so invisible all these years," his voice sounded excited, as if in awe of this city. "Nobody thought anyone could live here with the severe wind storms." I saw the hope on his face, the way it lit up his features as he beamed at me. I could tell he adored Dyrcsa and how it functioned.

I stepped further into the town, critically analysing this place now, my intrigue piqued. "So the... Druids you said? They don't hate each other?"

Archer joined me, a hand casually thrown over my shoulders as his head leaned in to mine, his long finger pointing at a patio where two Druids now sat, chatting amicably. "Does it look like it? I mean, I'm sure there are issues—no place is perfect—but nothing like back home."

"And what about the rest of them...?" My body tensed, praying there were no slaves here.

He placed his hands on my shoulders and turned me towards him, his twinkling eyes locking with mine. Excitement bubbled from him. "There are no slaves. Nonmagical people work the same jobs and live in the same buildings as the magical. Look." His finger drew my attention back towards the Druids, who had now been joined by another citizen who did not wear Druid garb. They raised their glass in cheers as the newest grinned wide.

"Magic... isn't evil?" I asked hesitantly.

"I don't think so, Holls," Archer broke off, and I could feel the heat of his stare burn a hole on my cheek, but I could not meet his eyes.

"But, but then..." My eyebrows furrowed as I turned towards him, and I could see the sadness, the confusion, the hatred, the curiosity, all the conflicting emotions I was feeling mirrored on him as he watched me process it all.

We had always believed magic was evil. That it corrupted all, eventually.

As I processed this, a deep sorrow filled me over the life I'd lived. What generations of my people had been fed to believe.

If magic itself was not evil, this meant that what Domers did to us, allowed to happen to us—that was solely their human side. The suffering, the poverty, the paranoia—that was all a result of choices Domers made to keep us in fear of magic.

If magic isn't inherently evil... then...

My fists clenched as blinding rage began to overtake my sadness. My body shook at the deceit.

Archer spoke softly, his hands rubbing my arms, "We can't let them get away with it. We deserve a future more like this." His outstretched arm gestured grandly to the city before us.

Does he want us to live here?

"We can create a better world, Torch."

I had never let myself hope that Edinguard would ever get better, never let myself dream of a future that did not include the indenture of Low-Towners. I had no intense loyalty to Low-Town; I never stuck my neck out for more than my own, out of necessity. "You want to overthrow the Domers?" My mouth hung open, certain I was misunderstanding. I couldn't believe Archer would risk everything.

"They have plans, Holls, and I really think it could work." Archer's eyebrows shot up in innocence, the purity of his hope so clear.

But I was not so convinced. I remembered how none of our neighbours had helped us, had come to check in on Grandma, how they had left teenagers to figure it out on their own. "Why would I risk everything for Low-Town? I owe them nothing."

Archer snickered, his mouth in a wry smile. "I appreciate the honesty, Holls."

I folded my arms, shrugging his arm off my shoulders. "Well, what has anyone done for me? You're talking in dreams, and I'm just being realistic."

He sighed, his hand rubbing the back of his neck. "I know. It's just—maybe there's something bigger than us. What's all this for, just to survive?"

Frowning, I considered the sentiment before I whispered, "Is this because I'm a... Dufort?"

"You should really come—"

"Hey!!" hollered a nearby store owner, deftly bending to peel off his shoe before throwing it over the patio railing. It skittered in the sand, evidently missing its intended target. The man gestured wildly with his arms, his frustration flushing his deeply sun-kissed skin. After a moment, he seemed to give up and returned to serving his patrons.

I watched as a little boy in filthy pants, holes at the knees, crept towards the patio, where his scrawny arm reached carefully to pilfer a half-eaten pastry left by a previous customer. I nodded towards him. "Are there poor here?"

"Of course. There's poverty everywhere." Archer gestured toward the boy, who was now grinning devilishly at his score as he crouched in a dark corner nearby. "His father gambles. Too much."

I nodded, understanding the debilitating nature of addiction.

"It's not perfect, Holls, but it proves Edinguard is the product of corrupt assholes. That magic doesn't need to be used to bend people's will."

I wondered then, like Slade had mentioned, whether the Duforts were as deserving of their legacy as the Domers had us believe.

Fury burned deep in the pit of my stomach, as if the last vestige of hope that Domers could one day become better had been scorched to ash. They had manipulated us using the threat of their magic—while Dyrcsans used their magic to protect, to help citizens prosper.

I could understand why we were never told about this city. It would have caused a riot.

"Do the Domers know about this place?" I asked.

"Yes. That was my first question when I came here," Archer admitted.

Wearily, I nodded, the weight of our city's inequality bearing down on me. Not only did Domers manipulate and abuse, they also knew another way of life existed successfully. And still they chose to keep our caste system.

A small part of me had hoped there was still some good in the Domers, in Slade and Ryker.

But even if they hadn't had a hand in the creation of the system, or even profited from our slave labour, at the very least, they were complacent. My grandmother always said idle complicity was just as bad as partaking in the sin.

I saw anew how Slade had never offered to use the Relic to heal the countless Townies that suffered with nearly nonexistent medical care. It was only to be used to heal his legs.

A true show of his ethics.

They're just like the rest of the Domers. Selfish, manipulative assholes.

I wondered how Dyrcsa might use the Relic—would it be shared equally? Maybe they deserved to have it. Maybe I would give these pieces to them and move on with my life.

Of one thing I was certain—whatever I chose, I would ensure my grandmother would be healed as part of the bargain.

My hand reached for Archer's elbow, "Can I see her? I know you said she was well taken care of, but I would like to see for myself." I was anxious to see her and couldn't wait any longer.

Cupping his hand over mine, Archer nodded, "Yeah... sure, Holls, let me just see what Top Dog says."

"Top Dog?" My face scrunched as I searched his face for answers.

Something flickered, so quickly I nearly missed it as it flashed across his features. It was so faint I wasn't sure I'd even seen anything, but yet my heckles rose, like my body could sense something hidden behind Archer's current, too-perfect smile.

"She's kind of the boss, Holls. See, your grandma is housed in the main bunker with all the state-of-the-art medical equipment, but it's also protected by defences that need the highest clearance," he spun me so I was facing to the East, his long arm directing where to focus. I could see a building in the distance, one in contrast to Dyrcsan architecture. It was made of concrete and glass, very modern and sleek.

But the word boss pulled my attention back to him, my neck craning to see him again, "Boss? Archer, who the fuck are these people? Are you working for them?"

He scratched the back of his head, his eyes slowly meeting mine, a slight grimace on his face. "I know this is going to sound bad, real bad, but you know you can trust me—"

"Just tell me," I interrupted, my hand waving to silence the excuses.

Archer blew a huge exhale through his pursed lips before continuing, "I-I've been working for the Mutts. Been a spy for them for a little while now, collecting intelligence on the Domers and their security systems—"

I flinched backward, his words slapping me in the face. "What?!"

His hands immediately came up to placate me, his eyes huge like saucers as he rushed to explain himself, "*Not* a spy on you–"

"The Mutts? Like the resistance group? All those stories we used to hear about in the factory?" I shook my head voraciously, unwilling to believe him. "But, they're not real! They're just ...stories!"

Archer hedged forward, halting as I took another step backward in response, "No, they're real. And active. Holls, we really might have a chance here. They want a revolution, and after I told them about the Inukviak Relic, they wanted to see you and recruit your help," Archer rushed, passion in his eyes. "Top Dog insisted on meeting with you as soon as possible."

"You what?" My mouth dropped open in disbelief as I took another few steps backward. "You told them?" *Do they know who I am then?*

"They're good people, you can trust them." Archer took another step toward me.

"Dont!"

Nodding as he raised his hand further he conceded another step back from me, giving me the physical space I needed to think straight.

"You were spying on me?!" Heat flushed my body as tears began to blur my vision, my eyelashes working rapidly to clear them away.

Archer motioned to step forward again, but halted himself midstep as my body recoiled from him, "No! Never. I only told them about you so that they would help me get you back."

My world was spinning out of control. I had been elated to find Archer safe, only to have to pull his dagger out of my back. I was even more lost than before and just as lonely; my most trusted friend had kept this huge part of his life from me.

"How can we trust them?!" I began to step away from him, my arms going up to guard myself. "How—how can I trust you? Why didn't you tell me?"

Archer opened his mouth to reply, but my fury spurred me on, "Were you just playing me this whole time?" I winced as my fingernails dug into my palms, surprising me with the pain. I hadn't realized I was clenching my fists.

"No, Torch, I—"

"Don't you fucking call me that," I threatened, emotion choking me. "How long have you been spying? On me?!"

"I didn't tell them anything that would put you in danger, I never would. I thought you'd be excited at a chance to take down the Domers. They're the enemy here. Not us. The information I gave them had nothing to do with you," Archer insisted as he closed the space between us again, his arms wrapping around mine.

I shrugged his touch off. "*Us?!* I thought *we* were us!"

"We are—

"So why didn't you tell me? And how could you tell them about me now, without even asking me first? Do you truly get how dangerous my identity is?!" I slammed my finger into his chest with every question, his body jerking back each time. I could barely look at him even though he looked remorseful.

His hand shot to the back of his head in anxiousness, a motion so achingly familiar to me, "I was gonna tell you but Top Dog wanted me to wait. I was always planning to bring you over, but all this happened before I had the chance."

I scoffed, my arms folded as I glanced back towards the uniquely contemporary concrete building, "So now you take orders from a dog. How is that any better than being ordered around by the Domers?"

"The Mutts are nothing like the Domers," Archer snapped back. "Don't act like I would do all this, risk all of this, if there wasn't a real shot at bringing down our caste system."

"No, just risking me." I spat. I didn't care if it was unfair.

Archer huffed, exasperation lacing his words, "Come on. I had to tell them so they'd help me get you out."

"I didn't ask for your help." I dragged my gaze back at him, leveling him with a look of disgust. I saw the hurt and frustration on his face, but I couldn't stop myself, the past few days eroding away what little self-control I had left. All that remained was a miserable bitch. "Maybe you came at just the right time to take the Relic."

Archer clenched his jaw as I saw him fight not to respond to my bait, holding my gaze as he remained silent.

I scoffed, frustration torrenting through me, "Did they know about the Relic? Is that what they're after?"

"No. That was news to everyone," Archer maintained.

"But what an ace up their sleeve now. The power to heal, and—and who knows what else." I'd heard enough. I couldn't even look Archer in the eye anymore, bile rising in my throat at his betrayal.

Snarling, I crossed my arms and averted my eyes, my body rigid as a board. He had broken my trust. Had spied on me. Had told my secrets to everyone. Had chosen their loyalty over mine.

Did he wait for me to get the second piece before rescuing me?

I felt stupider than ever. I was a pawn to everyone, and I seemed to be three steps behind at all times.

"Did you know who I was?" I choked out. "Is that why you befriended me to begin with?"

"Holls..." Archer's voice broke, and I looked back to see his pained expression. "No! I was your friend first and always will be." I thought I would feel better seeing him hurt, but it only worsened the pit of despair gnawing at my belly.

Tears welled in my eyes, the weight of his deceptions unbearable. He was the only person I would have said I'd have trusted with my life. I wanted to believe him now, but I needed time. Even if his intentions had been good, he still had kept all of this from me, feeding them information about me and my life without my consent.

I separated myself from him. I needed space.

"Please," Archer began, sorrow filling his trembling voice. "I thought I was doing the right thing. I didn't know it would evolve like this. That you could be the key to everything."

My head whipped up, "Why? Because of my dormant magic?"

Archer nodded hesitantly and I paled.

"Do they think I can get it back?" My shoulders shrugged upwards, my body preparing to hear what I had been fearing this whole time. Maybe I could handle the magic remaining in the Relic, but I was terrified of what would happen if it released back into me. Dashiell had gone mad from it. Surely it would ruin me.

My body shivered in dread.

He shrugged.

Leaning forward, my arm thrusting my pointer finger at him, "*Archer*. You don't get to lie to me now."

"They don't know. But they suspect. Why else would the O'Malleys be so relentless in their witch hunt? I wanted to bring you over to the Mutts to keep you safe."

I swayed as a dizzy spell threatened to topple me over, causing me to stumble backward a few steps, my hand cupping my head in an effort to steady myself. My skin felt clammy, perspiration breaking out in beads on the back of my neck, my forehead, my upper lip. I dropped down into a ball, my head hanging in my hands, my elbows propping me over my crouched legs as I struggled to breathe. My lungs felt like they weren't working, my chest burning from the shallow breaths I struggled to inhale.

Whimpering, I knew I was losing control, my anxiety pounding at the door with a battering ram.

How can I possibly handle Dufort magic when I can't even handle my anxiety?

Tears stung my eyes as my fists clenched my hair, my body rocking back and forth habitually. I tried to focus on taking deeper breaths but my body wouldn't listen and soon I was hyperventilating in panic.

Archer's warm hand rubbed soft circles along my lower back as his body came against me, his lean frame expanding and constricting with overexaggerated, deep breaths.

I focused on his breathing as slowly he co-regulated me back from the edge. A process so familiar to both of us. I hadn't realized how much I relied on him until now.

Until he had lost my trust. And that realisation stung. Badly.

Not to mention what we had done before this. The vulnerability, the intimacy.

I shuddered in repulsion at how naive I was. Cracking my eyes open, my hands cradled my chin as I worked to swallow down the bile rising in my throat.

His hand shyly grazed my elbow, and instinctively I shrugged him off, refusing to look at him. I couldn't handle seeing his remorse.

A brief pause, before Archer breathed, "Come and meet them, talk to them."

Sighing in exhaustion, I rose to stand, "What if I never wanted to bring down the Domers? What if I just wanted to get the hell away and never look back? I don't owe anyone shit."

"Nobody's forcing you to stay here. I would understand, either way. But I know you do want to bring them down, just like I do," Archer retorted as he rose, his round eyes shining in solemnity underneath his raised, hopeful brows. "We could live here and be safe. Be protected. Be *free*."

I sighed, turning my head away. *Doesn't he know I'll never be free? Not now.*

Grabbing my hands in enthusiasm, Archer turned me to once again face that atypical building in the distance, nodding his head towards it, "Come and talk to the Mutts. Then we can make a decision, *together*. I promise." As his head flitted back to face me, I felt dizzy, giddy even. Like how I felt before each new mission, the anticipation thundering adrenaline through my veins.

I wanted to argue for the freedom to run, but Archer knew me better than I was admitting. He was right—I needed to talk to the Mutts. For I, too, wanted Domer blood.

Something I'd never let myself dream of before. But maybe it was time I let hope triumph over despair. Maybe there was more to life than simply surviving. Maybe it was selfish of me to *not* use my power for more. I would be no better than a Domer if I hoarded my magic.

I would heal my grandmother with the Relic. That was my priority, and maybe joining up with the Mutts was my way of obtaining the final piece and keeping her safe.

But maybe I would also find my true purpose—shattering that fucking glass Dome and setting fire to everything inside.

Turn Over a New Thief

Despite Archer's offer to act as tour guide, I could not stomach pretending everything between us was okay. I needed space and time to try and reconcile our friendship with my sense of betrayal. And so I had refused his accompaniment, deciding to find my way to the Mutts' home base—called the Compound—myself. I would see grandma first and make sure she was okay before heading to meet with the Mutts' leader, Top Dog.

Dyrcsa was similar, in some senses, to Low-Town. Everyone seemed to dwell in the same style and size of homes. Many citizens looked like they'd lived a life of hard work. Multigenerational homes seemed common.

But so much of it was different to back home. Dyrcsans seemed to revile arrogant mansions and displays of wealth, instead showing their individualism through their attire, their jewellery, their makeup. Small, unassuming flourishes, unique to each citizen—their individuality expressed openly and without fear. Even the magic users I passed by did not seem to rely on it, for I had not seen another flash of magic since the ritual.

Two adorable little girls ran up to me as I walked and handed over the most beautifully pale pink lily before they giggled and ran away again. I lifted the flower to my nose to inhale the spicy fragrance. I had never seen this flower in real life—I'd only seen the ragged poster my teacher had pinned to the wall of our cramped classroom for reference. But it had been one of the few colourful pieces that broke up the dullness of my school, and I'd found myself drawn to it repeatedly, until I had memorised each and every image, along with its common and scientific names.

Lilium formosanum.

As I wound through the narrow, twisting streets, I noticed the multicoloured-bead entrances and the windows without glass or blinds, the laughter and conversations that floated out creating a lively bustle all around. The city pulsed with energy and vivaciousness, hummed a happiness I had never felt within my own people.

I watched as merchants chatted with customers over an abundance of fruits and vegetables I had never seen before. Intoxicating aromas wafted from massive pots and pans inside people's homes, and I watched, amazed, as neighbours came in and out without invitation and were openly welcomed. Food was offered without trade or force.

The Dyrcsans smiled warmly at me, and shyly I smiled back. A plump, middle-aged woman beckoned me over, nodding insistently until I relented and approached her.

"Child, I have not seen you before. Welcome. I am Dhalina," the stranger said, before pulling me into an almost suffocating embrace. She pulled back and examined me, her eyes roving over my too-sharp hips, my sunken cheeks, my protruding collarbone and clucked her disapproval.

I knew before it landed in my hands that this woman would not allow me to continue on without consuming her offered cuisine. I did not bother to play polite by refusing at first and instead eagerly gulped down the contents.

I'd thought the Domer food was exquisite, but this soup danced circles around those meals. There were so many delicious spices and flavourings in the soup that I stood there with my jaw hung open in disbelief.

"What is in this?" I wondered aloud.

Dhalina laughed softly at my reaction, and my cheeks flushed with embarrassment. "It is amazing what magic can add, no?" she teased.

My eyebrows scowled in confusion. "Magic?" *How could it affect the food? Was it safe to eat?*

"I don't mean spelling my soup, dear—in fact, I have no magic. But the Druids invoke magic to protect and enhance our crops. It makes the ingredients everyone uses second to nothing." Dhalina winked.

"I think I'd be obese if I ate this food every day," I muttered before returning for another gulp, content in believing I was safe to continue eating.

"You may come back here anytime, dear, for more food." Her eyes twinkled. "No cost."

There was always a cost back home. Perhaps that was the biggest difference between our societies.

I drained the last bit of soup. Laughing, Dhalina waved to me as I rejoined the pedestrians that milled about, once again heading towards my destination.

Scattered awnings of vibrantly coloured fabrics provided shade throughout the streets, where people met and conversed, some playing games using cards or stones. I watched as one boy moved a wooden token to a spot that resulted in an uproar of clapping and congratulations, before both players stood up to bow and shake hands. Coins of metal were slapped down onto the table angrily by the losers. The only games I'd known were the scams my father resorted to, leeching the last few Kroja from his fellow drunks and gamblers.

An elderly woman sat on a bench lined with cushions, her knotted fingers whirling as she wove a stunning blanket of rainbow threads. I could not look away, my eyes entranced by the bright hues, the total chaos of each colour exploding in delight. It made me think of my own grandmother, whose hands had seized up before my sixteenth birthday after a particularly gruelling weekend of sewing new khaki-coloured police uniforms.

My mind replayed my argument with Archer, dwelling over whether I could awaken the dormant magic inside me. I knew the Relic could heal... that my magic was bound within it. But I couldn't help but fear what else waited to be woken up.

I'd felt a surge of power when I wielded just two of the Relic pieces—I was certain my magic was not gone. Dormant, but alive. And powerful. Slade had called it holy magic—what did that mean? And yet Dashiell had gone mad from it. The two polarizing views didn't mesh. It didn't make sense.

The thought of inciting a revolution, of joining a resistance group to overthrow the evil in this world, seemed unattainable when I had no idea whether my body could control my magic. It had seemed much safer thinking the magic was forever caged within the Relic. Would the Relic magic release back into me? Into others? Were there other Duforts?

Once the magic was awoken, I knew there would be no turning back.

It would be a choice that would forever change me, for good and bad. Sentencing me to a life of magic, with the ability to heal—and whatever else.

Whatever else had driven Dashiell mad.

I needed to talk to my grandmother. She would guide me. Normally I would consult Archer too, but I couldn't face him yet.

But I found myself empathising with why he had played his reconnaissance role. Dyrcsa was an enticing dream. It was no wonder he was entranced by the Mutts and their mission. They were here, living in our ideal world.

Could we really fight for a future like this?

It still did not excuse his secrecy, how he'd withheld the truth. That would take time for me to forgive, if I ever fully could.

Abruptly, I stopped before a set of shallow stone stairs. Atop a small platform set in the centre of a town square, a glowing oval hummed. *This must be it.* Archer had told me to look for a massive shimmering ring.

An attendant stood nearby and must have noticed my hesitancy. "This is a portal. A gateway between places, intended for fast travel." I noticed his soft brown eyes crinkle as he smiled at me. "It is safe."

Nodding, I looked back toward the portal and couldn't help but stare in awe. I Imagined how useful portals would have been for our own industries. How advanced our trades could become, if magic like this could be harnessed to assist.

Grandma might still have been healthy. I might not have had to thieve.

I might not have been abandoned by my parents.

"What does it feel like?" I asked, but after having experienced the doors in Abraxas, I had a sense of how it might feel.

"Nothing, really. Cold, breezy, maybe. You just sort of shimmer through, and then you're there. Kinda like you walked through a completely dark room and popped out back in the light," the attendant responded matter-of-factly.

As I walked towards the portal, my stomach churned.

I had no idea what the Mutts would ask of me, whether they could be trusted. But if Archer trusted them, I owed it to him to give them a chance.

I knew, deep down, that I wanted to fight back. To join the resistance. To feel a greater sense of purpose. And that terrified me.

I'd learned to stifle my wants and my desires to protect myself.

But what else was I doing with my life? I felt trapped, suffocated by it all.

What if my magic could forge a new future, a new Edinguard?

What if the Mutts could help me harness it? Stop me from going mad like my ancestor?

I needed Grandma's guidance, needed her reassurance that this risk would be the right move. I prayed she'd be lucid once I got there.

With a nod to the attendant and a deep breath, emotions conflicting through me, I rolled my shoulders back, my mind set.

And so I stepped through.

Miss and Make Up

All I could smell was antiseptic and metal. As if the entire stronghold had been bleached to death, not a single living thing able to survive on its walls. Whether it was truly clean—or a facade to trick us into thinking it was—was a metaphor for what I was walking into.With one last hug and a kiss pressed on each of my cheeks, I rose and said my goodbyes to the last living family member I had before heading towards my next task: maintaining power in the negotiation with Top Dog.

I emerged at the base of broad concrete steps and noticed the Compound felt slick, barren even. The single-story structure had no intricate designs carved into the walls, no colour painted, no decoration of any kind. The windows were massive, tinted and triple paned to allow no outside eyes a view inside and the entrance was housed behind two giant slabs of steel. It was a modern fortress, designed to be impenetrable.

My only goal was to discover the Mutts' true intentions: why they banded together, what kept them together, and if their leader was worth following. And most importantly, I needed to decipher whether they aimed for the domination of Edinguard or if they fought for Low-Town's liberation.

I tried to shove the suspicion out of my mind, to give them an honest chance, as I ascended the steps. There was a keypad but Archer hadn't given me a code to enter and I was debating whether I should knock or wait for Archer when I heard conversation murmuring from inside. I sidestepped to the corner of the landing when the doors creaked open and two men clad in camo engrossed in conversation strode out, completely oblivious to me hidden behind the opened door. Seeing my chance, I snuck inside before the door shut.

As I headed down a sterile-looking corridor with recessed pot lights intensely illuminating the way, I craned my neck back and forth as I peeked into the windows on either side. Most of the workers here sported military garb, their camo and khaki-colored outfits adorned with gun holsters, utility belts far superior in quality to my own, and black helmets painted like dogs of different faces and fur. It made sense—they needed anonymity within a rebel alliance, but the unique paint jobs still allowed for recognition between members.

It also raised the hairs on my back as I wondered who was hidden under those masks. How easily a mole could be planted right under their own noses.

In one room, there were workers clad in long white doctor's coats hunched over microscopes, petri dishes, and vials of different-coloured liquids, as if their minds were solely focused and undisturbed. As if on cue, one of the scientists whipped their head to look directly at me. I watched as their blacked-out face shield dropped down to reveal violet-blue eyes. They scrutinised me intensely.

Okay, well that one isn't as focused on their work.

The scientist cocked their head to the side, as if in perplexity, before resuming their work.

A loud voice pulled my attention to another room, where a woman stalked back and forth, arguing heatedly with someone through the headset in her ear. Her ebony hair was braided in cornrows that trailed down to the small of her back with tiny hoops of silver threaded throughout. Her arms were exposed, unlike most others I'd seen, who seemed to cover up with a jacket or long-sleeved shirt. The cords of her muscles flexed as she paced relentlessly from one side to the other, her fury obvious from the hateful scowl down to the clenched fists at her sides. Intricate white tattoos wove down her neck and shoulder, stopping just above the zipper of her bulletproof vest.

Abruptly, she spun on her heel to exit the room as her finger pressed down on her headset, ending the call. As she rushed out, we nearly collided.

"Watch it," she warned, teeth bared. Wordlessly, I stepped aside as I watched her barge past me and down the hallway, until she was hailed by a scientist from the other room.

"Odette!" the scientist yelled at her, beckoning her over. Words were exchanged, and although I could not decipher what they said, both turned slowly towards me. I recognized those same violet-blue eyes from before. Nearly writhing under their scrutiny, I wondered if my reputation already preceded me.

"Hollyn!" Archer's voice shocked me, and I whirled around to see him striding towards me, thankful for an opportunity to break from the staredown.

With tension still hanging between us, my arms flailed awkwardly in some attempt between a double wave and a shrug. The energy between us felt stilted, as if I was a newborn foal just learning to walk. I saw Archer cut himself short, an uneasiness settling behind his eyes. I knew that look—knew he wanted to talk.

Before he could direct the discussion to our fight from earlier, I blurted out, "Is she awake?" Reuniting with my grandma was all that mattered right now. The drama between Archer and me could wait.

He nodded, and I swore I saw a sense of relief drift over his face. "Come on. Just up through here." A brief inclination of his head toward Odette and the scientist before we continued.

The Compound felt zoo-like as we reached the end of the long hallway, each room no bigger than a cell. Like tableaux of the innermost workings of this organisation, one window at a time. Glimpses into the mechanics of this machine. Fragments that only hinted at the cogs and wheels, but without the framework, were too out of context to portray the total truth.

And I hated acting off partials. I preferred to collect every piece of information I could scrounge before letting my emotions influence my decision. I had learned that the hard way, after going to the police to accuse my father of negligence without enough evidence to convict. He had used my passionate hate for him as a stake in my own coffin, claiming psychosis and whatever other shit his half-drunk mouth could verbalise. It hadn't taken me long to learn that whatever hopes I had of the police intervening on my behalf were pointless, my reputation and my word degenerated to rambling accusations from a crazy bitch that, according to him, didn't lift a finger to help with the finances. A freeloader, he'd called me.

But he was dead now. And the only part of my past that remained was in a room in the sick bay just past the doorway we had reached.

"She's awake now and pretty lucid from what they've told me. You ready?" Excitement for my reunion laced his voice. My eyes welled up unexpectedly in anticipation of seeing her again. I had watched her almost die, left her for what I thought was certain death, and now trembled as the door slid open, my body unable to stay calm. Relief and excitement flooded through me.

I sped to her glass door, the sensors swishing it open as she struggled to prop herself up bony arms. She was lying down in her bed, the stark-white linens tucked tightly around her slender body. She was settled in a private triage room with her own bathroom that was nearly as big as our entire place back home, although it felt entirely too spartan in comparison to the homes

I'd viewed walking through Dyrcsa. There was only a small table and a single chair stuffed against the windowed wall, but despite the austerity of the room, it was immaculately clean and that was more than I could ask for.

A large window filled the back wall to her right, casting a soft ambience to her pearl skin and a brassiness to her starkly chalky bob. Across from her, a TV was mounted on the wall, the flickering lights from whatever show was on flashing briefly in my peripherals. Our matching teary eyes met, and my breath caught but for a moment before my legs propelled me into a sobbing embrace. My shoulders quaked as we swayed softly back and forth, neither one of us relinquishing our hold, as if we could not risk being separated again.

"Oh baby, baby, shhhh," she murmured as she rubbed my back in comfort. I'd always loved when she did that. I knew right then and there that she was more lucid than she'd been in years.

As much as I wished to never move, I knew I needed to capitalise on her mental state before it receded. I needed her wisdom and sharp insight into who the Mutts were, who I was, and what my purpose should be moving forward. I had endless questions, but I knew Top Dog waited for me and I didn't want to risk insulting them by making them wait too long. But I'd begged for a quick visit with my grandma to ease my worries before the meeting, if only to focus me.

For just a moment longer, I savoured her endless love and comforting presence. Even if she was not my grandmother biologically, she would forever be family to me.

And in true Grandma fashion, she soothed my gut-wrenching guilt and anxiety with just a few words, before I could even begin to apologise for not going back to save her. "You should have left me. What good would it have been if both of us died there? And besides—this is the nicest bed I've slept in my entire life."

I laughed between hiccups of crying as I nodded, knowing deep down she would never have held it against me if I'd left without looking back, yet not allowing myself the grace to accept that without hearing it directly from her lined lips.

"I wish I could stay here with you forever, Grandma," I confessed.

"Me too, honey, me too. But that wouldn't make for much of a story, would it?" She winked at me, as if she knew the monstrous quest that I had already gone through, and what lay ahead of me.

Drawing in a raggedy breath, my eyes swollen from happy tears, I cleared my throat and fired off, "They taking good care of you, Grandma? Good food? You getting outside? Archer been visiting you?"

Her crooked hands coming up in surrender at the onslaught, she laughed as she appeased my worries. "Yes yes yes, baby. Everything's good. Don't you worry."

"And this... Top Dog?" I started, unsure how to ask for the answers I needed. Her eyes crinkled in understanding—she truly was wise far beyond what I could have hoped. She knew what I was digging for without me figuring out how to ask.

"She's popped in every day to check in on me, although never without those peculiar helmets on. All the others look like dogs, but her helmet resembles a wolf, you can't miss it," Grandma remarked.

She.

Top Dog was female. Interesting.

"From what she's shared with me, it seems like her intentions are true. She really does want to help us; her passion for the cause shows. Although I don't believe she would freely tell any evil plans, even in front of a semi-lucid old lady such as myself," Grandma chuckled to herself.

It seemed as though she believed in this Top Dog, at least on a superficial level. But to know her gut reaction was positive was reassuring.

It was all I could ask for. Until we knew more.

Grandma patted my hands, "Listen, honey, Archer told me about everything–" I scoffed, "Yeah about everything he's been hiding from me?" I clenched my jaw, the wounds still too fresh.

She nodded her head, her small smile not quite reaching her eyes, "I know he didn't handle it in the best way, but I think he just messed up. Archer has been loyal to you for years, he'd never choose them over you. Stick with that loyalty, and let him earn back the trust he lost. You two make quite the pair—and you're all each other has. Let his love guard you when this frail old body cannot."

"I just never thought he'd keep anything from me, Gram," I relished the feeling of her bony, cold hands in my own as if they were made of soft down, not wrinkly, weathered skin. I sighed a huge sigh, "And now he wants me to join these Mutts–and even told them I'm a Dufort!"

"Hush, baby, don't get worked up now. Archer was desperate to find you, and played whatever cards he could to convince them to save you. I don't think he thought much past that." She cradled my hands in hers and brought them softly to her lips to kiss. I planted a kiss atop her head in response, closing my eyes.

We stayed in that moment of silence for as long as we could until I heard faint footsteps echo closer. They must be coming to collect me for the meeting with Top Dog.

My eyes flashed open as I hurried to squeeze in my final questions before we were interrupted, "Should I join them?"

"What other choice do you have right now?" Grandma leaned back against her bed, her body propped up by pillows, "Go out on your own, without company or protection? Or do you stay with the numbers and increase your chances of survival?"

I nodded, her words of wisdom striking a chord in me. She was right—I didn't have much choice other than to join the Mutts. For my own survival.

"Will my magic come back?" I feared this question the most. If my magic was restored, everyone would want to kill me or use me.

"Hollyn, baby, listen to me. You need to assume it will, sooner or later. There's been talk for decades of the Domers trying to bring back the lost magic, each family trying to win this terrible war for power," Grandma warned. Exhaustion riddled her face, the many lines crinkling deeper than I remembered, and my heart ached over the toll my secret identity had taken on her. *She hid it so well from me, to keep me safe and oblivious.* I gulped down the emotion bubbling in my throat as I worked through intense feelings of love mixed with an incurable sense of guilt.

"A target has been painted in blood on your back, one you can never remove. We tried for as long as we could to keep it off you. But this day was inevitable. I'm sorry we couldn't stop it." She looked so saddened, her hands clasping mine as her thumbs traced the back of my hands in slow circles.

My eyebrows shot up, "What do you mean 'we,' Grandma? Do you mean my father—" Archer knocked before entering and before she had a chance to reply. "We should go. Sorry ladies, but I'm sure you can visit again after, Hollyn."

I twisted around to see him just barely stepped through the threshold. There was a hesitancy in his stance, like he felt bad interrupting our private moment. "Just five more minutes, Arch." I needed to hear the rest, to know who she referred to. There was more to the puzzle, I could feel it.

Archer's hand shot up to scratch the back of his head, a telltale sign that I wouldn't like his answer, "Top Dog really doesn't like waiting."

I huffed as I spun around so my body faced him, my skin flushing in frustration, "Well, I don't really fucking care–" Grandma cleared her throat, "Go, baby. I'll be here. And please stop using that language." She smiled fondly at me, her eyes shining bright with love. "We can chat more later."

I hesitated, worried she wouldn't be so coherent next time. And I wanted those answers.

She nodded again, her hands patting my back, "Go."

With one last hug and a kiss pressed on each of my cheeks, I rose and said my goodbyes to the last living family member I had before heading towards my next task: maintaining power in the negotiation with Top Dog.

Give the Benefit of the Clout

She was seated at the end of a long, ovular table in a room painted a deep mahogany, so dissimilar to the other starkly white rooms in the Compound. It gave the room a lived-in sort of ambience—like walking into the men's clubs I'd seen inside the Dome, the air rife with cigar smoke, decanters filled with amber liquors, the chairs made of pristine tawny leathers.

Behind the wolf painted in perfect likeness on her matte black helmet were floor-to-ceiling bookshelves filled with a spectrum of coloured covers, not unlike the one in Slade's home. I couldn't read any of the titles from the opposite side of the room, but I decided that access to this library would be another condition of my alliance, if I were to accept it.

I craved knowledge, my journey so far confirming my ignorance of so many things. Too many things.

I would gain power without magic too.

My strongest skill was being an excellent thief. I lacked muscle mass, weaponry. Training my brain was my best option, especially if we were going up against people like the O'Malleys. I had to be able to outsmart them—had no idea when or how my magic might return to me and could not rely solely on the possibility of its potential.

Top Dog watched me enter and find a seat at the middle of the table, my back against the windows rather than the doors. Years of looking over my shoulder had drilled that habit into me.

I turned towards her, working overtime to conceal my nervousness by clasping my hands together to stop the tremble threatening to show. I had to maintain power here. I had to make her work for me, never showing my own desperation for protection, for myself, for Grandma.

A mask of stoicism slid over my face, my lips downturned in suspicion and my eyes narrowed, my dark lashes dropping halfway to help conceal any emotions that might accidentally slip through. I'd learned how to plant ideas into my father's mind subtly, proffering them almost reluctantly in a way that caused him to believe, after careful navigation, that the ideas had been his all along. I prayed I could pull it off here too.

I knew, from the moment my feet entered this room, that we'd already begun our game of cat and mouse—and that she would not be such an easy target. So I waited, far past any length of comfortable silence, the soft tick tock of the grandfather clock behind me counting every second of tortured conversational standstill.

But still, I held firm, my eyes locked on her helmet, refusing to stand down. Grandma had said she never took her helmet off, but experiencing the audacity of it, that she declined to reveal her face even in this important meeting, irritated me more than I thought it would. As if, after everything I'd endured, my only real choice for a new alliance couldn't be bothered to take the first leap of faith and meet me as her true self.

And Archer was asking me to give her a chance.

"Your grandma has been welcomed like one of our own here. Were her accommodations to your liking?" Her slightly raspy voice asked. But not really looking for an answer, she continued, "We are a pack here and look after our own. And any other strays we bring in."

"Wow, you're really committed to the theme, aren't you?" I snorted.

Only a second of pause before she rebutted, "I think 'thank you' is universally accepted." She stretched her arms straight, her hands flat against the table as she cocked her head to the side. "When Archer came to us, pleading for not only your grandmother to be taken in, but for us to head to Abraxas? For his long-lost lover? It was a hard case to sell to the others."

"So what swayed the people's decision? My tumultuous family history? Or could you not bear to see Archer heartbroken a moment longer?" I joked, refusing to give her the gratitude she was fishing for. It would keep me in a state of indebtedness, and that wasn't a powerful position.

Top Dog scoffed, her arm bending to place her knuckles underneath her chin as she contemplated me in a brief moment of silence. *Hold it together, Hollyn.*

When she spoke next, there was a softness to her voice that surprised me. "It must be hard to believe humans can live together where each opinion is heard and respected. You've spent your entire life crushed under the thumb of others, your purpose nothing more than that of a drone to be used and discarded," Top Dog lamented. Was the sympathy genuine? Or was it all part of an act to soften me up?

Carefully scrutinizing my nail beds, I played the role of boredom perfectly. "Please continue to tell me about my own life." A slight roll of my eyes to really sell it.

Top Dog tapped her fingers, perhaps in irritation, but she did not take my bait. Her chest puffed slightly in pride as she continued on. "Despite how you may mistrust us, our purpose is true. We were created in reaction to the increasingly destitute conditions in Edinguard. We are the fail-safe against Domer expansion."

Pushing back my chair, I rose. "You know, call me jaded, but these types of mutinies haven't worked in the past. I'm not really interested in changing the world. I think it's best for my grandma and me to move along, not disturb what you've got going on here." I needed Top Dog to need *me*.

"You've never been outside Edinguard—you don't know anything around here. You would die within a week." She laughed, waving her hand in dismissal at my insane plan. "The food you'd take would last, sure, but the sandstorms... you'd never make it. And your poor grandmother! In her last moments on this planet, you would have her suffer so?"

My shoulders tensed and my jaw clenched, my teeth grinding each other as I pictured Grandma windburnt, her lips cracked and bloody, both of us slowly dying from dehydration. I couldn't let Top Dog know she had hit my weakness, so I swallowed my fears and leaned over, my hands gripping the table. "Then she can stay here. Only slow me down anyway. And besides, you'd keep her safe, right? One of the pack now."

Top Dog rose from her seat to grab a map off the table behind her and wordlessly slapped it down in front of me before perching on the table to my right. Her garb was all black and tighter than most seemed to wear, but a bulletproof vest protected her chest like all her subordinates.

"Give up the act, girl, and let us speak with candour. We need each other more than either of us cares to admit. Your grandmother is dying—don't be fooled by this moment of lucidity. Dyrcsan healers are far superior to those sawbones you're accustomed to back in Low-Town, and still they cannot heal her condition."

Her gear creaked as she leaned back, sitting taller. "That Relic of yours has the power to heal, yes. But to heal what your grandmother ails from... the Relic needs to be whole. And you need our help finding the final piece. Unless, of course, you think you can master this yourself." She jabbed at the map in front of me to draw my attention to the areas surrounding Dyrcsa.

She was right. I discovered that, were I able to somehow escape the clutches of sandy death, as she warned, there was nowhere to go. There was no way I could return back west to Edinguard. To the north, I would have to pass through the full expanse of the desert, and the south led only to a few seaport towns peppered along the long stretch of coast. I had neither a boat nor boating skills, let alone any ability to swim. To the east, harsh, niveous mountains barred further passage. Based on the altitude scaling, these mountains were thousands of feet high, with no towns or dwellings past the base to find shelter in.

My mind ran with fear, picturing my icy demise, my body frozen under a carpet of snowfall. My grandma falling down a steep cliff, pranging in a zigzag pattern off alternating crests, her tired body shattering. I pictured her bloody and ragged, bent in impossible angles far down below me, my body shaking, from frostbite seeping through my extremities, from the guilt of having dragged her through this impossible expedition.

I shuddered at the detail of my morbid thoughts.

I was fucked every which way. It would be like playing roulette with the reaper himself, his ghastly body eagerly waiting to see which slaughter I handpicked.

Top Dog was right, of course. I really had no other choice. I was a survivor. But the hardships I would face if I ventured out alone were insurmountable.

"What do you want from me?" I asked, then held my breath, awaiting her answer.

"What does anyone want with a Dufort? We want you as an ally, not an enemy," she confessed. "We promise you a life of honesty and true choice, more than you ever had back in your slums. You will never be just a weapon to us, for we all fight equally. A pack. We believe the Relic's power—*your* bound magic—can do more than just heal. So much more. And we want you to use it for our cause—for *good*."

My mind recoiled, my body wincing as if her words lashed at me. A deep-seated fear was born deep in my gut as I digested what she'd fed me. *More than heal?*

"What do you mean more than heal?" I breathed, my pulse pounding through my chest. I'd barely come to terms with the idea of gaining the power to heal. And there was more?

Top Dog leaned forward, her elbows coming to rest atop her thighs, "Did you really think the ability to heal would drive someone mad?"

I leaned back in my seat as I felt a cold sweat break out over my forehead as my body flushed with goose pimples. I'd heard whispers, voices urging me to act, voices that felt...bloodthirsty. What else would I be able to do once this magic reawoke? Was this magic evil? Would I become evil?

I'd barely been able to control myself when retrieving the Relic piece in Abraxas, the need to find the piece overpowering my need for survival. I shuddered thinking about how seductive it must feel to have the full extent of that power course through me.

How the fuck will I handle this magic?

The very real possibility that my magic was beyond my power, my control, left a cold dread in the pit of my belly. And I had no idea what else was included in this "holy" magic.

"We have some of the best scientific minds in Dyrcsa, and they believe reuniting the Inukviak Relic pieces may overpower the spell binding Dufort magic. We believe it may... release it back into the world. Into you." Top Dog stood up, returning to her seat at the head of the table once again, her elbows resting atop it, her fingers touching calmly in front of her at a point.

It's so fucking hard to gauge what she's thinking with that goddamn helmet.

"I'm supposed to believe that putting three shattered pieces together will undo a spell that's bound the most powerful magic for the last five hundred years?" I shook my head in disbelief. "There's no way it's that easy. And-and what if I don't want it?" Things were progressing rapidly. I felt a tightening in my chest and placed a hand over my heart to rub away the ache. I knew the signs—needed to get out, before I had a full-blown panic attack in front of her.

"I understand your life has been through quite an upheaval. Born a Townie, only to find out you are a Dufort, and now to learn you could repossess a power lost for half a millennium. A power more formidable than you could dream." Top Dog leaned back as she radiated arrogance, as if certain I would eventually agree. "It is quite a powerful position to find yourself in."

"But I never asked for this! I don't want to go mad," I pushed myself away from the table, my chair scratching against the floor as I rose and stepped away, as if physical distance would give my brain a moment to think and recover.

Her fist slammed down on the table. "Think, girl, *think*. The O'Malley's will never stop hunting you. And it is only a matter of time before they discover a way to harness the Dufort magic themselves!" My head whipped towards her, and I noted the clenched fists, the tenseness of her shoulders: I was edging her line of patience by continuing to deny reality.

"Then how have I survived this long?" I paced along the windows, my restless energy a physical manifestation of my turmoil. "If this has always been a possibility, I should have been dead long ago."

Out of the corner of my eye, I watched Top Dog roll her shoulders, cranking her head to the side as she forced her hands open. We both had lost control of our emotions. "Things have gotten worse, from what our sources tell us—ambitions expanding exponentially, the thirst for power growing unchecked in Edinguard." Top Dog rose and headed towards the door, her arm outstretched to invite me with her. "You have survived this long thanks to how well your identity was hidden. Someone went to great lengths to prevent people from finding out who you really are."

I hesitated, Top Dog's words reaffirming what Slade and Ryker had told me, before joining her at the threshold of the door.

"What if I say no?" I gazed up at her wolfish mask, my eyes desperate to see beyond the tinted shield. I could just heal Grandma and hand it over, be rid of the damned thing.

Nobody could use it without me—not until they figured a way around it all. It would give me some time to get away, go into hiding. *Do I want to stay hiding for the rest of my life?*

Top Dog leaned forward, her hand resting on my shoulder in an awkward attempt to comfort me. "You have a chance to change everything. It could guarantee an end to Domer rule. Don't you want that?"

I looked at her hand on me before shrugging it off. "What I *want* is the choice, but I keep getting forced one way or another." At every turn, there's been a new path, a new goal, a new enemy. I'd been damned before I was born.

She crossed her arms with a snort, any patience for my woes evaporated. "What the hell do you call this? Choosing to do nothing is just as bad as helping the enemy."

I inhaled sharply, surprised to find my grandma and Top Dog shared such a similar viewpoint. "I've gotten two of the three pieces—haven't I done enough? Now I have to harness a magic that made my ancestor go mad, or else be hunted forever? How is that any kind of choice?"

"The Dufort magic coming back is inevitable. It is a certainty, you need to understand that. You cannot change it now. All you can *choose* is how and when that happens."

My hand resting on my cocked hip, I hung my head in exhaustion. I was tired, overwhelmed, could not handle any more of this conversation.

"How did you feel, holding the Relic pieces? Did you feel the warmth of magic?" Top Dog urged, softly, her hand coming to guide my back as we strode into the hallway.

I turned to face her as she matched my pace. "Y-Yes. Like nothing I've ever felt before."

"Remember that warmth. Remember that magic can be good or bad, it all depends on how you use it."

Just like Slade said.

"You would not have to do this alone." Top Dog's voice was soft again, almost like a whisper. Could I trust her?

"I need some time," I informed her, halting our progression. "This is all... a lot to process."

A hand to my upper back, Top Dog murmured, "Of course. Take the night."

Nodding, I veered back through the Compound and I couldn't help but feel like yet again my future was not my own. I knew the risks of both choices—whether I regained my dormant magic or not. But could I live with myself if the world burned down around me and I did nothing to stop it?

Fake a Fresh Start

I walked back to my room in stunned silence, still grappling with the idea that the lost holy magic would be in my possession. Clashing emotions warred within me. Not only had I gained a new identity, I now was on the throes of obtaining a level of power I could never have imagined before. And perhaps one that could hurt, too.

To launch from one end of the power spectrum to the other—I feared what that would do to me. To my body, my mind, my heart.

Would it corrupt me? Would it cause insanity in me too?

I'd popped back in to check on my grandmother, desperate to talk with her about all of this, but she had been fast asleep. I dared not wake her; she needed all the rest she could get. I vowed to check in again later.

Worries festered deep inside over how I could keep her safe, keep myself and Archer safe, if I acquired that magic. Everyone would hunt me for it, whether to destroy that power once again or to harness it for themselves.

And it seemed like nobody cared what that future meant for me. Slade had kept me ignorant entirely. I wondered if he knew all of this. At least Top Dog had been honest about how she hoped to use it for her cause, promising me transparency.

Still, I couldn't help but feel like nothing more than a tool, a means for obtaining an end, just like back home. Even with more power than I could dream of, I would be barraged by others still trying to control me, exploit me.

Perhaps the best I could hope for were allies who were honest.

Slade and Ryker, whether they knew as much as Top Dog or not, had lied to me. I'd felt they were keeping something from me, and this confirmed there was so much more to my job than they had let on. Why was I surprised? Domers used everyone to get what they wanted.

How could I have been so fucking naive?

Again and again, I was surprised by the narcissism of the Domers. And again and again, I kept getting fucked over.

No fucking way would I let this keep happening.

Even though I didn't trust Top Dog yet, I decided I would join their cause. I needed her resources and manpower. And at least she gave me honesty.

I would work with the Mutts to obtain the final piece. I would wake up my magic.

Archer and Top Dog had been right. I had to choose to fight for more. To take control over my own life, to be proactive, not reactive.

It wasn't just about my survival anymore. This was bigger than me and mine, now.

Somehow I had to bring down the evil that plagued us before it spread like a cancer into the rest of the world.

And it seemed like my magic was our only hope.

Top Dog promised an early meeting tomorrow with the rest of the key members in her war room, where we would brainstorm our next steps in acquiring the final Inukviak Relic piece. Until then, I had the night to explore Dyrcsa in its evening splendour, the clear night sky aglow with vibrantly twinkling stars.

Archer and I had agreed to meet by the Trevani Fountain, one of the many magically unlimited fresh-water sources that provided the Dyrcsan people with their running water, sewers, and irrigation systems in an otherwise inhospitably arid environment.

My outfit was of a soft rose colour paired with a deep forest-green cloak made of velvet—apparently most people had a daytime and nighttime cloak, as the evenings were cooler. I was used to pelts of synthetic furs covering me from head to toe in our harsh winter months, frostbite threatening any exposed areas, and I remembered the aggravating itch that used to terrorize my pale skin, the patches of red rashes all over my body.

My hair was braided to look like a headband halo—an elegant updo my grandmother had taught me before her hands became too crooked and arthritic to move nimbly. I had donned my combat boots and my trusty utility belt, not willing to fully commit to the Dyrcsan look just yet. Pockets were great, and not enough clothing was made with them.

My boots tapped down quietly as I stepped from my quarters, the sand underneath muffling the sound as I surveyed my surroundings. Stringed lights wove back and forth in canopies over many of the houses, creating an ambient warmth for their welcoming front porches. People laughed in conversation, cats rubbed up against legs hoping for a scratch, lively music poured onto the streets as residents fell in and out of dance, their bodies instinctively reacting to the beat.

A night market had set up just past my quarters, the aromas of grilled food blowing towards me. I listened and watched as merchants emphatically bartered their wares. Large gold and silver coins were exchanged freely as goods were packaged with care. Low-Town markets often dissolved into a melee, people fighting over whatever fragments we could snatch before they were gone. We did not have the luxury of being choosy; we usually fought over damaged products and rotting food. We learned quickly what colour mould was edible and what colour would kill.

But better than nothing.

Not a piece of food I saw looked like anything but the ripest, plumpest, most perfect thing I'd ever seen. Apples were triple the size, potatoes almost as big as both of my hands, leafy greens so straight and crisp, I knew I could never look at my old food with any interest again.

And the meat—cuts of beef, poultry, fish, some pre seasoned by the butchers themselves. Fat pork rumps, thick-cut bacon, gigantic T-bone steaks, everything in my wildest dreams. So tender and juicy compared to the ground-up mystery meat, tongues, and gamey pieces I'd grown up eating.

As I trailed through the bustling tents, a cook tending one of the open grills began to barter with me. "You there! I have beef, on sale. Tender and marbled."

I shook my head. "I have no money. I'm sorry, no thanks."

The mouth-watering fragrance that wafted towards me nearly buckled me in ravenous hunger, the rumble in my stomach from years of near starvation reacting with a vengeance. I felt like I would never be satiated, like an endless pit had replaced my stomach, and I had to concentrate on quelling the bubbling. A tsunami of hunger had been unleashed after I'd tasted their magical fare.

But this middle-aged, plump man continued to beckon me, refusing to accept my polite rejection, until I approached him. "I have no money. I'm sorry—it really looks delicious!" I repeated in case he hadn't heard me.

"It is no problem, beautiful. You are hungry, I can see it in your eyes. Eat as much as you want. Drink. Be merry." The cook nodded his head in earnest and pushed a plate filled with cubes of steak towards me.

"Nothing is free." I politely shook my head, my cheeks flushing in embarrassment. Again, the people of Dyrcsa flooded me with kindness without expectations, and I had no idea how to receive the kindness. I was both suspicious and uncomfortable with the handouts.

His expression darkened with pity as he looked me up and down. "In Dyrcsa, there is. You are safe here. Eat."

"You want nothing in return?" I forced myself to soften my scowl.

"All I need is to see you enjoy my food, and I will have everything." He smiled warmly. "Please."

I gingerly took one and popped it into my mouth. An explosion of taste filled my tongue as I devoured the beef, swallowing hastily as I grabbed another piece without stopping for permission.

The cook chuckled as he offered another plate, this one filled with tender fish, chicken drumsticks, and crispy pork crackling. Delicious grease dirtied my mouth, the juices from each bite dripping down my chin, but I did not care as I ate to make up for a lifetime of minimal sustenance, the floodgates of my appetite releasing.

After a second drumstick, multiple slabs of salmon, and three servings of pork crackling, I sighed in satisfaction, my stomach gurgling, working overtime trying to digest the rich meats.

"I'm—I'm so sorry, I've eaten way too much." My cheeks flushed. "Let me repay you. Let me help. I-I can clean up or something."

Without missing a beat, the man placed a goblet of dark red wine into my hand as he pushed it towards me. "Unnecessary, but I will accept the offer. You can help clear off the tables, if that'll make you feel better."

I downed the wine in one gulp, the warmth of the liquid already stoking a small fire in my gut. I felt the heat touch my cheeks and nodded, before wiping my mouth with the back of my hand.

Grabbing the cleaning rag from the cook, I began to stack used dishes from nearby tables as I wiped off crumbs and grease marks, happy to have a means to repay the cook. Bending down, I picked up fallen debris, my mind focused on the menial task.

"—soon. They're coming, I'm telling you."

"And they want us to unlock—"

My butt hit one of the wrought-iron chairs nearby, causing it to grind against the table, and two young men seated at a table nearby bit off their conversation as their heads whipped my way. The surprise on their faces told me I'd overheard a snippet of something supposed to be kept secret.

Abruptly, they lifted the hoods of their cloaks and silently left coins on their table before heading into the night market and disappearing within the crowd.

"They're a weird bunch," admitted the cook, who had paused to watch them leave. "Never really talk to us, but they always pay and never cause a scene, so."

I nodded, standing back up and gathering the pile of dirty dishes. What they said nibbled at me, but without context, I could not draw any conclusions. As a clock nearby chimed its ninth dong, I jumped as I realised Archer was waiting for me. "Thank you again for the food." I nodded at the cook as I took my leave.

There was still a lot I needed to say to Archer if we were to work together. And I dreaded that conversation—the raw honesty and emotion, the vulnerability, the insecurities that would be involved. Everything I was great at stuffing down and compartmentalising.

But Archer and I deserved frankness and sincerity from each other. And I deserved to have my best friend back on my team. Grandma had said his intentions were good. He deserved to be able to make his own choices and to have his own secrets—I had to remember that.

The Mutts were bound to have discovered me and my identity at some point. He'd actually given me the power to control how that happened.

So I ambled onward until I recognized the old lady from earlier, whose beautiful rainbow-coloured blanket hung in all its unabashed glory behind her.

I stopped to admire it again, noticing how tiny shimmering threads of silver delicately popped, reflecting the rows of lights behind me. The lady smiled at me and pointed to the blanket, and I commended her workmanship wholeheartedly.

"I am an old woman," she started. "I do not care about negotiating. I saw you look at my afghan earlier. It is yours, if you still want it."

"Oh, I don't have any money. I couldn't," I protested.

"I imagined you didn't. I haven't seen you before, so I assumed you were new here. It does not change my offer," she assured me.

"I... can't. Everyone here is so kind, so willing to give. I will buy it from you when I have enough." I walked away before she could thrust it on me. My pride could not take any more of the Dyrcsans' hospitality without feeling indebted. It went against how I had been raised.

Owe nobody and expect nothing.

I already felt I'd overstepped that line with all the food I'd consumed without payment. I could not accept the blanket as well. I would earn the money I needed to purchase it. And I would earn that money honestly.

No more thieving. I hoped.

Splash.

A gorgeous, curly-haired toddler laughed gaily as her father scooped a handful of water and chased her around the fountain, trying to soak her. Her raven ringlets bounced as she scampered around, until her face lit up with an idea. Quickly, she halted, and seeking aquatic revenge, her little hands dunked under the water, trying earnestly to scoop it up but failing to stop it from seeping through the cracks of her fingers. As her father neared, she resorted to desperately heaving water like a cat kicking up its litter after relieving itself. The first two attempts at pawing the water didn't land, but the third one doused the dad right on his crotch.

The girl erupted into a fit of laughter as she pointed at him, shouting, "You peed your pants, Papi!" I found myself giggling with both of them, the wholesome scene touching me.

Shoes crunched on the sand behind the low bench I was perched on, and I whirled, jumping into an attack stance. My shoulders slacked and my hands dropped when I saw Archer's crooked smile, his amber eyes crinkled in amusement. "Good to see some of those instincts are still sharp as ever," he teased.

"Good thing you didn't touch me, or your ass would be flat on the ground," I retorted.

He nodded towards the father and daughter I'd been watching. "Cute, eh? It feels like you could actually have a family here without fearing for their survival."

"Yeah... until someone comes and fucks this place up too," I said cynically.

He and I had joked about having a family before, but it'd never felt like it could ever happen, like plans that could never truly be written in stone. Not with the way things were in Low-Town. We would never choose to raise a child there.

And now the thought of raising a child was impossible with the blood that coursed through my veins, knowing the target branded on me. Not until my magic was returned and I could defend my future unborn properly.

Archer handed me a cup of warm cocoa with a leaf made out of foamy milk floating on its surface, and I accepted it gratefully as we walked towards the fountain, watching the leaf sway and bank with the movement of my steps. Nervousness dripped off Archer, visible in the restless twitching of his body, the way he scratched behind his ear, the stiffness of his walking. I glanced at him and could see his facial expression play out an entire conversation to himself, assumingly preparing how to start this conversation with me. We reached the Fountain and sat atop the stone bench encircling it.

"They say if you make a wish here and give some money, the Priestess will grant your plea," Archer mentioned softly as he trailed his pointer finger through the crystal-clear liquid. I watched as little waves rippled out from his figure-eight motion.

"I've never believed any superstitious crap like that before. But after Top Dog and her team swooped in to rescue me as I was kneeling before the O'Malleys, convinced this was it, I came here right after and prayed before this fountain, begging for Her to save you." He pulled his hand from the water, and we watched the droplets drip from his fingertips. "And then Top Dog tells me the very next day about the insane energy readings the Druids picked up right by Abraxas, and my heart raced, I was so excited.I knew it was you."

His attention remained on the water, his chestnut brows furrowing as his eyes blinked rapidly to fight back the tears that began to cluster along his waterline.

"I'm so sorry, Holls, about everything. I wish I could have saved you from all of this. I knew about the Mutts, agreed to work for them before I even consulted you, but it wasn't right for me to hide that from you. You deserved to know as soon as I did," he began. "I should have given you a choice in all of this."

I sighed and sat down on the ledge of the fountain. But before I could respond, he continued on. "And I couldn't do anything to stop you from going to Abraxas, or working with those two Domers. They obviously didn't give a shit about you and only wanted you for your magic."

"I think that's pretty much what everyone will want from me now," I admitted.

"Well, not me. I don't give a shit about any powers you might have. I fell in love with you long before any of this." He searched my face, but I couldn't respond the way he wanted me to, not yet. He needed to hear my whole truth before we could possibly move forward.

I sighed heavily, looking down at my clasped hands, "You were the only person that hadn't let me down, outside of Grandma. I felt like I could trust you with my life, with anything. And I'm sorry, but you kind of shit on that trust." I glanced up at him and saw the agony that plagued him. There was no denying he felt remorseful and I took comfort in that.

He opened his mouth as if to respond but then snapped it shut and waited for me to continue when I held up a hand, "I know you say you didn't keep tabs on me, but you involved me in this without my consent. My identity was one of the few things that I had left, that nobody had taken from me, that remained hidden from most, and you gave that up. And to who? People I don't even know. People I don't trust."

I stood up, my hands wringing in frustration as my gaze stayed steadfast on the buildings ahead of me, refusing to meet Archer's gaze even as it pierced a burning hole through me.

"I've lost a father, I've lost my home, I've lost who I am in every sense, and my entire life is gone, with no chance of ever returning. I'm being forced to continue on in a world where I will be hunted for the rest of my life for something that will always be a part of me. Over a power that might ruin me and everyone around me. And the only person I thought I didn't have to worry about using and manipulating me has been keeping this from me all along." Tears threatening to spill, my jaw clenched in anger, I turned the full weight of my emotions towards Archer, refusing to swallow down the turmoil he had manufactured.

Don't you understand this hurts the most?

"My best friend, my *lover*, and you literally fucked me—"

"Holls, I didn't mean for us to—until—I was going to—"

I snarled through gritted teeth, "Doesn't matter. It still happened. You still let it happen. I deserved to know before that."

He dropped his head down, his chestnut curls bouncing from the motion, "You're right. That was fucking shitty of me. I never should have slept with you before telling you all of this."

I crossed my arms, my head whipping away as bile rose in my throat. It wasn't as though I was some virginal angel that had been robbed of her purity—the act of sex was not what angered me. It was the intimacy. The complete trust I'd given to Archer in those moments, unknowingly, while he had been hiding these secrets from me.

"And now I'm stuck in an impossible decision where I'm damned if I join the Mutts or damned if I don't."

Archer opened his mouth to protest, but I raised a hand to silence him. "If you're about to tell me we can run away together, stop. If I was planning to run, I'd already be gone and you know that. I also know it's suicide, whether you come with me or not. But if I had shown up here as a nobody, I could have remained a nobody, found a life here, or in another nearby city, safe in plain sight, at least for a while."

I turned back to face him, my hands gesturing wildly in anger. "But I can't now. You made sure of that. And maybe it would have come out soon enough anyway, but I could have at least made my own choices as to when that time came." Choking back the tears, I refused to lose control. It was easier to keep my guard up if I was angry.

Archer rose and approached me, his body fidgeting, as if he were desperate to hold me. He had never been the source of my pain or my anger before, and he seemed to have no idea how to navigate it.

I didn't care; it wasn't my job to guide him. I had one last thing to say.

"What hurts even more than all of that, though, is that not only am I caught in this web, but so is Grandma. They hold that over me. What if they threaten her or hurt her to get me to do what they want?"

Shock broke out over Archer's face, "I would never let that happen—"

"What could you possibly do to stop them? You have no money, no power, no magic." I bit my tongue before I veered into insults. I had been the recipient of venomous insults too often to know it didn't help.

And I still loved Archer, despite this.

I would always love Archer.

Sighing, I took in his downtrodden expression, the agony in his wide honey-coloured eyes, the slump of his shoulders, and I took a big breath, willing myself to let some of it go. I had said my piece, and he'd listened without contest or defence.

"I know your intentions were good. You're your own person, you are allowed to have your own secrets... your own choices." I placed a hand on his shoulder in comfort. "The truth is you're my best friend, and this is the first time you've ever done anything like this, so that's why it hurts so much. It might take me a while to get over this, but in your defence, in our entire lives, this is the first time you've ever done anything behind my back. And twenty-plus years of loyalty and love is not thrown out over one thing, as mistaken as it was."

I saw the slight pout of his lower lip, his eyebrows raised in contrition as he shook his head, "I'm sorry, Holls, really. I understand how poorly I handled all of this, and I promise you I won't let you down again."

"I feel so... lonely right now. I'm terrified. The possibility of gaining magic that drove my ancestors mad haunts me. I want my best friend back—I need him right now," I sobbed, the weight of it all breaking the dam holding back my tears. Archer wrapped me in a hug as my body shook, waves of sorrow cresting.

"Whatever happens, I'll help you through it." He held me until my tears were spent and my hiccuping breath returned to some normalcy.

"How can I possibly handle power like this, Arch? What if—what if I hurt people too?" *Will I go down in history as a psychopath too?* I turned my head to the side to watch the soft rippling as the Trevani Fountain spouted crystal-clear water.

"That was five hundred years ago. We know so much more now. We'll figure out how to control it."

I pulled back to look up at him. "What if I just *don't* unbind the magic?"

Archer hesitated. "I don't think that will stop the Domers from acquiring it. Now that we know who you really are, what your magic really is, I don't think we have any other choice than to obtain it for ourselves before they do." He pulled me back into an embrace, his hand rubbing slow circles along my spine as he continued. "Even if they need Dufort blood to access it—they would find a way soon enough. Better to arm yourself and get ahead of it."

I pushed against his chest to give us some space. "How could I have been so fucking *stupid*? How could I have believed Slade and Ryker didn't have another motive?" I slammed my fists against his chest in exasperation. "I was about to hand over a power that could destroy everyone. *My* magic. To a *Domer*."

I shoved him off me, angry at myself for being so gullible.

Archer smiled softly, love shining from his eyes, "Because despite what you've lived through, the horrors you endured with your father, from Edinguard—still, deep down, you are a good person. And you see the good in people. That is a strength, not a weakness."

"It sure doesn't feel like one," I huffed.

He chuckled, "One day it will, maybe not now. But I hope that never changes in you. It's one of the reasons I love you. You're strength and softness all in one."

I nodded at him, still unsure I agreed, but finding comfort in those soft amber eyes. "Will you help me? Make sure I don't go insane?"

With a lopsided grin, Archer wrapped his arms around my shoulders as I let him lead me back towards the bustle of Dyrcsa's nightlife. "You don't need to ask. I promise. Now let's go blow off a little steam. I'll show you how Dyrcsa comes alive at night."

Clan Plans and God Laughs

My head pounded as I cracked open one eye, the sunlight penetrating into the very corners of my skull. I slowly pushed into an upright position in bed, the sheets tangled from what looked like a torpedo of movement, but I couldn't remember sleeping with Archer.

God, I hoped not. How lamentable if I couldn't even stay away from him for one night.

Right now, it didn't matter—I needed to stop the room from spinning, or I was going to vomit. I cupped my head in my hands, closing my eyes as I steadied the world.

A knock came from my doorway before Archer's curly head bobbed through the beads, the sound amplified by my hangover to sound like tiny firecrackers erupting as each bead tapped into another. I shuddered as I opened one eye to peep through my hands. I dared not move more than that.

"Torch, your room get ransacked or what?" Archer joked as he took in the clothes strewn all over the room.

"If you think this is bad, keep shouting at me and see what else gets thrown all over this room," I warned half jokingly, half seriously. "There any magic that could help me feel not so fucking awful?"

I'd only ever been hungover twice before: once when I rage-drank my father's stash after he'd burned a cig on my hand in a drunken fit, and another time after Archer and I filled our first black-market mission.

Perhaps this was my father's one last laugh at my expense.

Not my father. I had no idea what to call the man I had lived with my entire life.

Victor, I guessed.

"Here, drink this." Archer handed me a cup of what looked like toxic sludge, and the odour alone gagged me, forcing me to hold my nose to keep the contents of my stomach down. "It works best if you plug your nose and drain it in one go."

Nodding, I took the muck and whipped my head back before my body could protest, swallowing the thick ooze. I let out a compulsive shudder as my eyes closed from the horrid taste. "God, what the hell's the point of magical food if shit still tastes like that," I whined.

Almost instantly, the turbulence raging war in my gut quieted, the headache softening to a dull, manageable hum.

"Oh wow, thanks, that's already helping," I marvelled. I was nervous to ask whether anything had happened between us and didn't know how to broach the topic. "Why did we drink so much?"

"I'd say it was more the mixing rather than the amount," Archer explained. "By the fourth type of liquor, your face was beet red and your eyes half-open, so I took you back and put you to bed."

Oh, so we didn't. I sighed in relief.

"Don't get me wrong, Torch, I loved having sex with you, but half-asleep just doesn't do it for me. What can I say? Call me old-fashioned." Archer chuckled and I reddened, embarrassed I even entertained the idea that he would do that to me.

I threw the covers off me and shakily stood up with a back-cracking stretch, my arms overhead. Archer stalked to the closet and picked out a steel-grey pair of linen pants and matching bustier and threw them onto my bed.

"So when do I get the fatigues?" I asked. The Dyrcsan clothing was beautiful, but I felt far more comfortable in clothes more battle-ready, like what Archer and the Mutts donned.

"Definitely before we head out, but I'm sure they'll talk gear and everything at the meeting," Archer replied.

The meeting.

Where I would meet the rest of the crew and discuss tactics for retrieving the final Inukviak Relic piece. Wherever it was.

"Who else will be there?" I dressed quickly, anxious over who I would be meeting, what the Mutts' plans were. What new challenges would await me.

"Top Dog, Malachai, myself, Knox, and... Odette. I'd watch out for her, though, she's a biter." I raised my eyebrows at him, unsure whether he was joking or not. My brief encounter with Odette had been anything but hospitable.

"Mal is the head scientist, and Knox is head of R&D. Odette is commander of most missions, unless Top Dog joins. And I do most of the preliminary analysis, just like I did for you."

"And my role?"

"Let's find out," Archer evaded.

I sat in the same chair in the same room as I had in my meeting with Top Dog, sunlight warming my back and yet shivering with nervousness. These were the big players seated at the table.

Odette studied me from my left, her gaze unrelenting, her scrutiny making me squeamish. She hadn't said a word yet, and I hadn't tried to instigate conversation either. Instead, I scrupulously worked on clearing out the dirt and sand stuck under my nails so as to avoid inviting anyone's interrogation.

Archer sat beside me, but I had warned him not to play the saviour on my behalf. I couldn't look weak and dependent on him. I had to show them I would not be pushed around. After all, once I had my powers back, I would be a force to be reckoned with. But I'd survived this long without spellwork. I was tough, calculated, agile. I could still hold my own, magic or not.

Mal, who sat across from me, I recognized as the violet-eyed scientist from earlier. Her platinum hair was shaved on one side, the other side pin-straight and draped to her shoulders like icicles suspended from eavestroughs.

Knox's face showed a warmth that was in contrast to the restrained fury of Odette and the careful blankness Mal maintained. I didn't know whether to trust him the most or the least.

Archer had given me a brief overview of each of them on our way over, and I'd been surprised to find out all three were magical. *Why do they care so much about the poor in Low-Town?*

Odette, to no one's surprise, harnessed the power of pure physicality—strength, defence, and speed were all in her wheelhouse. Just like the Makotovics back home.

Mal was her polar opposite, in both stature—she came to my chin at most, her body more like a prepubescent boy than woman—and in sorcery. Turned out her scientific prowess was substantial, as was her mental magic.

I wondered whether she was reading my thoughts now and sent out a mental *do nothing if you can hear me* to test the waters. The tiniest of smirks, immediately hidden behind that wall of disinterest, confirmed my suspicions. Archer had told me she was so powerful she could also move things telepathically on a grand scale—a rare feat even among her own kind. Most could move only small things, parlour tricks mostly.

I hadn't crossed paths with a Cabral back home, so her magic was quite a mystery to me. It kept me more at unease than Odette, despite the venom dripping from the latter. At least I knew what to expect with Odette and her magic.

Knox was the gentle giant of the group, at least a foot taller than my own average height and close to double my weight. His black hair was combed back off his soft face, his cheeks full and pink, his nose bulbous to match his chin. I guessed he was older than the rest of us–there was a maturity to him, a calmness even that the others didn't possess. Except Top Dog. He, just like Ryker and other Lagodas, could shapeshift.

Ryker.

My thoughts wandered to that beast of a man, his unrefined manners so unlike Knox's gentleness, almost as if Ryker's natural state was animal and he shifted to human when needed. He'd been impossible to understand. Each action he took was a roulette between helping and hindering me. His loyalty had been with Slade without contest—and yet he'd saved my life. Twice. Whether he'd done so out of self-interest or out of kindness, I had no idea. And now he was my enemy, so it didn't matter.

Are they my enemy?

A beep prompted the frosted glass door to slide open, and Top Dog, still hidden behind her wolf helmet, entered and sat in the same seat at the head of the table.

She held the final archetype: elemental. I knew firsthand how dangerous that made her, having barely escaped with my life from the flaming orbs the O'Malleys fired at me.

I wondered why nobody nonmagical held a seat at this table. Why all four of these people, who theoretically held all the power they'd ever need to succeed, wished to bring change to a world that gave them everything.

I promised myself I would ask them.

I had too many questions. Too many questions I was sure nobody would want to answer. Too many questions that would further ostracise my position. So I kept my mouth shut and waited, for now. The answers would come out eventually, or I would bide my time until the right opportunity to ask them arose.

Top Dog cleared her throat, drawing our attention, and, without a greeting or an introduction of me, began.

"The third piece is on the peak of Nihani Mountain. It is crucial we retrieve it as soon as possible. We are on the precipice of obtaining power beyond our hopes, power that could finally set our plan into motion."

All three whistled in enthusiasm, the sound startling me. Nobody back home cheered each other's successes, as that usually meant others suffered for it. Finite resources only covered so many people. Often a family achieving a full belly meant another starved.

"We still don't need *her*." Odette gestured towards me. "My soldiers are ready—let us try first."

Knox sighed and rubbed his forehead as Odette continued. "I don't know her, so I don't trust her. Probably wouldn't if I did." She looked me up and down, her eyebrows raised in challenge and her lip snarled in repulse.

There's her bite. I swallowed back my retort with restraint. But although what she said might have been harsh, it was the truth. I could respect someone who had nothing to hide, even if it meant enduring her spite until I'd proven my trustworthiness.

"Why sacrifice anyone? The lives we will save—our people's lives, O. Archer trusts her, so we can trust her," Mal reassured her. "Besides, think of what we could learn from unlocking this ancient magic. Maybe I could extract it and—"

"Ah yes, always fighting for science." Odette rolled her eyes, but a smile played on her lips, cutting any venom from her words.

"Oh please, just because you don't know the difference between lepidopterology and herpetology doesn't mean you can't understand how important this scientific advancement could be," Mal snorted, her eyebrows raised in challenge back at Odette. But I noticed a twinkle behind her eyes and I guessed these two were close.

"Shit, nobody knows the difference between those, Mal," Knox confessed before belly laughing, his whole body reverberating as his head fell backward.

"Enough." Top Dog passed out maps of the region, and I scanned until I found Nihani Mountain, nestled in the east, past the expansive desert Dyrcsa was surrounded by. I noted the region was named Celestia—I had never known it to exist until now.

Nihani Mountain looked like it was a daunting climb. It was the highest mountain in its range, and gauging from the snow detailed on the map, I could expect a bone-chilling expedition.

Winters were tough in Edinguard, but usually we still had four walls to hole up inside of, even if we couldn't afford heat. But out in Celestian lands, ascending the mountain would give us little escape from the elements. We'd have only the equipment we could carry, only caves and overhangs to find refuge in.

"Knox, inform Odette why we cannot afford to mobilise her unit on this mission, please," Top Dog commanded. The look on Odette's face could have killed, and I wondered whether these two women competed for command.

Knox plastered an apologetic smile on his face, evidently uncomfortable being stuck between two spitting hydra heads. "My spies have confirmed our suspicions about encroaching activity from Edinguard. They pretty much said it's only a matter of time before the Domers will try to take Dyrcsa. Things must be worse there than we thought." Knox turned towards me expectantly.

So Domer threat has already reached here. So that was why these people were choosing to fight. Why the magical were standing up, too.

"I mean... Yeah, it's shit. Food's been getting scarcer every year, and more people are dying since the O'Malleys increased their patrols. Or should I say executions," I said bluntly.

"All that killing, just to try and get to you. How's that make you feel?" Odette snarled.

"Probably as shitty as you feel knowing it's been happening for however long and you've done nothing to stop it," I snapped back. If Odette was an inferno, I would fight fire with fire.

I had endured twenty-six years of abuse. A loudmouth smart-ass wasn't going to be the needle that broke my back. I had evolved from that scared little girl years ago, and I wasn't going back.

Odette's brows furrowed, the whites of her eyes showing as her eyes widened in anger, her full upper lip curling in anger, "Listen you little shit, you don't know the first thing about who I am or what my history—"

"Enough!" Top Dog bellowed, her gloved fist slamming down onto the table like a judge hammering his gavel. "Enough of this schoolgirl bullshit! We are royally fucked if we cannot succeed in this, and you're bickering like idiots!" Top Dog rose to continue her rant. "This isn't a fucking game! We have to be prepared for the kind of weather that will kill us, not to mention whatever magic defends the final piece. We have *no* idea what's in store for us. Every single one of us could die."

"Then why the fuck are you placing our lives in the hands of this anorexic bitch?" Odette roared. "She won't even make it up the mountain—and then what was the point?"

"O, we voted on it. The popular vote won. Those are our rules, and we have to live by them, or we're no better than the tyranny we're trying to overthrow," Malachai reminded her.

"Fuck the popular vote!" Odette couldn't stop, her inferno imploding. "We don't *need* this magic!" A vein popped out on her forehead to match those bulging on her neck.

"Come on, Odette. Of course we do. If not us, then they'll have it," Knox countered. "Then imagine what will happen to us all."

"How do we know *she* won't do the same?" Odette threw her hands up. "Or what if she can't control this magic? There are too many risks! Why am I the only one that sees it this way?"

I felt Archer spring forward in his seat, seemingly unable to restrain his need to defend me any longer. "Because she is a good person. And we will help her control it! Besides, does my word mean nothing? I vouched for her and still do."

"So we're supposed to believe that because you two fucked, she's trustworthy?" Odette spat on the floor. "I don't trust you either. You're almost as new as her!"

"Why am I not surprised? You trust nobody. Do you even know what that feeling is? Or is your heart entirely dead?" Archer retorted.

Odette rose to her feet, her chair flying backward into the wall behind her, leaving a sizable dent. Her nostrils flared in unfettered fury, and I half expected steam to blow out like the machines in our factories after an impossibly long day of work.

Knox's massive frame rose with impressive speed, his docile face now beginning to harden in frustration and exhaustion. Clearly they'd had this argument before. "Odette, we don't have time for this. We could be attacked any day. We need to get planning—we're leaving tomorrow."

Odette huffed, her arms folded, but she stayed in the room, leaning against the wall near where her chair had gouged it.

He'd been able to subdue her rage. I took in Knox again, piecing together more of the intricacies at play here. I noticed a brief pause before Top Dog tore her gaze from him, her leather glove clenching her map tightly, and continued, "That's right. So twenty-four hours to gather our equipment, coordinate our route, share our knowledge, and secure our exit plan."

Twenty-four hours—I couldn't believe it. "You mean the Domers are coming here right now?"

A grave nod from Knox. "We've been keeping tabs for a while. They've been quietly raising a legion of soldiers to invade us. We're the next closest city, and they've driven Edinguard into the ground. As you are well aware."

"Holls, they're planning to conquer Dyrcsa and extract every last drop of wealth from the people and the land. They drained us of everything like leeches, and now they're on the hunt for their next prey," Archer said coldly, his hand placed on top of mine. "That's why I joined. I can't let that... that *evil* happen to others. I won't." His fingers intertwined mine until our hands made a fist.

I nodded. That need for justice raged inside me too. His words struck chords in my soul. We would stop them.

But I had to ask. "Why are Archer and I the only nonmagical here? You all fight for Low-Town, and yet none hold a position of power?"

Odette lurched forward. "What did they tell you?!"

"What? Who—" I brought my hands up in defence, bewildered.

Odette strode towards the table. "Who told you!" Her wild eyes ripped around the room, demanding the perpetrator step forward. I was clueless.

"I don't know what you're talking about," I stammered, shaking my head as I looked to Archer to fill in my missing information.

Archer shook his head subtly at me, and I took that as a sign to drop it. That there was more to the story he'd tell me at a later time.

Mal's tiny hand softly grazed Odette's arm. "Nobody would, O. And it wasn't your fault." The two women exchanged a look, and I saw a softening in Odette, who then returned to her spot against the wall.

What was that about?

Clearing her throat, Top Dog continued. "I will be staying back just in case their attack coincides with when you are all on mission. We will need my battle experience to lead the Dyrcsan

Druids and whoever else we can rally to arms. Odette, you will lead this expedition." She did not wait for a reply, as it was not up for debate.

"You five will go in quickly and quietly. You will extract the final piece, and you will return here before anything else. You will *not* put the pieces together prior to your return, do you understand?" Her voice was sharp, almost as if fear propelled her orders.

Again they all whistled, but this time my lips curled into a circle in a failed attempt to join in. I'd work on that.

"So how are we getting in?" Malachai asked.

"The Druids are creating a new portal to the Silver Steppe for us to use. From there, we ascend. I hope you all are comfortable with ice climbing. The first half will have a trail, but the second half will have some frozen crags," Top Dog commented. "We can't portal up the mountain–the distance is too far, and as you all know, we can only portal to places we've been to before. Nobody has ascended Nihani." She nodded towards Odette and Mal, "And we need to ensure we can portal back if things go badly." Top Dog's focus flopped to me, and again I wished I could read her expression.

"It will be a priority that Hollyn makes it to the top. If we can assume the third piece will be like the other two, then we will need her to retrieve it," Archer looked at me and I nodded back.

"I'm not carrying dead weight. She better hold her own," Odette dismissed.

"*She* can handle herself," I responded snarkily, resulting in an accusatory glare from Odette.

Knox pushed back his chair, the wood scraping against the floor, before rocking his massive weight forward to stand. The chair audibly groaned a sigh of relief. "But Archer is right—the pieces, according to our information, are guarded by a barrier that only responds to Dufort blood. Hollyn's survival is paramount." His brown eyes, so similar in colour to the minced meat pies my grandmother used to bake for us, held mine. He subtly nodded at me, and I was surprised to find myself eager to impress him.

Odette rolled her eyes and huffed. I didn't dare gamble my life in her hands.

"I will get to work on synthesising some weatherproof clothing and triple-checking our climbing gear," Knox stated as he grabbed the map in front of him, evidently ready to get back to work. "Hollyn and Archer, the most we can spare is a stun gun for each of you. We cannot risk an avalanche, so no bullets."

Malachai raised her hand, as if we were in school. "I will prepare the perishables, something that will last the elements and provide as many nutrients as possible to fuel our journey."

Her finger pointing, Top Dog requested, "Archer, you find us a map of the mountain—try to get as detailed as possible. I want a visible route if possible. Odette, you check in with your troops here. Inform them of our expectations for guarding the city, and then link up with Archer to assess the best path for our trek."

"What should I do?" I asked, wanting a purpose too.

"You will gather the first-aid kit and ensure its completeness," Top Dog replied. I nodded.

"We will meet back here tomorrow morning at dawn, where you will change into your gear and head out. So get some rest, you will need it. And fill up on food." She looked towards me, and despite not seeing her face, I knew she was assessing my too-thin frame, as if calculating my chances of survival.

I had a feeling that no matter how much we prepared, we were walking into the jaws of death.

I perused the outdoor market, my eyes scanning for the herbs and plants I knew to be helpful remedies. The poor healthcare provided by our "doctors" left much for us to cure ourselves. Agaricus was a mushroom that I had ground up and mixed into a salve many times to aid with mild frostbite. I was also searching for calendula oil that I could craft into an ointment that helped treat infection. There were gauzes, bandages, and various pills ready to be packed into the kit, but Grandma had always said I was a natural healer, so I added my homemade remedies to my own utility belt, just in case our first-aid pack was lost.

I requested cantharis oil and a few other tea leaves from the vendor and handed over the silver coins Archer had given me after learning of my intentions. The afternoon sun cast long shadows behind me as adrenaline coursed through my body. I would barely sleep tonight, as usual before each mission I undertook. I wondered whether consuming sleeping aids would help, but decided against it, not wanting to risk anything but complete clarity in the morning.

I retreated back to my room, where a serving tray containing a bowl of piping hot stew, a heavy mug of spicy tea, and a pile of plump fruit and flaky pastries, packed full of jams and fruit purees spilling out, had been left waiting at the foot of my bed. A folded note lay beside it, with my name scrolled in cursive.

Eat it all. You will need the extra calories.

E.

Puzzled over who "E" was, I searched the other rooms in the building but found nobody. I quickly ran out the front door, hoping to find my mystery giver, but life continued on, not a soul focused on my bewilderment.

Shrugging, I returned to the delicious spread and began devouring it, intent on consuming everything, down to the last crumb. Whoever "E" was, they were right. I would need every extra calorie. I had to survive this mission.

Everything relied on me. On my survival.

I went to bed, my gut swirling in tension, my body restless, and awoke in the early morning ragged and achy, as if I had barely slept a wink. Groggily, I left my room, darkness still lingering in the sky as I ventured to the Compound, not waiting for Archer to awaken.

I needed these quiet moments alone to focus myself and calm the quells storming inside. I would find comfort in my singularity.

It was do or die, and I had no plans on dying.

Two Down Run to Go

Bitter, bone-chilling wind lashed my face, my eyes protect-ed behind military-grade night vision goggles, ready to be turned on when darkness reigned. Any wrong steps would be suicide, as Odette had informed us, if we *were too stupid to follow simple fucking orders.*

Sure-footedness was one of the many transferable skills, I was realising, that my life of thievery had afforded me. That and adaptability in response to last-minute changes and challenges, which I was sure would come into play soon enough.

I thought of my grandmother, who had been battling a par-ticularly muddled episode before I'd left and hadn't remem-bered who I was nor where we were. The medics had been forced to sedate her as panic turned into manic hysteria—we couldn't risk a heart attack or stroke. I'd resorted to sleeping tonics back home from time to time. Making that choice never got easier.

My inner demons antagonised me with worries of her slipping into a coma, of her not waking up again.

I knew it was the best course of action every time, yet I fed those beasts of paranoia deep within as if they were at a buffet.

We stood at the base of the looming mountain dominating our view, and I couldn't help but feel like krill moments before being vacuumed inside the enormous mouth of a blue whale. The elements and the terrain held the upper hand here, and I had to respect and remember the power of this natural wonder—and whatever creatures found refuge on it.

"Let's do one last pack check," Mal requested.

Each of us carried a small pack filled with shiny, flimsy fabric they told me was a thermal blanket. Food rations had been divided between us equally, and weird tubes of variously coloured liquids were wrapped securely inside, along with our map copies, fire starters, and medical supplies. Underneath the massive coat that swallowed me, my trusty utility belt stowed my chosen herbs and remedies, as well as my pouch of Dustclox and the Relic pieces.

I'd vehemently refused to give the pieces up for safekeeping in the Compound, even under intense pressure from Top Dog. It was *my* job to secure the Relic.

I never handed over my end of the bargain without first receiving payment, and I wasn't about to hand over the keys to unlocking my magical future and saving my grandmother in return for promises from a near stranger. So they rested inside my belt, separate from the pack that burdened my back. I never used backpacks on a job for a reason—they felt cumbersome, like a foreign limb that hindered my own balance and agility. If I had to release the bag to survive, I would without hesitation. So in the belt the Relic pieces went, safe from being severed.

Clad in white thermal camouflage, my head completely covered save for holes for my eyes and mouth, and with Thermpaks stuffed in my wool socks and thick waterproof gloves, I was awkwardly bulky, but warm. For now.

"Oh fuck, Mal, we don't need a third check." Odette spun on her heels and headed up the winding, snow-covered rocky path. "Come on, we need to start."

I saw Mal shake her head, a smile playing on her lips, "Fine. You win." She waved her arm for us to join in single file behind her as we all clasped the carabiners onto the safety rope tying us together. On Odette's hand signal, we began moving swiftly forward as one.

Knox, whose breath blasted the back of my neck like a furnace, lumbered behind me untethered, his massive polar bear paws thumping with each step. He looked almost adorable with his pack secured on his back like a horse's saddle, and I yearned to touch his dazzling alabaster fur, though I resisted such an intimate gesture. But I shuddered when I saw the size of his claws and gauged the supreme damage he could unleash in this form.

Jagged rock crescendoed up from the snow-covered valley we trudged through, the drifting powder erasing our footprints almost as quickly as they were created. Blizzard-like conditions wreaked havoc on our visibility, most of us relying on the tether attaching us to each other. Rays of sunlight were just beginning to peek out from behind the craggy peaks, chasing away the shadows of night, and I welcomed the warmth that defended me from the piercing gusts of glacial wind that tried to penetrate my gear through any gaps and cracks it could find.

"Mal, you think you can make me dream about lying on a beach, somewhere hot?" Archer joked, his voice crackling through the comms.

Mal chuckled, "Sorry, Arch, if I could risk consuming that much magic, I would."

"Ahh, worth a shot anyway," Archer teased. "Maybe Top Dog should have come, cast a nice fire for us, eh?"

Odette snorted. "You think Top Dog could climb this? She's older than us. Her body probably can't do it."

"How old?" I asked, eager to find out more about who hid behind the wolf mask.

A pause from Odette, as if she contemplated ignoring me. "Nobody knows, nobody has seen her without the helmet. But one of our first lessons in training is to assess our enemies for weaknesses. Trust me—her body isn't at its peak."

"And you guys trust someone whose face you've never seen?" I was baffled.

Odette's head turned to the side, "I don't need to see someone's face to know if they're a lying piece of shit." My cheeks reddened beneath my face covering, embarrassed Odette could make me feel so small. I was thankful nobody was paying any attention to me.

"Easy, O," Mal's hand softly touched Odette's back. "It's true though, Top Dog has never led us astray before. Science requires repetitive testing to confirm a hypothesis. Every test, she's stayed true."

Knox huffed and I turned to watch his giant snout sway up and down in agreement.

We continued on our zigzagging adventure as the sun inched higher into the sky, its full brilliance shining without apology. A murder of crows cawed as they circled overhead, assessing us, before they ventured on to what I assumed was greener pastures. It would take us half the morning to reach the end of the valley, and then our real climb would begin.

Odette stopped abruptly, the rest of us too slow to stop before bumping into each other.

Two pulls of the rope.

That was our signal to stay quiet and get low. So we dropped to the ground, our bodies as compact as we could make them while our leader assessed the situation.

A sharp crack of ice broke the silence as a giant drift of icy snow broke off one of the cliffs and crashed below, the sound echoing as it bounced off the surrounding escarpments. More cracks, like branches lopped from their trunks, followed as we stood rooted in place.

Fuck.

We couldn't afford an avalanche, especially in our position. We were exposed and far too low to not be swallowed.

Another massive fissure rifted before us, the snow beginning to rip away from the mountain.

"Mal," Odette urged.

Our smallest member stood, her gloves stretched out before her in focus as the mass of snow descended. I watched, my breath caught in both fear and awe, as I witnessed my first example of mental magic. They'd said her power was immense, but it was another thing to see it.

Mal was suspending the barrage of snow midair.

With a momentous throw of her arms, she heaved it behind us, saving us from this first wave.

But the avalanche was inevitable.

A deluge thundered down towards us, swallowing everything in its path. The waves of incoming snow looked like wild horses racing.

Mal whipped around, her hands ready to target another falling mound, but it fell and crested towards us like a tsunami of snow and ice.

We had only a few moments before it would consume us.

"Mal!" Odette panicked.

My body vibrated from the thunderous rumbling, the approaching wind whipping snow at us. I gasped, shutting my eyes and tucking my head to brace for impact.

A low hum sounded as the wind ceased abruptly.

I opened my eyes to witness Mal straining with effort as she halted the onslaught; an invisible wall had formed, wave after wave of snow and ice crashing into it.

Mal's feet slid back a few inches as she maintained her protective shield, her magic expending to suspend each flake and shard before it could reach us. With a grunt of exertion, she thrust her hands away from each other, and the wall began to part, a chasm forming down the middle.

She was parting the onslaught of snow, creating a pathway through which we could continue as she diverted it to either side of us.

I marvelled at the scope of her power.

A small river of blood began to leak from Mal's nose, the red stark against the black of her ski mask. We all watched, helpless, as she endured the avalanche's wrath.

It felt like an eternity.

Finally, it ceased, the mountains once again tranquil and idyllic. She dropped to her knees, heaving deep breaths, and I wondered how much magic a person could harness before it was exhausted, before it could be channelled again.

Knox huffed twice before Mal raised a hand to abate his worries. She rose to her feet shakily. "I'm good. We should keep going."

Odette only paused a moment before rushing us up and onward, the desire to be free of this vulnerable valley propelling us into an unrelenting pace.

Banks of snow consumed me up to my knees as I struggled to maintain Odette's unforgiving charge. Knox's snout poked my back after I stumbled through an exceptionally deep section and fell behind. We had forgone Blizzboots, as they were too bulky once we reached our ice climb, but we suffered for it now as we sank deeply with each step.

We reached the end of the valley by midday, where we set up a small fire out of the bramble and dead tree branches we could scrounge at the foot of the mountain. My legs wobbled as I sat down and rummaged through my pack for the pre-allocated lunch food: an energy bar and a vial of pink liquid. Mal had insisted on the pink, claiming she'd crafted a slow-releasing energy booster that stimulated the mitochondria in our cells. With my basic education, I could make no sense of her description, but I chose to trust in her and in everyone else as they downed theirs without a second thought.

The Thermpaks' warmth was beginning to dwindle in its fight against the bitter cold, despite the strength of the high sun beating down on us. A chill had begun to seep into my bones, my body lacking any fat to insulate me. Frostbite would be quick in these conditions, my lips already drying out from windburn.

The liquid burned slightly as the pink juice flowed down my throat and settled into my belly. I could feel a flush throughout my body in response, which helped to ward off the frigidity that threatened to ravage me. I had to be careful not to give in, not to let that malevolent blanket of frostiness extinguish my fire.

I knew the dangers of the bitter cold. How important it was not to be seduced by the comforting lull of slumber that whispered in your ear, that promised an easing of the torture you endured. Mental strength—the strength of a survivor—would carry me through. Not my body, not magic. My mind: the power of hope, resilience, and persistence.

Gale force winds nearly snuffed out our small fire as we all huddled around it and wolfed down our nourishment. Time worked against us, each minute diminishing our chances of survival. So we rushed to refuel, Odette already impatiently standing paces away up the incline, vibrating in restless energy.

"You doing okay?" Archer placed his hand on my arm and I nodded. If I wasn't okay now, still at the start of our climb, I would be dead before long. It was only going to get worse from here.

Mal was frozen in place, her mind elsewhere, and I worried, not only for her, but for us. If she continued to decline, we would be severely handicapped, burdened in carrying her and her equipment.

I prayed her energy drink worked as well as she claimed it did.

"Everyone, get your cramps on. It will be icy and uneven to the summit," Odette directed.

The brutal climb would begin shortly, our trail at times promising to be nothing more than ridges and loose rock. Near the top, we would be scaling a bluff to complete our ascent. We'd picked out a likely-looking place on our map for us to make camp for the night, but that still was at least half a grueling day away. Up.

I double-checked the carabiner that latched the harness around my waist to the paracord that connected us, our makeshift safety net if anyone slipped and fell. We did not attach Knox, his monstrous weight guaranteed to drag us all down with him if he fell. He trusted in his instincts, and so did we. We had no other choice.

"Thank you, Mal. For saving us." I knew we wouldn't be here right now had she not protected us. I wasn't sure Mal heard me, though, as she didn't even look at me, her eyes glassy and distant. *Is she sick? Tired?*

A quiet uneasiness settled in, and I felt the need to start conversation to fill the silence. I attempted conversation again with Mal, knowing Odette would not respond, and Knox had gone to check on something.

A slow blink, before her head finally turned towards me, and I realised her mind was far away. She opened her mouth, but before she could respond, Odette kicked snow over our fire, smoke billowing as its flames extinguished under the wintry blanket. "We should get going."

Any chance for conversation died like the last burning embers that marked our passage, and we rose, our next chapter of challenges calling to us through the whisper of whistling winds.

Night an Uphill Battle

We marched like lemmings, our heads downcast to hide from the blizzard that hounded us. My legs burned from exertion, the unforgiving ascent pushing my body far past its limit, especially after the last couple of days. That energy drink was my saving grace and the only thing preventing my legs from seizing up from exhaustion.

Years of malnutrition had prevented me from building the muscle mass needed to endure this impossible journey. I feared for the night, worried that my body would not rise after lying down for whatever slumber we could muster in these blistering conditions.

But we were still a few hours away from sunset—from the real cold—and our trail had become increasingly more intricate.

One wrong step and...

"This is our ridge walk. All eyes down. Everyone follows my *exact* footprints," Odette ordered, and without another moment to breathe, she urged us onward with a "go."

I chanced only a quick glance at the knife-edge path ahead, but my anxiety skyrocketed as my eyes travelled down the steep rocky cliffs that bordered either side. I did not dare follow them all the way down to the ground, trying to stop myself from entering into a complete panic.

A gentle tug pulled my torso forward, ripping my attention back, and I jutted my arms out for added precautionary balance. Whether from the frigid air or the adrenaline pumping, my teeth chattered as I took my first gingerly step, like a tightrope walker performing for their whistling audience. Only the whistles here were from the white-out snowstorm threatening to fling me off the edge. And the audience members were deadly boulders waiting for my body to plummet towards them.

Inch by inch we travelled along, our boots crunching on the mixture of shale, ice, and compacted snow. Everyone was silent, their focus razor sharp. Every few steps, rocks would loosen under one of our feet and cascade down, jumping and spinning in a weird dance, the sound delicately echoing.

We were making slow but steady progress; minutes felt like hours as we walked the line. We were centipede legs prowling forward, our tether cord the vertebrae that held us together.

The high sun had passed its peak, our shadows slowly growing as we continued on. I heard Knox huff and whip his head towards a massive bird soaring high in the sky, its wingspan causing an eclipse as it briefly passed by.

His sudden movement caused me to shift my balance, and my feet slid, my left slipping down the rocky ramp. I squatted down to steady myself with my hands before I fell into a straddle.

Heaving a sigh of relief, I took a moment to compose myself. But before I could rise, the others unknowingly continued hiking and yanked me forward onto my chest. My arms and feet scrambled to find holds before I slid headfirst to my death. "Stop!" I shrieked.

"Holls?!" Archer whipped around to assess, but the tug was just enough movement to push me over the edge, my one hand losing its grip as my nightmare came to fruition.

My limbs thrashed, searching desperately for anything to halt my momentum. But the more I flailed in desperation, the more loose rock detached. My right foot finally hooked the edge, and my right arm wobbled from bearing my body weight at such an awkward angle. I'd barely recovered from my arduous climb in Abraxas, my muscles still deeply strained and my body bruised.

Archer dropped low, straddling the edge as he twisted awkwardly to try and pull me up from my rope, the others following suit. But my arms could not hold on long enough, and I plunged down headfirst.

I slid down the jagged terrain, the rough texture ripping into my jacket until I lost all grip, my body jerking as I hung suspended from the noose around my waist. I was dangling, pain shooting up my back from the jolt.

Panic rose as my feet pedalled, trying to get some stability to turn myself around, but the rope around my waist prevented me from twisting my upper body enough to grab anything behind me.

"Odette, pull her up!" Archer shouted.

"I can't from here. There's not enough room for all of us to stand on the ledge," Odette replied. "Hollyn, you are going to have to get up yourself."

The harness dug into my pelvis unapologetically as my frantic movements worsened the pain. My eyes squinted as my fingers tried to wedge space between me and the harness, trying to alleviate the pressure.

My scrambling was futile and only caused more damage. So in a moment of clarity, I tucked my legs up so I formed a ball, and relished in the change in pressure on my hips. I breathed some relief, but then remembered I still hung helplessly, hundreds of feet above a most brutal death.

"Mal, can you help her out?" Archer asked frantically.

"I-I can't—I'm sorry," Mal replied somberly. "I don't have enough power."

"Fuck. Hollyn, let me try to turn around and get you." Archer began to shift, my body swaying and twisting in response.

"She's going to have to do this herself," Odette repeated.

"Even if you don't want to help—" Archer spat.

"Just stop. I can do this, just stop moving the damn rope," I told them as my legs worked to halt my sway. Knox huffed and I shook my head at him, "You'll never be able to get down here."

Focus. One step at a time. This isn't the first rope you've hung from.

Once I steadied my body, I took another deep breath to focus myself. I had to do this myself—there was no other choice.

I worked to dig one heel into the rock behind me, my knee bending and testing its support. Once I was confident I had enough traction, in one swift motion, I pushed off the cliff and flipped over, my hands and feet quickly punching into the snowy cliff like support posts being hammered into the ground.

Now climb.

My body took the initiative as I shifted to reach up with one hand, my opposite leg following suit. I silenced the fatigue in my arms and focused on utilising more of my lower body strength in compensation as I followed with my other limbs.

I hadn't fallen more than twenty feet, but the climb felt arduous. My foot twisted as it dug in search of the solid rock that lay beneath the loose, but it was a precarious method—I unleashed a torrent of stone and slipped, my foothold vanishing beneath me.

Quickly, I found another spot, not willing to risk my weight on only three spots of support. Gingerly, I nuzzled my toe in until it scraped the solid boulder, and I charged upward. My gloved fingers finally curled over the lip, and with one last spring from my legs, I vaulted over the ledge and landed in a bear hug.

"You okay, Torch?!" I could hear the fear in Archer's voice and knew how his face looked–eyebrows skyward, amber eyes doe-like, his full-lips pressed together in worry.

I sagged in relief for a moment before I pushed myself to an upright position and checked myself over. "Yeah." Another deep breath.

A draft of brisk wind infiltrated my coat, sending a chill down my spine. I couldn't see the slash but knew it was fairly big and I worried how I would keep warm. We hadn't packed spare coats—we couldn't afford to carry that added weight.

Rising, I urged us forward, deciding I would address the problem once we stopped and made camp. There was nothing we could do until we were past this cliff.

We continued on without incident, finally reaching solid ground once again. Our shadows were long as the sun began to lose its battle against the night sky.

"We just have this steep incline until we reach our camp spot. We're a bit behind schedule, so let's power through—we don't want to be climbing in the darkness," Archer stated, pointing to his map.

Despite the severity of our situation, a part of me felt alive. I lived for thrills. I felt like an explorer conquering new lands. The great unknown was both daunting and exciting.

Archer looked the part, like a wintry cartographer consulting his trusty map, carefully confirming our route.

"Knox, be on the lookout," Odette directed as she turned back to face us. Her eyes were hooded in darkness, adding a sinister foreboding to her warning.

"For what?" I asked. *Does she see something?*

"For anything. For nothing, if we're lucky." Her response sent a shiver down my spine. What we had endured so far had been excruciating, but it felt as though it was only the tip of the iceberg. I did not wish to wait for whatever demons hunted us unknowingly from afar.

And so we continued on, our trudge up the massive mountain painstakingly vertical.

I had not known fatigue. Real fatigue.

Not like this.

My hips ground in protest, my legs having gone numb awhile back. My arms pumped to try to propel me forward with momentum and to help lift my boots up out of the knee-deep snow with each step.

A cold sweat plastered my forehead and upper lip while my lungs scorched with each icy inhale. I could no longer take deep breaths, the pain of the cold air far worse than surviving on shallow puffs. But the payoff was a mild, constant headache and a slight dizziness.

The gap in my coat prevented me from retaining any of the heat my thin body produced, and I realised how critical fixing it would be if I wanted to survive.

To survive.

No longer were we talking in maybes, in hypotheticals.

Death was a reality up here, and it hunted us. Waiting. Biding its time to strike.

The rope encircling my waist jerked me forward, my movements a beat too slow to stay on Odette's unforgiving pace. The rest of us were slowing down, but not her. Whether it was due to her physical magic or her natural fitness, I didn't know.

Either way, she was nearly dragging us by the time we reached the mouth of the cave where we would seek refuge for the night.

I slumped down onto the ground once inside the cave, sagging with exhaustion against my pack. Knox transformed back into his human state, no magic left to expend. He likely wouldn't be able to transform again for a while, he'd told us. But we hadn't known what lurked in these mountains and had chosen the extra defence his great bear form could provide to get us this far.

From now on, it would be up to Odette's magic, the other two in need of rest and time to recover.

There were no branches, no twigs, nothing with which we could make a fire, so we enveloped ourselves in our thermal blankets to stave off the tremors that convulsed our bodies. I marvelled at the efficacy of the thin, shiny fabric and thought about how impactful fabric like this would have been back home. Too many homeless, frozen to death on the worst winter days. So many of us had nothing more to offer, no extra space to provide, no trust left to give. Charity was a luxury that only the rich could afford to give.

Once I'd warmed up enough, I dared to take off my coat to inspect the damage as I hid underneath the blanket, trying not to draw any attention to my problem. I didn't want to be seen as weak by Odette, nor have Archer do something chivalrously stupid like offer me his coat instead.

Multiple gashes marred the back. None of our packs had a needle or thread, and being stuck in the middle of the snowy mountains, we had no natural fibres to use either.

In short, my jacket was ruined.

Why don't you stuff it with the thermal blanket?

I glanced up and around, unsure whether someone had spoken, or if I was hearing whispers from the Relic again. But it hadn't sounded like before, and when I found Mal's attention on me, I understood and silently thanked her for the idea. I would stuff myself like a turkey; if I couldn't fix the holes, I'd fill them. I was especially thankful she'd chosen to speak telepathically and hadn't alerted anyone to my problem.

I felt a kinship begin to form with Malachai, and I wondered if I could one day fit in with this crew. I smiled tentatively at her, relieved when she returned it.

"You asked me why I joined earlier," Mal began, her voice soft, weak still.

I nodded. "I just find it interesting so many magical people have devoted their lives to fighting a system that keeps them in power." My hands went up as I realised how that sounded. "I-I didn't mean for it to sound... like that. It's just—I like to think everything through."

Fortunately, Malachai smiled knowingly. "I can understand that. Like testing a hypothesis." Huddling like a ball, her knees up and under her chin, the shiny blanket wrapped around her, she looked so small. Like a child. "Truth is, my reasoning was selfish at the beginning. I wanted to seek revenge... still do."

I felt Odette tense, and I guessed she didn't want me to know Mal's story.

Mirroring Malachai, I huddled deeper into my blanket as well. "I can understand that. I do too."

A soft whistle from Knox, as if confirming he, too, sought revenge.

Surprising me with her openness, Mal continued. "My sister was beaten and raped by Bryce O'Malley—he had taken a liking to her, and nothing we did could stop his assaults." Tears welled in her eyes as emotion choked her off. "That bald-headed fuck destroyed her."

Was that the bald man who nearly killed me back in Edinguard?

She continued before I could muster up anything in response. "We lived inside that Dome. The mirage of perfection. We should have been the lucky ones, and yet my sister endured that abuse for years, both of us too terrified to fight back against them."

"If I'd had the courage to..." Mal struggled to finish her thoughts, tears streaking down her face. Had her sister died?

I didn't ask—Mal had divulged enough. But I floundered for words to say, to provide some solace for the painful wounds that she had made visible. So I settled on, "Thank you. For sharing."

"Enough," Odette commanded, approaching Mal's softly weeping form and enveloping her in a hug, surprising me with her softness. It was clear that the Mutts shared a deep bond, and my heart tugged, envious of the family they had created for themselves.

That had to be a good sign—to fight together and still like each other. It reassured me in my choice to join them.

And it surprised me to hear of Domer abuse amongst their own.

We were all broken. Misfits, cast away before we could disrupt their way of life. But these misfits had banded together, a common goal uniting all of us.

Ruination. Complete and total upheaval.

Most of us didn't say much after—we were exhausted, famished, and mentally drained. The whiz of the wind echoed around us as we chomped on our food—meat sticks, fruit bars, nut squares, and another coloured drink. This time, Mal told us to consume the blue one; it would aid in muscle recovery and facilitate a flush of the built-up lactic acid in our bodies.

Outside, the pale waxing moon glowed softly in the night sky, shyly flirting behind a blanket of dark clouds. More snow was imminent.

One by one, we fell asleep. Our chests became accordions, expanding and compressing with each soft, rumbling snore. Our bodies cuddled together to maximize body heat, and I was lucky enough to be in the centre.

I prayed we would not be snowed in when we woke up.

Put the Scary on Top

C^{aaaww!}

The piercing sound woke me abruptly, and I blinked my eyes rapidly to banish the fog of sleep.

That damn bird again.

The first few rays of golden light were just breaking through the mountainous horizon, almost blinding in their glory, amplified in their reflection off the fresh snowy powder. It was eerily still; the brutal winds had finally ceased, and no other sounds of life could be heard this high up.

I walked to the mouth of the cave to take in the scene, scouting for enemies or threats. My thief's mind was never fully at rest, always on alert, always anticipating danger before it could blindside me. From up here, you could see the expanse of the valley below, where the three mountains met, the landscape barren and alabaster without vegetation. We were so high, my eyes played tricks on me, making me doubt how elevated we truly were—it seemed like such a short distance straight to the ground. But my tired body reminded me how far we'd travelled.

Odette was already awake, diligently packing her bag and scarfing down her morning protein bar. I studied her face, visible without her thermal mask, and watched as her brows furrowed in concentration, her sooty eyelashes stark against her dark skin. Her long braids were gathered in a low ponytail, and her full lower lip looked as weathered as mine felt.

Her face seemed incapable of masking any of her emotions, as I watched her frustration over zipping up a pocket increase as her scowl deepened. I wondered about her story, of what I had unknowingly brought up earlier that had caused such a strong reaction from her. I wondered what trauma she bore that had forced her to become so angry with the world. Even her braids were so tight that I could see where they pulled slightly on her hairline as if fearful themselves of disobeying her orders to stay put.

But Mal had shown me kindness, vulnerability, even trust. So I knew there had to be a lot more than a short fuse inside Odette. And I was curious to find out her true self.

"Do you fucking mind?" she snarled my way, although the venom I had initially felt now seemed a little diluted. Maybe I'd become accustomed to her anger.

"Sorry." I was too tired to take on her wrath so early in the morning.

"Maybe you should be doing the same." Her icy gaze met mine, and I froze like prey hearing the menacing crackle of its predator's footsteps approaching, awaiting the first strike. "Unless you're too busy." Sarcasm dripped from her.

"You're right." I strode back to my bag and began to repack the remnants of our gear, leaving out the thermal blanket to stuff into my coat's holes. I hadn't the energy to engage in a debate with her, so I bit my tongue, like I had so many times in front of my father. My head pounded, the talons of a migraine having firmly dug in, whether from the cold, the stress, the proximity to the final Relic piece, or a combination of all.

"*Some* of us understand how fucking crucial this mission is," Odette muttered under her breath.

I sat back on my heels and took the bait. "You don't think I understand the gravity of the situation? I have just as much at stake, probably more. I'm the one that has to take in this magic—"

"Yeah, no, I'm not listening to a sob story about obtaining more power than any of us could imagine. Give me a fucking break," Odette interrupted.

"What is your problem with me?" I asked, my voice rising in frustration, nearing my breaking point of quiet patience.

"My *problem* with you is that we've been slaving away for years. *Years.* Busting our balls planning missions, training soldiers, gathering intel, compiling a goddamn textbook on the assholes of Edinguard. I finally feel like we're ready to go on the attack. I've been dreaming about this moment for what feels like an eternity. All the blood, sweat, and tears about to finally pay off." Odette stalked toward me, each step eliciting a shudder up my spine.

"And then you show up, out of nowhere, with the key to the fucking world at your fingertips, and *all* our plans change at the last goddamn minute to centre around you." Her accusatory finger pierced right through me. "Who the fuck are you, and why the fuck am I putting everyone's lives in your scrawny-ass, incapable hands?"

"We've gone over this, O—this is our best chance at seeing our vision come to fruition," Mal's voice spoke up calmly. Behind us, the others were all now awake and stiff with tension.

"It doesn't matter. None of it matters if *she* has other plans. Everyone is so fucking obsessed with magic. More, more, *more*," Odette snarled with disgust. "It was banished for a reason, and we're risking our asses to unleash it back into the world. Into someone most of us don't even know! Why am I the only one that thinks this is stupid?" Her hands were raised in bewilderment and her mouth gaped open, as if she were gifted with vision when everyone else was blind, the answer so openly obvious.

"You don't think I want to see the Domers fail? My entire life, I've wanted to see those assholes fall from grace. They have tormented me and mine for as long as I can remember. I am a *good goddamn person*." I'd had enough. I was tired of being accused.

"And then what? You'll rule? What if we start disagreeing? If the Mutts no longer serve your goals?" Odette fired off hypotheticals, the proverbial cork dissolving as everything that she was squashing down poured out.

Rule? I had never once considered a future where I would rule anything.

Am I going to become that *powerful?*

"That's a risk you're already taking with Top Dog—" Archer began, as he walked to stand beside me.

"At least I know her. And she can't harness this magic."

"This magic is coming, whether you want it to or not!" I hollered. My calm was shot and my patience was tried.

Knox agreed with me. "It's true. My intel has told me as much—they're coming for it, O. *Them.* I know you don't know Hollyn very well, but you do know the Domers. You know how awful they are. You know that if they get that magic, we are truly, absolutely, without-a-doubt dead. They will find a way to use it."

"My troops and I can take them down. If we could just infiltrate their base—"

He shook his head with a calmness that belied the frustration on his face, "That won't stop them from obtaining this magic. You know they'll find a way to take it. When have they ever not gotten what they've wanted in life?"

"Yes, but if we can kill enough of them—"

Rising to cup Odette's face, Mal spoke to her gently. "We can't try it again, O. Not after what we lost... *who* we lost." Odette grimaced, her body flinching. *Did they lose one of their team?*

Responding only to Mal, her voice low and uncharacteristically quiet, Odette said, "He didn't fucking listen to me. And I told Top Dog he wasn't ready. With only that gun..."

"I know." Mal rubbed Odette's cheek with her thumb before pulling her into a gentle kiss.

Was this another Mutt? Was he without magic too?

I shook my head, my mental and physical fatigue almost too much to bear. I walked back towards the cave opening, letting the breathtaking wintry stillness calm me, focus me. It was so beautiful and so lonely. As I turned back to face the others, I stood confidently, resolute in my purpose. I just had to convince the others. "I know you don't know me... at first, all I ever wanted was the chance to save my grandmother."

I zipped up my jacket, pulling my mask down over my face once again before I continued. "But now I finally feel like my people have a fighting chance to be able to have a future. To dream, have hope. To learn a trade, or become a doctor—find a purpose that fills their souls. To one day bring children into this world that won't die from malnutrition and illness."

Refastening my harness and triple-checking my utility belt, I brought my gaze up to meet each of their eyes. "And if this magic can make that happen, then I will keep fighting until it's mine and can be used for good." I hoped they all saw the sincerity in my eyes. I was committed to this now, and forever.

Archer, forever at my side, placed his hand on my shoulder, his back to the others but facing me. "I know you. I know you are good. Magic won't change that." I met his gaze, a small smile playing on my lips.

He was my family. He never gave up on me, and I wouldn't give up on him.

I fought for him and his future too. Our future.

I hoped Odette believed me. And I hoped I fulfilled my own expectations.

"Let's go," Odette said, after a lengthy pause. She refused to meet my eyes, a look of dissatisfaction still upon her face.

We were close, if my pounding headache was any indication.

Just like in Abraxas, the proximity of the final Relic piece incurred an intensifying, blinding migraine that I knew would be insatiable until the pieces were together.

The magic's pull was formidable, my focus streamlining towards its location. The others didn't know how close we were, couldn't truly feel it, deep in their core.

And man, was my core alive. It was molten hot, blazing in anticipation of this climactic moment. My body pulsed as each snow-covered step brought me closer, my breath puffing like a starved dog panting, begging for a bite of its owner's tantalising meal.

There was no biting wind, no piercing howl rampaging our senses. It was deathly still, almost as if Nihani Mountain had abated the raging snowstorm and unravelled the red carpet for us.

So our final ascent began as the easiest leg of our journey. Mal and Knox had regained some of their powers, but we dared not waste any until we reached the peak. We had no idea what awaited us.

We wove like a snake around the curving, snow-packed path we cut, the air thinner and the oxygen lower. Our packs were lighter, mercifully, making our pace fairly fast.

"If anyone would have told me months ago I'd one day climb Nihani Mountain, I would have called them crazy," Knox mused. He was a source of lightness, a wonderful balance to Odette's grave seriousness; it was enjoyable having his quips on our final stretch.

"If anyone would have told me I'd be outside of Edinguard, I would have bought them another drink," I joked. We enjoyed the brief moment of levity before our world was changed forever, for good or bad.

"If anyone would have told me I'd be leading you idiots up this mountain instead of defending my city, I would have knocked their asses out," Odette drawled.

"If—"

A monstrous roar cut Archer off. It was guttural, like a mixture of a lion's warning howl and a vixen's shriek. A flock of birds that had been perched on a cliff, basking in the sun, scattered in fear.

Our bodies went rigid, the muscles in my neck and shoulders bunching, my eyes widening as we scanned for the source of the unknown sound. This was the unexpected, the variable in our equation. We'd expected a surprise—and it sounded like this surprise was furiously famished. Fortunately, it also sounded like it was still a fair distance away.

First, we had to scale this mountain. And so we continued onward, wary and alert of what might greet us at the top. When we finally reached our ice climb, we dropped our packs to the ground and pulled out our extra equipment. We'd been suited up with carabiners, extra harnesses, rope, and ice picks.

I stepped into my harness and tightened the straps snuggly around my hips and waist before clipping the thick metal ring by my belly to both of the ropes. Knox would be the caboose, his larger frame acting as the anchor if any of us slipped and fell.

We stood at the base, staring up the length of the daunting vertical climb that loomed over us. We would have to climb this in unison, spread out horizontally like gems set in the band of a ring.

"Slow and steady, guys," Knox reassured us. "Really make sure those picks are dug in deep, and kick your feet in to make footholds on each step."

I let loose a giant, shaky breath and steeled my nerves as I took a quick glance down the rope. Odette already had one boot up, her powerful frame steady and at ease, as if she were simply about to climb the rungs of a ladder.

Archer, beside her, fidgeted as he checked his harness obsessively over and over—there was a reason he stuck to comms and backup during our missions. He was deathly afraid of heights, and I sympathised with the knots that must be twisting his gut relentlessly. Mal was zoned out, staring up towards the finish line, her mouth moving in either prayer or magical incantation.

She turned towards me, a wry smile on her mouth. "I don't really believe in a 'Priestess'—scientifically, it just doesn't make sense. But I figured hey, what the hell, it couldn't hurt to send up a little message just in case, right?" I appreciated her trying to lighten the mood and wondered whether the distraught look on my face or the anxious thoughts in my mind had tipped her off that I was nervous.

"If the Priestess is real, she sure likes to sit back and watch. I wouldn't count on Her divine intervention," I quipped back. Many people believed the Priestess to be their mothering saviour, that her divine intervention could be called upon to save you in the darkest moments.

But my life had been filled with more dark than light, and I never felt like anyone lovingly watched over me from above.

"After all of this, Hollyn, *you* might be a god—"

"Let's move," Odette ordered, her thin patience incapable of delaying any further. Her eyes were focused on me again. Wary, always wary.

And so we secured our footing and pushed off, our connection to terra firma effectively severed.

It had been an hour from my best estimate, based on the position of the rising sun. Not quite midday, but encroaching on it, the intensity of the light impossible to hide from.

And stuck on the scarp of Nihani, we were defenceless against its blinding, beating rays. Sweat pooled inside my gear before it froze from the subzero temperatures. Stray strands of hair that had escaped my thermal mask were now icicles, and my weather-beaten lips pulsed in agony, desperate for moisture.

I'd removed the heating pads that were stuffed inside my gloves and boots, as they'd lost their efficacy overnight. I wanted to feel as close to bare contact as possible on this climb. I needed to feel my fingers and toes as they dug and clung, but I sorely missed the extra warmth the pads had provided. I could feel the tips of my digits begin to go numb, but powered through, the top of the cliff within sight.

I looked down briefly, and my head immediately dizzied from vertigo as I baulked at our elevation. If that bird were still around, I could have reached out and grabbed it, we were so high.

My palms and forearms ached, not conditioned to the extreme pressure they were under, and my legs were so exhausted they quivered trying to pick up my upper body's slack. But that was nothing compared to the crescendoing migraine obliterating my skull. Nausea bubbled in my gut, my body rebelling against the pain.

I fantasised about the week-long slumber I vowed I would take after this mission.

Groans of exertion and panting filled my ears, only the periodic crackling of our comms interrupting the noises. Even Odette had slowed her pace, although likely to accommodate the rest of us.

Thunk.

My ice pick bit into the frozen rock and shavings sprayed my face, making me choke and cough. I spit out the minuscule shards of frosty terrain filling my mouth with flavours of dirt and metal. I hoisted my body up, the cords of my lean muscles rippling in effort, and kicked my boot into its next foothold—but slipped as my foot slid with the packed snow it evicted. My hands slid down the handles, and I felt my breath catch as my heart pounded.

I quickly solidified my grip, my biceps burning to hold my weight with my arms now bent at ninety degrees. My face grimaced in effort until my foot created a new step and I found my footing again.

Nobody seemed to have noticed, thankfully. I was not helpless and despised how I'd felt during this entire mission: ever the damsel in distress.

I could do this. Myself.

The lip of the climb was tantalisingly close—only a few more minutes of gruelling toil before we'd be on flat land.

As if in silent cue, our tired bodies sped up in unison, the end so near it breathed a second, third, even fourth wind into us, propelling us towards our goal.

My hand finally curled over the edge as snow sprinkled down around us like dust settling. With one final heave, I hurled my waist over the edge and shimmied until my knees could give me the leverage I needed to thrust safely onto my stomach. One by one, I felt the others flop down beside me, the gentle tug of the cord around me the only indication as my eyes were closed in exhausted relief.

I sucked the crisp air deep into my lungs, hoping the breathwork would dispel the endless throbbing that all but lived in my muscles. My head welcomed the icy pillow it lay against, the cold soothing some of the splitting pain that now spewed like lightning bolts down my neck and spine.

We lay there but for a moment.

One beautifully calm moment.

Until the wailing monster from earlier shattered our serenity with its scream. I'd been wrong before—it wasn't a roar or a shriek. It was a scream.

A bloodcurdling, shudder-inducing, ear-splitting scream.

A sound so horrible I would never forget it.

A sound of something in insurmountable agony.

A sound that was no more than ten feet from us.

Snatch Victory from the Jaws of the Beast

M y head whipped up and I froze.

What stood before us was horrifying.

It was like nothing I had ever seen, ever heard of before.

It stood on four feet, its terrifying glory easily looming over ten feet tall, not including the height of its twisted horns that curled up and out like gnarled tree roots. It was covered in blue fur, from the tip of its menacing snout down to the tops of its massive, bird-like feet. Blades of frosted glass shot out of its shoulders and feet like spiked armour.

Pools of saliva gushed out the sides of its heavily toothed mouth, and its eyes were milky white save for the large blood-red pupil dilating as it flicked between each of us, processing, assessing. Its wolflike ears twitched and rotated as they analysed every sound, every vibration I imagined the humongous organs detected.

One of its taloned toes was as big as my head. One swipe from it would gut me like a fish, my insides falling out, no hope for survival.

It shrieked again, a warning to the trespassers that lay before it.

We didn't move, hoping perhaps it was nearly blind.

It rose onto its back legs before it charged at us, the colossal beast surprisingly fast for only using its sinewy hind limbs. We watched as the beast stretched its arms wide, more blades bursting through its dense fur, until deadly spikes filed in a line down its outer arms. It curled its hands into gigantic spearheads as its feet pounded the earth, each massive step shaking the ground beneath us.

I lay there almost in awe of the mythical beast that pounded towards me. My mind could not process what I was seeing, my body rooted, frozen in fear.

It was seconds away, and still I could not will myself to move. I was lost in those haunting eyes, my migraine growing unbearably. White-hot pain filled me, nearly blinding me in its fury, and I could not get away.

In that moment, I realised it was the Relic. It was close by, the obsession with it ensnaring me, overpowering my rationale.

And it was preventing me from getting the hell out of this beast's way.

Just a few steps from me, it began to crouch into a low lunge, one gigantic arm raised up, ready to deliver its bone-crunching blow, when I saw it, dangling from a cord around its neck.

The final piece.

The onyx piece flopped against the beast's chest like a carrot hanging in front of a horse, and my arms stretched out desperately to reach for it.

I was so close. If I just waited one more second.

Strong hands gripped my arms and dragged me out of the monster's path, the beast's lengthy nails whooshing past my face a millisecond too late.

My body was dragged through the snow, the cold wet seeping up my coat, yet my eyes did not waver in their focus on the Inukviak piece.

"Wake the fuck up, Hollyn," Odette bellowed at me as her hands flipped me over and shook me in frustration.

I could barely hear her over the throbbing in my skull, the sweet whispers from the Relic enchanting me, consuming me. I knew all my pain would evaporate once I fused the three pieces together.

Dormant parts of me I never knew existed vibrated to life in reaction to the final piece, like I'd unlocked new doors that had spent decades being barred, the key hopelessly lost. Until now.

Every cell in my being burst awake. I was a shooting star, imploding from within, ready to show the world my fiery glory, no longer willing to hide in the anonymity of the night sky.

Another piercing howl slapped me awake, the beast's rage from missing its intended target evident. First I needed to survive. And I would have to slay this monster in order to steal what hung around its thick neck.

I shot to my feet, but the harness around my hips ground into me as I remembered we were all connected.

We would have to do this together.

"Up," I ordered, clarity penetrating the murky fog in my brain as I began to concoct a plan.

I scanned our surroundings, noting a cavern in the distance, the lack of any trees we could use for cover. We were on a plateau, with not much room to navigate. It would be tight; every move had to be perfect.

"Hurry, to the cave!" I began to dash, stumbling from the slower reactions of the others, and reminded myself we were only as fast as our slowest.

I felt its pounding advance as it sent tremors rippling towards us, and I worked to quell the panic rising in my throat, my body twitching in restless energy, waiting infuriatingly for Mal, our physically slowest, to gain steady footing.

"Grab each others' hands. GO!" I hollered. My hands clenched Archer's and Knox's in a vise grip as I funnelled the last reserves of energy into our mad dash towards covered ground. It wasn't long before the rest of us were nearly dragging Malachai, her feet barely making contact as we flew towards our goal.

It was gaining on us, the intensity of the quakes under our feet spiking as it covered the distance quickly. Too quickly.

We weren't going to make it in time.

We had to adapt. Now.

I felt the brute once again raise an expansive arm, heard it unsheathe its icy blades, ready to cause deadly destruction.

Wait for it.

Just a few more seconds.

"Drop!" I screamed, but my body delayed, the intoxication of the Relic's proximity inebriating me. The weight of the others' bodies pulled me into a prone position, much less gracefully than I had planned.

Its serrated swipe whipped above us in a horizontal arc, the gust of wind pulling my mask back to obstruct my view. I ripped off the black cover. I would endure the freezing cold and hoped the fight would be swift.

Odette followed suit, as did Archer, both of their gazes locked on me, awaiting their next orders.

Despite Odette's warfare experience, she looked to me to lead this.

Thunk.

The monster had cleaved down this time, inches from my arm, and without another thought we rose and sprinted.

Except Knox wasn't with me.

I looked down at the severed ropes that hung from my right hip and then back at Knox's huge frame—still lying on his stomach. The rest of us were escaping, but the beast's bloodlust had converged on Knox, who had been left to defend himself, helplessly still in his nonmagical human form.

"Stop!" I shrieked as my heels dug in to halt our progress. "We need to split up and distract it!" I unclasped the harness and ropes, my fingers flying deftly in panic as I bellowed and thundered to draw the beast's attention.

Those haunting bleached eyes shifted my way, and hoping the others would understand my unspoken plan, I bolted in the opposite direction of my teammates. I couldn't afford to turn around to gauge the beast's nearness—I had to rely on the crescendoing vibrations of its feet and hope my plan would save Knox's life.

I was dripping in sweat, but still I charged onward, no destination to race to.

I was nearing the edge of the plateau, the monster's strides right on my heels, the hairs on the back of my neck erect with perceived danger.

C'mon, Archer. Anybody.

I heard the clink of the blades pop open, felt them whizzing right for me, and I dropped to the ground again, narrowly ducking the swing.

But another swing came immediately after, and I was not prepared for it.

It sliced my bulky coat, the teeth ripping through the down filling and across the flesh of my back. I shrieked as white-hot pain thundered through me. I felt the wet blood ooze down my back as I blinked away tears, terrified to lose sight of the beast. And it was none too quickly, for I had to roll away from a third attack immediately and stagger to a standing position.

My hands found the stun gun on my hip, and I charged the towering giant before it could sweep for me again. I used my speed to catch it off guard, and my stunner connected with its birdlike foot, flooding the maximum amount of volts up its leg.

It convulsed as the energy infiltrated the rest of its body, and I gained confidence as I watched it stumble down to a lunge position.

The beast's convulsions loosened the Inukviak piece from around its neck.

My eyes homed in on the falling object, my hands forgetting to continue to press the stun gun's trigger. Soft whispers from the shard pervaded my senses as everything else around me dimmed.

Come, we will help you kill it. Unleash us.

I took two steps toward it before I was punched halfway across the plateau.

My body slammed onto my back, and white-hot pain erupted from the fresh gashes. Hot blood oozed down my back, droplets trickling out of my coat to taint the pristine alabaster snow.

I writhed in agony.

It charged for me again, but my back shouted in pain with every effort I took to try and get up.

My limbs failed me, and I lay there, watching the horrid creature close the distance. Fast.

I heard the others shouting to distract it, but the fresh scent of blood had dilated its ruby pupils until they glowed like infrared dots, its nostrils flaring to track my scent.

I dragged my body, trying to crawl my way out of its rampage.

It snarled its enormous mouth, baring its yellowed fangs at me in rage.

It was going to kill me—nothing would stop its pursuit.

I could smell the toxic odour spewing from its muzzle and nearly gagged. I watched as its hands formed twin spearheads, ready to impale me.

But then it stumbled, tripped over something.

Archer had thrown himself in front of the brute's feet, using his own body as a tripwire.

It flew forward, its front arms bracing the impact, reminding me of a demonic, horned gorilla. Before it could seek revenge on Archer, Odette vaulted onto its back and unleashed her fury, her fists pummelling the creature quicker than my eyes could follow the motion.

It roared in fury, its back arching away as it suffered her unrelenting onslaught.

Mal and Knox had reached me, their hands pulling me up from under my arms. Like a newborn foal, I swayed unsteadily, the blood loss enveloping me in a dizzy spell.

"Thanks."

"Let's get you back into that cavern there, I can take a look at—"

Mal jerked suddenly forward in front of me, the tip of the beast's claws poking through her shoulder, before it ripped it back out, her body tugged backward with the motion.

Blood gushed out, gurgling like a babbling brook, down her camo jacket. Her eyes were wide in surprise, her back still to the enemy. She crumbled to her knees, deathly white, before she slumped over.

None of us had been paying attention, assuming the others had the beast occupied.

But I spied Odette's body across the other side of the plateau, face down in a bank of deep snow. Motionless.

Archer was struggling to stand, his beautiful face marred by a gash ripped diagonally across his features, blood oozing down like strawberry preserves.

I couldn't let them die.

Not like this.

Knox fell to Mal's dying body, covering her from further attack.

I could not watch another person die in front of me.

Not for this fucking Relic.

So I ran straight for the beast, despite the protests from the gashes and aches of my body. Straight towards its terrifying mouth, with no weapons save for my stun gun.

I anticipated its swing. And its follow-up.

I slid through the snow headfirst, my arms outstretched, not daring to land on my damaged back. I rolled away from its second attack, and using the rush of adrenaline coursing through my veins, I sprang up underneath the monster and slammed up my stun gun.

Right under it, into its exposed soft belly.

Within seconds, its knees buckled and it howled in excruciating pain. Within a minute, it was silently convulsing on its side, its disgusting mouth foaming as its eyes rolled backward, the red dots all but invisible.

I broke contact only for a moment before reconnecting the gun with its chest.

I continued until I smelled charred flesh.

I only stopped once Archer found his way to me, his gentle hand placed over mine, still pressing the trigger. "That's enough."

Those hideous eyes were closed. I released my finger.

I leaned over, my hand bracing against one of his bony antlers to reach towards the Relic. Just like in Abraxas, an invisible veil rippled away as a magical barrier deteriorated. I ripped the Relic free.

As soon as my hand held the piece, my migraine disappeared, a warming calm flushing through my body. My energy seemed revived, my muscles felt stronger, my mind sharpened somehow.

I felt whole.

And I hadn't even put the pieces together, remembering our promise to Top Dog to keep them separate until our return.

But fuck, did I want to.

A scream broke my concentration.

We rushed over to Mal, whose body was cradled so lovingly in Odette's arms, swaying as silent tears fell from her dark eyes. "Help her!" she shrieked.

"I've given her all the medicine we have. We need to get her home *now*," Knox urged.

"Something's wrong with her. The black markings." Odette revealed Mal's shoulder, where a webbing of black veins dispersed from the wound like splintering glass. "No, no, no, don't let her die!"

"We can give her anti-tox at home, O. We need to get home," Knox argued.

"She *is* our fucking way home!" Odette flew into hysteria. "I can't create the portal without her!"

Knox swore under his breath. He looked at Mal, and my stomach dropped at what was written on his face.

He didn't think Mal was going to make it.

"Let me try something." I ripped through my pack, searching for the ingredients I needed to make a detoxing salve. "I should have saved her. I was right there, I should have been paying attention. I'm so sorry." I looked to Odette, the main target of my piss-poor apology, but for once, she didn't respond as she continued to weep and sway, Mal's face nearly as white as the tundra around us.

I rushed to mix my calendula oil with my ground-up agaricus mushroom and cantharis oil, until a thick paste had formed in the container. I crudely scooped the tincture with my stirring finger and slopped it on her gaping wound—thankfully, the bleeding had almost stopped, allowing my paste to stick.

Mal groaned, sweat dripping down her brows as my fingers touched her wound repeatedly; Odette had removed her mask for comfort, but also to monitor her paling, clammy skin.

I drenched and filled the ugly wound with every last bit of my tincture.

She writhed in pain as my medicine began to work, leeching the toxins from her body.

"It's going to look worse before it gets better," I informed everyone. I removed my jacket, unstuffed the thermal blanket from the holes, and wrapped it around Mal's shoulder in a makeshift sling to keep her arm as still as possible and to provide some protection to the wound.

"What did you do?" Odette asked me quietly.

"I purchased some extra ingredients for my pack, just in case. Just stuff that I've used before, when it was too expensive to visit the doctor. It's worked for me before, but a wound like that–" I snapped my mouth shut, nervous I was putting my foot in my mouth.

Odette just nodded, her head turned away from me. Mal had gone still again, her shallow breath laboured but at least steady.

"The fuck?!" Archer exclaimed, his finger pointing towards the monster's corpse.

Except it wasn't a monster.

It was a human.

What. The. Fuck.

Archer ran over and I followed suit, my work on Mal completed.

Did I kill someone? It was one thing to kill a monster—it was an entirely different thing to have killed a human. Was the human trapped in that terrible form? Cursed? My mind raced as my body hurried over to it.

Archer bent down to roll him over, and we gasped at the handsome middle-aged man that lay unconscious before us. His thick brows were furrowed, his lips open slightly, and a thick, curly beard covered the lower half of his face, continuing down towards his chest.

Archer bent forward to place his ear near the stranger's nose and mouth to listen for breathing as he removed one glove to feel the stranger's neck for a pulse.

"It's there. Weak, but he's alive," Archer confirmed.

"W-who is this? What happened? I don't..." I shook my head in disbelief as waves of guilt crashed over me. "He was a monster. It was self-defence."

"Hollyn, you had to do what you did, or none of us would be here," Archer reassured me. His eyes held mine in comfort, and I could tell he was sincere.

"We should bring him back... help him heal."

"Yes," he replied. "I'm sure everyone will want the answers he has too."

Archer removed his coat, doing his best to slide it under the naked man to use as a sled. We each took one of the coat's sleeves, and wrenching them with both hands, we began to tug him back towards the others.

We had made it halfway, the coat straining under the pressure, when a gust of wind slapped us in the face.

The bird from before had landed right before us, its gigantic wingspan stretched wide as it tilted its head up towards the sky and cawed. Its feathers were all shades of browns, beiges, and whites. They looked so familiar.

The harpy's head drew back down, its smoky grey eyes locking in on me. Perched on its back was Slade, wrapped in a trench coat of speckled white fur, like the hide of a snow leopard.

"Hello again."

Come Pain or Shine

Without further delay, we passed through.

I watched as Ryker's avian form shed its feathers and lush silvery fur burst forth. His wings shortened to become two more legs, the claws on his paws sinking into the patch of snow they landed on. His beak softened into a snout with whiskers poking out, and his mouth sprouted formidable canines aptly shaped to shred and devour. His ears lengthened atop his head, twitching in every which direction, on constant alert to every sound and vibration.

The only constant were those eyes. Like unbent steel, rigid and unforgiving.

As a giant arctic wolf, so big that Slade remained perched on him, his wise gaze subtly assessed his surroundings. I watched his eyes linger on the cavern we had found shelter in moments before, take in the barrenness of the plateau we were confined on, gauge the sharp, fatal plummet off the cliff edges. Plumes of smoke exhaled from his flared nostrils as his paws stretched into the thick blanket of snow we stood upon, no doubt testing his grip, perhaps even checking for ice.

His eyes settled back on Archer, the naked man, and me—on our separation from the others, a fair distance away. Far enough that we were at a big disadvantage, and he and Slade seemed to quickly understand that.

Slade's bright blue eyes found mine, and any friendliness from earlier was missing. They had a menacing feel instead, and my spine crept in worry—I feared those eyes. There was urgency, frustration, even panic in them, and I did not wish to find out to what lengths Slade would go to snatch the Relic from me. Ryker might have been the physically daunting opponent, but Slade was cunning. And I had no sense of his moral compass, whether he was willing to hurt me, even kill me if necessary.

"You know how this will play out, Hollyn. Why not save everyone and hand it over?" Slade's voice was flat, almost bored. As if he did not truly consider us a threat.

"Don't." Archer was firm.

"Half of you are hurt. You will be no match for Ryker."

"I'd die before I'd let you get it," Archer spat.

Slade sighed, exhaustion flickering over his face before his facade concealed that glimpse of honest emotion. He was once again unreadable, impossible to predict.

"Give me the fucking Relic, Hollyn."

"She won't—"

"Am I *talking* to you?!" Slade roared. His calculated coolness had finally erupted, no hint of the smiles and calmness we'd become accustomed to. His hands massaged his temples as he closed his eyes briefly.

"He's right though, I'm not going to give it to you. I need this—and I would never trust some Domer scum." I spat on the ground to emphasise my disgust. "You fucking lied to me."

"And you took the Relic and ran. Left us there." Slade's voice was cold, his eyes frosty. They must have thought I'd planned to double-cross them the whole time.

"What about my magic, huh?! You just happened to forget to tell me what this Relic really is?" I felt my cheeks flush, my rising anger manifesting physically.

"We were going to tell you, but then you went behind our backs," Slade snapped in rising anger.

"Fuck your deal," I snarled. "I deserved to know everything *from the start.*"

"You wouldn't have agreed and you know it." Gripping Ryker's mane in his hands, he leaned forward, his teeth bared in frustration. "Do you know what it's like to be useless like this?" He gestured towards his paralyzed lower half. "To be carried around like a twenty-eight-year-old man-baby?"

"I don't give a shit about your problems."

"You would try anything too, if you'd felt the utter uselessness I have. Remembered the freedom you once had—and will never have again without that Relic's power." His jaw flexed, before he gulped hard, as if swallowing emotion threatening to bubble over. I had never considered how difficult it must have been for him to become paralyzed.But it still didn't make up for the fact that he had been using me, lying to me, putting my life on the line. And I didn't quite believe he wanted the Relic only to heal himself. He was a Domer, he would do anything for more power.

"Stop pretending like you aren't really after the holy magic." I shook my head, my hands curled into fists. "It's never been about your paralysis. It's always been about the magic. *My* magic. Healing your legs was just a nice side effect."

"There could be a lot worse people to wield that Relic's magic—"

"See, Hollyn. We knew he was power-hungry just like all the other assholes hunting us." Archer's vindication was obvious; he had never trusted those two and his gut was being proven correct.

Hollyn.

My eyes darted towards Mal's limp body, cradled in Odette's arms.

Put the Relic together.

What?! I responded in my head. *But Top Dog told us to wait.*

No choice. Get ready to run to me.

Ryker prowled towards us slowly, the confident wolf subtly cutting us off from the others.

"They won't make it here in time," Slade warned me. They knew we were sitting ducks, outmatched by Ryker's lupine form in brawn and speed.

"I'll die before I let you hurt her," Archer promised, drawing a sharp glance from me. His jaw was set and his hands curled and I knew he wasn't joking. The sharp glint in his eyes lacked all the warmth typically swirling in those amber orbs. Ryker growled, his wolf snout exposing his canines in challenge. Those two would kill each other without hesitation, no love lost between them.

"If I agree to hand over the Relic, you must let me heal Mal first." I spun toward the others, Ryker and Slade turning to look at the huddled group. With my back to them, my hands found the pouch on my utility belt, and deftly I pulled the pieces out—and without another thought, placed the third piece in its missing position.

Immediately, a brilliant warmth seeped through my body from the Relic and I felt my eyes dilate as I nearly writhed in ecstasy. I shuddered as I felt the power within begin to unlock, bit by bit, like the grooves of a lock.

"Hollyn, you can't!" Archer whispered, his mouth open slightly in disbelief.

"Trust me," I breathed.

The duo's eyes returned to me, and I bit the inside of my cheek to regain composure.

"We can't let you leave here with it," Slade stated, his eyes hard like unbent steel. He outstretched his hand, palm up, his jaw set with determination.

I could feel my skin flush as my senses awakened, my eyes taking in colours I hadn't noticed before–the slight green hue

that encircled one of Slade's pupils, the streaks of silver and
navy that wove through Ryker's fur, the rosy kiss of Archer's
windburnt cheeks. I swallowed hard, trying to shove down the
overwhelming sensations, praying Slade didn't notice.

"Give it to me, Hollyn," Slade seethed through gritted teeth.
"Don't do this."

He cannot take us. We cannot let him.

My hand cupped the side of my head as whispers once again
pervaded my thoughts, intoxicating me with their promises and
desires. Shutting my eyes, I shook my head to try to banish them.

"No." Although I wasn't sure who I was responding to.
Maybe both.

When I opened my eyes again, I saw Slade's puzzled expression, the furrow of his golden brows as he scanned me from head
to toe. As his gaze rose back to meet my eyes, I could see him put
the pieces together. Saw the understanding wash over him.

He knew I was harnessing the magic.

Slade leaned forward, his hand outstretched, his eyes widely
opened, "Hollyn!"

Run.

The duo charged at us, Ryker's enormous fangs greeting me
as he closed the gap between us. It threw off my plan to run first,
and I scrambled to escape the clutches of that intimidating jaw.
My legs felt like jelly as I pushed off one foot then the other, my
body nearly useless with exhaustion.

I dashed towards Mal, the thundering of Ryker's paws following close behind. His hot breath blew on my neck as I was

tackled from my left, Slade's long body landing awkwardly on my chest, pinning me on my back.

I grimaced in pain, the breath knocked out of me from the impact, but I watched in amazement as Slade began to softly glow white, his sapphire eyes blazing and wide in surprise.

I felt what was happening before my mind could understand.

Like a vacuum, the Relic's magical warmth torrented through me, funnelling into Slade, his mouth agape as his stiff body consumed my magic, his hands gripped knuckle-white on my jacket.

I heard roars, snarling fangs snapping, growls of effort, but they sounded far in the distance. My vision blurred as tears began to well from the sheer magnitude of force passing through my body from the Relic to Slade. My eyes fell shut.

And then it stopped. Slade's weight lifted off me, and air filled my lungs as I gasped.

I blinked my eyes open to see Archer throwing Slade away from me and Knox, back in bear form, viciously grappling Ryker, snow and saliva spraying like geysers.

Get up. Now's our chance!

I rolled over to my side, lying but for a moment to get my bearings before I pulled myself to my wobbling feet. I took one last glance at Ryker and Knox, who were engrossed in their savage brawl, then turned my attention to Slade and Archer.

I saw Archer posed in his fighting stance, legs wide, knees bent, arms up to protect his face, and marvelled as I watched Slade roll onto his knees and rise.

He was standing.

Standing.

My mind nearly exploded at the miracle before me, as if I'd never truly fathomed the power of the holy magic. A part of me had remained sceptical of it, believing the stories had evolved more into tales of fiction than fact.

But his legs were healed, as evidenced by the graceful, experimental movements he tested; he swung his legs in all directions, bent his knees, and finished with a spinning roundhouse kick, his lean body looking so natural in the motions.

And I'd believed Ryker to be the physically formidable opponent. This guy was a master of his fighting form, and we had just restored his arsenal of weapons.

"Go!" Archer's eyes never left Slade as he craned his neck to release a crack before squaring up again.

"Archer—"

"*Go.*"

I bolted for Mal and Odette, not wanting to lose the chance Archer was creating for me. Behind me, I heard the grunts and thuds of Archer and Slade engaging in combat, my ears trying to decipher who landed which blow as I raced towards the women.

If just touching me healed Slade, then I need to reach Malachai.

Odette was glued to the spot, torn between her desire to help fight and her need to protect her frail lover. Once I dropped down beside Mal, whose breath was shallow but constant, her eyes fluttering in effort fighting an internal battle I could not see,

I released Odette. Her body shimmered as she flew towards the melee, her superhuman speed swift and powerful like a blast of wind.

I unzipped Mal's jacket and placed my hands on her wound, intending to focus the magic as quickly as possible. As soon as contact was made, I felt the crest of power surge through my fingertips that held the Relic, across my body, and down the hand placed softly on Mal's chest.

That same soft white glow highlighted Mal's body as her eyes snapped open, her back arching as the Relic showered her with its healing powers. I watched as the gaping, oozing wound began to fuse itself back together, like a knitter weaving threads. My breathing sped up and my eyes widened as I began to feel overwhelmed from facilitating the Relic's power.

Behind me a snarl of agony sounded, and I prayed it was not from one of our own.

Malachai lurched forward suddenly, breaking our connection, and I swayed backward from the movement.

"Th-thanks," she breathed, the colour flushing back into her face.

"Do you have enough strength to make the portal?" With a nod, she raised her hands as her mouth began mumbling incoherent words—I assumed the beginning of the portal spell.

I finally turned to see how the others had fared and gasped at the scene.

Archer groaned on his side, blood splattered all over as he cradled the giant gash on his arm, undoubtedly from the dual-bladed staff Slade now deftly wielded. *Where the hell did that come from?*

Odette's speed was outstanding as she charged Slade, who exerted tremendous effort as he tried to parry her barrage. It wasn't long before Odette had broken through Slade's defences, her punches landing audible grunts and gasps from him as blood began to sputter from his nose and lip, speckling red onto his furred coat.

But she was surprised by Ryker, who'd outmatched Knox briefly, his wolf fangs locking onto her calf, halting her attack.

Odette's head whipped back towards Mal, the only evidence of their telepathic conversation, before she slammed her elbow down on Ryker's snout, who whimpered in pain and released her. She then turned towards Slade and charged him, her furious fists landing blows to his gut before his human reflexes could offer a defence.

With one final blow, she uppercut Slade, his body flying back ten feet and landing on his back.

Ryker charged Odette with a fury intent on revenge for his partner's pain, but the forgotten Knox speared him, his giant bear head tucked down to slam into Ryker's undefended side, sending him flying back too. Knox roared powerfully, the sound rumbling across the plateau enough to shake the loose rocks within the cavern.

Racing to Archer, I helped shoulder his weight as we all dashed back to the cavern. Odette stopped briefly to pick up the unconscious man, carrying him back with us as Knox kept one last eye on the other two, still slowly rising to their feet.

When we reached the cave, we watched as Odette's outstretched hands fluttered, her mouth moving to join in on invoking the portal spell.

A ring of cobalt blue started to form, the neon glow cutting into the air like a knife slicing through pie. Each inch appeared in a trail of chasing light until the circle was completed, and a shimmery veil manifested inside. It crackled and flashed and almost blinked out.

"What's wrong?" I shouted over the noise. It didn't look or feel right.

"I don't think we have enough power," Mal responded. "We're going to have to hold it while you guys head through. It's not stable."

"Stop! Give me that Relic, Hollyn!" Slade was standing beside Ryker, but his voice sounded panicked. Scared, even. "If you don't, a lot of people will die!"

I didn't listen to his pleas. Domers didn't care about the deaths of anyone else.

We needed to head home. Now.

"Holls, help me!" Archer gestured urgently for me to grab the unconscious man, slipping from his injured grasp. We dragged him through the portal, the cool, gel-like texture rippling over our bodies as we entered the darkness.

I was still not used to the void; all my senses strained to sense anything, desperate to hear some noise, smell, some sound.

But it was over quickly, and we collapsed on the Silver Steppe, safely on the other side of the portal.

A deafening crackle in my ear prompted a shriek of pain. I wrenched the comms off me, the blue haze of portal magic clearly having caused some sort of malfunction. Archer followed suit.

Knox emerged from the void just moments after us, almost stumbling over our prone bodies. We rushed to stand up, Knox now naked in human form. He scooped up our stranger, and we waited tensely for the last two to follow.

A howl blasted from the peak of the mountain.

The ring crackled and blinked, no other sound or sight penetrating through.

It burst with light then disappeared, the low hum of energy gone.

"What's wrong? Where are they?!" Archer shouted.

"I-I don't know—they were coming right behind me!" Knox stuttered.

We huddled around, our next steps uncertain if the women didn't make it through.

"Should we go back?" I asked half-heartedly, knowing the safety of the Relic would trump any rescue mission.

"We'll give them a couple more minutes," Knox whispered softly, his brown eyes stormy with worry.

The former guardian beast groaned softly, and my anxiety skyrocketed. We couldn't let him wake up before we returned; his renewed hostility would be the straw that broke this mission's back. It'd be impossible to restrain him and drag him back to Dyrcsa.

I caught Archer's gaze, my worries reflected in his eyes. He still held his gouged arm, his hand cupping the injury that marred his tricep, and I felt a wash of guilt swallow me.

Guilt over my identity and the destruction it was creating in its wake.

Guilt over being the priority of the mission, of making Archer and the others expendable if need be.

Guilt over agreeing to work with Slade, of adding more danger to an already treacherous situation.

Before my mental state could collapse in shame and remorse, the portal tore back into existence, the neon glow brighter than a solar flare, forcing us to shield our eyes with our arms.

Malachai and Odette hurled out of the portal mid-jump, nearly crashing into us.

The ring sputtered, sounding as if the energy was overcharging, ready to blow, the light intensifying until, with a loud bang, it burst into nothingness.

Knox burst into laughter and picked up the women in a massive bear hug. "Oh thank God," he murmured as he squeezed and shook them back and forth.

"Put. Me. Down. You. Moose," Odette snarled with gritted teeth, her lungs crushing under Knox's embrace.

With a plop, he released them, apologising and sobering with the memory of Mal's injury. The urgency of getting home.

With a dull flicker and a low hum, the ring back to Dyrcsa turned on, like a waxing moon, inch by slow inch, adding to its length until it formed a complete halo.

A Battle of Kills

"Grandma!" I shrieked as I barreled through the portal. Our fears had come true. The Domers were invading Dyrcsa.

Gunfire rained down as bombs and other explosions obliterated all around us, debris spraying through the air like raindrops of sand and stone. The portal had brought us back to the heart of the city, but there was no attendant to greet us. A severe wind ripped through, whipping my hair into my face and blasting sand into my mouth and eyes. The magical shield that warded away the inhabitable climate seemed to have vanished, as the sandstorm intensified with each gust, gaining more and more momentum.

If we didn't die by Domer hands, we would die if we couldn't replace the wards in time.

I heard the sounds of warfare—the screams of agony, the cries for mercy, the shouts of rage—and flashbacks of O'Malley raids flooded me.

War did not shock me; I had seen death. But this carnage was on a whole other scale. Everywhere I looked, Domer soldiers were advancing. And in their wake, an entire culture was being massacred.

Assassinations occurred with the blink of an eye, the flick of a hand, the curl of fingers. A Druid was stuck, hesitating, between trying to save a family that cowered by his feet and answering the call for backup from another Druid struggling to keep a cluster of soldiers from advancing.

Walls of houses crumbled as buildings collapsed in on themselves, the shrieks of agony and panic muffled under mounds of sandstone. I trembled as I saw a mother fall to her knees, helplessly trying to move the rubble that now suffocated her trapped family underneath.

Bullets whizzed through the air, my hair whipping as too many came too close for comfort. Hiding behind upraised arms I could do nothing but watch the anarchy around me, gasping as another Druid was gunned down mercilessly from behind. The light from the flames incinerating the city peaked through the bullet holes that pierced through, before her body collapsed like a wet rag, her haunting eyes finding mine moments before wheezing her final breath.

Despite the Druids fighting heroically, they were no match for the pure evil the Domers, clad in their symbolically appropriate all black, brought forth. There were no pauses, no hesitations as Domer soldiers massacred every inch of the city. Children, the elderly, families were brutally slain all around me.

It seemed like we had landed right at the feet of the assault.

The hounds had arrived, their bloodlust rampant in the search for the Relic. *My* Relic.

I tried to make contact with Top Dog, but the comms only crackled and sputtered in response. Did the Portal fuck them up?

I looked to the others, who were rooted in place, as if we all debated joining the fray though we knew keeping the Relic safe was most important.

But I could not hide away and watch this city burn down around me. I would not.

I'd run for too long. Hidden for too long.

So without warning, I shed my cumbersome mountain gear, snatching the stun gun still holstered on Mal and ran towards the action, adrenaline pumping me towards death itself.

"Holls!" I heard Archer shout behind me, but I did not stop. I would not let them ruin another city. I heard Mal yell as I blazed towards the fight.

Droves of Domer soldiers advanced as they gunned down rebelling Dyrcsans and destroyed their homes. In the centre of each brigade, magic flew forth from a commander's fingers; tongues of flames licked across everything and everyone they touched, bolts of lightning erupted their targets with a deafening crack, spikes of jagged earth perforated unsuspecting victims. It appeared as though the O'Malleys were leading each group of soldiers, their armed guards surrounding them in protection.

Unless we could behead the snake, we would never be able to take down the units.

I could feel the powerful heat radiating from the buildings caught aflame, warming my face as I got closer, the torrential winds spreading the fire quickly. I spotted a few Druids caught between snuffing out flames with jets of water and knocking back advancing troops. But they were too close, and I watched, helplessly, as one Druid was incinerated into nothing more than charred bones and scorched rags.

The remaining Druids surrendered the burning buildings to turn their vengeance towards the troops, their geysers of water crystallising into honed icicles that impaled multiple soldiers within seconds. The troops could do nothing, the icicles far too slim to destroy by gunfire before they were pierced through.

One of the Druids paused, his arms outstretched as the glow of magic gathered around him, enlarging his icicle into a massive spear before shooting it forth and into the commander.

It impaled his chest, carrying him backward and staking into the ground. His limp body sagged against the spike—before the spear shattered, sending thousands of ice shrapnel outward, slicing and gashing the rest of his unit, soldiers dropping everywhere.

Perhaps the Druids can hold their own.

The building to my right exploded from within, and I was thrown into the building to my left. I felt every bone in my body crunch in pain. My neck ached from the whiplash. My ears rang from the deafening noise, my mind disoriented.

Familiar hands shook me alert, until my gaze focused on honey-coloured eyes. Archer's concerned face hovered over mine as he pulled me up and nearly dragged me out of there. We retreated through a back alley and into a different town square.

"The fuck are you doing!" he roared at me, his face red.

"I can't let these people die and do nothing!" I screamed back as I shoved him off me. "Where are the others?" My head whipped around, searching for the familiar dark braids of Odette or the massive frame of Knox.

"Mal and Knox took our captor back to the Compound, and Odette is battling another front. We need to get back to the Compound now, before another legion arrives," Archer insisted.

"Papi!" a little girl screamed as her father was restrained by roots bursting up from the ground, like nature's own handcuffs arresting a suspect. The roots twined around his wrists and feet as an extra-thick tuber wrapped around his neck, completely immobilising him.

It was the father and daughter I'd seen playing by the fountain when Archer and I met in town. I raced towards them, stun gun ready.

"G-go!" the man squeaked out before his oxygen was cut off, his face turning beet red with strain. The little girl's raven curls shook as she refused to leave him, her arms clutching her dolly in terror. She wet herself as another blast from a neighbouring building erupted.

"No!" I screamed as I dashed to the base of the roots. I cranked them with all the electricity the stun gun would allow, shredding through most of the vines. I grabbed a jagged rock from the ground and smashed the last few attached tentacles, a crunch telling me each of my swings connected with my intended targets. I hacked away until the father was finally released, and I watched the lopped-off portions disintegrate back into magic dust, the roots sucked back beneath the broken ground.

The man scooped up his petrified daughter, both weeping in relief. The father sobbed, "Thank you."

"We need to go!" I reminded them, before pointing them towards the Compound. "Go there, we will retreat there. Stay hidden, stay safe!"

"*We* need to retreat, Hollyn! Or all of this is for nothing!" Archer insisted as he caught up to me. I could see him considering dragging me if I didn't cooperate.

"I can heal people!" I argued.

Crash. A roof collapsed nearby as the insanity of war breathed down our necks.

"If anyone sees that Relic, you'll be captured within seconds! You cannot let them have it, Hollyn."

I knew he was right. I was more of a liability than a help out here, especially considering the precious cargo I carried.

"Then let's help as many wounded as we can back to the Compound, and I can heal them there," I offered as a compromise.

A shot rang out, and white-hot pain exploded through my stomach.

I didn't know what had happened until I saw Archer's expression of pure fear. The way his eyes dropped down to my stomach. The blanching of his face. The way his mouth hung open in disbelief.

I felt the warmth seep from my wound and wet my fingers. Darkness encroached on my peripherals as my mind felt thick and sluggish, like my thoughts had to swim through molasses to reach me.

A numbness had spread from my core, crawling out to cover every inch of my body.

My legs buckled and I fell backward into Archer's arms as he caught me in a crouch.

"No, no, no, no, no!" Archer placed a hand on my wound to try and stifle the blood, but it was futile, his hand covered and slick already from the blood spewing from me.

"Where's the Relic?!" he yelled, but my eyes were rolling backward, and I couldn't form words, my tongue too heavy to function. He frantically patted my pants and belt until he found it hidden safely in one of the pockets.

He ripped the zipper open. "Here. Here, just hold it. That's how it works, right?" He enclosed my fingers around the Relic, his warm hands wrapped around mine. "Right?! Dammit, Hollyn!"

Darkness called to me, peaceful slumber so enticing. I yearned to give in to it.

But then light filled me, chasing away its opposition.

My body writhed in pleasure as peace and hope and love and every other beautiful feeling flooded me. I was enveloped in toasty comfort—like a perfect summer day, the sun beating down on me.

I felt the familiar pull of magic from the Relic like before, but this time it remained within me, filling me up. It did not drain me; it gave me life.

I felt invincible.

I could feel the cells of my body weave back together, erasing the gaping hole in my abdomen, like time in reverse.

My eyes popped open as I snapped up to a seated position. Archer's face flooded with relief and love, like the threat of losing me again would have killed him. I looked at my upturned palms as if I could see the electricity surging through me. The power was almost impossible to contain.

The feeling was addictive.

The soldiers had closed in on us while I was down—I felt shots whiz past our heads.

Rage consumed me. *Kill them*, whispers counselled. *Make them pay.*

I turned to meet my enemies as I took in the annihilation they were creating. I saw the faces of the fleeing Dyrcsans, terror and panic sending them in frenzied sprints.

I watched Dhalina be dragged out of her house and shoved to her knees in preparation for execution, blood already gushing from a wound at the side of her head.

I looked on as women and children were engulfed in flames, asphyxiated by tentacles, gunned down from behind. One soldier was taunting a man, slowly impaling an icicle through his chest inch by inch. I saw another soldier rip open the bodice of a young mother, exposing her to everyone, her body flushing in embarrassment as the Domers groped and leered.

I watched that beautiful rainbow-coloured afghan ignite in flames, burning down to nothing more than ashes before being trampled by encroaching soldiers.

These people had welcomed me, without prejudice or suspicion. They had given freely to me, with no expectation of anything in return.

I had brought this to them. Had sentenced them to this fate when I had chosen to stay here.

And I lost it.

A shriek ripped from my throat as I channelled the energy inside me. A white shroud emerged around me as my hair lifted, the dirt around my feet levitating. Like a black hole, I drew energy from the Relic until it filled me to my limit and I knew I could not take in any more.

At the sight of my gathering magic, the soldiers all around us shifted their aim to me, their intended targets forgotten as I readied my assault.

They fired.

The bullets lodged into the white shield of light surrounding me and fell like dead flies to the ground.

They'd drawn first blood, and now they must die.

With another shriek, I shot my hands out, catapulting my magic at them.

Bursts of light ruptured in unison as multiple soldiers imploded. They splattered like crimson globs of paint, chunks of flesh littering the streets and buildings around them. One by one, soldiers evaporated within seconds, their screams of suffering drowning out the battle raging around us as my hands made quick work of every Domer I could see. I was a puppeteer, and every time my fingers twitched, another's fate ended.

A new commander emerged, her face ghostly white as she watched her unit disintegrate within seconds with no idea how to stop it. Dozens of her soldiers became nothing more than slabs of bloody flesh, splinters of bone, clumps of scorched hair.

I did not stop, aiming at every Domer I could spot. I channelled my anguish into every explosion that barraged the enemy unit.

Decades of misery, of hatred towards the Domers, poured out of me, supercharging every ripple of holy magic that I detonated inside of them.

There was no stopping me, my emotions overrun and impossible to choke down.

I was seeing red, each eruption only feeding into my bloodlust.

Nobody was safe.

More soldiers came out from Dyrcsan homes, drawn to the sound of the explosive light magic, only to fall prey to my hands. They were shredded and blown apart before they could escape.

The commander finally jumped into action, blasting flames at me, but my shield was impenetrable.

I felt my body begin to tire, unaccustomed to channelling energy of this magnitude. My core was piping hot, burning from invoking the magic, as I edged my body's limit. But there were still a few more.

I could not let them live.

I saved the last bit of magic my body could handle for the commander.

I turned my attention towards her. I revelled as I made her eyes bulge and her mouth open, my brilliant white light beaming out of her as I envisioned her burning from the inside out. I pictured her blood boiling from the heat.

Her body steamed as her bones broke down, melting in the lava torrenting inside her. Her face drooped, the skin dissolving, and her bloodcurdling screams began to gurgle. Her fatigues and bulletproof vest caught ablaze until the licks of fire reached her hair, singeing her tied-back locks, until nothing but a bloody scalp remained. Her bones liquefied and her body collapsed into a steaming, oozing puddle.

I fell to my knees, gasping for air, my body unable to harness any more power. I felt empty without it, but Archer's hands pulled me to my feet and rushed me back towards the Compound before another unit reached us.

The smell of charred flesh gagged me as we escaped; the stillness after was haunting.

I shoved the Relic back into my pocket, not sure if I ever wanted to invoke its power again. I had felt immortal. But I had also felt insatiable in my need to execute everyone. *Could I have stopped myself?*

Blasts continued to rang out in the near distance, and I knew despite halting some, there were still too many Domers advancing to stop. Archer nearly dragged me as my body stumbled and stuttered trying to find the energy to keep up.

Finally, I caught a glimpse of the portal to the Compound and nearly cried as I put everything I had left into reaching our goal.

But as we neared, I noticed an odd hum that echoed and narrowed my eyes when I realized the portal was flickering unsteadily. Something was wrong.

"Have they reached the Compound already?" I suddenly had a feeling of lead in the pit of my stomach. A cold sweat broke out over my upper lip. If the Domers had already gotten into the Compound...

Look Who's Shocking

Our boots jumped the concrete front steps three at a time, our arms pumping to propel us as quickly as possible. Blood streaks, scorch marks, and gun holes throughout the hallway painted a picture of a brutal battle, a tapestry of artillery and magic aftereffects–all signs that the Domers had already reached the Compound. *Is this our last stand? How are they already here?*

I had only stopped one unit. One of many, I began to realise soberly.

The corridor lined with rooms that I walked through for the first time just a few days earlier now stood empty and dark, the lights smashed, our boots crunching the shards of glass littering the floor.

We took quick, silent strides, both of our bodies falling into a standing crouch, ready for anything. Some of the doors were hanging suspended by only one hinge. Some of the rooms looked ransacked, the beds upturned violently. I spied the lab where Mal had watched me, those violet eyes assessing me with her scientific mind. No scientists remained, most of the equipment shattered, doors and safes unlocked and rummaged through.

Are they looking for something?

The safe against the back wall of the lab was open, last wisps of liquid nitrogen leaking out. Slots big enough for what might have been test tubes were now empty. One of the lights above us flickered, the last vestiges of power trying to relight, but with a sudden crackle and flash, it gasped its last breath.

"They're already inside," Archer confirmed our worries, as if I couldn't see the evidence myself. "Where's Top Dog?" His brows furrowed in confusion. I could see the worry in his eyes, and I wondered if he was contemplating if Top Dog had abandoned them.

I definitely wondered about it. She was tasked with protecting this city and was nowhere to be seen. *Did she leave them to die?*

"We need to find her too," I nodded vigorously. She needed to explain how this happened.

Leaving the lab, we raced towards the end of the hallway, not wanting to risk any more delays in finding Grandma. If they were already inside... I shuddered, refusing to allow my mind to go any further. I wouldn't give up on her, not now that I was so close.

Just as our hands reached for the exit, the entrance behind us blasted open, the door ripping off its hinges and slamming against the wall.

"Don't move."

We slowly turned around to face our newest enemies. A unit of soldiers filed in, the commander a beastly man with pock-marks all over his face. His greasy hair was combed back and his thick moustache hid his thin upper lip. He had forgone sleeves, instead preferring to showcase his massive corded arms.

"Biggs, Wyatt, seize them," he ordered two of his lackeys. Two men clad in all black advanced towards us, their guns poised and ready for us to make a mistake.

I dared not risk anything as I wasn't confident I could invoke the Relic magic again. I might be willing to risk my life, but I would not risk Archer's.

So they advanced on us until they were tying our hands behind our backs with ZipTags, our weapons seized. They shoved us forward, forcing us to head back to their commander. We had no choice but to obey.

"Pretty little thing, isn't she?" the commander observed as he trailed his fingers down the side of my face, before grabbing my jaw and wrenching my head from side to side. He looked me over far too thoroughly, like a farmer inspecting his prized mare.

Archer bucked in anger.

"Oh, looks like I struck a chord," the commander mused. He punched me in the gut, and I doubled over in pain as he slammed into my freshly healed gun wound. My eyes saw stars as I sputtered for breath between gasps of agony. Archer tried to wrench free in fury, but to no avail. He spat at the commander.

"Looks like you didn't learn." He backhanded my face and my mouth sprayed blood. Pain exploded from my jaw and bolted down my neck. Already my cheek felt inflamed, and I blinked away the tears filling my eyes.

Archer stilled himself to avoid further provocation.

"Good dog."

The commander's massive hands perched on his hips as he roared in laughter, madness gleaming in his eyes. The other soldiers soon joined in—they seemed scared to not follow along.

I spat blood on his boot. "Fuck you."

Immediately his hand gripped my throat, his lip curling in rage, until I gasped and writhed as he crushed my windpipe. "You need to learn when to keep your mouth shut, bitch." My hands struggled against the plastic binds, my wrists burning. Another punch to my stomach, and I nearly blacked out, regretting my choice.

"Maybe I will show you a better use for that pretty mouth of yours." His hand gripped my jaw painfully as he yanked me towards him, my neck cracking in pain. He crushed my lips with a painful kiss, his stubble shredding my windburnt lips. I could taste nothing but cigarette smoke and whisky, almost gagging.

Before I could, he shoved me away. "Nah, you'd like that too much, wouldn't you, you slut." The pack of hyenas joined him in laughter.

But their merriment was cut short when a tidal wave of water crashed over all of us, washing us down the hall.

I bobbed underwater, my inability to swim mixed with my restraints a recipe for disaster. My legs flailed instinctively to try and bring me to the surface as Archer and I floated down the hallway and crashed into the back door. The wave disappeared as quickly as it came, water escaping through the door rapidly, and I sputtered remnants out of my lungs as I lay drenched on the floor.

"Get them!" I heard the large asshole bark.

I heard a snap and saw that Archer had cut open his restraints on a piece of metal jutting out from the edge of the door. "Quickly!" His hurried hand waved me over, and in seconds I sawed through my own ZipTags. I rolled my wrists in appreciation of their freedom, burns already marking where the ties had rubbed against my skin.

A small group of Druids and Mutts had filled the entrance behind us, catching the enemy by surprise. And in the middle was Top Dog, her hands out in front of her as she invoked another element for a follow-up attack. She led her Druids in an incantation, and in seconds a fire snake blazed into existence, its tongue crackling and hissing in ravaged hunger. Groans emitted from the water soaked soldiers strewn around the hallway as they struggled to upright themselves, but Top Dog didn't wait for their recovery, seizing the element of surprise.

The magic-wielders focused, their arms outstretched towards the flamed viper, each of them funnelling more magic into it until multiple heads burst forth, becoming a hydra.

"Three... Two... One!" Top Dog bellowed, and their hands came together in prayer, their heads bowing briefly, before they curled their hands into fists.

With a shriek the blazing beast erupted outward, each of its heads shooting toward a soldier. We heard the blood curdling screams, the crackle of their outfits and gear melting and disintegrating before the hydra burst into flames and disappeared behind a wall of smoke.

I sighed in relief as the grey cleared away.

But to our horror the commander remained, his sleeveless arms the colour of liquid metal. He withstood the monster, his physical powers morphing his skin into some type of heat-resistant metal.

Top Dog called to her soldiers to ready again. The commander belly-laughed, shaking his head.

"You've had your fun—now it's my turn." And in a blink, he'd closed the gap between them, his metal fists grabbing Top Dog by the lapels and lifting her off her feet. He rammed a metal fist at her helmet multiple times in quick succession, shattering the front.

Her Druids gathered electric energy between their palms.

"I will snap her neck," the Domer threatened. Top Dog shook her head at them.

"Where is the Relic?" he demanded.

Top Dog remained silent, so the brute shook her violently. "I will ask only one more time. Where. Is. It."

"You... forget..." she squeaked out, her jacket choking her as she hung in midair, reeling from the punches.

He rolled his eyes, confident in his invincibility. "And what have I forgotten?"

"Metal... conducts... electricity." She placed both hands on his temples, her body cracking with electricity as she poured it all through his skull, his body seizing from the amps flowing through him.

My ears heard him drop to the ground before my eyes readjusted from the dazzling radiance. Smoke wisped from his body, now slumped on the hallway floor with the others.

We strode over to Top Dog, already ordering some of her people to head back out into the fray and enlisting others in gathering the remaining survivors that hadn't found refuge inside the Compound yet. I overheard Top Dog tell a subordinate, "That should be all of them."

I let loose a huge breath I didn't know I was holding in. If Top Dog said the Compound was safe again, then my grandma would be, too.

I can go check on Grandma and then help fight.

Archer tried to thank Top Dog, but her back was to us, her focus still on delegating her people. After clearing his throat he tried again. "How can we help?"

She looked over her shoulder at us briefly, and I noticed the hole in her helmet was not big enough for me to see her face entirely. "You can help with reinforcing these walls and doors. We make our last stand here."

Archer and I nodded at each other, our next mission set.

"Not you, Hollyn."

I opened my mouth to protest, but she interrupted me. "You need to protect your grandma. You will be no help with your mind distracted by her wellbeing."

"Is-is she okay?!" I hadn't thought that maybe soldiers had already reached her room and my body tensed.

"Yes. For now."

I closed my eyes briefly in relief, nodding, "Let me check that she's okay, then I'll come back and help. That should be enough time for my mag—"

Top Dog whirled to face me, only her hazel eyes visible, but flashing in rage. "What do you mean? Enough time for your what?"

I took a slight step back, startled. "I-I can help people, heal them—"

"Did you put the Relic together?!" The whites of Top Dog's eyeballs shone through the darkness of her cracked helmet, her voice harsh with anger. "What did I say? You were specifically ordered *not* to do that! You don't know what kind of risks—"

"We had to. Mal was hurt... badly and—"

"I explicitly said not to put it together!" she roared.

"We had no choice!" Archer defended me, his hand placed protectively on my chest.

"Do you know what could have happened?!" Top Dog closed the gap between us, her hands gripping my shoulders hard, "We have *no* idea the magnitude of this magic! What damage it could have caused!"

I shrugged off her hands, "I couldn't sit there and let her *die*." Stepping forward so that my face was inches from those angry hazel eyes, my arms curled into fists at my side. "Is that what you would have wanted?!"

She huffed, staring me down from behind her distorted mask, before turning her head away in frustrated defeat. But she whipped back just a moment later, her palm open. "Give the Relic to me now then. At least we can minimize whatever else may come."

I furrowed my brows, suspicion creeping up my spine. "No."

"Hollyn, we need to keep it stowed away safely."

"Then it stays with me."

A pause again, this time a bit longer. Assessing her options of how this would play out, I assumed. I was rigid in defiance, staring down my nose at her, silently challenging her to dare take it from me.

"I could just strike you down here and steal it from you," Top Dog stated coldly.

I rolled my shoulders back, grabbing the Relic from its pocket, willing the magic to reemerge in me, begging and pleading for its comforting warmth to flood me once again.

Just to show her that I was not to be fucked with.

I concentrated on that magical feeling, on welcoming it back into me, in visualising the Relic once again illuminating in power, and I chuckled when I felt the initial crests of its strength torrent through my body. Through my very veins.

Strands of my hair hovered in weightlessness, the alabaster shimmering veil fabricating around me like the translucent wings of an angel. "Fucking try it," I snarled.

The air around us was heavy with tension, all activity ceasing as nobody dared interrupt our power struggle. From the stories Archer had told me, no one had ever challenged Top Dog so openly like this, her iron fist ruthless. She did not allow such open insubordination, but I no longer feared her.

With that power surging through me, I feared nothing.

To our surprise, Top Dog started to chuckle softly, crescendoing until she bucked her head back into full belly-laughing. Her raspy laugh continued on for a minute, until she finally calmed down, settling her attention back on me.

Her hands raised to each side of her helmet and tugged until they pulled it off.

Brilliant russet curls cascaded down her back, stopping just below her armpits. Hazel eyes, flecked with streaks of gold, were encased with long, dark eyelashes, her straight eyebrows slanted slightly upward like a bird's open wings.

Soft freckles splattered her nose, cheeks, and forehead. Freckles just like mine, that appeared during the long summer days of sunshine.

Hair made of copper, like my grandma used to tell me.

"I guess you really are my daughter after all."

Be in for a Block

I stared, dumbfounded, at the striking woman in front of me. Who shared so many similar features.

My *mother*.

Physically, it couldn't be doubted. I saw Archer's head whip back and forth between us, comparing and contrasting the insane claim.

"You're probably wondering why I didn't say anything earlier," she mused, her expression scrunched in regret, guilt even.

Words escaped me.

Top Dog paced back and forth, her hands animating wildly to emphasize her story, "I had to be sure... I've... had quite a few rumours surrounding your identity. People who've pretended to be you, hoping to win my favour to try and infiltrate our ranks and destroy us from the inside out. People who have tried to blackmail me." She paused, her boots squeaking as she twisted to face me, now rooted in spot. There was a coldness to her expression, an emotional detachment to her.

"You'll have to excuse me if at first I didn't believe who you were. Who Archer had said you were." Top Dog nodded toward him, her arms crossed. "Despite how similar we look, I've had people use glamours before to try to convince me. I've been burned too many times."

What was that expression? Fool me once, shame on you, fool me twice, shame on me?

Turning to face Archer I asked, "Did you know?" My gut wrenched as I waited for his answer, praying he hadn't. That he hadn't kept this from me. Not another secret.

If he had, this would finish us. I could not stop that.

He shook his head vehemently, "No!" And I could tell from the bewilderment on his face he was just as shocked over this as I. I nodded after a moment, accepting his answer.

"I keep my identity hidden," Top Dog affirmed, her hands circling in front of her face. "Nobody has seen my face for a long time. You can understand the target I have on my back."

I let loose a ragged breath. I didn't think I could have handled another betrayal.

"How—But when did—so you're—" I huffed in frustration as so many questions whipped through my mind I couldn't formulate one entirely.

A small smile, her hand patting against her chest, "My story is long, but I will give you the points you deserve to know right now and save the rest for another time when we're not under siege." A distant explosion rattled as if on cue. "Your father—your real father—and I were lovers doomed from the start. He was a Dufort, I was an O'Malley. We fell in love hard and fast, something that was illegal—the union of two magical bloodlines. As you know, Edinguard survives on the precipice of mutually assured destruction, and two bloodlines coming together like that... well, they feared the power that a child from a union like that could have." She stared off to my right, her eyes glazed, lost in memories of forbidden love.

"But we couldn't keep away from each other—like two magnets, we were drawn to each other, and nothing could stop us." She refocused on me, as her cheeks flushed slightly. "So we met in secret, our passion burning brighter with each meeting, until before long I was pregnant. With you." She rubbed her belly in memory, her head hanging down to look in fondness.

After a moment, she seemed to remember herself, straightening up and dropping her hand, "I knew they would hunt you down if they found out. Knew that we couldn't stop the wrath of the Domers, the paranoia ugly and vicious even among our own kin. So I ran away... from your father, from Edinguard, from all of it. I nearly died making my way to Dyrcsa, but they took me in as one of their own, protecting me until I gave birth to you."

I inhaled sharply, surprised to hear she had snuck us out. That I hadn't been abandoned from the start.

She stepped tentatively towards me until I could see the flecks of gold in her hazel eyes, "But I feared that as long as you were with me, you would never be safe. And I couldn't curse you with a life like that." She stretched out a hesitant hand to cup my face. I recoiled slightly, the gesture strange, both of us unaccustomed to the maternal motion. She dropped her hand back down, disappointment streaking across her face before turning away from me.

"So I brought you back to Edinguard, and... left you with Victor, his wife, and her mother. I told them who you were, what it meant. The wife felt for you and agreed to look after you until I could come back. I couldn't afford to leave you with anyone who was tied to me. I knew they had learned of my escape, so I figured they would never look for you right under their noses in Edinguard."

She chose Victor? My hands rubbed along my thighs as I recounted the scars that marred my limbs, scars caused by Victor. My mother let this happen to me?

I shook my head in disbelief, certain Top Dog must be mistaken, "My mom died in childbirth." I couldn't believe my own mother would think I was safer away from her.

Top Dog turned sharply toward me, "I very much did not. That's just the story we created to sever any ties to your father and me."

My hands came to my hips, my brows furrowed, "But I have pictures of my mother. We have the same red hair—family hair, my father told me."

"He is not your father, girl," she spat. *Who is my father? Is he alive?* I was desperate to ask these questions, but Top Dog continued on. "We went to great lengths, altered every document we could to support our story, to hide our tracks. We specifically found another woman with our hair colour, just to sell it." Forged records, just like what Slade had discovered.

I swayed as dizziness threatened to swarm me. My hands clasped each other to wring in distress from the anxiety building within me. Another secret. Another level of deception.

I was staring into the eyes of my mother—who had abandoned me, had never come back for me. The shock that had fogged my brain was beginning to clear as feelings of hurt and anger burned through.

One hand cupped my forehead as the other wildly flailed. "I'm sorry, but am I supposed to believe I just happened to join a rebellion group that is led by my long-lost *mother?* That I was left for twenty-six years with an abusive drunk in order to *keep me safe*?!" I guffawed in hysteria, the story sounding even more insane out loud. "I-I can't fucking do this right now."

I backpedalled a few more steps, my body creating space, as if to protect my mental state from its impending breakdown. "I'm going to my grandma... I—I mean—when the fuck were you going to tell me?"

"When I could be sure. When the time was right." She responded matter-of-factly, as if we were discussing something as impersonal as deciding what to eat for dinner.

"Did you know how much I suffered?" Tears welled in the corner of my eyes as I stood my ground. "Did you ever check on me? Do you know what he used to do to me? Over and over."

I couldn't stop the anger bubbling over inside. Tumultuous emotions raged and clashed through me—shock, hope, anger, frustration, abandonment.

"I didn't know... he wasn't an alcoholic then. They seemed happy."

"So you just left me?! Abandoned me, never—never checking on how I was doing? Do you understand what that did to me? I spent my entire life feeling unworthy of love, because you left me with that asshole." I could barely see through the gush of tears filling my eyes, streaming down my face.

"I couldn't contact you or else I'd risk the O'Malleys finding you—"

"Well they did anyway. And I was completely fucking unprepared for it. You think I wouldn't have rather had my mother with me?!"

"I... fucked up. I admit that. It was so hard to give you up, I hope you know—"

"But I don't know that. All I know is that my mother abandoned me. Left me with a horrible person, and left me completely ignorant of any of the truth about who I am, *what* I am." My mind reeled, my hands going to my head as I shook it, the throes of a panic attack threatening to consume me. "I could have *died*. I've struggled for so long just to get enough food on the table." So many excuses spewing out from her mouth made me sick.

A hesitant step forward, one arm outstretched towards me, before she changed her mind and dropped it. "I'm sorry it turned out this way, I was young and didn't know what else I could do. I wanted to keep you safe the only way I knew how."

"You had my entire life to come back for me. I was worth it... I *am* worth it." My teeth gritted as years of pain poured out. "My grandma did more for me than you've ever done. And I'm not even related to her. *She* gave me the love I never got from you. The love I needed and deserved."

Pain wrenched her face, "I should have come for you sooner, you're right."

I spat at her feet, wishing my saliva were acid that would burn her toes right off.

Another blast rattled the Compound, but this time it came from up ahead, beyond the door.

From up near the medical bay.

Grandma.

I turned towards Archer, quickly reminded of my true purpose. I wasn't going to let this new information, as earth-shattering as it was, prevent me from protecting my family.

And Grandma *was* my family—the only true familial figure that had been there for me. Even if we did not share blood, she'd raised me as her own. She had been there for me my whole life.

"I will kill you if you try to stop me from going to her," I warned Top Dog and was surprised to realise I spoke the truth. I felt no maternal loyalty to her, and if I had to choose between them both, I'd pick Grandma every time.

Top Dog hesitated, uncertainty flecking in her eyes as she took me in, the Relic held in my ironclad grip. She didn't know my true powers, but I silently dared her to find out. With a nod, she looked away, and Archer took my arm, steering me towards the exit.

I stared at Archer as we approached the doors, tenderness welling up toward him. Despite having worked under Top Dog for a while, in that singular gesture, he declared his loyalty to me.

He chose me over her.

Maybe one day there wouldn't be a choice, but for now, he was acknowledging my emotions were valid, without a word letting everyone know I came first—not this job.

And I truly loved him for that.

My family: Grandma and Archer. They were who mattered, who I needed to protect.

With one last glance at my mother, who watched us, frozen in place, conflicting emotions of pain, anger, frustration, and sadness painted on her face, the door swished open and we headed out towards the medical bay.

But smoke choked us as we headed down the corridor, screams echoing from around the corner.

We slammed our backs against the wall perpendicular to the bend, doing our best to hide ourselves within the shadows as we listened for what stood between us and Grandma.

"Sir? There's another one here. He may be in a coma."

"Take him as a hostage. He must be important if they're holding him here."

"Yes, sir." I heard a fist slam against someone's chest in salute.

"How do we get past them?" Archer whispered. I shook my head, unsure—they were close to Grandma's room, advancing this way.

They must have infiltrated the Compound from the rear.

The stomping of their boots reverberated down towards us, each step looming closer, sounds of thrashing and clashing as they systematically ransacked each room one by one.

"Here you are."

I heard my grandmother scream.

I barrelled around the corner, pragmatism be damned, to come face to face with a small unit of soldiers, all in black uniforms, who whipped their guns towards me, shouting to halt immediately. My legs shuffled to a stop as I watched a bald middle-aged man with a goatee, clad in an all-black suit, drag her out of her room by her shoulder-length grey bob.

Her nightgown billowed below her, her thin fingers scratching at the unforgiving hands nearly ripping the hair out of her scalp. Her eyes squinted shut in torment, her feet stumbling to gain a foothold.

I knew this bald man—he'd been the one leading the attack when we narrowly escaped Edinguard.

"Don't fucking move!" one of the nameless soldiers warned me, and I raised my hands in peace, signalling for Archer to also stop in his tracks. I restrained myself from yelling to her, not wanting to give them the knowledge of our relationship, if they hadn't already connected us.

"We've been looking for you, Hollyn." His deep voice rumbled, lacking any shred of warmth. He held up his hand, palm facing upward, and a blazing orb popped into existence.

The man from Edinguard. Bryce?

"Why does it seem like if I do... this..." He held the fiery ball against my grandmother's veiny, translucent arm, charring her skin as she writhed in agony, her eyes and mouth gaping open like a fish out of water. "I will get what I want?"

"Don't you fucking touch her!" I screamed. I saw Archer's body buckle in barely constrained rage in my peripherals—she was family to him as well.

"Like this?" he teased me with an evil smirk, this time pressing the blazes against her liver-spotted chest. Grandma's eyes rolled back into her head, and my body jerked towards her, terrified for her, as I shrieked in anguish. I knew the signs.

If she gets hit again, she'll have another episode.

"Okay! Stop! Stop... What do you want?" I bided my time as my brain tried to concoct a plan of extraction and escape. I knew what they wanted.

Bryce rolled his eyes melodramatically, as if acting on a stage, the ending of this scene already written to his inevitable win. "Don't act stupid. The Relic."

I debated whether I should try to draw on the Relic's power again, but the magic felt quiet. Too quiet, after I had peacocked at my mother. I didn't know if I could invoke it quickly enough to free her before they could attack. I couldn't risk aggravating Bryce with my grandmother's life hanging in his clutches.

I could try to draw out this interaction, hoping backup would arrive in time. But there was no guarantee of anyone coming, or of the backup having enough power to help. My mind whirred through all the possibilities, but nothing guaranteed her safety.

I looked at Archer, whose helpless expression mirrored my own. He couldn't help, either, held at gunpoint.

My best chance was to hand over the Relic.

Bryce's face hardened over my too long hesitation. "Don't play coy with me, bitch. Hand it over, or the next time my ball of fun will meet her face." His leather-gloved hands flicked towards me, and the soldier nearest him headed in my direction, his gun targeted directly at my forehead.

"Don't do it... honey..." Grandma sputtered out before the man backhanded her into silence.

"No!" I shrieked, running towards her, but the soldier in front of me moved to grab my shoulders. My body remembered its brief training under Ryker, and instinctively I grabbed his arm, yanking him over me as I pivoted my feet, my other hand slamming down onto his elbow.

With a thud and a grunt, the soldier buckled before me. Immediately, I wrapped my arms around his neck from behind, just as I had done to Archer in the ring, and I began to choke him out.

"I'll kill him, I swear!" I threatened the bald man. My throat felt hoarse.

Gasps trailed up from the soldier, his hands scrambling to dig space to breathe.

The bald man thought for a moment, then shrugged in acceptance.

I baulked at his nonchalance—he didn't care whether his soldier lived or died. I threw the man away, not willing to kill senselessly, the threat useless anyway. I took another couple steps before the other soldiers raised their weapons at me, and I stopped dead in my tracks.

I couldn't help her if I was dead, and I didn't know whether the Relic would be able to keep me alive—or worse, bring me back from the dead.

So I watched, helplessly, as my grandmother began to flail, subtly at first, like the tremors from chills, and the suited man turned to watch her in disgust, unaware of what was starting. Waves of violent quaking overtook her nervous system, her body uncontrollable as her eyes rolled back completely, until nothing but the haunting whites stared back. The sudden movements surprised her captor, who released her, letting her body drop to the ground—which slammed her head against the pearly tiled floor. Blood pooled slowly from behind her head as her mouth filled with foam, her hands folded rigidly against her chest.

Blood kept gathering, her body now splashing in the puddle.

"Please! Let me help her, I'll give it to you after." I was willing to bargain everything away at this point.

"Before," he responded, completely undisturbed by the sounds of impending death escaping my grandmother.

"I need it to heal her!" I hollered back. "*Please!*" I dug my nails into my hands and felt the skin break.

Still her body contorted just as violently, no signs of the episode slowing down. I once read that it took mere minutes before a seizure could cause permanent brain damage.

"Hollyn! You–" Archer was cut off as another soldier bound and gagged him. I searched his face, trying to figure out what he was going to say. Hand it over? Don't?

"Don't care. Give it to me or we watch her die. Then I kill you and take it from your dead body." He smiled menacingly at me, gathering pleasure from my misery.

I whimpered as I realised I was backed into a corner with no way out. "Promise me I can heal her."

"Tick, tock. Tick, tock." His smile was purely evil as he wagged his finger back and forth like the arm of a grandfather clock.

"Okay! Okay." Tears welled in my eyes and my cheeks flushed. I knew I was choosing for my own needs, but my resolve crumbled with each convulsion of Grandma's body.

I rummaged in my pocket, retrieving the Relic to hand over to the soldier in my face. It plunked into his hand, my fingers lingering before I released it.

The soldier wrapped his fingers around it and headed back towards his leader, and I raced to my grandmother's side, offering what little comfort I could while she lived through this nightmare. I had no medicine left to give her, no tea or tonics either. But perhaps I could help her through it, comfort her through the pain.

"Please, bring it to me, I just need a few minutes. You can guard it. Please!" I begged the bald man.

"Hmm... nah." He turned away, before calling over his shoulder to his grunts. "Oh and kill them. It's getting... gross." He curled his lip in distaste.

"You fucking bastard!!" I shrieked at his back before the barrel of a machine gun stared down at me.

This was it, I admitted to myself.

I've failed everyone.

I closed my eyes, accepting my fate.

I heard my grandma's body quell into stillness, the shallow labouring of her breath barely perceptible. I grasped her cool hand, finding some peace in being by her side in the end.

The metal jostled in the soldier's hand as his finger pulled the trigger.

Dead Gran Walking

It detonated in a brilliant explosion, like a supernova combusting in the night sky, the energy violently tossing everyone in the room.

Click. Click. Click.

I heard multiple bullets release from the cartridge.

I waited for the darkness, the nothingness, the afterlife, but it didn't come.

I opened one eye to find the bullets hovering inches from my head, twirling but stuck, spinning as if in invisible molasses.

I heard the howl of an unleashed beast, finally released from its cage, ready to sink its teeth into everything in its path.

I saw Odette flying through the air as she landed on one of the soldiers, her face the picture of insanity as she savagely bit a soldier's nose clean off. Blood sprayed all over her face as she spit the discarded chunk onto the floor, leaving the soldier to sink to his knees in shock as he slowly lost consciousness. She immediately shielded herself in diamond-like skin to protect from the fire the bald man shot at her. She batted the attack away effortlessly.

The bullets hovering in my face suddenly shot back towards my executor, piercing his chest and head. He dropped, dead within seconds.

Stand up—move! Mal's voice sounded in my head.

But my body seemed frozen in place next to my grandmother, my eyes tracking the fight around me as I clutched her hand. Behind Odette, a huge tiger barrelled down the hallway and catapulted himself into the air, his ferocious, predatory jaws sinking into another soldier. *Knox.* The man's scream bubbled as blood filled his mouth, his body crunching beneath the sheer weight of Knox in his big cat form.

A bullet grazed the tiger's side and he roared in pain. My head whipped to see a now unbound Archer tackle the culprit before he could finish Knox off, and they slammed into the wall. Odette moved to assist him, and I finally snapped out of my stupor.

I searched for the bald man—his lips were flying and I realised he was invoking a spell. I rose to chase after him, but he released his power before I could catch him.

My hands grasped at my throat as I gasped for air.

Each of us stumbled down, the oxygen draining from our lungs. Even nearly invincible Odette could not defend herself against it.

I wheezed and rasped as my lungs began to burn, panic shooting through my body, my nerves fraying as my mind freaked out. My grandma's laboured breathing choked off, the gaps between gasps for breath getting longer. Too long.

But I was immobile, rooted in my own agony.

Mal raised her hand as she shakily attempted to levitate one of the discarded guns, slowly rotating it towards the bald man. But he *tsked* at her and crunched his hands together, choking us further until Mal dropped the gun.

I saw stars as darkness invaded my peripherals.

An invisible wall of air whipped through the corridor, knocking him off balance just enough to release the grip he held over us. Top Dog strode around the corner.

I gasped a raggedy breath, my mouth gaping open, trying to take in as much oxygen as humanly possible.

"Leave them alone, Bryce!" she growled at the bald man, her palms sparking with electric energy. So it was him.

"Oh... Cousin Eleanor. Such a displeasure to see you," he sneered at her.

Eleanor... E?

My eyebrows shot up in surprise. She'd said she was an O'Malley, but this confirmed her story. The idea that the two of them shared blood filled me with unease—Bryce was evil incarnate.

Then—are we related? The thought was horrifying.

"You're surrounded. Give it up and maybe I will spare you," Top Dog ordered, her jaw set, no love in those hazel eyes. "Or maybe I'll kill you." She ripped electricity towards him, but he deftly blocked the attack with his own shield of impenetrable air.

Odette had snuck up on Bryce in the meantime, but as her first punch connected, the contact shot her flying back as his wall suddenly electrified.

"Try that shit again, bitch, and I will kill every one of you." The arrogance was gone from Bryce's face now, pure hatred in its place.

"Give me the Relic. Please!" I hoped he would concede, but deep down I knew my effort was futile. He would die before he'd hand it back.

But I only had a few more moments before it was too late. "Please!" I shrieked at him again, tears streaming down my face.

How could I have been so stupid in handing it over? What have I done?

"Ha! You idiot. Such a dumb little girl, all for your geriatric, dying grandma." He barked with laughter as my cheeks flushed in embarrassment. I'd chosen my own needs over everyone else's, and he was twisting the knife deep into that fresh wound.

"The O'Malleys will never be able to use it. Your mission is useless," Top Dog exclaimed.

"Well, my dear cousin, that's why we also came for *this*." Bryce pulled out a test tube of dark navy liquid, and I wondered if that was what had been in the safe inside the lab.

My mother gritted her teeth, her eyes seething with anger at him. Puzzled, I looked between the others, not understanding what importance the vial held. Only Archer looked as confused as I.

Bryce must have noticed my look of bewilderment as he smiled evilly at Top Dog again. "What? You didn't tell her? That you've been testing ways to extract singular magical compounds from inanimate objects so you would be able to harness the holy power yourself? Oops, my big mouth." He hovered a hand before his mouth in comically exaggerated surprise, evidently relishing being the bearer of this news.

I caught Mal's eyes, briefly, before she cast them down in guilt.

Are they trying to take my magic from me?

Bryce followed my gaze, and his eyebrows lifted in surprise as he crooned, "Malachai. So lovely to see you again. How much you look like your sister... only uglier."

If looks could kill, Bryce would have died tenfold from the look Mal levelled at him.

He turned his venomous attention back towards me, his gloved hands drumming against his mouth. "Unfortunately, I cannot, in good conscience, let a known living Dufort remain alive. That's a variable we just simply will not risk."

Maintaining his shield, he let loose in an inferno that blasted us back. The fiery storm scorched my forearms, protectively raised in front of my head, the heat charring chunks of my hair and skin off. I screeched in agony as I felt layers of skin incinerated.

I heard Archer's scream echo mine, my skin bubbling as the blaze reached my face. My cheeks burned, and I could feel the skin cells die as the extreme heat swallowed one side of my face. My throat ached from the screams that ripped from me, the pain so blinding I wished I were dead.

I felt one of my eyes engulfed in the flames, and suddenly I lost vision in it. Whimpering, I sank to my knees, the torture so intense I could do nothing but scream and twitch.

Blissfully, another tsunami crested through the hallway, this time gentle enough it didn't wash me away. The cold water extinguished the flames, soothing the charred skin now covering my arms and face. I welcomed the coolness, sobbing from the relief as my body started shaking in the first throes of shock.

Blinking my one good eye open, I saw Top Dog stamping out the firestorm. I saw Mal's naked head, her ice-colored hair singed down to her burnt scalp. I saw Odette, whose metallic body had withstood the fire, but who'd been caught unawares by my mother's deluge, lay sputtering the water out of her lungs.

I looked at Knox, large patches of fur burned off and replaced with ruby-red sores, his bullet wound giving him an awkward limping gait. I spied Archer, his back scorched, the synthetic materials of his coat melted into his skin like acid.

I took in my mother, poised for an attack, her arm like a scorpion's raised tail. But the exhaustion in her face, in the sag of her limbs, in the dimness in her eyes, was telling. I didn't know how much fight she had left in her.

In the chaos, my grandmother had been washed backward, and before any of us had recovered enough to stop it, Bryce had cunningly taken her hostage, his bulging arm wound tightly around her frail neck, her toes barely grazing the floor. Her eyes did not flicker, her limbs were limp.

He formed icicles that hovered inches from my grandmother's forehead, like a tiara of death, daring us to make a move as he slowly inched away from us.

We hesitated, none of us wishing to see my grandma sacrificed. Cold dread filled my stomach at what would happen if we couldn't stop Bryce from leaving here with the Relic. Before I was forced to choose, more of the Domers broke through the Compound entrance, effectively pincering us in.

"And suddenly, dear cousin, your luck turns for the worse," Bryce taunted as he approached the door ahead of us.

"Kill them all," he commanded his new subordinates. "Such a pity, really, but I'm bored and ought to go, or else I'd do it myself." He took his final steps, until he was standing in the doorframe, and waved to us as if he were a friendly neighbour bidding us farewell.

And then he looked at me, an ugly smirk on his face, and I could see the decision he'd made before it happened.

My body lurched forward as I screamed, "No!!!"

The tiny halo of icicles flashed, the lights behind Bryce reflecting their luminescence as they impaled my grandma's skull.

Bryce dropped her like a used rag, worthless and beyond repair, before striding deeper into the Compound.

I wailed as I rushed towards her, battle erupting around me. I had tunnel vision, my only focus reaching my grandma. Sinking to my knees, I cradled her upper body in my arms.

"Grandma!" I lightly tapped on her cheek, as if rousing her from slumber. "Grandma, come on, wake up."

I placed my palm over her wounds to try and halt the bleeding, but there were too many for me to cover them all, and the ones I could cover showed no signs of slowing even as I compressed.

Her eyelids remained shut, not even a flutter of response, but still I attempted to wake her. "It's me, Grandma, it's Hollyn. You're safe now. You don't have to say anything, just open your eyes." I tried to stifle my sobbing as my hands desperately searched for a pulse. I couldn't feel one, so I held my hand in front of her mouth and nose, hopeful to detect even a faint blow of air coming from them.

But my hands felt nothing.

"Grandma come on—wake *up*." My voice was hoarse with emotion. "Don't do this to me. Don't, don't, don't, don't..."

My lungs rapidly inhaled, the panic attack that'd been threatening me finally taking over. My heart pounded so heavily I thought it would break through my chest. My body was rigid with immobility, paralyzed by the overwhelming sensations. It felt like someone was wrenching my heart from within.

"No, no, no, no," I muttered repeatedly. Shaking her violently now, I refused to believe it. "Please, just—come on, Grandma.

I'm here now, I'm so sorry. I'm so sorry, I'm so sorry..." My head shot backward as I wept, my body rocking back and forth in mourning.

She was gone.

All of this had been for her. And she was gone at the precipice of success.

Murdered by Bryce.

A howl erupted from me as my grief poured out. Streams of tears flooded my face, dripping from my nose, channelling into my mouth. I could taste the salt of my misery.

"Grandma—I... You can't—I can't do this without you." My hand grabbed at my chest as heightened palpitations threatened to burst through, a clammy sweat breaking out across my forehead and upper lip.

Hands shook me, but I paid them no heed.

"-llyn!"

I couldn't get enough air, each breath getting more rapid and more shallow as I began to whimper in fear. I couldn't get my attack under control.

"Hollyn!" My body was shaken again, harder this time. Enough to whip my neck forward and bring my attention to whoever was shaking me.

Amber eyes, reddened from sorrow, blocked my view. A giant gash slashed diagonally across from eye to mouth. It took me a moment before I recognized who knelt in front of me. I grabbed his arms in mania. "You have to help her!!!"

"Holls... I'm so sorry—"

"Maybe there's some magic still in me." I held her limp body, willing the magic to fill me again, pleading for its warmth. I promised anything and everything, my soul included, to bring her back.

I focused everything in me into coaxing the holy magic alive.

But, my body remained cold. Powerless.

Uselessly human.

"Why?! Why won't it work," I squeaked at Archer teary-eyed, although we both knew the answer. "Why?"

I wept. And wept and wept, praying over and over to heal her. Tears streamed down my face as time stood still, the battle around me diminishing to nothingness.

My reason for everything I had gone through. My reason for having survived the life I'd had thus far.

Gone.

Executed without a second thought.

I leaned forward over her thin body, my forehead resting against her shoulder, and I breathed in her familiar scent. That was home to me. Her smell—like baby powder mixed with dirt. The dichotomy of her life, of softness and hardship. A smell I would never experience again. My shoulders silently quaked as I curled over her lifeless body.

"I'm sorry, Hollyn." Archer held me as a new wave of weeping rocked through me. "I'm so sorry."

He held me until finally the wave of grief crested and began to ebb.

I pulled away from him to look again at her frail body.

I petted her, softly, as I laid her peacefully on her back, her arms folded nobly on her chest. I straightened her nightgown to save her modesty, even as her body lay cold and unknowing.

An explosion blasted behind me, rousing me into focus.

I noticed for the first time that the others were caught deep in battle with Bryce's reinforcements. I watched the bloodbath as the Mutts fought valiantly to keep them at bay—all working to keep me safe while I mourned. More tears fell as I grappled waves of grief, touched by the thoughtfulness of Mal, Odette, and the others.

Suddenly I shot to my feet, my new plan forming. "We can still catch him. Get the Relic back! Maybe we can bring her back!"

"How?" Archer looked at me with pity in his eyes. "Hollyn, she's–"

Exasperated by Archer's logical mind, I blurted, "I d-don't know! But we have to try!" And before he could convince me otherwise, I sprinted forward.

I had no plan, no weapon.

I would probably die, but I did not give a fuck.

I would retrieve the Relic or die trying. It was my only option. My only chance to keep her with me.

He must be in the next room, the Dining Hall. I had to catch him.

But when I followed Bryce, I screeched to a stop as I witnessed Slade and Bryce at a standstill, Ryker brooding in bored arrogance off to the side. Standing in the open space between rows of simple, plastic tables and chairs, the three halted their conversation and spun to face me, surprise plastered on all of their faces.

A part of me flushed with excitement that perhaps these two were here to help, but then Slade held out his hand to Bryce in familiar expectation. Bryce's eyes shifted towards Ryker as if sizing him up in human form, then ran over Slade, miraculously standing.

"No, I don't think I will be keeping up my end of the bargain."

"Bargain?!" I shrieked and Slade glanced at me, a hard glint in his eyes, before returning to focus on Bryce. Shock paralyzed me—Slade had made a deal behind my back. A deal with this bald-headed asshole.

"It's not what you—" Slade started through gritted teeth, anger rolling off him.

Taking advantage of the distraction, Bryce ripped out slabs of the cement floor and enclosed Ryker in a thick cage. I heard his muffled roar from within as his hands slammed against the walls. The cage was too small to allow him to transform into anything strong enough to possibly break through. Slade's surprised outrage was evident as he charged at Bryce, but he shielded himself from the onslaught.

I charged at Bryce too, my emotions completely unhinged as I battered my shoulder against his force field. But it was like ramming into solid rock, and my small frame stumbled backward from the impact.

"I'll fucking kill you!!" I roared. I pounded my fist against his shield over and over, making zero progress but incapable of tethering my rage.

"I thought you would've been dead by now." He frowned at me in calm disappointment.

"I won't stop until I kill you myself!" I bellowed in his face as I slammed into his field again with the full force of my body. A faint flicker rippled in his shield.

Bryce huffed, the threat of me without the Relic barely a blip on his radar. "Goodbye."

The shield exploded outward, sending Slade and me flying through the air. I landed awkwardly on my tailbone, pain shooting up my back. I heard Slade's grunt as his body was pinwheeled into the jagged corners of Ryker's pen.

As I wobbled, pushing myself up to a seated position, I watched Archer's charging frame get rocketed back through the doorway, sailing through the air and out of sight.

"Archer!" I yelled.

"It ends now." Bryce lifted his hand, my death blazing atop his fingertips. My body tensed, waiting. Biding my time.

His fire roared forth, but seconds before I was engulfed, I rolled out of the way, the heat charring the floor just past my ear. I sprang to my feet and ran in a zigzag pattern, my best attempt at avoiding another blast as Bryce prepared another spell to unleash.

But a resounding roar drew my attention. Knox, in his full tiger-striped glory, sprinted at Bryce, his massive paws masterfully dodging each burst of flame sent forth to singe his advance. When Knox's fangs were within arm's reach, Bryce defaulted to his shield. But it sputtered, not forming entirely, to his shock and dismay.

His magic is draining.

He was knocked back, his arms held in front of him protectively as Knox sank his fangs into his forearm. Bone crunched, the coppery smell of blood bursting forth. Bryce screamed in agony, his bald head now dripping in sweat as he stumbled backward, the Relic popping out of his pocket and clinking to the ground.

I sprang for it, but I was still too far away.

The two fighters found it before I could reach it.

Knox slammed a paw over part of the Relic as Bryce's fingers reached out to grab the other side. As Knox's other paw rose to swipe at him, Bryce's fingers crackled with a bolt of lightning.

Before their attacks could land, the Relic began to shine, its silvery veins illuminating. Its glow intensified, building, peaking, until the Relic itself began to shake, as if it could no longer contain its own glory.

Hell Hath No Fury Like a Woman Reborn

"Oh darling, keep your hands steady when you pour that or it'll go all over!" My grandmother laughed gaily down at me.

Both my small hands were gripping the well-worn measuring cup, the incremental numbers rubbed off almost entirely. But my grandma did not need the guidelines; her skillful hands were masters of baking. My tiny arms wobbled as they strained to tip the flour over into the plastic bowl below. I felt the scrunch of my face and the tip of my tongue poking out the side of my mouth as I concentrated on not making a mess.

Our front door slammed open, the hinges moaning under the duress, the rickety wood shaking from the impact. It was a miracle it still stood, considering the absolute onslaught it endured under my father's heavy hand.

The sound startled me, my hands quivering just enough to spill some of the brimming ingredient onto the table my grandmother and I were huddled around.

I heard my father snort in derision. "Can't even pour flour without making a ssscene, you uselessss twat?"

"Don't start—" my grandma protested.

"You coddle her, she's as useless assss one of those... those street urchins. You've ruined her." He sneered at her as I meekly cowered, praying to melt into the wall behind me. Anything to end this tirade—but knowing my father, it was just the beginning.

My hand rubbed my cheek, the last victim of his drunken rampage.

"You oughta toughen up, girl, if you hope to be annnnything. I oughta beat you just for reminding me how hopelesssss you are."

My grandma's warm, knobby hands cupped my head, turning my attention towards her loving expression.

You are perfect, she mouthed to me.

My father hiccuped as he stumbled to the icebox, bored of us already, hanging heavily against the open door. His massive hands rummaged for another drink, knocking two of the cans out to roll across the floor. He swore in annoyance, bending over to chase the moving targets like a drunk fat cat stumbling after a mouse too swift and too sober. His face reddened as bright as a tomato—although it'd been months since we'd been able to afford such lavish produce.

I scanned the well-stocked beer, comprehending even as a child what his addiction sacrificed for us.

Grandma softly rubbed my shoulders, murmuring words of reassurance and comfort as she coaxed me to continue helping her bake. She was making my favourite: carrot cake. Although we couldn't afford icing, I knew it would be spectacular.

Having finally caught the runaways, my father swayed over to us, more bored without an audience. He looked at me with disgust—there was no masking it—and knocked over the bowl, spilling the flour my grandmother had been hoarding for this occasion.

"Oopsss," he chuckled.

"That was all we have!" she cried in frustration, her hands slapping down on the table. My shoulders winced out of instinct even before his backhand rocked her off her chair.

"SSShut the hell up or I'll kick you outtt of here tonight!" he roared back, his swollen, alcoholic nose flaring in anger. My desperate eyes locked with my grandma's, pleading for her to be quiet—I couldn't lose her.

It was my seventh birthday.

My ears rang from the blast, my eyes blinking rapidly to shoo away the twinkling stars filling my vision as I came to. I didn't know why that particular memory had played in my mind, but it seemed to taunt me—I hadn't been able to stop the bad guy then either.

My skull throbbed and I swore my brain was swollen from rattling inside. Every muscle, every fibre felt like it couldn't possibly take another hit, my entire body shutting down from all the trauma. I tried to move my fingers, my hand stretched above my head, the bones in my hip cold against the concrete floor. What was once a smooth surface felt broken, chasms of concrete split like an open zipper of a coat, exposing the soft ground hidden beneath.

I strained to pull my head up, my neck bobbing under the weight, as if it was lifting a cast of gold instead of bruised flesh and bone.

Thick, smoky dust prevented me from seeing anyone or anything more than inches in front of me, but I didn't doubt the devastation that tiny Relic had created.

I prayed for Knox's safety but I hoped for Bryce's death.

I heard banging.

"Hollyn!" Archer was yelling in panic, following it with a spree of bangs, desperate to know I was alive.

In the haze of my mind, I couldn't understand why he didn't come to me. My mouth opened, but words failed to form, and instead I fell into a coughing fit. The deafening ringing in my ears started to subside as the dust and smoke trickled down, settling, like parting curtains opening the stage.

Slade was struggling to stand as he pulled himself from the deep indent his body left in Ryker's cage. It was just enough weakness for Ryker to take advantage.

I watched with my one good eye, blinking the dust away, as Ryker and Slade burrowed, ripped, and tore, shoving and throwing loose cement chunks until Ryker's massively muscular upper body burst through their man-made hole, then dragged the rest of himself to freedom.

More hysterical banging and shouting ripped my attention back to the entrance—completely barricaded by heavy wedges of concrete and cement, Archer and the others sealed on the other side. It would take even Mal and Odette some time to break through, if they even had any magic left to use.

Knox, now human, lay naked and still, his heavily damaged back to me. I couldn't make out whether he was breathing or not.

Bryce, who lay on his side, was vomiting weakly, his eyes fluttering, barely open, his head lolling around.

I found my way to my hands and knees and dry heaved as nausea began to overpower the shock keeping everything else at bay. I purged whatever remnants of food were left in my stomach. I heaved again, then wiped my mouth with the back of my hand.

Shakily, I stood, intent on reaching Knox before Bryce could gather himself and attack.

"Hollyn, are you okay?" Slade shouted at me from across the room.

"Fuck you," I croaked back.

Bryce grunted and writhed on the ground as I continued towards Knox, but something glossy caught my eye.

Tiny pieces of Relic. Shrapnel left over from the explosion.

I raced towards one, pleading there was still some power stored within these little chunks.

"Don't touch any!" Ryker warned as I knelt before it.

"This will save her!" I didn't hesitate as my hand scooped up the biggest shard.

It flickered softly at first, but then the glow began to build again, terror growing inside of me as I numbly watched the potential of a round two come alive.

None of us were ready when the remnant exploded again.

The current lifted me into the air, my back arching while my toes remained connected to the ground. My chest pressed up to the ceiling, my arms outstretched at my sides as I was swarmed with the current.

Synapses sparked all throughout my body, my core over-heating with energy. I could not move as the familiar magical warmth flooded me—but unlike earlier, it was unhinged. Nothing was containing its intensity, its vibrancy.

My severely weakened state couldn't handle it; it was like being electrocuted and incinerated from the inside out.

My senses heightened to the supernatural as dozens of whispers raced in my head. The throbbing in my skull was so intense it felt like my brain would burst through it. My heart pounded so rapidly it skipped beats. My toes and fingers were burning, and I could feel the blood inside of me flood through each and every spider web of vein and artery.

I fought to crack open my eye, finding Ryker and Bryce gaping at me. They all seemed untouched by the magic.

Everyone—except Slade.

Whose body hovered midair like me own. Whose body glowed a brilliant white.

Whose eyes, closed in ecstasy, shed tears.

And then a crack resonated in the building and the power calmed, wrapping me in contained glory.

The beast had been tamed within.

I fell to my knees and turned up my palms, seeing again that familiar white glow hovering around them.

It's back.

My exhaustion was washing away with every breath, my blind eye regaining its vision.

The holy magic was healing me, but this time, the source was not contained within the Relic.

It was contained within me.

I looked up to see Slade meet my gaze.

I could feel the power pulsing from him.

It was within him too.

Bed and Cord

His cobalt irises glowed like wolf eyes peeking out from the forest, reflective in the moonlight. A soft white haze, same as mine, rippled around him, matching the intensity I felt within.

How?

"I was injured retrieving the first piece, Hollyn. I couldn't make the trek into Abraxas or up Nihani Mountain in my paralyzed state." Slade's leather shoes softly lowered to the ground. "As I'm sure you've realised now, I too have Dufort blood, although we are not truly related." Slade's calm had returned, his quiet confidence supported by his regained magic.

My mouth hung open, "You?" It was all I could muster.

First Top Dog, and now Slade–these people were my family? My blood? Were there others?

Had he been hoping to obtain it all, trying to snake me out of my own magic?

"I am not a bad person!" Slade's arm thrust away from him, obviously seeing the disgust snarling my face. "I was going to tell you eventually. Everything." He searched the room, spotting luminescent powder on the ground, and stalked towards it. But there was nothing left of the Relic, so he directed his gaze back at me.

I sneered, "Oh, please. You wanted it all for yourself, didn't you?" I hadn't considered anyone else obtaining this magic, too. Did he know how to control it? What did he plan to use it for?

Would he kill me?

Slade curled his fist, his jaw set in indignation, "This is *my* birthright, too. Why are you allowed to have this power, and I'm not?"

I scoffed, "Because you're a Domer! All you people have ever done is destroy others—"

"I am not like the others!" Stepping closer, I could see the frustration, even the hurt he hid so well. "I thought that we could work together, train together. Another Dufort—" Slade snapped his mouth shut, his cheeks flushing slightly as if embarrassed to admit of his hope for us to join forces.

He wanted to work with me? It must have crushed him when I had left him and Ryker in Abraxas.

"I've had to make tough choices, just like you. You're no saint," he commented bitterly.

"But you made a deal with him!" I flung a finger at Bryce, now standing, assessing us. "And you allowed *this*"—I gestured around me—"to happen. Look at all the homes you've destroyed. The lives you've sacrificed!"

Anger flashed over Slade's face as he stopped just before me. "I *tried* to get you to give me the damn Relic before any of this happened." His eyes flicked to Bryce. "I wouldn't have had to make a deal for the Relic if you hadn't reneged on your end."

"I didn't plan any of that!" I admitted, closing the last gap between us. Boldly, I pointed my finger against his chest. "They saved me. I was stranded—while you two were waiting for me to do all the work!"

Shock plastered Slade's face, as if he really believed I had orchestrated such a grand exit strategy. "You weren't going to double-cross us?"

I hesitated, knowing I had been planning an escape at some point. Slade was quick to pick up on the unspoken, scowling at me.

"Oh fuck you—I owed you nothing. As if I would hand over the Relic to you." I was face to face with Slade, my growing hatred burning in my palms, a force field of light sparking as manifestation of my hostility toward him and everything he had unknowingly set into motion. "You let this happen. My grandmother is *dead* because of this."

Remembering her body, I whirled my head back towards the previous hallway, but my stomach sank when I saw the threshold still buried in a mountain of debris. There would be no way I could reach her yet. *Soon*, I promised her.

"We made a deal, and you double-crossed me. I had to. *You* lied to *me*," Slade reminded me again, both of us adamant the other was at fault.

"What did you expect?! You left my family there to *die*. You were ready to kill us on that mountain. You *let this happen*!" My face flushed in rage, my eyebrows scowling so hard I felt the muscles between them shaking in exertion.

"The O'Malleys had been planning to infiltrate Dyrcsa for a while now—don't act like I wanted this! If I'd gotten the Relic earlier, I could have kept them at bay. If you'd just listened to me, dammit!"

"Fuck you!" I spat at him. "They had my grandmother! What else was I supposed to do?!" I shoved with both hands against his hard chest. He didn't move an inch.

A chunk of cement crunched beneath a shoe, and our attention whipped to Bryce, who was surreptitiously backpedalling, capitalising on Slade and I caught up in our own argument. I was certain we were walled in, but I wasn't stupid enough to give Bryce enough space to test my theory.

Bryce was the real reason she was dead. He was the true enemy, and we were letting him escape from his overdue retribution.

"Move another foot and die." My voice dropped low in restrained abhorrence. For a moment, I almost believed he would stay. But I hadn't anticipated his moves earlier.

I wouldn't make that mistake again.

Before he could take another step, I let go of the restraint I had been holding, releasing the stifling emotions of the last twenty-four hours, channelling them into my magic—and exploding it at Bryce.

He was wrenched backward, his back arched as his body froze in midair. I debated how I would end him. What would give me even a fraction of satisfaction—whether I would blast him to bits, liquefy his skeletal frame, ignite him and burn him from within.

"H-Help me," he pleaded to Slade.

Slade slowly perused Bryce from head to toe, deliberately stretching out the tension until finally he responded, mocking him. "No, I don't think I will."

Slade's hands shot out in front of him, both of us simultaneously unloading energy. Geysers of light pierced through Bryce, his body illuminating as every cell was overcharged with our magic. His entire being vibrated, his frame becoming indecipherable in all our light's glory. His screams of agony were cut short as beacons of light burst through from his core, lasering holes through him.

He was vaporised from the inside out.

But what we'd started could no longer be contained, and our magic continued to deluge out of us, despite Bryce being nothing more than dust particles. Our combined magic was so intense that it seemed to rebound between us—before bouncing back our way.

Slade and I were blown backward again, our own power reflected back onto us.

Like karma finding its revenge for our sins.

I was drowsy as I rolled to my side, blinking back to consciousness, however long it had been. The sheer magnitude of our combined magic had knocked me unconscious, and I fought to not return to the darkness.

"Holls! HOLLS!" I heard Archer's renewed desperation. "We're almost through, hang in there!"

"Ar... cher," I squeaked out, but it was nearly inaudible. "Knox..." I blacked out, the last image I saw of Knox, motionless, his battered back still to me.

Sharp talons encircled my waist, firm but painless, as the wind rushing against my face woke me.

My groggy eyes cracked open a fraction. It was all my strength could muster.

I shrieked as I looked down at the great storm clouds weaving together to form a steel blanket beneath me—and realised I was hundreds of feet in the air.

I passed out again.

I awoke with a jolt, my body shooting upright, but I was halted by the glowing bindings wrapped tightly around my wrists and ankles, leashing me to a bed. I jostled them in panic as my mind took in my surroundings.

I was on some kind of makeshift medical cot, surrounded by turquoise tented walls coming to a high peak in the center. My bed stood on an intricately woven rug of wine and navy-coloured wool, one of many that covered the sandy floor. I could feel the dusting of sand that the wind had blown onto me scrape me uncomfortably. *Are we in the desert?* The blankets that were piled upon me, to help stave off the crisp air, seemed handmade and similar to those I saw in Dyrcsa. My bound hands shot forth fingers to investigate the rough woolen texture. *Are we still in Dyrcsa?*

A few plain cots on the other side of the room were neatly made, only the slight sag in the pillows any indication of their being used. Hanging from the ceiling were three paper lanterns, their warm glow casting flickering shadows on the ground below. I was reminded of the fires that raged through Dyrcsa. I shuddered at the haunting memories.

The tent flapped in the wind, its whistle drowning out any other sounds, despite my ears straining to figure out where I was. I was alone within the spacious dwelling, but I knew I couldn't truly be alone.

"Any... now..." I could barely hear fragments over the wind as someone reported just outside of my door.

The front flap's zipper suddenly moved, zooming around the perimeter, and I quickly snapped my eyes shut. Loose lips flapped louder when they believed no eavesdroppers were listening.

The muffled steps of six boots entered my domain, one much more graceful than the others.

"Good morning, princess," Ryker drawled at me.

My eyes flashed open, and I snarled at my captors as I rattled my bindings. "Now I'm your fucking prisoner?!" I took in Slade, back in his too-cool, cocky persona, dressed in cargo pants, combat boots, and a Henley shirt, a plaid chequered scarf draped around his neck, his golden skin a touch pink from windburn.

My eyes roved over Ryker, once again topless, with the same khaki cargo pants on, his boots lazily unlaced and his face covered in a dark shadow of beard. His grin showcased the stark contrast between his white teeth and his olive skin.

And then I noticed Knox, with a sling over one arm, his ruddy face and neck patched with new skin healing over his injuries, beaming from ear to ear in genuine happiness.

"Knox! You're okay!" I could not prevent a smile from breaking out as I mirrored his own affection. Our short time together had been intense, but it had birthed a real connection and trust between us. I was surprised to feel so happy seeing those plump cheeks, that pushed back head of raven-coloured hair. "Why did you let them tie me up like a psychopath?!" I asked him, refusing to hold a conversation with the other two. "After everything they did to your city—"

"It was for your own good," Ryker interrupted.

"It was for *your* own good. If I could, I'd be—"

"Really, Hollyn, it was to protect you. And us," Knox assured me, halting me from spiralling. "We didn't know what your magic would do when you were unconscious, so those binds around your hands and ankles have tethered your magic until we knew it would be safe."

How long was I out?

"Knox, get me out of these things. I'm going to kill these two." My eyes narrowed in disgust as I finally met Slade's. "We have to get back to Dyrcsa." I jostled the restraints again, but could make no ground.

"A lot has happened while you've been asleep, we'll get you caught up—" Slade began.

"I'm not going anywhere with you. I'm going back to my grandmother, to Archer. Maybe I can still heal her." I refused to listen to anything he said. Now that I had this magic in me, I would get back to my grandma, see if I could bring her back. I had no idea, but I was desperate to try. "You got what you wanted out of me. Leave me the fuck alone." Slade scowled darkly before turning his head away, his arms crossing in dismissal.

I heard Ryker sigh and I brought my gaze back to the brute who looked too serious for my liking, "You need to hear what's happened."

"No. I need to be with my family. Take me back, or let me go and I'll get there myself."

"Hollyn..." Knox hesitated, and the look in his eyes brought on a cold sweat. "They have Archer."

I bolted upright, the shackles on my limbs digging into my wrists and ankles. "What?! Who?"

My family. My love.

The only person I had left.

Tears threatened the corners of my eyes as a fresh wave of grief washed through me. I choked it back, refusing to let Slade see me out of control.

He walked over to me and unfastened my restraints without making eye contact with me, then returned to the entrance. "Them. The O'Malleys."

"But—but Bryce is dead—we killed him, didn't we?" Finally his sapphire eyes found mine and we silently stared at each other, remembering what our combined magic had done to him, to us. Slade's eyes darkened and his expression pinched and I wondered if he felt guilty for what he had done. Certainly not to Bryce, but to Dyrcsa.

"Yeah, and guess who's fucking pissed over that?" Ryker remarked dryly.

I swallowed, lost over who had taken him.

Slade popped his head out of the tent, beckoning whoever was out there to come inside. A man dressed similarly but wielding an assault rifle came inside carrying my own desert combat attire and a tray of cured meat, dried fruits, and a hunk of bread. *Who the hell were these guys? More soldiers? But whose?*

"Bryce's father: Cyrus O'Malley," Knox said quietly, his chocolate eyes downcast in worry.

What had I done?

In my need to avenge my grandma, I had provoked another, perhaps deadlier person. I couldn't get ahead, each decision I made seemed to make everything worse.

Whispers filled my head again, promising me a glorious retribution. I felt the magic urge me into action, trying to convince me to invoke it, but I stifled it aggressively. Fearfully.

I needed Archer, or else this magic would consume me.

"I know you probably don't want to work with us," Slade admitted, his jaw tense like he didn't want to hear it confirmed. "But right now, if we *don't* stick together, they will hunt us down and they will kill us. Don't think you're invincible. They have hunted Duforts for over five hundred years. Magic or no magic, they will not stop until we are dead. The only hope we have is to face this new adversity together. And perhaps, if I can help you get Archer back... maybe there's a chance." Slade curled his golden hair behind an ear, a rare tell of his anxiousness.

"A chance for what?" I questioned.

Slade shrugged his shoulders. "Nothing. Never mind."

Knox sat on my bed, his weight sinking the corner by my feet. "I know I didn't know Archer for very long, but he's a good man. And one of the pack. We *will* get him back." His large hand patted mine, and I found it surprisingly comforting, despite the fact we were strangers only days ago.

Ryker turned, his boot grinding the sand underneath. "We'll leave you to get ready and eat. But hurry—we have a long day ahead of us."

And with that, the three men exited, leaving me bewildered and alone.

Where was I?

Where were we headed?

And most importantly, could I save Archer in time? Or would I fail him like I had my grandmother?

I scarfed down the food and rushed to get dressed, running my fingers through my matted hair before I pulled back the tent door and stepped out into the unknown, the dull hum of my magic thrumming through me in comfort.

I would not fail him too.

I was smarter than that girl who I used to be. I was more confident. I was more powerful.

I was a Dufort.

Acknowledgements

To be sitting here writing acknowledgements for a book I've published is entirely surreal. When I decided to write *A Thief Reborn*, it began as a self-imposed challenge to see whether I could practice what I preached. And I quickly and brutally learned that teaching middle-graders how to write was vastly different from penning my own novel. By writing this story while on maternity leave, in the throes of sleepless nights, endless dirty diapers, the constant give of motherhood, I found myself again. I found the confidence to take a risk that I had always been too scared to take for fear of disaster and disappointment. I found an identity beyond mother or teacher. I found a creative purpose that filled me with joy and childlike excitement. And if I've ever learned anything from anyone, you chase that feeling!

This book, to me, inspires a journey of self-love, of finding oneself whilst lost amidst the drudgery of the underpaid and overworked lifestyle—a theme with which so many of us resonate. Hollyn, through the catalyst of her forbidden, enigmatic magic, discovers her worth, begins to overcome the scars left by domestic violence, and realizes that life should be lived with purpose and hope, even if it's terrifying and risky. I hope you, reader, realize that your worth is so much bigger than how small it might feel on your worst days. Be like Hollyn and find the courage to push yourself past simply surviving, whatever that looks like to you.

My hope is that Hollyn is a relatable heroine for you all, one who struggles with anxiety, who carries *bags* of emotional baggage and trauma, whose actions have dark and fatal consequences because those were the characters I always loved most in books. The complexities, the grey matter, the characters susceptible to fallacies, vices and irrationalities, and yet still managed to find the light in all that darkness. It was almost like I needed my characters to be tested and to stumble, so that their redemption arc was that much more satisfying.

There are many others whose hard work and tireless ear played an instrumental role in the completion of *A Thief Reborn*, and it would be a disservice to them to not take a moment to recognize their efforts and patience.

To Patrick, who supported my dream and gave me the support and space to chase this. Without you stepping up and looking after the kids so many times so that I could sneak in an hour or two of writing, I would not be writing this. I would have given up, frustrated and broken. You never once doubted I could do this, encouraging me at every step and I thank you for it. Our family of five relies on your steady presence and joyful spirit more than you'll ever know.

To my family, who listened to me prattle on in the brainstorming stages, who inspired and proffered ideas and suggestions to fill my initial plot holes. You all were the original ARC readers when it was nothing more than a word document of scrambled thoughts. I could not have done this without your guidance and your unrelenting belief in me. Imposter-syndrome rears its ugly head far too often for indie authors, and it was your words of calming that helped me cage the beast.

To Jennifer, who pumped my tires in the best way possible. To be the first person to read my story in its initial, raw, ugly phase speaks volumes to the undying trust I have in you. You were the soundboard for my worries, my ideas, my questions about every step of this process. Besties don't let besties give up on their dreams and you never let me.

To Kara, my editor and saving grace. To find someone who so perfectly understood Hollyn and her story was perhaps the biggest relief of it all. You were able to help me transform my story into something so much more elevated, succinct and cohesive. Everything you suggested I felt was a great alteration or addition and I respect your work so much. You have a forever client in me!

To my kids, may you look at this and respect this journey not by the success of its sales, but of the courage it took and the hard work and perserverance needed to complete it. I hope one day you find something that excites you the way writing does for me, and you pursue it unconditionally. Know that you will always have my support.

And finally to you, reader, I thank you from the bottom of my heart. How lucky I am to have friends and family who without hesitation have shown up to support my work. I know how much harder it can seem to take a risk on a novice, a newbie, and I appreciate all the words of encouragement, the reviews and the overall excitement so many of you have shown me! I can't wait to continue Hollyn's journey with you.